Billionaires & Babies

MAUREEN CHILD

KATHERINE GARBERA

EMILY McKAY

MILLS
& BOON

First published in Great Britain 2012
by Mills & Boon, an imprint of Harlequin (UK) Limited,
Eton House, 18-24 Paradise Road, Richmond, Surrey TW9 1SR

BILLIONAIRES & BABIES © by Harlequin Enterprises II B.V./S.à.r.l 2012

Baby Bonanza, Baby Business and Baby on the Billionaire's Doorstep were published in Great Britain by Harlequin (UK) Limited.

Baby Bonanza © Maureen Child 2008
Baby Business © Katherine Garbera 2008
Baby on the Billionaire's Doorstep © Emily McKaskle 2008

ISBN: 978 0 263 89711 1
ebook ISBN: 978 1 408 97080 5

05-1212

Printed and bound in Spain
by Blackprint CPI, Barcelona

BABY BONANZA

BY
MAUREEN CHILD

Maureen Child is a California native who loves to travel. Every chance they get, she and her husband are taking off on another research trip. The author of more than sixty books, Maureen loves a happy ending and still swears that she has the best job in the world. She lives in Southern California with her husband, two children and a golden retriever with delusions of grandeur.

To the ladies at Long Beach Care Center—
Christabel, Barbara and all of the others who give such
loving care to the patients—including my uncle—
who need it the most. You really are amazing.

One

"Ow!" Jenna Baker hopped on her right foot and clutched at the bruised toes on her left one. Shooting a furious glare at the bolted-down table in her so-tiny-that-claustrophobics-would-die cabin, she called down silent curses on the head of the man who was the reason for this cruise from hell.

Nick Falco.

His image rose up in her mind, and just for a second Jenna enjoyed the nearly instant wash of heat that whipped through her. But the heat was gone a moment later, to be replaced by a cold fury.

Better all around if she concentrated on *that* particular emotion. After all, unlike every other passenger aboard *Falcon's Pride,* she hadn't come aboard the floating orgy to party. She was here for a reason. A damn good one.

While her aching toes throbbed in concert with her heartbeat, Jenna cautiously stood on both feet and took the step and a half that brought her to a minuscule closet. She'd already hung up her clothes, and the few outfits she'd brought with her looked crowded in the narrow wardrobe. Snatching a pale yellow blouse off the attached-to-the-rod hanger, she carried it to the bathroom, just another step away.

It was the size of an airplane bathroom, only it also contained a shower stall designed to fit pygmies. In fact, the opening of the sliding door was so slender, Jenna had slapped one arm across her breasts when leaving the shower, half-afraid she'd scrape her nipples off.

"Really nice, Nick," she muttered, "when you upgraded this old boat and turned it into your flagship, you might have put a little extra thought into those people who *aren't* living in the owner's penthouse on the top deck."

But she told herself that was typical enough. She'd known what Nick was like even before she'd met him on that sultry summer night more than a year ago. He was a man devoted to seeing his cruise line become the premier one in the world. He did what he had to do when he had to do it. And he didn't make apologies for it.

She'd been working for him when she met him. An assistant cruise director on one of the other cruise ships in the Falcon line. She'd loved the job, loved the idea of travel and stupidly, had fallen in love with the boss. All because of a romantic moonlight encounter and Nick's undeniable charm.

Jenna had known darn well that the boss would never get involved with an employee. So when the sexy, gorgeous Nick Falco had stumbled across her on the Pavilion Deck and assumed she was a guest, she hadn't corrected him. She should have and she knew it, but what woman wouldn't have been swept away by a chiseled jaw, ice-blue eyes and thick black hair that just tempted a woman to tangle her fingers in it?

She sighed a little, set her hands on the sides of the soapdish-size sink and remembered how it had been from the first moment he'd touched her. *Magic.* Pure and simple. Her skin had sizzled, her blood had sung and her heart had beaten so frantically, it had been hard to breathe. He'd swept her into a dance, there in the starlight, with the Hawaiian breeze caressing them and the music from the deck below floating on the air like a sigh.

One dance became two, and the feel of his arms around her had seduced Jenna into a lie that had come back to haunt her not a week later. She fell into an affair. A blistering, over-the-top sexual affair that had rocked her soul even as it battered her heart.

And when, one week into that affair, Nick had discovered from someone else that she actually worked for him, he'd broken it off, refused to hear her out, and once they were back in port, he'd fired her.

The sting of that…dismissal felt as fresh as the day it had happened.

"Oh, God. What am I doing here?" She blew out a breath as her stomach began to twist and ripple with the nerves that had been shivering through her for months. If there were any other way to do this, she would have. After all, it wasn't as if she were looking forward to seeing Nick again.

Gritting her teeth, she lifted her chin, turned sharply and cracked her elbow into the doorjamb. Wincing, she stared into her reflection in the slim rectangular mirror and said, "You're here because it's the right thing. The *only* thing. Besides, it's not like he left you any choice."

She had to talk to the man and it wasn't exactly easy to get access to him. Since he lived aboard the flagship of his cruise line, she couldn't confront him on dry land. And the few times he was in port in San Pedro, California, he locked himself up in a penthouse apartment with tighter security than the White House. When she couldn't talk to him in person, she'd tried phone calls. And when they failed, she'd taken to e-mailing him. At least twice a week for the last six months, she'd sent him e-mails that he apparently deleted without opening. The man was being so impossible, Jenna'd finally been forced to make a reservation on *Falcon's Pride* and take a cruise she didn't want and couldn't afford.

She hadn't been on board a ship in more than a year and so even the slight rolling sensation of the big cruise liner made her knees a little rubbery. There was a time when she'd loved being on ship. When she'd enjoyed the adventure of a job that was never the same two days in a row. When she'd awakened every morning to a new view out her porthole.

"Of course," she admitted wryly, "that was when I *had* a porthole." Now she was so far belowdecks, in the cheapest cabin she'd been able to find, she had no window at all and it felt as though she'd been sealed up in the bowels of the ship. She was forced to keep a light on at all times, because otherwise, the dark was so complete, it was like being inside a vacuum. No sensory input at all.

Weird and strangely unsettling.

Maybe if she'd been able to get some sleep, she'd feel different. But she'd been jolted out of bed late the night before by the horrific clank and groan of the anchor chain being lifted. It had sounded as if the ship itself was being torn apart by giant hands, and once that image had planted itself in her brain, she hadn't been able to sleep again.

"All because of Nick," she told the woman in the glass and was gratified to see her nod in agreement. "Mr. Gazillionaire, too busy, too important to answer his e-mail." Did he even remember her? Did he look at her name on the e-mail address and wonder who the heck she was? She frowned into the mirror, then shook her head. "No. He didn't forget. He knows who I am. He's not reading the e-mails on purpose, just to make me crazy. He couldn't have forgotten that week."

Despite the way it had ended, that one week with Nick Falco had turned Jenna's life around and upside down. It was simply impossible that she was the only one affected that strongly.

"So instead, he's being Mr. Smooth and Charming," she said. "Probably romancing some other silly woman, who, like me, won't notice until it's too late that he's *nobody's* fantasy."

Oh, God.

That was a lie.

The truth was, she thought with an inner groan, he actually *was* any woman's fantasy. Tall, gorgeous, with thick, black hair, pale blue eyes and a smile that was both charming and wicked, Nick Falco was enough to make a woman's toes curl even *before* she knew what kind of lover he was.

Jenna let her forehead thunk against the mirror. "Maybe this wasn't such a great idea," she whispered as her insides fisted and other parts of her heated up just on the strength of memories alone.

She closed her eyes as vivid mental images churned through her mind—nights with Nick, dancing on the Pavilion Deck beneath an awning of stars. A late-night picnic, alone on the bow of the ship, with the night crowded close. Dining on his balcony, sipping champagne, spilling a few drops and Nick licking them from the valley between her breasts. Lying in his bed, wrapped in his arms, his whispers promising tantalizing delights.

What did it say about her that simply the memories of that man could still elicit a shiver of want in her, more than a year later? Jenna didn't think she really wanted an answer to that question. She hadn't boarded this ship for the sake of lust or for what had once been. Sex wasn't part of the equation this time and she was just going to have to find a way to deal with her past while fighting for her future. So, deliberately, she dismissed the tantalizing images from her mind in favor of her reality. Opening her eyes, she stared into the mirror and steeled herself for what was to come.

The past had brought her here, but she had no intention of stirring up old passions.

Her life was different now. She wasn't at loose ends, looking for adventure. She was a woman with a purpose, and Nick was going to listen to her whether he wanted to or not.

"Too busy to answer his e-mail, is he?" she muttered. "Thinks if he ignores me long enough I'll simply disappear? Well, then, he's got quite the surprise coming, doesn't he?"

She brushed her teeth, slapped some makeup on and ran a brush through her long, straight, light brown hair before braiding it into a single thick rope that lay against her back. Inching sideways out the bathroom door, she carefully made her way to the built-in dresser underneath a television bolted high on the wall. She grabbed a pair of white shorts, tugged them on and then tucked the ends of her yellow shirt into the waistband. She stepped into a pair of sandals, grabbed her purse and checked to make sure the sealed, small blue envelope was still inside. Then she took the two steps to her cabin door.

She opened her door, stepped into the stingy hallway and bumped into a room service waiter. "Sorry, sorry!"

"My fault," he insisted, hoisting the tray he carried high enough that Jenna could duck under it and slip past him. "These older hallways just weren't made for a lot of foot traffic." He glanced up and down the short hall, then back to Jenna. "Even with the ship's refit, there are sections that—" He stopped, as if remembering he was an employee of the Falcon Line and really shouldn't be dissing the ship.

"Guess not." Jenna smiled back at the guy. He looked about twenty and had the shine of excitement in his eyes. She was willing to bet this was his first cruise. "So, do you like working for Falcon Cruises?"

He lowered the tray to chest level, shrugged and said, "It's my first day, but so far, yeah. I really do. But…" He stopped, turned a look over his shoulder at the dimly lit hall as if making sure no one could overhear him.

Jenna could have reassured him. There were only five cabins down here in the belly of the ship and only hers and the one across the hall from her were occupied. "But?" she prompted.

"It's a little creepy down here, don't you think? I mean, you can hear the water battering against the hull and it's so…dark."

She'd been thinking the same thing only moments before and still she said, "Well, it's got to be better than crew quarters, right? I mean, I used to work on ships and we were always on the lowest deck."

"Not us," he said, "crew quarters are one deck up from here."

"Fabulous," Jenna muttered, thinking that even the people who *worked* for Nick Falco were getting more sleep on this cruise than she was.

The door opened and a fortyish woman in a robe poked her head out and smiled. "Oh, thank God," the older blonde said. "I heard voices out here and I was half-afraid the ship was haunted."

"No, ma'am." The waiter stiffened to attention as if just remembering what he'd come below for. He shot Jenna a hopeful look, clearly asking that she not rat him out for standing around having a conversation. "I've got breakfast for two here, as you requested."

"Great," the blonde said, opening the door wider. "Just…" She stopped. "I have no idea where you can put it. Find a place, okay?"

While the waiter disappeared into the cabin, the blonde stuck out one hand to Jenna. "Hi, I'm Mary Curran. My husband, Joe, and I are on vacation."

"Jenna Baker," she said, shaking the other woman's hand. "Maybe I'll see you abovedecks?"

"Won't see much of me down here, I can tell you," Mary admitted with a shudder as she tightened the sash on her blue terry-cloth robe. "Way too creepy, but—" she shrugged "—the important thing is, we're on a cruise. We only have to sleep here, after all, and I intend to get our money's worth out of this trip."

"Funny," Jenna said with a smile. "I was just telling myself the same thing."

She left Mary to her breakfast and headed for the elevator that would carry her up and out of the darkness. She clutched the envelope that she would have delivered to Nick and steeled herself for the day to come. The elevator lurched into motion and she tapped her foot as she rose from the bowels of the ship. What she needed now was some air, lots of coffee and a pastry or two. Then, later, after Nick had read her letter, she would be ready. Ready to face the beast. To beard the lion in his den. To look into Nick's pale blue eyes and demand that he do the right thing.

"Or," Jenna swore as the doors shushed open and she stepped into the sunlight and tipped her face up to the sky, "I will *so* make him pay."

"The sound system for the stage on the Calypso Deck has a hiccup or two, but the techs say they'll have it fixed before showtime."

"Good." Nick Falco sat back in his maroon leather chair and folded his hands atop his belly as he listened to his assistant, Teresa Hogan, rattle off her daily report. It was only late morning and together they'd already handled a half-dozen crises. "I don't want any major issues," he told her. "I know this is the shakedown cruise, but I don't want our passengers feeling like they're guinea pigs."

"They won't. The ship's looking good and you know it," Teresa said with a confident smile. "We've got a few minor glitches, but nothing we can't handle. If there were real trouble, we never would have left port last night."

"I know," he said, glancing over his shoulder at the white caps dancing across the surface of the ocean. "Just make sure we stay one step ahead of any of those glitches."

"Don't I always?"

"Yeah," he said with a nod of approval. "You do."

Teresa was in her late fifties, had short, dark hair, sharp green eyes and the organizational skills of a field general. She took crap from no one, Nick included, and had the loyalty and tenacity of a hungry pit bull. She'd been with him for eight years—ever since her husband had died and she'd come looking for a job that would give her adventure.

She'd gotten it. And she'd also become Nick's trusted right arm.

"The master chef on the Paradise Deck is complaining about the new Vikings," she was saying, flipping through the papers attached to her ever present clipboard.

Nick snorted. "Most expensive stoves on the planet and there's something wrong with them?"

She smirked a little. "According to Chef Michele," Teresa said, "ze stove is not hot enough."

Not a full day out at sea and already he was getting flak from temperamental artistes. "Tell him as long as ze heat is hot, he should do what I'm paying him to do."

"Already done."

One of Nick's eyebrows lifted. "Then why tell me at all?"

"You're the boss."

"Nice of you to remember that occasionally," he said, and sat forward, rolling his chair closer to the desk where a small mountain of personal correspondence waited for his attention.

Ignoring that jibe, Teresa checked her papers again and said, "The captain says the weather outlook is great and we're making all speed to Cabo. Should be there by ten in the morning tomorrow."

"That's good." Nick picked up the first envelope on the stack in front of him. Idly, he tapped the edge of it against his desk as Teresa talked. And while she ran down the list of problems, complaints and compliments, he let his gaze shift around his office. Here on the Splendor Deck, just one deck below the bridge, the views were tremendous. Which was why he'd wanted both his office and his luxurious owner's suite on this deck. He'd insisted on lots of glass. He liked the wide spread of the ocean all around him. Gave him a sense of freedom even while he was working.

There were comfortable chairs, low-slung tables and a fully stocked wet bar across the room. The few paintings hanging on the dark blue walls were bright splotches of color, and the gleaming wood floors shone in sunlight that was only partially dimmed by the tinted glass.

This was the ship's maiden voyage under the Falcon name. Nick had bought it from a competitor who was going out of business, and over the past six months had had it completely refitted and refurbished to be the queen of his own cruise line. *Falcon's Pride,* he'd called her, and so far she was living up to her name.

He'd gotten reports from his employees on the reaction from the passengers as they'd boarded the day before in the L.A. port of San Pedro. Though most of the guests on board were young and looking to party, even they had been impressed with the ship's luxurious decor and overall feel.

Nick had purchased his first ship ten years before, and had quickly built the Falcon Line into the primary party destination in the world. *Falcon's Pride* was going to take that reputation and enhance it. His passengers wanted fun. Excitement. A two-week-long party. And he was going to see that they got it.

He hired only the best chefs, the hottest bands and the greatest lounge acts. His employees were young and attractive—his mind shifted tracks around that thought and instantly, he was reminded of one former employee in particular. A woman he'd let get under his skin until the night he'd discovered her lies. He hadn't seen or spoken to her since, but he was a hell of a lot more careful these days about who he got involved with.

"Are you even listening to me?"

Nick cleared his thoughts instantly, half-irritated that he was still thinking about Jenna Baker more than a year since he'd last seen her. He glanced up at Teresa and gave her a smile that should have charmed her. "Guess not. Why don't we take care of the rest of this business after lunch."

"Sure," she said, and checked her wristwatch. "I've got an appointment on the Verandah Deck. One of the cruise directors has a problem with the karaoke machine."

"Fine. Handle it." He turned his attention to the stack of hand-delivered correspondence on his desk and just managed to stifle a sigh. Never failed. Every cruise, Nick was inundated with invitations from female passengers to join them for dinner or private parties or for drinks in the moonlight.

"Oh," Teresa said, handing over a pale blue envelope. "One of the stewards gave me this on my way in." She smiled as she handed it over. "Yet another lonely lady looking for companionship? Seems you're still the world's favorite love god."

Nick knew she was just giving him a hard time—like always—yet this time her words dug at him. Shifting uncomfortably in his chair, he thought about it, tried to figure out why. He was no monk, God knew. And over the years he'd accepted a lot of invitations from women who didn't expect anything more than a good time and impersonal sex.

But damned if he could bring himself to get interested in the latest flurry of one-night-stand invitations, either. The cards and letters had been sitting on his desk since early this morning and he hadn't bothered to open one yet. He knew what he'd find when he started going through them.

Panties. Cabin keys. Sexy photos designed to tempt.

And not a damned one of them would mean anything to him.

Hell, what did that say about him? Laughing silently at himself, Nick acknowledged that he really didn't want to know. Maybe he'd been spending too much time working lately. Maybe what he needed was just what these ladies were offering. He'd go through the batch of invites, pick out the most intriguing one and spend a few relaxing hours with a willing woman.

Just what the doctor ordered.

Teresa was still holding the envelope out to him and there was confusion in her eyes. He didn't want her asking any questions, so he took the envelope and idly slid his finger under the seal. Deliberately giving her a grin and a wink, he said, "You think it's easy being the dream of millions?"

Now Teresa snorted and, shaking her head, muttering something about delusional males, she left the office.

When she was gone, he sat back and thoughtfully looked at the letter in his hand. Pale blue envelope, tidy handwriting. Too small to hold a pair of lacy thong panties. Too narrow to be hiding away a photo. Just the right size for a cabin key card though.

"Well, then," he said softly, "let's see who you are. Hope you included a photo of yourself. I don't do blind dates."

Chuckling, Nick pulled the card from the envelope and glanced down at it. There was a photo all right. Laughter died instantly as he looked at the picture of two babies with black hair and pale blue eyes.

"What the hell?" Even while his brain started racing and his heartbeat stuttered in his chest, he read the scrawled message beneath the photo:

"Congratulations, Daddy. It's twins."

Two

She wasn't ready to give up the sun.

Jenna set her coffee cup down on the glass-topped table, turned her face to the sky and let the warm, late-morning sunshine pour over her like a blessing. Despite the fact that there were people around her, laughing, talking, diving into the pool, sending walls of water up in splashing waves, she felt alone in the light. And she really wasn't ready to sink back into the belly of the ship.

But she'd sent her note to Nick. And she'd told him where to find her. In that tiny, less-than-closet-size cabin. So she'd better be there when he arrived. With a sigh, she stood, slung her bag over her left shoulder and threaded her way through the crowds lounging on the Verandah Deck.

Someone touched her arm and Jenna stopped.

"Leaving already?" Mary Curran was smiling at her, and Jenna returned that smile with one of her own.

"Yeah. I have to get back down to my cabin. I um, have to meet someone there." At least, she was fairly certain Nick would show up. But what if he didn't? What if he didn't care about the fact that he was the father of her twin sons? What if he dismissed her note as easily as he'd deleted all of her attempts at e-mail communication?

A small, hard knot formed in the pit of her stomach. She'd like to see him try, that's all. They were on a ship in the middle of the ocean. How was he going to escape her? Nope. Come what may, she was going to have her say. She was going to face him down, at last, and tell him what she'd come to say.

"Oh God, honey." Mary grimaced and gave a dramatic shudder. "Do you really want to have a conversation down in the pit?"

Jenna laughed. "The pit?"

"That's what my husband, Joe, christened it in the middle of the night when he nearly broke his shin trying to get to the bathroom."

Grinning, Jenna said, "I guess the name fits all right. But yeah. I have to do it there. It's too private to be done up here."

Mary's eyes warmed as she looked at Jenna and said, "Well, then, go do whatever it is you have to do. Maybe I'll see you back in the sunshine later?"

Jenna nodded. She knew how cruise passengers tended to bond together. She'd seen it herself in the time she'd actually worked for Falcon Cruises. Friendships formed fast and furiously. People who were in relatively tight quarters—stuck on a ship in the middle of the ocean—tended to get to know each other more quickly than they might on dry land.

Shipboard romances happened, sure—just look what had happened to her. But more often, it was other kinds of relationships that bloomed and took hold. And right about now, Jenna decided, she could use a friendly face.

"You bet," she said, giving Mary a wide smile. "How about margaritas on the Calypso Deck? About five?"

Delighted, Mary beamed at her. "I'll be there."

As Jenna walked toward the elevator, she told herself that after her upcoming chat with Nick, she was probably going to *need* a margarita or two.

Nick jolted to his feet so fast, his desk chair shot backward, the wheels whirring against the wood floor until the chair slammed into the glass wall behind him.

"Is this a *joke?*"

Nick held the pale blue card in one tight fist and stared down at two tiny faces. The babies were identical except for their expressions. One looked into the camera and grinned, displaying a lot of gum and one deep dimple. The other was watching the picture taker with a serious, almost thoughtful look on his face.

And they both looked a hell of a lot like *him*.

"Twins?"

In an instant, emotions he could hardly name raced

through him. Anger, frustration, confusion and back to anger again. How the hell could he be a father? Nobody he knew had been pregnant. This couldn't be happening. He glanced up at the empty office as if half expecting someone to jump out, shout, "You've just been punk'd," and let him off the hook. But there were no cameras. There was no joke.

This was someone's idea of serious.

Well, hell, he told himself, it wasn't the first time some woman had tried to slap him with a paternity suit. But it was for damn sure the first time the gauntlet had been thrown down in such an imaginative way.

"Who, though?" He grabbed the envelope up, but only his name was scrawled across the front in a small, feminine hand. Turning over the card he still held, he saw more of that writing:

"We need to talk. Come to cabin 2A on the Riviera Deck."

"Riviera Deck." Though he hated like hell to admit it, he wasn't sure which deck that was. He had a lot of ships in his line and this was his first sail on this particular one. Though he meant to make *Falcon's Pride* his home, he hadn't had the chance yet to explore it from stem to stern as he did all the ships that carried his name.

For now, he stalked across the room to the framed set of detailed ship plans hanging on the far wall of his office. He'd had one done for each of the ships in his line. He liked looking at them, liked knowing that he was familiar with every inch of every ship. Liked knowing that he'd succeeded in creating the dream he'd started more than ten years before.

But at the moment, Nick wasn't thinking of his cruise line or of business at all. Now all he wanted to do was find the woman who'd sent him this card so he could assure himself that this was all some sort of mistake.

Narrowing his pale blue eyes, he ran one finger down the decks until he found the one he was looking for. Then he frowned. According to this, the Riviera Deck was *below* crew quarters.

"What the hell is going on?" Tucking the card with the pictures of the babies into the breast pocket of his white, short-sleeved shirt, he half turned toward the office door and bellowed, *"Teresa!"*

The door flew open a few seconds later and his assistant rushed in, eyes wide in stunned surprise. "Geez, what's wrong? Are we on fire or something?"

He ignored the attempt at humor, as well as the look of puzzlement on her face. Stabbing one finger against the glass-covered ship plans, he said only, "Look at this."

She hurried across the room, glanced at the plans, then shifted a look at him. "What exactly am I looking at?"

"This." He tapped his finger against the lowest deck on the diagram. "The Riviera Deck."

"Uh-huh."

"There are people staying down there."

"Oh."

Pleased that she'd caught on so fast, Nick said, "When the ship came out of refit ready for passengers,

I said specifically that those lower cabins weren't to be used."

"Yeah, you did, boss." She actually winced, whipped out her PDA and punched a few keys. "I'll do some checking. Find out what happened."

"You do that," he said, irritated as hell that someone, somewhere, hadn't paid attention to him. "For right now, though, find out how many of those cabins are occupied."

"Right."

While Teresa worked her electronic wizardry, Nick looked back at the framed plans and shook his head. Those lower cabins were too old, too small to be used on one of his ships. Sure, they'd undergone some refurbishing during the refit, but having them and using them were two different things. Those cabins, small and dark and cramped, weren't the kind of image Nick wanted associated with his cruise line.

"Boss?" Teresa looked at him. "According to the registry, only two of the five cabins are being used."

"That's something, anyway. Who's down there?"

"1A is occupied by a Joe and Mary Curran."

He didn't know any Currans and besides, the card had come from whoever was in the only other occupied cabin on that deck.

So he waited.

"2A is…" Teresa's voice trailed off and Nick watched as his usually unflappable assistant chewed at her bottom lip.

That couldn't be good.

"What is it?" When she didn't answer right away, he demanded, "Just tell me who's in the other cabin."

"Jenna," Teresa said and blew out a breath. "Jenna Baker's in 2A, Nick."

Nick made record time getting down to the Riviera Deck, and by the time he reached it, he'd already made the decision to close up this deck permanently. Damned if he'd house his paying guests in what amounted to little more than steerage.

Stepping off the elevator, he hit his head on a low cross beam and muttered a curse. The creaks and groans of the big ship as it pushed through the waves echoed through the narrow passageway like ghosts howling. The sound of the water against the hull was a crushing heartbeat and it was so damned dark in the abbreviated hallway, even the lights in the wall sconces barely made a dent in the blackness. And the hall itself was so narrow he practically had to traverse it sideways. True, it was good business to make sure you provided less expensive rooms, but he'd deal with that another way. He'd be damned if his passengers would leave a cruise blinking at the sun like bats.

With his head pounding, his temper straining on a tight leash, he stopped in front of 2A, took a breath and raised his right fist to knock. Before he could, the narrow door was wrenched open and there she stood.

Jenna Baker.

She shouldn't have still been able to affect him. He'd had her after all. Had her and then let her go more than a year ago. So why then was he suddenly struck by the turquoise-blue of her eyes? Why did that tight, firm mouth make him want to kiss her until her lips eased apart and let him back in? Why did the fact that she looked furious make his blood steam in his veins? What the hell did *she* have to be mad about?

"I heard you in the hall," she said.

"Good ears," he conceded. "Considering all the other noises down here."

A brief, tight smile curved her mouth. "Yeah, it's lovely living in the belly of the beast. When they raise anchor it's like a symphony."

He hadn't considered that, but he was willing to bet the noise was horrific. Just another reason to seal up these rooms and never use them again. However, that was for another time. What he wanted now were answers.

"Good one," he said. "That's why you're here, then? To talk about the ship?"

"You know why I'm here."

He lifted one hand to the doorjamb and leaned in toward her. "I know what you'd like me to think. The question is, why? Why now? What're you after, Jenna?"

"I'm not going to talk about this in the hall."

"Fine." He stepped inside, moving past her, but the quarters were so cramped, their chests brushed together and he could almost feel his skin sizzle.

It had been like that from the beginning. The moment he'd touched her that first night in the moonlight, he'd felt a slam of something that was damn near molten sliding through him. And it seemed that time hadn't eased it back any.

He got a grip on his hormones, took two steps until he was at the side of a bed built for a sixth-grader, then turned around to glare at her. God, the cabin was so small it felt as though the walls were closing in on him and, truth to tell, they wouldn't have far to move. He felt as if he should be slouching to avoid skimming the top of his head along the ceiling. Every light in the cabin was on and it still looked like twilight.

But Nick wasn't here for the ambience and there was nothing he could do about the rooms at the moment. Now all he wanted was an explanation. He waited for her to shut the door, sealing the two of them into the tiny cracker box of a room before he said, "What's the game this time, Jenna?"

"This isn't a game, Nick," she said, folding her arms over her chest. "It wasn't a game then, either."

"Right." He laughed and tried not to breathe deep. The scent of her was already inside him, the tiny room making him even more aware of it than he would have been ordinarily. "You didn't *want* to lie to me. You had no choice."

Her features tightened. "Do we really have to go over the old argument again?"

He thought about it for a moment, then shook his head. He didn't want to look at the past. Hell. He didn't want to be here *now*. "No, we don't. So why don't you just say what it is you have to say so we can be done."

"Always the charmer," she quipped.

He shifted from one foot to the other and banged his elbow on the wall. "Jenna…"

"Fine. You got my note?"

He reached into the pocket of his shirt, pulled out the card, glanced at the pictures of the babies, then handed it to her. "Yeah. I got it. Now how about you explain it?"

She looked down at those two tiny faces and he saw her lips curve slightly even as her eyes warmed. But that moment passed quickly as she lifted her gaze to him and skewered him with it. "I would have thought the word *daddy* was fairly self-explanatory."

"Explain, anyway."

"Fine." Jenna walked across the tiny room, bumped Nick out of her way with a nudge from her hip that had him hitting the wall and then bent down to drag a suitcase out from under her bed. The fact that she could actually *feel* his gaze on her butt while she did it only annoyed her.

She would not pay any attention to the rush of heat she felt just being close to him again. She would certainly not acknowledge the jump and stutter of her heartbeat, and if certain other of her body parts were warm and tingling, she wasn't going to admit to that, either.

Dragging the suitcase out, she went to lift it, but Nick was there first, pushing her fingers aside to hoist the bag onto the bed. If her skin was humming from that one idle touch, he didn't have to know it, did he?

She unzipped the bag, pulled out a blue leather scrapbook and handed it to him. "Here. Take a look. Then we'll talk more."

The book seemed tiny in his big, tanned hands. He

barely glanced at it before shooting a hard look at her again. "What's this about?"

"Look at it, Nick."

He did. The moment she'd been waiting so long for stretched out as the seconds ticked past. She held her breath and watched his face, the changing expressions written there as he flipped through the pages of pictures she'd scrapbooked specifically for this purpose. It was a chronicle of sorts. Of her life since losing her job, discovering she was pregnant and then the birth of the twins. In twenty hand-decorated pages, she'd brought him up to speed on the last year and a half of her life.

Up to speed on his sons. The children he'd created and had never met.

The only reason she was here, visiting a man who'd shattered her heart without a backward glance.

When he was finished, his gaze lifted to hers and she could have sworn she saw icicles in his eyes.

"I'm supposed to believe that I'm the father of your babies?"

"Take another look at them, Nick. They both look just like you."

He did, but his features remained twisted into a cynical expression even while his eyes flashed with banked emotion. "Lots of people have black hair and blue eyes."

"Not all of them have dimples in their left cheek." She reached out, flipped to a specific page and pointed. "Both of your sons do. Just like yours."

He ran one finger over the picture of the boys as if he could somehow touch them with the motion, and that small action touched something in Jenna. For one brief instant, Nick Falco looked almost…vulnerable.

It didn't last long, though. His mouth worked as if he were trying to bite back words fighting desperately to get out. Finally, as if coming to some inner decision, he nodded, blew out a breath and said, "For the sake of argument, let's say they are mine."

"They are."

"So why didn't you tell me before? Why the hell would you wait until they're, what…?"

"Four months old."

He looked at the pictures again, closed the book and held on to it in one tight fist. "Four months old and you didn't think I should know?"

So much for the tiny kernel of warmth she'd almost experienced.

"You're amazing. You ignore me for months and now you're upset that I didn't contact you?"

"What're you talking about?"

Jenna shook her head and silently thanked heaven that she'd been smart enough to not only keep a log of every e-mail she'd ever sent him, but had thought to print them all out and bring them along. Dipping back into the suitcase, she whipped a thick manila envelope out and laid it atop the scrapbook he was still holding. "There. E-mails. Every one I sent you. They're all dated. You can see that I sent one at least once a week. Sometimes twice. I've been trying to get hold of you for more than a year, Nick."

He opened the envelope as she talked, and flipped quickly through the printouts.

"I—" He frowned down at the stack of papers.

She took advantage of his momentary speechlessness. "I've been trying to reach you since I first found out I was pregnant, Nick."

"How was I supposed to know that *this* is what you were trying to tell me?"

"You might have read one or two of them," Jenna pointed out and managed to hide the hurt in her voice.

He scowled at her. "How the hell could I have guessed you were trying to tell me I was a father? I just thought you were after money."

She hissed in a breath as the insult of that slapped at her. Bubbling with fury, Jenna really had to fight the urge to give him a swift kick. How like Nick to assume that any woman who was with him was only in it for what she could get from him. But then, he'd spent most of the past ten years surrounding himself with the very users he'd suspected her of being. People who wanted to be seen with him because he was one of the world's most eligible billionaires. Those hangers-on wanted to be in his inner circle because that's where the excitement was and it made them feel important, to be a part of Nick's world.

All Jenna had wanted was his arms around her. His kiss. His whispers in the middle of the night. Naturally, he hadn't believed her.

Now things were different. He had responsibilities that she was here to see he stood up to. After all, she hadn't come here for herself. She'd come for her kids. For *his* sons.

"I wasn't interested in your money back then, Nick. But things have changed and now, I *am* after money," she said and saw sparks flare in his icy eyes. "It's called child support, Nick. And your sons deserve it."

He stared at her. "Child support."

"That's right." She lifted her chin even higher. "If I only had myself to think about, I wouldn't be here, believe me. So don't worry, I'm not here to take advantage of you. I'm not looking for a huge chunk of the Falco bank account."

"Is that right?"

"That's right. I started my own business and it's doing fine," she said, a hint of pride slipping into her tone while she spoke. "But twins make every expense doubled and I just can't do it all on my own." Lifting her gaze to meet his, she said, "When you never responded to my e-mails, I told myself you didn't deserve to know your babies. And if I weren't feeling a little desperate I wouldn't be here at all. Trust me, if you think I'm enjoying being here like this, you're crazy."

"So you would have hidden them from me?" His voice was low, soft and just a little dangerous.

Jenna wasn't worried. Nick might be an arrogant, self-satisfied jerk, but physically dangerous to her or any other woman, he wasn't. "If you mean would I hide the fact that their father couldn't care less about them from my sons…then, yes. That's just what I'll do."

"If they are my sons," he whispered, "no one will keep me from them."

A flicker of uneasiness sputtered in Jenna's chest, but she told herself not to react. Physical threats meant nothing, but the thought of him challenging her for custody of their children did. Even as she considered it, though, she let the worry dissipate. Babies weren't part of Nick's world, and no matter what he said at the moment, he would never give up the life he had for one that included double diaper duty.

"Nick, we both know you have no interest in being a father."

"You have no idea what I do or don't care about, Jenna." He moved in close, taking that one small step that brought his body flush to hers. Jenna hadn't been prepared for the move and sucked in a gulp of air as his chest pressed into hers.

She looked up into his eyes and felt her knees wobble a little at the intensity of his stare. He cupped her cheek in one hand, and the heat of his skin seeped into hers, causing a flush of warmth that slid through her like sweet syrup.

"I promise you, though," he murmured, dipping his head in as if he were going to kiss her and stopping just a breath away from her lips, "you will find out."

Three

She ducked her head and slapped his hand away and even *that* contact felt too damn good. Nick stepped back and away from her, which, in that cabin, meant that he was halfway out the door. So once he felt as though he could look at her without wanting to wrap his hands in her hair and pull her mouth to his, he shifted his gaze to hers.

"I don't have the time to go through this right now."

She smirked at him, folded her arms over her chest in a classic defensive posture. "Oh, sure, worlds to conquer, women to seduce. Busy, busy."

"Clever as ever, I see." He didn't even want to admit to himself how much he'd missed that smart mouth of hers. Always a retort. Always a dig, putting him in his place, deflating his ego before it had a chance to expand.

There weren't many people like Jenna in his life. Mostly, those he knew were too busy kissing his ass to argue with him. Everyone but Teresa, that is. And of course, Jenna. But she wasn't a part of his life anymore.

"We'll have dinner tonight. My suite."

"I don't think so."

"You came here to talk to me, right?"

"Yes, but—"

"So we'll talk. Seven o'clock."

Before she could argue, stall or whatever else might come into her too-quick mind, he opened the door and left her cabin. He took a breath in the dark hall, then headed for the elevator that would take him out of the bowels of the ship back into the light.

By five o'clock, she was more than ready to meet Mary for margaritas.

Jenna'd left her tiny, hideous, airless cabin only a few minutes after Nick had. Frankly, his presence had been practically imprinted on the minuscule space and had made the cabin seem even smaller than it actually was. And she hadn't thought that would have been possible.

But he'd shaken her more than she'd thought he would. Just being near him again had awakened feelings and emotions she'd trained herself more than a year ago to ignore. Now they were back and she wasn't sure how to handle them. After all, it wasn't as if she had a lot of experience with this sort of thing. Before Nick, there'd been only one other man in her life, and he hadn't come close to affecting her in the way Nick had. Of course, since Nick, the only men in her life preferred drooling on her shoulder to slow dances in the dark.

Just thinking about her boys brought an ache to Jenna's heart. She'd never left them before, and though she knew the twins were in good hands, she hated not being with them.

"But I'm on this boat for their sakes," she reminded herself sternly.

With that thought in mind, her gaze swept the interior of Captain Jack's Bar and Lounge. Like everywhere else on this ship, Nick hadn't skimped. The walls were pale wood that gleamed in the light glinting down on the crowd from overhead chandeliers shaped like ship's wheels. The bar was a slinky curve of pale wood with a granite top the color of molten honey.

Conversations flowed in a low rumble of sound that was punctuated by the occasional clink of crystal or a high-pitched laugh. First day at sea and already the party had begun.

Well, for everyone but Jenna. She hadn't exactly been in celebration mode after Nick left her cabin.

In fact, Jenna'd spent most of the day lying on a chaise on the Verandah Deck, trying to get lost in the book she'd picked up in the gift shop. But she couldn't concentrate on the words long enough to make any progress. Time and again, her thoughts had returned to Nick. His face. His eyes. The cool dismissal on his face when he'd first seen the pictures of their sons.

She didn't know what was coming next, and the worry over it had gnawed at her insides all day. Which was why she'd decided to keep her margarita date with Mary. Jenna had spent too much time alone today, with too much time for thinking. What she needed now was some distraction. A little tequila-flavored relaxation sounded great. Especially since she had dinner with Nick to look forward to.

"Oh God," she whispered as her stomach fisted into knots again.

"Jenna!"

A woman's voice called out to her, and Jenna turned in that direction. She spotted Mary, standing up at one of the tables along the wall, waving and smiling at her. Gratefully Jenna headed her way, threading a path through the milling crowd. When she reached the table, she slid onto a chair and smiled at the margarita already waiting for her.

"Hope you don't mind. I ordered one for you as soon as I got here," Mary told her, taking a big gulp of her own oversize drink.

"Mind?" Jenna said, reaching for her frosty glass, "Are you kidding? This is fabulous." When she'd taken a long, deep gulp of the icy drink, she sat back and looked at her new friend.

Mary was practically bouncing in her seat, and her eyes were shining with excitement. Her blond hair looked wind tousled and her skin was a pale red, as if she'd had plenty of sun today. "I've been looking for you all over this ship," she said, grinning like a loon. "I had to see you. Find out where they put you."

Jenna blinked and shook her head. "What do you mean? Put me? Where *who* put me?"

Mary stretched one hand out and grabbed Jenna's for a quick squeeze. "Oh my God. You haven't been back down to the pit all day, have you?"

"No way," Jenna said on a sigh. "After my meeting, I came topside and I've been putting off going back down by hanging out on the Verandah Deck."

"So you don't know."

"Know what?" Jenna was beginning to think that maybe Mary had had a few margaritas too many. "What're you talking about?"

"It's the most incredible thing. I really can't believe it myself and I've seen it." She slapped one hand to her pale blue blouse and groaned like she was in the midst of an orgasm.

"Mary...what is going on?"

"Right, right." The blonde picked up her drink, took a big gulp and said, "It happened early this afternoon. Joe and I were up on the Promenade, you know, looking at all the shops. Well," she admitted, "I was looking, Joe was being dragged reluctantly along behind me. And when we came out of the Crystal Candle—which you should really check out, they have some amazing stuff in there—"

Jenna wondered if there was a way to get Mary to stay on track long enough to tell her what was happening. But probably not, so she took a sip of her drink and prepared to wait it out. She didn't have to wait long.

"When we came out," Mary was saying, "there was a ship steward waiting for us. He said, 'Mr. and Mrs. Curran?' all official-sounding and for a second I wondered what we'd done wrong, but we hadn't done anything and so Joe says, 'What's this about?' and the steward only told us to go with him."

"Mary…"

Her new friend grinned. "I'm getting to it. Really. It's just that it's all so incredible—right." She waved one hand to let Jenna know she was back on track, then she went right back to her story. "The steward takes us up to the owner's suite—you know, Nick Falco?"

"Yeah," Jenna murmured. "I know who he is."

"Who in the English-speaking world doesn't?" Mary said on a laugh, then continued. "So we're standing there in the middle of a suite that looks like a palace or something and Nick Falco himself comes up to us, introduces himself and *apologizes* about our cabin in the pit."

"What?" Jenna just stared at the other woman, not sure what to make of all this.

"I know! I was completely floored, let me tell you. I was almost speechless and Joe can tell you that that almost never happens." She paused for another gulp of her drink and when she finished it, held up one hand for the waitress to bring another. "So there we are and Mr. Falco's being so nice and so sincere about how he feels so badly about the state of the rooms on the Riviera Deck—and can you believe how badly misnamed that deck is?—and he *insists* on upgrading us."

"Upgrading?"

"Seriously upgrading," Mary said as she thanked the waitress for her fresh margarita. She waited until the server had disappeared with her empty glass before continuing. "So I'm happy, because hey, that tiny cabin is just so hideous. And I'm expecting a middle-grade cabin with maybe a porthole, which would be *great*. But that's not what we got."

"It's not?" Jenna set her glass down onto the table and watched as Mary's eyes actually sparkled even harder than they had been.

"Oh, no. Mr. Falco said that most of the cabins were already full, which is how we got stuck in those tiny ones in the first place. So he moved us into a *luxury suite!*"

"He did?"

"It's on the Splendor Deck. The same level as Mr. Falco's himself. And Jenna, our suite is amazing! It's bigger than my *house*. Plus, he said our entire cruise is on him. He's refunding what we paid for that hideous cabin and insisting that we pay *nothing* on this trip."

"Wow." Nick had always taken great pride in keeping his passengers happy, but this was…well, to use Mary's word, *amazing*. Cruise passengers usually looked forward to a bill at the end of a cruise that could amount to several hundred dollars. Oh, the food and accommodations were taken care of when you rented your cabin. But incidentals could really pile up on a person if they weren't paying attention.

By doing this, Nick had given Mary and her husband a cruising experience that most people would never know. Maybe there was more heart to the man than she'd once believed.

"He's just so nice," Mary was saying, stirring her slender straw through the icy confection of her margarita. "Somehow, I thought a man that rich and that famous and that playboylike would be sort of…I don't know, snotty. But he wasn't at all. He was really thoughtful and kind, and I can't believe this is all really happening."

"It's terrific, Mary," Jenna said sincerely. Even if she and Nick had their problems, she could respect and admire him for what he'd done for these people.

"I'm really hoping your upgrade will have you somewhere near us, Jenna. Maybe you should go and see a steward about it, find out where they're moving you."

"Oh," Jenna said with a shake of her head, "I don't think I'll be moving." She couldn't see Nick doing her any favors. Not with the hostility that had been spilled between them only a few hours ago. And though she was happy for Mary and her husband, Jenna wasn't looking forward to being the only resident on the lowest deck of the ship. Now it would not only be small and dark, but small and dark and creepy.

"Of course you will," Mary countered. "They wouldn't move us and *not* you. That wouldn't make any sense at all."

Jenna just smiled. She wasn't about to go into her past history with Nick at the moment. So there was nothing she could really say to her new friend, other than, "I'll find out when I go downstairs to change. I've got a dinner appointment in about," she checked her wristwatch, "an hour and a half. So let's just have our drinks and you can tell me all about your new suite before I have to leave."

Mary frowned briefly, then shrugged. "Okay, but if you haven't been upgraded, I'm going to be really upset."

"Don't be." Jenna smiled and, to distract her, asked, "Do you have a balcony?"

"Two!" Mary crowed a little, grinned like a kid on Christmas morning and said, "Joe and I are going to have dinner on one of them tonight. Out under the stars…mmm. Time for a little romance now that we're out of the pit!"

Romance.

As Mary talked about the plans she and her husband had made for a night of seduction, Jenna smiled. She wished her friend well, but as for herself, she'd tried romance and had gotten bitten in the butt for her trouble. Nope, she was through with the hearts-and-flowers thing. All she wanted now was Nick's assurance that he would do the right thing and allow her to raise her sons the way she wanted to.

Her cabin was locked.

"What the—" Jenna slid her key card into the slot, whipped it out again and…nothing. The red light on the lock still shone as if it was taunting her. She knew it wouldn't do any good, but still, she grabbed the door handle and twisted it hard before shaking it, as if she could somehow convince the damn thing to open for her.

But nothing changed.

She glanced over her shoulder at what had been the Curran cabin, but no help would be found there. The happy couple were comfortably ensconced in their floating palace. "Which is all fine and good for *them*," Jenna muttered. "But what about *me?*"

Giving up, she turned around, leaned back against her closed door and looked up and down the narrow, dark corridor. This was just great. Alone in the pit. No way to call for help. She'd have to go back topside and find a ship phone.

"Perfect. Just perfect." Her head was a little swimmy from the margaritas and her stomach was twisted in knots of expectation over the upcoming dinner with Nick, and now she couldn't even take a shower and change clothes. "This is going so well."

She stabbed the elevator button and when the door opened instantly, she stepped inside. The Muzak pumping through the speakers was a simply hideous orchestral rendition of "Stairway to Heaven" and didn't do a thing to calm her down.

Jenna exited onto the Promenade Deck and was instantly swallowed by the crowd of passengers wandering around the shops. The lobby area was done in glass and wood with a skylight installed in the domed ceiling overhead that displayed a blue summer sky studded with white, puffy clouds.

But she wasn't exactly on a sightseeing mission. She plowed through the crowd to a booth where one of Nick's employees stood ready to help passengers with answers to their questions. The man in the red shirt and white slacks wearing a name tag that read Jeff gave Jenna a welcoming smile as he asked, "How can I help you?"

She tried not to take her frustration out on him. After all, he was trying to help. "Hi, I'm Jenna Baker, and I'm in cabin 2A on the Riviera deck and—"

"Jenna Baker?" he interrupted her quickly, frowned a little, then checked a clipboard on the desk in front of him.

"Yes," she said, attempting to draw his attention back to her. "I just came from my cabin and my key card didn't work, so—"

"Ms. Baker," he said, his attitude changing from flirtatious and friendly to crisp professionalism. "There's a notation here asking that you be escorted to the Splendor Deck."

Where Mary's new cabin was. So Nick had upgraded Jenna, as well? Unexpected and frankly, a relief. A suite would be much more comfortable than the closet she'd been assigned.

But… "All of my things are still in my cabin, so I really need to get in there to pack and—"

"No, ma'am," Jeff said quickly, smiling again. "Your cabin was packed up by the staff and your luggage has already been moved. If you'll just take that elevator—" he paused to point at a bank of elevators opposite them "—to the Splendor Deck, you'll be met and directed to your new cabin."

Strange. She didn't know how she felt about someone else rooting through her things, but if it meant she could get into a shower, change clothes and get ready for her meeting with Nick, then she'd go with it. "Okay then, and, um, thanks."

"It's a pleasure, Ms. Baker. I hope you enjoy your stay with Falcon Cruises."

"Uh-huh." She waved distractedly and headed for the elevators. Not much chance of her enjoying her cruise when she was here to do battle with the King of Cruise Lines. Nope, the most she could hope for was getting out of the pit and into a nicer cabin courtesy of one Mr. Nick Falco.

When the elevator stopped on the Splendor Deck, Jenna stepped out into a wide, lushly carpeted hallway. The ceiling was tinted glass, open to the skies but dark enough to keep people from frying in direct sunlight. The walls were the color of rich cream and dotted with paintings of tropical islands, ships at sea and even simple ocean scenes with whitecaps that looked real enough to wet your fingers if you reached out to touch them.

The one thing she didn't see was someone to tell her where to go now that she was here. But almost before that thought formed in her mind, Jenna heard the sound of footsteps hurrying toward her. She turned and buried her surprise when she recognized Teresa Hogan, Nick's assistant.

"Jenna. It's good to see you," the older woman said, striding to her with long, determined steps. Her smile looked real, her sharp green eyes were warm and when she reached out a hand in welcome, Jenna was happy to take it.

"Nice to see you, too, Teresa." They'd met during that magical week with Nick more than a year ago.

Ordinarily, as just an assistant to the cruise director, Jenna never would have come into contact with the big boss's righthand woman. But as the woman having an affair with Nick, Jenna'd met Teresa almost right away.

Teresa had been friendly enough, until the truth about Jenna being one of Nick's employees had come out. Then the coolly efficient Teresa had drawn a line in the sand, metaphorically speaking. She chose to defend Nick and make sure Jenna never had the chance to get near him again.

At the time, it had made Jenna furious, now she could understand that loyalty. And even appreciate it in a way.

"How've you been?" Jenna smiled as she asked, determined to keep the friendly tone that Teresa had begun.

"Busy." The older woman shrugged. "You know the boss. He keeps us hopping."

"Yes," Jenna mused. "He always did."

A long, uncomfortable moment passed before Teresa said, "So, you know about the cabins on the Riviera Deck being sealed."

"That's why I'm here," Jenna said, shooting a glance up and down the long, empty hallway. "I saw Mary Curran earlier, she told me she and her husband had been upgraded. And then I went to my cabin and couldn't get in. Jeff at information sent me here."

"Good." Teresa nodded and her short, dark hair didn't so much as dip with the movement. She pointed behind Jenna to the end of the wide, plush hall. "The Currans' suite is right along there. And now if you'll come with me, I'll take you to your new cabin. We can talk as we go."

They headed off in the opposite direction of the Currans'. Walking toward the bow of the great ship, Jenna casually glanced at the artwork as she passed it and tried to figure out what was going on. Being escorted by the owner's assistant seemed unusual. Shouldn't a steward have been put in charge of seeing her to her new accommodations? But did it really matter? Jenna followed along in Teresa's wake, hurrying to keep up with the woman who seemed always to be in high gear.

"You can imagine," Teresa said over her shoulder, "that Nick was appalled to find out the cabins on the lowest deck had been rented."

"Appalled, huh?" Jenna rolled her eyes. Clearly Teresa was still faithful to the boss. "Then why rent them at all?"

Teresa's steps hitched a little as she acknowledged, "It was a mistake. The cabins below were supposed to have been sealed before leaving port for this maiden voyage. The person responsible for going against the boss's orders was reprimanded."

"Shot at dawn? Or just fired without references?" Jenna asked in a low-pitched voice.

Teresa stopped dead and Jenna almost ran right into her.

"Nick doesn't fire indiscriminately and you know it." Teresa lifted her chin pointedly as she moved to protect her boss. "*You* lied to him. That's why you were fired, Jenna."

A flush stole through her. Yes, she'd lied. She hadn't meant to, but that's what had happened. And she hadn't been able to find a way out of the lie once it had begun. Still, he might have listened to her once the bag was open and the cat was out.

"He could have let me explain," Jenna argued and met that cool green stare steadily.

Just for an instant the harsh planes of Teresa's expression softened a bit. She shook her head and blew out a breath. "Look, Nick's not perfect—"

"Quite the admission coming from you."

Teresa smiled tightly. "True. I do defend him. I do what I can to help him. He's a good boss. And he's been good to me. I'm not saying that how he handled the… situation with you was right—"

Jenna stopped her, holding up both hands. "You know what? Never mind. It was more than a year ago. It's over and done. And whatever Nick and I had has ended, too."

Teresa cocked her head to one side and looked at her thoughtfully. "You really think so, hmm?"

"Trust me on this," Jenna said as they started walking again. "Nick is *so* over me."

"If you say so." Teresa stopped in front of a set of double doors. Waving one hand at them as if she were a game show hostess displaying a brand-new refrigerator, she said, "Here we are. Your new quarters. I hope you like them."

"I'm sure they'll be great. Way better than the Riviera Deck anyway."

"Oh," Teresa said with a smile, "that's certainly a fair

statement. You go on in, your things have been un-packed. I'm sure I'll be seeing you again."

"Okay." Jenna stood in the hall and watched as Teresa strode briskly down the long hallway. There was something going on here, she thought, she just couldn't quite puzzle it out yet.

Then she glanced at her wristwatch, saw she had less than an hour to get ready for her dinner with Nick and opened the door with the key card Teresa had given her.

She walked inside, took a deep breath and almost genuflected.

The room was incredible—huge, and sprawlingly spacious, with glass walls that displayed a view of the ocean that stretched out into infinity. The wide blue sky was splashed with white clouds and the roiling sea re-flected that deep blue back up at it.

Pale wood floors shone with an old gold gleam and the furniture scattered around the room looked designed for comfort. There was a fireplace on one wall, a wet bar in the corner and what looked to be priceless works of art dotting the walls. There were vases filled with glorious arrangements of fresh flowers that scented the air until she felt as if she were walking in a garden.

"This can't be my cabin," Jenna whispered, whip-ping her head from side to side as she tried to take in everything at once. "Okay, sure, upgraded to a suite. But this is the Taj Mahal of suites. There has to be a mistake, that's all."

"There's no mistake," Nick said as he walked easily into the room and gave her a smile that even from across the room was tempting enough to make her gasp. "This is my suite and it's where you'll be staying."

Four

"You can't be serious." Jenna took one instinctive step back, but couldn't go anywhere unless she turned, opened the door and sprinted down that long hallway.

"Damn serious," he said, and walked toward her like a man with all the time in the world.

He wore a dark blue, long-sleeved shirt, open at the collar, sleeves rolled back to his elbows. His black slacks had a knife-sharp crease in them, and his black shoes shone. But it was his eyes that held her. That pale blue gaze fixed on her as if he could see straight through her. As if he were looking for all of her secrets and wouldn't give up the quest until he had them.

"Nick, this is a bad idea," she said, and silently congratulated herself on keeping her tone even.

"Why's that?" He spread both hands out and shrugged. "You came to my boat. You tell me I'm the father of your children and insist we have to talk. So now you're here. We can talk."

Talk. Yeah.

In a floating palace that looked designed for seduction. Meeting Nick in her tiny cabin hadn't exactly been easy, but at least down there, there'd been no distractions. No easy opulence. No sensory overload of beauty.

This was a bad idea. Jenna knew it. Felt it. And didn't have a single clue how to get out of it.

"We shouldn't be staying together," she said finally, and winced because even to her she sounded like a prissy librarian or something.

"We'll be staying in the same cabin. Not together. There's a difference." He was so close now all he had to do was reach out and he could touch her.

If he did, she'd be a goner though, and she knew it.

"What's the matter, Jenna?" he asked. "Don't trust yourself alone with me?"

"Oh, please." She choked out a half laugh that she desperately hoped sounded convincing. "Could you get over yourself for a minute here?"

He gave her a slow smile that dug out the dimple in his left cheek and lit wicked lights in his eyes. Jenna's stomach flip-flopped and her mouth went dry.

"I'm not the one having a problem."

Did he have to smell so good?

"No problem," she said, lifting her chin and forcing

herself to look him dead in the eye. "Trust me when I say all I want from you is what your kids deserve."

The smile on Nick's face faded away as her words slammed home. Was he a father? Were those twin boys his? He had to know. To do that, he needed some time with Jenna. He needed to talk to her, figure out what she was after, make a decision about where to go from here.

Funny, Nick had been waiting all afternoon to enjoy that look of stunned disbelief on Jenna's face when she first walked into his suite and realized that she'd be staying with him. Payback for how he must have looked when he'd first seen the photo of the babies she claimed were his sons. But he hadn't enjoyed it as much as he'd thought. Because there were other considerations. Bigger considerations.

His sons. Nick's insides twisted into knots that were beginning to feel almost familiar. Countless times during the day, he'd looked at the photo of the babies he still carried in his shirt pocket. Countless times he'd asked himself if it was really possible that he was a father.

And though he wasn't prepared to take Jenna's word for his paternity, he had to admit that it wasn't likely she'd have come here to the ship, signing up for a cruise if it wasn't true. Not that he thought she'd have any qualms about lying—she'd lied to him when she first met him after all—but *this* lie was too easily found out.

So he was willing to accept the possibility. Which left him exactly where? *That* was the question that had been circling in his mind all afternoon, and he was no closer to an answer now than he had been earlier.

He looked her up and down and could admit at least to himself that she looked damn good to him. Her dark blond hair was a little windblown, stray tendrils pulling away from her braid to lay against her face. Her eyes were wide and gleaming with suspicion, and, strangely enough, that didn't do a damn thing to mitigate the attraction he felt as he drew in a breath that carried her scent deep into his lungs.

"I'll stay here, but I'm not sleeping with you," she announced suddenly.

Nick shook his head and smiled. "Don't flatter yourself. I said you're staying in my suite, not my bed. As it happens, there are three bedrooms here besides my own. Your things have been unpacked in one of them."

She frowned a little and the flush of color in her cheeks faded a bit. "Oh."

"Disappointed?" Nick asked, feeling a quick jolt of something hot and reckless punch through him.

"Please," she countered quickly. "You're not exactly irresistible, Nick."

He frowned at that, but since he didn't actually believe her, he let it go.

"I'm actually grateful to be out of that hole at the bottom of the ship," she added, glancing around at the suite before shifting her gaze back to his. "And if staying here is the price I have to pay for your attention, then I'll pay."

One dark eyebrow lifted. "How very brave of you to put up with such appalling conditions as these."

"Look," Jenna told him, "if you don't mind, it's been

a long day. So how about you just tell me which room
is mine so I can take a shower. Then we'll talk."

"Fine. This way." He turned, pointed and said,
"Down that hall. First door on the left."

"Thanks."

"My bedroom's at the end of the hall on the right."

She stopped, looked back at him over her shoulder
and said, "I'll make a note."

"You do that," he whispered as she left the room,
shoulders squared, chin lifted, steps long and slow, as
if she were being marched to her death.

His gaze dropped to the curve of her behind and
something inside him stirred into life. Something he
hadn't felt since the last time he'd seen Jenna. Something he'd thought he was long past.

He still wanted her.

Spinning around, Nick stalked across the room to the
wide bank of windows that displayed an awe-inspiring
view of the sea. His gaze locked on the horizon as he
fought to control the raging tide of lust rising inside him.

Jenna Baker.

She'd turned him inside out more than a year ago. Ever
since, he'd been haunted by memories of their time
together until he wasn't sure if what he was remembering was real or just fevered imaginings offered by a mind
that couldn't seem to let go of the woman who'd lied to
him. And Nick wasn't a man to forget something like
that. Now she was back again. Here, trapped on his
ship in the middle of the ocean with nowhere to go to
escape him.

Yes, they had plenty to talk about—and if her children were indeed his sons, then there were a lot of decisions to be made. But, he told himself as he shoved both hands into his slacks pockets and smiled faintly at the sunlight glinting on the vast expanse of the sea, there would be enough time for him to have her again.

To feel her under him. To lay claim to her body once more. To drive her past the edge of reason. Then, when he was satisfied that he'd gotten her out from under his skin, he'd kick her loose and she'd be out of his life once and for all. He wouldn't even allow her to be a memory this time.

In Neptune's Garden, the elegant restaurant on the Splendor Deck, Jenna watched as Nick worked the room.

As the owner of the ship, he wasn't exactly expected to mingle with the passengers, but Nick was an executive like no other. He not only mingled, he seemed to enjoy himself. And with her arm tucked through his, Jenna felt like a queen moving through an adoring crowd.

Again and again, as they walked to their table, Nick stopped to chat with people sitting at the white linen–covered tables. Making sure they were enjoying the ship, asking if there was anything they needed and didn't have, if there was anything that the crew could do to make their stay more pleasurable.

Of course the single women on board were more than anxious to meet the gorgeous, wealthy, eligible Nick Falco. And the fact that Jenna was on his arm didn't dissuade them from flirting desperately.

"It's a beautiful ship, Mr. Falco," one woman said with a sigh as she shook his hand. She tossed her thick black hair back over her shoulder and licked her lips.

"Thank you," he said, smiling at her and the two other women seated with her. "I'm happy you're enjoying yourselves. If there's anything you need, please be sure to speak to a steward."

"Oh," the brunette cooed, "we will. I promise."

Jenna just managed to keep from rolling her eyes. All three women were looking at Nick as if he were the first steak they'd stumbled on after leaving a spa dinner of spinach leaves and lemon slices. And he was eating it up, of course.

When he turned to go, he led her on through the crowd and Jenna swore she could feel the death stare from those women boring into her back.

"Well, that was tacky," she murmured.

"Tacky?"

"The way she practically drooled on you."

"Ah," Nick said, flashing a quick grin at her as he opened his right hand—the hand the brunette had shaken and clung to. A cabin key card rested in the center of his palm and the number P230 was scrawled across the top in ink. "So I'm guessing this makes it even tackier."

"Oh, for God's sake," Jenna snapped, wanting to spin around and shoot a few daggers at the brunette with no class. "I was *with* you. For all she knew I was your girlfriend."

His pale blue eyes sparkled and his grin widened

enough that the dimple in his left cheek was a deep cleft. "Jealous?"

She tried to pull her hand free of the crook of his arm, but he held her tight. Frowning, she said, "No. Not jealous. Just irritated."

"By her? Or by me?"

"A little of both." She tipped her head back to look up at him. "Why didn't you give the key back to her?"

He looked genuinely surprised at the suggestion. "Why would I embarrass her in front of her friends?"

Jenna snorted indelicately. "I'm guessing it's next to impossible to embarrass a woman like *that*."

"This really bothers you."

It always had, she thought. When she first went to work for Falcon Cruise Lines, she'd heard all the stories. About how on every cruise there were women lining up to take their place in Nick's bed. He was a player, no doubt. But for some reason, Jenna had allowed herself to be swept up in the magic of the moment. She'd somehow convinced herself that what they'd had together was different from what he found with countless other women.

Apparently, she'd been wrong about a few things.

"One question," she said, keeping her voice low enough that no one they passed could possibly overhear.

"Okay."

"Are you planning on using that key?"

He only looked at her for a long moment or two, then sighing, he stopped a waiter, handed over the key card and whispered something Jenna didn't quite catch. Then he turned to her. "That answer your question?"

"Depends," she said. "What did you tell him?"

"To return the card to the brunette with my thanks and my regrets."

A small puddle of warmth settled in Jenna's chest and even though she knew it was foolish, she couldn't quite seem to quash it. "Thank you."

He dipped his head in a faint mockery of a bow. "I find there's only one woman I'm interested in talking to at the moment."

"Nick…"

"Here we are," he said, interrupting whatever she would have said as he seated her in the navy blue leather booth that was kept reserved for him. "Jenna, let's have some dinner and get started on that talk you wanted."

Jenna slid behind the linen-draped table and watched him as he moved around to take a seat beside her. "All right, Nick. First let me ask you something, though."

"What?"

"All the people you talked to as we came through the restaurant…all the women you flirted with…" Jenna shook her head as she looked at him. "You haven't changed a bit, have you?"

His features tightened as he looked at her, and in the flickering light of the single candle in the middle of their table, his eyes looked just a little dangerous. "Oh, I've changed some," he told her softly, and the tone of his voice rippled across her skin like someone had spilled a glass of ice water on her. "These days I'm a little more careful who I spend time with. I don't take a woman's word for it anymore when she tells me who she is. Now

I check her out. Don't want to run across another liar, after all."

Jenna flushed. She felt the heat of it stain her skin and she was grateful for the dim lighting in the restaurant. Folding her hands together in her lap, she looked at the snowy expanse of the table linen and said, "Okay, I'm going to say this again. I didn't set out to lie to you back then, Nick."

"So it just happened?"

"Well," she said, lifting her gaze reluctantly to his, "yes."

"Right." He nodded, gave her a smirk that came nowhere near being a real smile and added, "Couldn't figure out a way to tell me that you actually worked for me, so you just let it slide. Let me think you were a passenger."

Yes, she had. She'd been swept away by the moonlight and the most gorgeous man she'd ever seen in her life. "I never said I was. You assumed I was a passenger."

"And you said nothing to clear that up."

True. All true. If she'd simply told the truth, then their week together never would have happened. She never would have known what it was like to be in his arms. Never would have imagined a future of some kind between them. Never would have gotten pregnant. Never would have given birth to the two little boys she couldn't imagine living without.

Because of that, it was hard to feel guilty about what she'd done.

"Nick, let's not rehash the past, all right? I said I

was sorry at the time. I can't change anything. And you know, you didn't exactly act like Prince Charming at the time, either."

"You're blaming me?"

"You wouldn't even talk to me," she reminded him. "You found out the truth and shut me out and down so fast I was half surprised you didn't have me thrown overboard to swim home."

He shifted uncomfortably, worked his jaw as if words were clamoring to get out and he was fighting the impulse to shout them. "What did you expect me to do?"

"All I wanted was to explain myself."

"There was nothing you could have said."

"Well," she said softly, "we'll never know for sure, will we?" Then she sighed and said, "We're not solving anything here, so let's just let the past go, okay? What happened, happened. Now we need to talk about what *is*."

"Right." He signaled to a waiter, then looked at her again. "So let's talk. Tell me about your sons."

"*Your* sons," she corrected, lifting her chin a little as if readying to fight.

"That's yet to be proved to me."

"Why would I lie?"

"Hmm. Interesting question," he said. "I could say you've lied before, but then we've already agreed not to talk about the past."

Jenna wasn't sure if she wanted to sigh in frustration or kick him hard under the table. This was so much more difficult than she'd thought it would be. Somehow,

Jenna had convinced herself that Nick would believe her. That he would look at the pictures of the babies and somehow *know* instinctively that these were his sons. She should have known better.

All around them the clink of fine crystal and the muted conversations of the other diners provided a background swell of sound that was more white noise than anything else. Through the windows lining one side of the restaurant, the night was black and the sea endless. The shimmer of colored lights hanging from the edges of the deck looked almost like a rainbow that only shone at night.

And beside her, the man who'd haunted her dreams and forged a new life for her sat waiting, watchful.

As she started to speak, a waiter approached with a bottle of champagne nestled inside a gleaming silver bucket. Jenna closed her mouth and bit her lip as the waiter poured a sip of the frothy wine into a flute and presented it to Nick for tasting. Approved, the wine was then poured first for her, then for Nick. Once the waiter had disappeared into the throng again, Jenna reached for her champagne and took a sip, hoping to ease the sudden dryness in her throat.

"So?" Nick prodded, his voice a low rumble of sound that seemed to slide inside her. "Tell me about the twins."

"What do you want to know?"

He shot her a look. "Everything."

Nodding, Jenna took a breath. Normally, she was more than happy to talk about her sons. She'd even been known to bore complete strangers in the grocery store with tales of their exploits. But tonight was different. Important. This was the father of her children. She had to make him understand that. Believe it. So choosing her words carefully, she started simply and said, "Their names are Jacob and Cooper."

He frowned a little and took a sip of his own champagne. "Family names?"

"My grandfathers," she said, just a touch defensively as if she was prepared to go toe to toe with him to guard her right to name her sons whatever she wanted.

"That was nice of you," he said after a second or two and took the wind out of her sails. "Go on."

While around them people laughed and talked and relaxed together, a tight knot of tension coiled about their table. Jenna's voice was soft, Nick leaned in closer to hear her and his nearness made her breath hitch in her chest.

"Jacob's sunny and happy all the time. He smiles from the minute he wakes up until the moment I put him down for the night." She smiled, too, just thinking of her babies. "Cooper's different. He's more…thoughtful, I guess. His smiles are rarer and all the more precious because of it. He's always watching. Studying. I'd love to know what he's thinking most of the time because even at four months, he seems almost a philosopher."

His gaze was locked on her and Jenna could see both of her sons in Nick's face. They looked so much like him, she couldn't understand how he could doubt even for a moment that they were his.

"Where are they now?"

"My sister Maxie's watching them." And was probably harried and exhausted. "The boys are crazy about her and she loves them both to death. They're fine."

"Then why did you get tense all of a sudden?"

She blew out a breath, slumped back against the booth and admitted, "It's the first time I've been away from them. It feels…wrong, somehow. And I miss them. A lot."

His eyes narrowed on her and he picked up his glass for a sip of wine. Watching her over the rim of the glass, he swallowed, then set the flute back onto the table. "Can't be easy, being a single mother."

"No, it's not," she admitted, thinking now about just how tired she was every night by the time she had the boys in bed. It had been so long since she'd been awake past eight o'clock at night that it was odd to her now, sitting here in a restaurant at nine. This was what it had been like before, though. When she'd only had herself to worry about. When she hadn't had two little boys depending on her.

God, how had she ever been able to stand the quiet? The emptiness in her little house? She couldn't even imagine being without her sons now.

"But," she added when he didn't say anything else, "along with all the work, a single mom gets all the perks to herself, too. I don't have to share the little moments. I'm the one to see them smile for the first time. To see them waking up to the world around them."

"So since you're not looking to share the good moments, that means you're not interested in having me involved in the twins' lives," he said thoughtfully. "All you really want is child support?"

She stiffened a little. Jenna hadn't even considered that Nick might want to be drawn into their sons' lives. He wasn't the hearth-and-home kind of guy. He was the party man. The guy you dated, but didn't bring home to mom.

"You and I both know you don't have any interest in being a father, Nick."

"Is that right? And how would you know that?"

"Well—"

He inclined his head at her speechlessness. "Exactly. You don't know me any more than I know you."

"You're wrong. I know that you're not the kind of man to tie himself down in one place. That week we were together you told me yourself you had no plans to ever get married and settle down."

"Who said anything about getting married?"

Jenna sucked in a breath and told herself to slow down. She was walking through a minefield here. "I didn't mean—"

"Forget it," he said.

Another waiter appeared, this time delivering a dinner that Nick had clearly ordered earlier. Surprised, Jenna looked down at the serving of breast of chicken and fettucine in mushroom sauce before lifting her gaze to his in question.

"I remembered you liked it," he said with a shrug.

What was she supposed to do with that? She wondered. He pretended to not care anything about her, yet he remembered more than a year later what her favorite foods were? Why? Why would he recall something so small?

Once the waiter was gone, Nick started talking again. "So answer me this. When you found out you were pregnant, why'd you go through with it?"

"Excuse me?"

He shrugged. "You were alone. A lot of women in that position wouldn't have done what you did. Giving birth, deciding to raise the babies on her own."

"They were mine," she said, as if that explained everything, and in her mind it did. Never for a moment had she considered ending her pregnancy. She'd tried to reach Nick of course, but when she couldn't, she'd hunkered down and started building a life for her and her children.

"No regrets?"

"Only the one about coming on this ship," she muttered.

He smiled faintly, laid his napkin across his lap and, picking up his knife and fork, sliced into his filet mignon. "I heard that."

"I meant you to." As Jenna used her fork to slide the fettucine noodles around her plate, she said, "Nick, my sons are the most important things in the world to me. I'll do whatever I have to to make sure they're safe."

"Good for you."

She took a bite of her dinner and, though she could tell it was cooked to perfection, the delicate sauce and chicken tasted like sawdust in her mouth.

"I'll want a DNA test."

"Of course," she said. "I've already had the boys' blood tests done at a local lab. You can send your sample in to them and they'll do the comparison testing."

"I'll take care of it tomorrow."

"What?" She shook her head, looked at him and said, "Don't you have to wait until we're back in San Pedro?"

"No, I'm not going to wait. I want this question settled as quickly as possible." He continued to eat, as though what they were discussing wasn't affecting him in the slightest. "We dock at Cabo in the morning. You and I will go ashore, find a lab and have them fax the findings to the lab in San Pedro."

"We will?" She hadn't planned on spending a lot of time with Nick, after all. She'd only come on board to tell him about the boys and frankly, she'd thought he wouldn't want anything more to do with her after that. Instead, he'd moved her into his suite and now was proposing that they spend even more time together.

"Until this is taken care of to my satisfaction," Nick told her softly, "I'm not letting you out of my sight. The two of us are going to be joined at the hip. So you might as well start getting used to it."

Five

Once the ship had docked and most of the passengers had disembarked for their day of shopping, sailing and exploring the city of Cabo San Lucas, Nick got busy. He'd already had Teresa make a few calls, and the lab at the local hospital was expecting them.

The sun was hot and bright and the scent of the sea greeted them the moment he and Jenna stepped out on deck. Ordinarily Nick would have been enjoying this. He loved this part of cruising. Docking in a port, exploring the city, revisiting favorite sites, discovering new ones.

But today was different. Today he was on a mission, so he wasn't going to notice the relaxed, party atmosphere of Cabo. Just as he wasn't going to notice the way Jenna's pale green sundress clung to her body or the way her legs looked in those high-heeled sandals. He had no interest in the fact that her dark blond hair looked like spilled honey as it flowed down over her shoulders and he really wasn't noticing her scent or the way it seemed to waft its way to him on the slightest breeze.

Having her stay in his suite had seemed like a good idea yesterday. But the knowledge that she was so close, that she was just down the hall from him, alone in her bed, had taunted him all night long. Now his eyes felt gritty, his temper was too close to the surface and his body was hard and achy.

Way to go, Falcon, he told himself.

"So where are we going?" she asked as he laid his hand at the small of her back to guide her down the gangplank to shore. Damn, just the tips of his fingers against her spine was enough to make him want to forget all about this appointment and drag her back to his cabin instead.

Gritting his teeth, he pushed that image out of his mind.

"Teresa called the hospital here," he muttered. "The lab's expecting us. They'll take a DNA sample, run it and fax the results to your lab. We should have an answer in a day or two."

She actually stumbled and he grabbed her arm in an instinctive move. "That fast?"

"Money talks," he said with a shrug. He'd learned long ago that with enough money, a man could accomplish anything. Way of the world. And for the first time, he was damned glad he was rich enough to demand fast action. Nick wanted this question of paternity settled.

Like now. He couldn't stop thinking about those babies. Couldn't seem to stop looking at the picture she'd given him of them.

Couldn't stop wondering how their very existence was going to affect—change—his life. So he needed to know if he was going to be a father or if he was simply going to be suing Jenna Baker for everything she had for lying to him. Again.

Her heels clicked against the gangway and sounded like a frantic heartbeat. He wondered if she was nervous. Wondered if she really was lying and was now worried about being found out. Had she thought he'd simply accept her word that her sons belonged to him? Surely not.

At the bottom of the gangway, a taxi was waiting. Silently blessing Teresa's efficiency, Nick opened the door for Jenna, and when she was inside, slid in after her. In short, sharp sentences spoken in nearly fluent Spanish, Nick told the driver where to go.

"I didn't know you spoke Spanish," she said as he settled onto the bench seat beside her.

"There's a lot about me you don't know," he said.

"I guess so."

Of course, the same could be said about what he knew of her. He remembered clearly their time together more than a year before. But in those stolen moments, he'd been more intent on burying himself inside her than discovering her thoughts, her hopes, her dreams. He'd told himself then that there would be plenty of time for them to discover each other. He couldn't have guessed that in one short week he'd find her, want her and then lose her.

Yet, even with the passion simmering between them, Nick could recall brief conversations when she'd talked about her home, her family. He'd thought at the time that she was different from the other women he knew. That she was more sincere. That she was more interested in *him,* the man, than she was in what he was. How much he had.

Of course, that little fantasy had been exploded pretty quickly.

He dropped into silence again as the cab took off. He didn't want to talk to her. Didn't want to think about anything but what he was about to do. With a simple check of his DNA, his life could be altered irrevocably forever. His chest was tight and his mind was racing. Cabo was no more than a colorful blur outside his window as they headed for the lab and a date with destiny.

In a few seconds the cab was swallowed by the bustling port city. At the dock and on the main drive that ran along the ocean, Cabo San Lucas was beautiful. The hotels, the restaurants and bars, everything was new and shone to perfection, the better to tempt the tourists who streamed into the city every year.

But just a few short blocks from the port and Cabo was a big city like any other. The streets were crowded with cars, and pedestrians leaped off the sidewalks and ran across the street with complete abandon, trusting that the drivers would somehow keep from running them down. Narrower, cobblestoned side streets spilled off the bigger avenues and from there came the tantalizing scents of frying onions, spices and grilling meat.

Restaurants and bars crowded together, their chipped stucco facades looking a little tattered as tourists milled up and down the sidewalks, cameras clutched in sunburned fists. As the cab driver steered his car through the maze of traffic, Nick idly glanced out the window and noted the open-air markets gathered together under dark green awnings. Under that umbrella were at least thirty booths where you could buy everything from turquoise jewelry to painted ceramic burros.

Cabo was a tourist town and the locals did everything they could to keep those vacation dollars in the city.

"Strange, isn't it?" she mused, and Nick turned his head to look at her. She was staring out her window at the city and he half wondered if she was speaking to him or to herself. "All of the opulence on the beach and just a few blocks away…"

"It's a city, like any other," he said.

She turned her head to meet his gaze. "It's just a little disappointing to see the real world beneath the glitz."

"There's always a hidden side. To everything. And everyone," he said, staring into her eyes, wondering what she was feeling. Wondering why he even cared.

"What's hidden beneath your facade, then?" she asked.

Nick forced a smile. "I'm the exception to the rule," he told her. "What you see is what you get with me. There are no hidden depths. No mysteries to be solved. No secrets. No lies."

Her features tightened slightly. "I don't believe that," she said. "You're not as shallow as you pretend to be, Nick. I remember too much to buy into that."

"Then your memory is wrong. Don't look for something that isn't there, Jenna," he said softly, just in case their driver spoke English. "I'm not a lonely rich boy looking for love." He leaned in toward her, keeping his gaze locked with hers, and added, "I'm doing this DNA test for my own sake. If those babies are mine, then I need to know. But I'm not the white-picket-fence kind of guy. So don't go building castles in the air. You'll get trapped in the rubble when they collapse."

Jenna felt a chill as she looked into those icy blue eyes of his. All night she'd lain in her bed, thinking about him, wondering if she'd done the right thing by coming to Nick. By telling him about their sons. Now she was faced with the very real possibility that she'd made a huge mistake.

Once he was convinced that the boys were his, then what? Would he really be satisfied with writing out a child support check every month? Or would he demand time with his children? And if he did, how would she fit him into their lives?

Picturing Nick spending time in her tiny house in Seal Beach was almost impossible. His lifestyle was so far removed from hers they might as well be from different planets.

"Nick," she said, "I know there's a part of you that thinks I'm lying about all of this. But I'm not." She paused, watched his reaction and didn't see a thing that made her feel any better, so she continued. "So, before you take this DNA test, I want you to promise me something."

He laughed shortly, but there wasn't a single spark of humor lighting his eyes. "Why would I do that?"

"No reason I can think of, but I'm still asking."

"What?" he asked, sitting back, dropping one hand to rest on his knee. "What's this promise?"

She tried again to read his expression, but his features were shuttered, closing her out so completely it was as if she were alone in the cab. But he was listening and that was something, she supposed.

"I want you to promise me that whatever happens, you won't take out what you feel for me on our sons."

He tipped his head to one side, studied her for a long moment or two, then as she held her breath, waiting for his response, he finally nodded. "All right. I give you my word. What's between you and me won't affect how I treat your sons."

Jenna gave him a small smile. "Thank you."

"But if they *are* my sons," he added quietly, "you and I have a lot of talking to do."

The DNA test was done quickly, and before she knew it, Jenna and Nick were back in the cab, heading for the docks again. Her stomach was churning as her mind raced, and being locked inside a car hurtling down a crowded street wasn't helping. She needed to walk. Needed to breathe. Needed to escape the trapped feeling that held her in a tight grip.

Turning to Nick, she blurted suddenly, "Can we get out? Walk the rest of the way to the dock?"

He glanced at her, and whatever he saw in her face must have convinced him because he nodded, then spoke to the driver in Spanish. A moment later the cab pulled to the curb. Jenna jumped out of the car as if she were on springs and took a deep breath of cool, ocean air while Nick paid their fare.

Tourists and locals alike crowded the sidewalk and streamed past her as if she were a statue. She tucked her purse under her left arm and turned her face into the breeze sliding down the street from the sea.

"It's still several blocks to the ship," Nick said as he joined her on the sidewalk. "You going to be able to make it in those shoes?"

Jenna glanced down at the heeled sandals she wore then lifted her gaze back to his. "I'll make it. I just— needed to get out of that cab and move around a little."

"I don't remember you being so anxious," he said.

She laughed a little and sounded nervous even to herself. "Not anxious, really. It's just that since the boys were born, I'm not used to being still. They keep me running all day long, and sitting in the back of that cab, I felt like I was in a cage or something and it didn't help that neither one of us was talking and we'd just come from the lab, so my brain was in overdrive and—"

He interrupted the frantic flow of words by holding up one hand. "I get it. And I could use some air, too. So why don't we start walking?"

"Good. That'd be good." God, she hadn't meant to go on a stream of consciousness there. If he hadn't stopped her, heaven only knew what would have come out of her mouth. As it was, he was looking at her like she was a stick of dynamite with a burning fuse.

He took her arm to turn her around, and the sizzle of heat that sprang up from his touch was enough to boil her blood and make her gasp for air. So not a good sign.

Music spilled from the open doorway of a cantina and a couple of drunk, college-age tourists stumbled out onto the sidewalk. Nick pulled Jenna tight against him and steered her past them, but when they were in the clear, he didn't release her. Not that she minded.

"So what's a typical day for you now?" he asked as they moved along the sidewalk, a part of, yet separate from, the colorful crowd of locals and tourists.

"Typical?" Jenna laughed in spite of the fact that every nerve ending was on fire and lit from within due to Nick's arm wrapped tightly around her waist. "I learned pretty quickly that with babies in the house there's no such thing as typical."

She risked a glance at him, and his blue eyes connected with hers for a heart-stopping second. Then he nodded and said, "Okay, then describe one of your untypical days for me."

"Well, for one thing, my days start a lot earlier than they used to," she said. "The twins sleep through the night now, thank God, but they're up and raring to go by six every morning."

"That can't be easy." His arm around her waist loosened a bit, but he didn't let her go and Jenna felt almost as if they were a real couple. Which was just dangerous thinking.

"No," she said quickly, to rein her imagination back in with cold, dry facts. Their lives were so different, he'd never be able to understand what her world was like. He woke up when he felt like it, had breakfast brought to his room and then spent the rest of his day wandering a plush cruise ship, making sure his guests were happy.

She, on the other hand…

"There are two diapers that need changing, two little bodies who need dressing and two mouths clamoring for their morning bottle. There are two cribs in the room they share and I go back and forth between them, sort of on autopilot." She smiled to herself as images of her sons filled her mind. Yes, it was a lot of work. Yes, she was tired a lot of the time. And no, she wouldn't change any of it.

"How do you manage taking care of two of them?"

"You get into a rhythm," she said with a shrug that belied just how difficult it had been to *find* that rhythm. "Cooper's more patient than his brother, but I try not to use that as an excuse to always take care of Jacob first. So, I trade off. One morning I deal with Cooper first thing and the next, it's Jacob's turn. I feed one, then the other and then get them into their playpen so I can start the first of the day's laundry loads."

"You leave them alone in a playpen?"

Instantly defensive, Jenna shot him a glare. "They're safe and happy and it's not as if I just toss them into a cage and go off to party. I'm right there with them. But I have to be able to get things done and I can't exactly leave them on the floor unattended, now, can I?"

"Hey, hey," he said, tightening his grip around her waist a little. "That wasn't a criticism…"

She gave him a hard look.

"Okay," he acknowledged, "maybe it was. But I didn't mean it to be. Can't be easy. A single mother with two babies."

"No, it's not," she admitted and her hackles slowly lowered. "But we manage. We have playtime and the two of them are so bright and so interested in everything…." She shook her head. "It's amazing, really, watching them wake up to the world a little more each day."

"Must be."

He was saying the right things, but his tone carried a diffidence she didn't much like. But then how could she blame him? He didn't believe yet that the boys were his sons. Of course, he would hold himself back, refusing to be drawn in until it had been proven to him that he was their father.

"When they take their naps, I work."

"Yeah," he said, guiding her around a pothole big enough to swallow them both, "you said you had your own business. What do you do?"

"Gift baskets," she said, lifting her chin a little. "I design and make specialty gift baskets. I have a few corporate clients, and I get a lot of business over the Internet."

"How'd you get into that?" he asked, and Jenna was almost sure he really was interested.

"I started out by making them up for friends. Birthdays, baby showers, housewarming, that sort of thing," she said. "It sort of took off from there. People started asking me to make them baskets, and after a while I realized I was running a business. It's great, though, because it lets me be home with the boys."

"And you like that."

Not a question, a statement. She stopped walking, looked up at him and said, "Yes, I like it. I couldn't bear the thought of the boys being in day care. I want to be the one to see all of their firsts. Crawling, walking, speaking. I want to hear their giggles and dry their tears. I want to be at the heart of their lives."

He studied her for a long minute or two, his gaze moving over her face as if he were trying to imprint her image on his mind. Or trying to read her thoughts to see if she had really meant everything she just said.

"Most women wouldn't want to be trapped in a house with two screaming babies all day," he finally said.

Instantly Jenna bristled. "*A,* the women you know aren't exactly the maternal type, now, are they? *B,* the boys don't scream all day and *C,* spending time with my kids isn't a trap. It's a gift. One I'm thankful for every single day. You don't know me, Nick. So don't pretend you do."

One dark eyebrow lifted, and an amused glint shone in those pale eyes of his. "I wasn't trying to insult you," he said softly. "I…admire what you're doing. What you feel for your sons. All I meant was, that what you said was nice to hear."

"Oh." Well, didn't she feel like an idiot? "I'm sorry. I guess I'm a little quick on the trigger."

"A little?" He laughed shortly, and started walking again, keeping his arm locked about her waist as if concerned she might wander off. "The words *Mother Grizzly* come to mind."

Even Jenna had to chuckle. "You're right, you know. I learned the moment the boys were born. I was so electrified just by looking at them…to know they'd come from me. It's an amazing feeling. Two tiny boys— one minute they're not there, and the next, they're breathing and crying and completely capturing my heart. I fell in love so completely, so desperately, that I knew instantly I would never allow anyone or anything to hurt them. *Nobody* criticizes my kids. Nobody."

"Yeah," he said, with a thoughtful look in his eyes. "I get it."

His hand at her waist flexed and his fingers began to rub gently, and through the thin fabric of her summery dress, Jenna swore she could feel his skin on hers. Her heartbeat jumped into high gear, and her breathing was labored. Meeting his gaze, she saw confusion written there and she had to ask, "What is it? What's wrong?"

Quickly he said, "Nothing. It's just…" He stopped, though, before he could explain. Then, shaking his head, he said, "Come on, we've still got a long walk ahead of us."

A half hour later Jenna's feet were aching and she was seriously regretting jumping out of that cab. But there were compensations, too. Such as walking beside Nick, his arm around her waist as if they were really a couple. She knew she should step out of his grasp, but truthfully, she was enjoying the feel of him pressed closely to her too much to do it.

It had been so long since their week together. And in the time since, she hadn't been with anyone else. Well, she'd been pregnant for a good part of that time, so not much chance of hooking with someone new. But even if she hadn't been, she wouldn't have been looking. Nick had carved himself into her heart and soul in that one short week and had made it nearly impossible for her to think about being with anyone else.

Which was really too bad when she thought about it. Because he'd made it clear they weren't going to be getting together again. Not that she wanted that, or anything....

"Oh!" She stopped suddenly as they came abreast of the street market they'd passed on their way to the lab. An excellent way to clear her mind of any more disturbing thoughts of Nick. "Let's look in here."

Frowning some, like any man would when faced with a woman who wanted to shop, Nick said, "What could you possibly want to buy here? It's a tourist trap."

"That's what makes it fun," she told him, and slipped out of his grasp to walk beneath the awning and into the aisle that wound its way past at least thirty different booths.

She wandered through the crowd, sensing Nick's presence behind her. She glanced at tables set up with sterling silver rings and necklaces, leather coin purses and crocheted shawls that hung in colorful bunches from a rope stretched across the front of a booth. She smiled at the man selling tacos and ignored the rumbling of her stomach as she moved on to a booth selling T-shirts.

Nick came up behind her and looked over her head at the display of tacky shirts silk-screened with images of Cabo, sport fishing and the local cantinas. Shaking his head at the mystery that was women, he wondered why in the hell she'd chosen to shop here.

"Need a new wardrobe?" he asked, dipping his head so that his voice whispered directly into her ear.

She jumped a little, and he enjoyed the fact that he made her nervous. He'd felt it all day. That hum of tension simmering around her. When he touched her, he felt the heat and felt her response that fed the fires burning inside him. The moment he'd wrapped his arm around her waist, he'd known it was a mistake. But the feel of her body curved against his had felt good enough that he hadn't wanted to let her go.

Which irritated the hell out of him.

He'd learned his lesson with her a year ago. She'd lied to him about who she was. Who was to say she hadn't lied about her response to him? Wasn't lying still? But even as he thought that, he wondered if anyone could manufacture the kind of heat that spiraled up between them when their bodies brushed against each other.

"The shirts aren't for me," she was saying, and Nick pushed his thoughts aside to pay attention. "I thought maybe there'd be something small enough for the boys to—here!"

She pulled a shirt out from a stack and it was so

small, Nick could hardly believe that it could actually be worn. There was a grinning cartoon burro on the front and the words Baby Burros Need Love Too stenciled underneath it. "It's so cute! Don't you think so?"

Nick's breath caught hard in his chest as she turned her face up to his and smiled so brightly the shine in her eyes nearly blinded him. He'd given women diamonds and seen less of a display of joy. If this was an act, he thought, she should be getting an Oscar.

"Yeah," he said. "I guess it is." Then he looked past her to the woman who ran the booth and in Spanish told her they'd be needing two of the shirts.

Smiling, the woman found another matching shirt, dropped them both in a sack and held them out. Nick paid for the shirts before Jenna could dig in her purse. Then he took hold of her hand and, carrying the bag, led her back out onto the street.

"You didn't have to buy them," she told him once they were on their way to the dock again.

"Call it my first present to my sons."

She stumbled a little and he tightened his hold on her hand, steadying her even while he felt his own balance getting shaky.

"So you believe me?"

Nick felt a cold, hard knot settle into the pit of his stomach. He looked into Jenna's eyes and couldn't find the slightest sign of deception. Was she too good at hiding her secrets? Or were there no secrets to hide? Soon enough, he'd know for sure. But for now "I'm starting to."

Six

Three days later the ship docked in Acapulco.

"Oh, come on," Mary Curran urged, "come ashore with Joe and me. He's going scuba diving of all things, and I'd love some company while I spend all the money we saved by having this cruise comped."

Laughing, Jenna shook her head and sat back on the sofa in the living room of Nick's spectacular suite. "No, thanks. I think I'm going to stay aboard and relax."

Mary sighed in defeat. "How you can relax when you're staying in this suite with Nick Falco is beyond me. Heck, I've been married for twenty years and just looking at the guy gives me hot flashes."

Jenna knew just what her friend meant. For the past few days she and Nick had been practically in each other's pockets. They'd spent nearly every minute together, and when they were here in this suite, the spacious accommodations seemed to shrink to the size of a closet.

Jenna felt as if she were standing on a tight wire, uneasily balanced over a vat of lava. She was filled with heat constantly and knew that with the slightest wrong move, she could be immolated.

God, great imagery.

"Hello? Earth to Jenna?"

"Sorry." Jenna smiled, pushed one hand through her hair and blew out an unsteady breath. "Guess my mind was wandering."

"Uh-huh, and I've got a good idea where it wandered *to*."

"What?"

"Oh, honey, you've got it bad, don't you?" Mary leaned forward and squeezed Jenna's hand briefly.

Embarrassed and just a little concerned that Mary might be right, Jenna immediately argued. "I don't know what you mean."

"Sure you don't." Mary's smile broadened. "I say Nick's name and your eyes flash."

"Oh God…"

"Hey, what's the trouble? You're both single. And you're clearly attracted to each other. I mean, I saw Nick's face last night at dinner whenever he looked at you."

The four of them had had dinner together the night before, and though Jenna had been sure it would be an uncomfortable couple of hours—given the tension between her and Nick—they'd all had a good time. In fact, seeing Nick interacting with Joe Curran, hearing him laugh and tell stories about past cruises had really opened Jenna's eyes.

For so long, she'd thought of him only as a player. A man only interested in getting as many women as possible into his bed. A man who wasn't interested in anything that wasn't about momentary pleasure.

Now she'd seen glimpses of a different man. One who could enjoy himself with people who weren't members of the "celebrity crowd." A guy who could buy silly T-shirts for babies he wasn't even sure were his. A guy who could still turn her into a puddle of want with a glance.

"Do you want to talk about it?" Mary asked quietly.

Jenna took a long, deep breath and looked around the room to avoid meeting Mary's too-knowing gaze. Muted sunlight, diffused by the tinted glass, filled the room, creating shadows in the corners. It was quiet now, with Nick somewhere out on deck and the hum of the ship's powerful engines silenced while in port.

Shifting her gaze to Mary's, Jenna thought about spilling the whole story. Actually she could really use someone to talk to, and Mary had, in the past several days, already proven to be a good friend. But she couldn't get into it now. Didn't want to explain how she and Nick had come together, made two sons and then drifted apart. That was far too long a story.

"Thanks," she said, meaning it. "But I don't think so.

Anyway, you don't have time to listen. Joe will be waiting for you."

Mary frowned at her, but apparently realized that Jenna didn't feel like talking. Standing up, she said, "Okay, I'll go. But if you decide you need someone to talk to…"

"I'll remember. Thanks."

Then Mary left and Jenna was alone. Alone with her thoughts, racing frantically through her mind. Alone with the desire that was a carefully banked fire deep inside. Suddenly antsy, she jumped to her feet, crossed the room and left the suite. She'd just go up on deck. Sit in the sun. Try not to think. Try to relax.

The business of running a cruise line kept Nick moving from the time he got up until late at night. People on the outside looking in probably assumed that he led a life of leisure. And sure, there was still time for that. But the truth was he had to stay on top of everything. This cruise line was his life. The one thing he had. The most important thing in the world to him. He'd worked his ass off to get this far, to make his mark. And he wasn't about to start slowing down now.

"If the band isn't working, contact Luis Felipe here in town," he told Teresa, and wasn't surprised to see her make a note on her PDA. "He knows all the local bands in Acapulco. He could hook us up with someone who could take over for the rest of the cruise."

The band they'd hired in L.A. was proving to be more trouble than they were worth. With their rock star attitudes, they were demanding all sorts of perks that hadn't been agreed on in their contracts. Plus, they'd been cutting short their last show of the evening because they said there weren't enough people in attendance to make it worthwhile. Not their call, Nick thought. They'd been hired to do a job, and they'd do it or they'd get off the ship in Mexico and find their own way home.

"Got it," Teresa said. "Want me to tell the band their days are numbered?"

"Yeah. We'll be in port forty-eight hours. Give 'em twenty-four to clean up their act—if they don't, tell 'em to pack their bags."

"Will do." She paused, and Nick turned to look at her. They were standing at the bow of the ship on the Splendor Deck, mainly because Nick hadn't felt like being cooped up in his office. And he couldn't go to his suite because Jenna was there. Being in the same room with her without reacting to her presence was becoming more of a challenge.

The last few days had been hell. Being with her every day, sleeping down the hall from her at night, knowing she was there, stretched out on a king-size bed, probably wearing what she used to—a tank top and a pair of tiny, bikini panties—had practically killed him. He'd taken more cold showers in the last three days than he had in the past ten years.

His plan to seduce Jenna and then lose her was backfiring. He was the one getting seduced. He was the one nearly being strangled with throttled-back desire. And he was getting damned sick of it. It was time to make a move. Time to take her to bed. Before they got the results of that DNA test.

Tonight, he decided. Tonight he'd have Jenna Baker back in his bed. Where he'd wanted her for the past year.

"Boss?"

He was almost surprised to hear Teresa's voice. Hell, he'd forgotten where the hell he was and what he was doing. Just thinking about Jenna had his body hard and aching.

"What is it?" He half turned away from the woman and hoped she wouldn't notice the very evident proof of just how hungry for Jenna he really was.

"The lab in Cabo called. They faxed the results of the DNA test to the lab in L.A."

"Good." His stomach fisted, but he willed it to loosen. Nothing to do about it now but wait for the results. Which would probably arrive by tomorrow. So, yeah. Tonight was the night.

"Do you want me to tell Jenna?"

Nick frowned at his assistant, then let the expression fade away. Wasn't her fault he felt like he was tied up in knots. "No, thanks. I'll do it."

"Okay." Teresa took a deep breath, held it, then blew it out. "Look, I know this is none of my business…"

"Never stopped you before," he muttered with a smile.

"No, I guess not," she admitted, swiping one hand through her wind-tousled hair. "So let me just say, I don't think Jenna's trying to play you."

He went perfectly still. From the shore came the sounds of car horns honking and a swell of noise that only a crowd of tourists released for the day could make. Waves slapped halfheartedly at the hull of the ship, and the wind whipped his hair into his eyes.

He pushed it aside as he looked at Teresa. "Is that right?"

She lifted her chin, squared her shoulders and looked him dead in the eye. "That's right. She's just not the type to do something like this. She never did give a damn about your money or who you were."

"Teresa—" He didn't want to talk about this and he didn't actually care what his assistant thought of Jenna. But knowing Teresa, there was just no way to stop her. An instant later, he was proved right.

"—still talking. And if I'm going to get fired for shooting my mouth off," she added quickly, "then I'm going to get it all said no matter what you think."

"Fine. Finish."

"I didn't say anything when you fired her, remember. I even agreed with you to a point—yes, Jenna should have told you she worked for you, but from her point of view I can see why she didn't."

"That's great, thanks."

She ignored his quips and kept talking. "I didn't even say anything when you were so miserable after she left that it was like working for a panther with one foot caught in a steel trap."

"Hey—"

"But I'm saying it now," she told him, and even wagged a finger at him as if he were a misbehaving ten-year-old. "You can fire me for it if you want to, but you'll never get another assistant as good as I am and you know it…."

Gritting his teeth because he knew she was right, Nick nodded and ordered, "Spit it out then."

"Jenna's not the kind to lie."

A bark of laughter shot from his throat.

"Okay, fine, she didn't tell you she was an employee. But that was one mistake. Remember, I knew her then, too, Nick. She's a nice kid with a good heart."

He shifted uncomfortably because he didn't want her to be right. It was much easier on him to think of Jenna as a liar and a manipulator. Those kind of women he knew how to deal with. A nice woman? What the hell was he supposed to do with one of those?

"And," Teresa added pointedly, "I saw the pictures of your sons—"

"That hasn't been confirmed yet," he said quickly.

"They look just like you," she countered.

"All babies look like Winston Churchill," Nick argued, despite the fact that he knew damn well she was right.

"Yeah?" She smiled and shook her head. "Winston never looked that good in his life, I guarantee it. They've got your eyes. Your hair. Your dimples." Teresa paused, reached out and laid one hand on his forearm. "She's not lying to you, Nick. You're a father. And you're going to have to figure out how you want to deal with that."

He turned his face toward the sea and let the wind slap at him. The wide stretch of openness laid out in front of him was usually balm enough to calm his soul and soothe whatever tensions were crowded inside him. But it wasn't working now. And maybe it never would again.

Because if he was a father…then his involvement with those kids wasn't going to be relegated to writing a check every month. He'd be damned if his children were going to grow up not knowing him. Whether Jenna wanted him around or not, he wasn't going anywhere. He was going to be a part of their lives, even if that meant he had to take them away from their mother to do it.

The ship felt deserted.

With most of the passengers still on shore exploring Acapulco, Jenna wandered decks that made her feel as if she were on board a ghost ship. That evening, she was back in Nick's suite and feeling on edge. She'd showered, changed into a simple, blue summer dress and was now fighting the fidgets as she waited for Nick to come back to the suite for dinner.

Funny, she'd spent nearly every waking moment with him over the past few days, feeling her inner tension mount incrementally. She'd convinced herself that what she needed was time to herself. Time away from Nick, to relax. Unwind a little, before the stress of being so close to him made her snap.

So she'd had that time to herself today and she was more tense than ever.

"Oh, you're in bad shape, Jenna," she whispered as she walked out onto Nick's balcony. She was a wreck when she was with him, and when she wasn't, she missed him. Her hair lifted off her neck in the wind, and the hem of her dress fluttered about her knees. Her sandals made a soft click of sound as she walked across the floor and she wrapped her arms around herself more for comfort than warmth.

From belowdecks, a soft sigh of music from the ballroom reached her, and the notes played on the cool ocean breeze, as if they'd searched her out deliberately. The plaintive instrumental seeped into her soul and made her feel wistful. What if coming on this trip had been a big mistake? What if telling Nick about their sons hadn't been the right thing to do? What if—she stopped her wildly careening thoughts and told herself it was too late to worry about any of that now. The deed was done. What would happen would happen and there wasn't a damn thing she could do about it now.

She sighed, leaned on the balcony railing and stared out at the sea. Moonlight danced on the surface of the water in a shimmer of pale silver. Clouds scuttled across a star-splashed sky, and the ever-present wind lifted her hair from her shoulders with a gentle touch.

"This reminds me of something."

Nick's deep voice rumbled along Jenna's spine, and she had to pull in a deep breath before she turned her head to look at him. He stood in the open doorway to the balcony. Hands in his pockets, he wore black slacks, a gleaming white shirt and a black jacket that looked as if it had been expertly tailored. His dark hair was wind ruffled, his pale eyes were intense, and his jaw was tight.

Her heart tumbled in her chest.

"What's that?" she whispered, amazed that she'd been able to squeeze out a few words.

He stepped out onto the balcony, and with slow, measured steps, walked toward her. "The night we met," he said, taking a place beside her at the railing. "Remember?"

How could she forget? She'd been standing on the Pavilion Deck of *Falcon's Treasure,* the ship she'd been working on at the time. That corner of the ship had been dark and deserted, since most of the passengers preferred spending time in the crowded dance club at the other end of the deck.

So Jenna had claimed that shadowy spot as her own and had gone there nearly every night to stand and watch the sea while the music from the club drifted around her. She'd never run into anyone else there, until the night Nick had stumbled across her.

"I remember," she said, risking a sidelong glance at him. She shouldn't have. He was too close. His eyes too sharp, his mouth too lickable. His scent too rich and too tempting. Her insides twisted and she dropped both hands to the cold, iron railing, holding tight.

"You were dancing, alone in the dark," he said, as if she hadn't spoken at all. As if he were prompting her memory. "You didn't notice me, so I watched you as you swayed to the music, tipping your head back, your hair sliding across your shoulders."

"Nick…"

"You had a smile on your face," he said, his voice

lower now, deeper, and she wouldn't have thought that was possible. "As if you were looking up into the eyes of your lover."

Jenna swallowed hard and shifted uneasily as her body blossomed with heat. With need. "Don't do this, Nick...."

"And I wanted to be the lover you smiled at. The lover you danced with in the dark." He ran the tip of one finger down the length of her arm, and Jenna shivered at the sizzle of something deliciously hot and wicked sliding through her system.

She sucked in a gulp of air, but it didn't help. Her mind was still spinning, her heart racing and her body lighting up like Times Square on New Year's Eve. "Why are you doing this?" she whispered, and heard the desperate plea in her own voice.

"Because I still want you," he said, moving even closer, dropping his hands onto her shoulders and turning her until she was facing him, until their bodies were so close only a single lick of flame separated them. "Because I watched you standing in the moonlight and knew that if I didn't touch you, I'd explode. I want you. Just as I did then. Maybe more."

Oh, she felt the same way. Everything in Jenna clamored at her to move into him. To lean her body against his. To feel the strength and warmth of him surrounding her. But she held back. Determined to fight. To hold on to the reins of the desire that had once steered her down a road that became more rocky the further along she went.

"It would be a mistake," she said, shaking her head, trying to ignore the swell of music, the slide of the trombone, the wail of the saxophone, that seemed to call to something raw and wild inside her. "You know it would."

"No," he said, sliding his hands up, along her shoulders, up the length of her throat, to cup her face between his palms. "This time would be different. This time, we know who we are. This time we know what we're getting into. It's just need, Jenna." His gaze moved over her features, and her breath caught and held in a strangled knot in her chest. "We both feel it. We both want this. Why deny ourselves?"

Why indeed?

Her mind fought with her traitorous body, and Jenna knew that rational thought was going to lose. The need was too great. The desire too hot. The temptation too strong. She did want him. She'd wanted him from the moment she first saw him more than a year ago. She'd missed him, dreamed of him, and now that he was here, touching her, was she really going to turn him down? Walk away? Go to her solitary bed and pray she dreamed of him again?

No.

Was she going to regret this?

Maybe. Eventually.

Was she going to do it?

Oh, yeah.

"There are probably plenty of reasons to deny ourselves," she finally whispered. "But I don't care about any of them." Then she went up on her toes as Nick smiled and flashes of hunger shone in his eyes.

"Atta girl," he murmured and took her mouth in a kiss that stole her breath and set her soul on fire.

His tongue slipped between her lips, stealing into her warmth, awakening feelings that had lain dormant for more than a year. His arms slid around her waist, pulling her in tight. Jenna lifted her own arms and linked them around his neck, holding him to her, silently demanding he deepen the kiss, take more from her.

He did.

His arms tightened until she could hardly draw breath. But who needed air? Jenna groaned, moved into him, pressing her body along his, and she felt the hard length of him jutting against her. That was enough to send even more spirals of heat dancing through her bloodstream.

Again and again, his tongue dipped into her mouth, tasting, exploring, divining her secrets. She gave as well as took, tangling her tongue with his, feeling the molten desire quickening within. He loosened his grip on her and she nearly moaned, but then his hands were moving, up and down her spine, defining every line, every curve. When his palms cupped her bottom and held her to him, she sighed into his mouth and gave herself up to the wonder of his touch.

"I need you," he whispered, dropping his mouth to the line of her jaw, nibbling at her throat.

She turned her head, allowing him easier access, and closed her eyes at the magic of the moment.

Around them, music swelled and the ocean breeze held the two of them in a cool embrace. Moonlight poured down on them from a black, starlit sky, and when Nick lifted his head and looked down at her, Jenna was trapped in his gaze. She read the fire in his eyes, sensed the tautly controlled tension vibrating through his body and felt his need as surely as she did her own.

"Now. Here." He lifted his hands high enough to take hold of the zipper, then slid it down, baring her back to the night wind. Then he pushed the thin straps of her dress down over her shoulders, and Jenna was suddenly glad she hadn't worn a bra beneath that thin, summer fabric.

Now there was nothing separating her from his touch. From the warmth of his hands. He cupped her breasts in his palms and rubbed her tender, aching nipples until she felt the tug and pull right down to the soles of her feet. She swayed into him, letting her head fall back and her eyes close as she concentrated solely on what he was doing to her.

It was everything. His touch, his scent filled her, overwhelming her with a desire that was so much more than she'd once felt for him. In the year since she'd seen him, she'd grown, changed, and now that she was with him again, *she* was more, so she was able to *feel* more.

"Beautiful," he said, his voice no more than a raw scrape of sound. His gaze locked on her breasts, he said, "Even more beautiful than I remembered."

"Nick," she whispered brokenly, "I want—"

"I know," he said, dipping his head, taking first one hardened nipple, then the other into his mouth. His lips and tongue worked that tender flesh, nibbling, licking, suckling, until Jenna's head was spinning and she knew that without his grip on her, she would have fallen into a heap of sensation at his feet.

He pushed her dress the rest of the way down, letting it fall onto the floor, and Jenna was standing in the moonlight, wearing only her high-heeled sandals and her white silk bikini panties. And she felt too covered. Felt as if the fragile lace of her underwear were chafing her skin. All she wanted on her now was Nick. She wanted to lie beneath him, feel his body cover hers, feel him push himself deeply inside her.

She loved him. Heaven help her, she still loved him. Why was it that only Nick could do this to her? Why was he the man her heart yearned for? And what was she going to do about it?

Then he touched her more deeply and those thoughts fled along with any others. All she could do was feel.

"Please," she said on a groan, "please, I need…"

"I need it, too," he told her, lifting her head, looking down into her eyes as he slid one hand down the length of her body, fingertips lightly dusting across her skin. He reached the elastic band of her panties and dipped his hand beneath it to cup her heat.

Jenna rocked into him, leaning hard against him, but Nick didn't let her rest. Instead, he turned her around until her back was pressed to his front and she was facing the wide emptiness of the moonlit sea.

He used one hand to tease and tweak her nipples while the other explored her damp heat. His fingers dipped lower, smoothing across her most tender, sensitive flesh with a feathery caress that only fed the flames threatening to devour her.

Jenna groaned again, lost for words. Her mind had splintered, no thoughts were gathering. She was empty but for the sensations he created. He dipped his head and whispered into her ear, "Watch the sea. See the moonlight. Lose yourself in them while I lose myself in you...."

She did what he asked, fighting to keep her eyes open, and focused on the shimmering sea as he dipped first one finger and then another into her heat. Jenna's breath hitched and she wanted to close her eyes, the better to focus on what he was doing, but she didn't. Instead, she stared unseeing at the broad expanse of sea and sky stretching out into infinity in front of her and fought to breathe as his magic fingers pushed her along a road of sensual pleasure.

He stroked, he delved, he rubbed. His fingers moved over her skin as a concert pianist would touch a grand piano. Her body was his instrument, and she felt his expert's touch with a grateful heart. Again and again, he pushed her, his fingers stroking her from the inside while his thumb tortured one particularly sensitive spot. And while Jenna moaned and twisted in his grasp, her eyes locked on the shimmering sea, she let herself go. She dropped any sense of embarrassment or worry. She pushed aside every stray thought of censure that leaped into her mind, and she devoted herself to the sensory overload she was experiencing.

"Come for me," Nick whispered, his voice no more

than a hush in her ear. His breath dusted her face, her neck, while his fingers continued the gentle, determined invasion. "Let me see you. Let me feel you go over."

His voice was a temptation. Because she was so close to a climax. Her knees trembled. Her body weakened even as it strove to reach the peak Nick was pushing her toward. Her breath came in ragged gasps, her heartbeat thundered in her ears and the tension coiling within was almost more than she could bear. And when she thought she wouldn't survive another moment, she cried out his name and splintered in his arms. Her body shattered, she rode the exquisite wave of completion until she fell at the end only to be caught and held in his strong arms.

Jenna dropped her head onto his shoulder, swallowed hard and fought to speak. "That was—"

"Only the beginning," Nick finished for her and picked her up, swinging her into his arms and stalking back into the suite. He was teetering on the edge of reason. Touching her, feeling her climax roar through her, sensing her surrender, had all come together to build a fire inside him like nothing he'd ever known before.

Seduction had been the plan.

But whose?

He'd thought to use her, feed the need that she'd caused, then be able to let her go. Get her out of his head, out of his blood. But those moments with her on the balcony only made him want more. He had to have her under him, writhing beneath him as he took her.

She lay curled against his chest, in a trusting manner that tore at him even as it touched something inside him he hadn't been aware of. She was trouble. He knew it. Felt it. And couldn't stop himself from wanting.

From having.

In his bedroom Nick strode to the bed, reached down with one hand and grabbed the heavy, black duvet in one fist. Then he tossed it to the foot of the mattress and forgot about it. He laid Jenna down on the white sheets and looked at her for a long moment. The moonlight caressed her here, as well, sliding in through the wide bank of glass that lined his bedroom suite. A silvery glow coated her skin as she stretched like a satisfied cat before smiling up at him.

"Come to me, Nick," she urged, lifting both arms in welcome.

He didn't need a second invitation. Tearing off his clothes, he joined her on the bed, covered her body with his and surrendered to the inevitable. More than a year ago, their first encounter had ended in his bed. Now, it seemed, they'd come full circle.

Nick ran his hands up and down her body and knew he'd never be able to touch her enough. He drew a breath and savored her scent. Dipped his head and tasted her skin at the base of her throat. Her pulse jolted beneath his mouth and he knew she was as eager as he, as needy as he.

He touched her core, delving his fingers into her heat again, and she lifted her hips from the bed, rocking into his hand, moaning and whispering to him.

His body ached and clamored for release. Every inch of him was humming, just touching her. Lying beside her. Jenna. Always Jenna who did this to him. Who turned him into a man possessed, a man who could think of nothing beyond claiming what he knew to be his.

With that thought, Nick tore away from her arms, ignoring the soft sound of disappointment that slipped from her throat. Tugging the drawer on the bedside table open, he reached in, grabbed a condom and, in a few quick seconds, sheathed himself. Then he turned back to her, levering himself over her, positioning himself between her thighs.

He gave her a quick smile. "Last time we forgot that part and look what happened."

"You're right," she said, reaching down to stroke his length, her fingers sliding over the thin layer of latex in a caress that had Nick gulping for air. "Now, will you come to me?"

He spread her thighs farther apart, leaned in close and locked his gaze with hers as his body entered hers. Inch by inch, he invaded her, torturing them both with his deliberately slow thrust.

Her hips moved beneath him, her eyes squeezed shut and she bit her bottom lip. Reaching up, her hands found his upper arms and held on, her short nails digging into his skin, and that was the last straw. The final touch that sent Nick over the edge of reason.

He pushed himself deep inside her and groaned at the tight, hot feel of her body holding his. His hips rocked, setting a rhythm that was both as old as time and new and exciting. She held on tighter, harder, her nails biting into his flesh with a stinging sensation that was counterpoint to the incredible delight of being within her.

Nick moved and she moved with him. Their rhythm set, they danced together, bodies joined, melded, becoming one as they reached for the same, shattering end that awaited them. He stared down into her eyes, losing himself in their depths. She met his gaze and held it until finally, as he felt her body begin to fist around his, she closed her eyes, shrieked his name and shuddered violently as her body exploded from the inside.

His own release came a scant moment later, and Nick heard himself shout as the tremendous relief spilled through him again and again, as if the pleasure would never end.

When he collapsed atop her, he still wasn't sure just who had seduced whom.

Seven

It was a long night.

As if they'd destroyed the invisible barrier keeping them separate, Jenna and Nick came together again and again during the night. Until finally, exhausted, they fell into sleep just before dawn.

When Jenna woke several hours later, she was alone in the big bed. Pushing her hair out of her eyes, she sat up, clutched the silky white sheet to her chest and stared around Nick's room as if half expecting him to appear from the shadows. But he didn't.

Carefully, since her muscles ached, she scooted off the bed, wandered down the hall to her own room and walked directly to the bathroom. As she took a long, hot shower, her mind drifted back to the night before and she wondered if things would be different between them now. But if she thought about that, hoped for it, how much more disappointed would she be if it didn't happen?

Nick had made no promises.

Just as he had made no promises last year during their one amazing week together.

So basically, Jenna told herself, she'd made the same mistake she had before. She'd fallen into bed with a man she loved—despite the fact that he didn't love her.

"Oh, man." She rested her forehead against the aqua and white tiles while the hot, pulsing streams of water pounded against her back. "Jenna, if you're going to make mistakes, and hey, everyone does…at least make *new* ones."

Out of the shower, she dried off and dressed in a pair of white shorts and a dark green tank top. Then she sat on her bed and tried to figure out her next move. The only problem was, she didn't have a clue what to do about what was happening in her world. This had all seemed like such a simple idea. Come to Nick. Tell him about the boys. Go home and slide back into her life.

But now, everything felt…complicated.

Muttering under her breath about stupid decisions and consequences, Jenna glanced at the clock on the bedside table and noticed the phone. Instantly her heart lifted. That's what she needed, she realized. She needed to touch base with the real world. To talk to her sister. To listen to her sons cooing.

Grabbing the receiver, she immediately got the ship's operator, gave them the number she wanted and waited while the phone on the other end of the line rang and rang. Finally, though, Maxie picked up and breathlessly said, "I don't have time for salesmen."

Laughing, Jenna eased back against the headboard of her bed and said, "Hello to you, too."

"Oh, Jenna, it's you." Maxie chuckled a little. "Sorry about that, but your babies are making me a little insane."

She jolted away from the headboard, frowning at the phone in her hand. "Are they okay?"

"*They're* fine," Maxie assured her. "I'm the one who's going to be dead soon. How do you do this every day? If I ever forget to tell you how amazing I think you are, remind me of this moment."

"Thanks, I will. So the boys are good?"

"Happy as clams," her sister said, then paused and idly asked, "although, how do we know clams are happy? It's not like they smile or whistle or something...."

"One of the great mysteries of the universe."

"Amen."

In the background, Jenna heard both the television set blaring and at least one baby crying. "Who is that crying?" she asked.

"Jacob," Maxie told her and her voice was muffled for a minute. "I'm holding Cooper and giving him a bottle and Jake wants his turn. Not exactly rating a ten on the patience scale, that boy."

"True, Jake is a little less easygoing than Cooper." Jenna was quiet then as Maxie brought her up to date on the twins' lives. She smiled as she listened, but her heart ached a little, too. She wanted to be there, holding her sons, soothing them, feeding them. And the fact that she wasn't literally tore at her.

"Bottom line, everything's good here," her sister said finally. "How about you? How did Nick take the news?"

"He doesn't believe me."

"Well, there's a shocker."

Jenna rolled her eyes. Maxie wasn't a big fan of Nick Falco. But then, her sister had been wined, dined and then dumped by a rich guy a couple of years before, and ever since then she didn't have a lot of faith in men in general—and rich men in particular.

"He took the DNA test, though, and was going to have the results faxed to our lab. He should have proof even he can't deny in the next day or two."

"Good. Then you're coming home, right?"

"Yeah." Jenna plucked at the hem of her shorts with her fingertips. She wouldn't stay on board ship for the whole cruise. She'd done what she'd come here to do, and staying around Nick any longer than was necessary was only going to make things even more complicated than they already were.

"I love my nephews," Maxie was saying, "but I think they're as ready to see you as I am."

"I miss them so much." Her heart pinged again as she listened to the angry sound of Jake's cry.

"Uh-huh, now tell me why you really called."

Jenna scowled. "I called to check on my sons."

"Oh, that was part of it. Now let's hear the rest," Maxie said.

"I don't know what you mean."

"Hold on, have to switch babies. Cooper's finished and it's Jake's turn."

Jenna waited and listened to her sister talking to both of the boys, obviously laying Cooper down and picking Jake up as the infant's cries were now louder and more demanding. She smiled to herself when his crying abruptly shut off and knew that he was occupied with his bottle.

"Okay, I'm back," Maxie said a moment later. "Now, tell me what happened between you and Nick."

"What do you mean?"

"You know exactly what I mean and the fact that you're avoiding the question tells me just what happened," her sister said. "You slept with him again, didn't you?"

Jenna's head dropped to the headboard behind her and she stared unseeing up at the ceiling.

"Jenna…"

"There wasn't a lot of sleeping, but yeah."

"Damn it, Jenna—"

She sat up. "I already know it was a mistake, so if you don't mind…"

"A mistake? Forgetting to buy bread at the market is a mistake. Sleeping with a guy who's already dumped you once is a disaster."

"Well, thanks so much," Jenna said drily. "That makes me feel so much better."

Maxie blew out a breath, whispered, "It's okay, Jake, I'm not yelling at you. I'm yelling at your mommy."

Then she said louder, "Fine. Sorry for yelling. But Jenna, you know nothing good can come of this."

"I know." Hadn't she awoken in an empty bed, with no sign of the tender lover she'd spent the night with? Nick couldn't have been more blatant in letting her know just how unimportant she was to him. "God, I know."

"Come home," Maxie urged.

"I will. Soon."

"Now."

"No," Jenna said, shaking her head as she swung her legs off the bed and sat up straight. "I have to talk to him."

"Haven't you said everything there is to say?"

Probably, Jenna thought. After all, it wasn't as if she was going to tell him she loved him. And wasn't that the only piece of information he was missing? Hadn't she done what she'd come here to do? Hadn't she accomplished her mission and more?

"Maxie…"

Her sister blew out a breath, and Jenna could almost see her rolling her eyes.

"I just don't want to see you destroyed again," Maxie finally said. "He's not the guy for you, Jenna, and somewhere deep inside, you know it. You're only asking to get kicked in the teeth again."

The fact that her sister was right didn't change anything. Jenna knew she couldn't leave until she'd seen Nick again. Found out what last night had meant to him, if anything. She had to prove to herself one way or the other that there was no future for them. It was the only way she'd ever be able to let go and make a life for herself and her children.

"If I get hurt again, I'll recover," she said, her voice firming as she continued. "I appreciate you worrying about me, Maxie, but I've got to see this through. So I'll call you when I'm on my way home. Are you sure you're okay to take care of the boys for another couple of days?"

There was a long moment of silence before her sister said, "Yeah. We're fine."

"What about work?" Maxie was a medical transcriber. She worked out of her home, which was a big bonus for those times when Jenna needed a babysitter fast. Like now.

"I work around the babies' nap schedules. I'm keeping up. Don't worry about it."

"Okay, thanks."

"Jenna? Just be careful, okay?"

The door to the suite opened and a maid stepped in. She spotted Jenna, made an apologetic gesture and started to back out again.

"No, wait. It's okay, you can come in now." Then to her sister, she said, "The maid's here, I've got to go. I'll call you soon. And kiss the boys for me, okay?"

When she hung up, Jenna didn't know if she felt better or worse. It was good to know her sons were fine, but Maxie's words kept rattling around in her brain. Yes, her sister was prejudiced against wealthy men, but she had a point, too. Jenna *had* been nearly destroyed after she and Nick had split apart a year ago.

This time, though, she had the distinct feeling that the pain of losing him was going to be much, much worse.

Nick had never thought of himself as a coward.

Hell, he'd fought his way to the top of the financial world. He'd carved out an empire with nothing more than his guts and a dream. He'd created a world that was everything he'd ever wanted.

And yet…a couple of hours ago, he'd slipped out of bed and left Jenna sleeping alone in his room because he hadn't wanted to talk to her.

"Women," he muttered, leaning on the railing at the bow of the Splendor Deck, letting his gaze slide over the shoreline of Acapulco, "always want to *talk* the morning after. Always have to analyze and pick apart everything you'd done and said the night before."

But there was nothing to analyze, he reminded himself. He'd had her, just as he'd planned, and now he was through—also as he'd planned.

Of course his body tightened and his stomach fisted at the thought, but that didn't matter. What mattered was that he'd had Jenna under him, over him, around him, and now he could let her go completely. No more haunted dreams. No more thinking about her at stray moments.

It was finished.

Scowling, he watched as surfers rode the waves into shore while tourists on towels baked themselves to a cherry-red color on the beach. Brightly striped umbrellas were unfurled at intervals along the sand, and waiters dressed in white moved among the crowd delivering tropical drinks.

So if it was finished, why the hell was he still thinking about her?

Because, he silently acknowledged, that night with her had been unlike anything he'd experienced since the last time they'd been together. Nick wasn't a monk. And since he was single, he saw no problem in indulging himself with as many women as he wanted. But no woman had ever gotten to him the way Jenna had.

She made him feel things he had no interest in. Made him want more than he should. That thought both intrigued and bothered him. He wasn't looking for anything more than casual sex with a willing woman. And nothing about Jenna was casual. He already knew that.

So the best thing he could do was stay the hell away from her.

Better for both of them. He pushed away from the railing in disgust. But damned if he'd hide out on his own blasted ship. He'd find Jenna, tell her that he wasn't interested in a replay of last night—and *now* who was lying? Turning, he was in time to see Jenna walking toward him, and everything in him tightened uncomfortably.

In the late-morning sunlight, she looked beautiful. Her blond hair hung loose about her shoulders. Her tank top clung to her breasts—no bra—and his mouth went dry. Her white shorts made her lightly tanned skin look the color of warmed honey. Her dark blue eyes were locked on him, and Nick had to force himself to stand still. To not go to her, pull her up close to him and taste that delectable mouth of hers again.

She hitched her purse a little higher on one bare shoulder and tightened her grip on the strap when she stopped directly in front of him. Whipping her hair back out of her eyes, she looked up at him and said, "I wondered where you disappeared to."

"I had some things to take care of," Nick told her and it was partially true. He'd already fired the band that had refused to clean up their act, hired another one and was expected at a meeting with the harbormaster in a half hour.

But he'd still been avoiding her.

"Look, Nick—"

"Jenna—" he said at the same time, wanting to cut off any attempt by her to romanticize the night before. Bad enough he'd done too much thinking about it already.

"Me first, okay?" she spoke up quickly, before he had a chance to continue. She gave him a half smile, and Nick braced himself for the whole what-do-I-mean-to-you, question-and-answer session. This was why he normally went only for the women who, like him, were looking for nothing more complex than one night of fun. Women like Jenna just weren't on his radar, usually. For good reason.

"I just want to say," she started, then paused for a quick look around to make sure they were alone. They were, since this end of the Splendor Deck was attached to his suite and not accessible to passengers. "Last night was a mistake."

"What?" Not what he'd been expecting.

"We shouldn't have," she said, shaking her head. "Sex with you was not why I came here. It wasn't part of my plan, and right now, I'm really regretting that it happened at all."

Instantly outrage pumped through him. She *regretted* being with him? How the hell was that possible? He'd been there. He'd heard her whimpers, moans and screams. He'd *felt* her surrender. He'd trembled with the force of her climaxes and knew damn well she'd had as good a time as he had. So how the hell could she be regretting it?

More, how could he dump her as per the plan if she was dumping him first?

"Is that right?" he managed to say through gritted teeth.

"Oh, come on, Nick," she said, frowning a bit. "You know as well as I do that it shouldn't have happened. You're only interested in relationships that last the length of a cruise, and I'm a single mom. I'm in no position to be anybody's babe of the month."

"Babe of the month?" He was insulted, and the fact that he'd been about to tell her almost exactly what she was saying to him wasn't lost on him.

She blew out a breath and tightened the already death grip she had on the strap of her purse. "I'm just saying that it won't happen again. I mean, what happened last night. With us. You and me. Not again."

"Yeah, I get it." And now that she'd said that, he wanted her more than ever. Wasn't that a bitch of a thing to admit? Not that he'd give her the satisfaction of knowing what he was thinking. "Probably best that way."

"It is," she said, but her voice sounded a little wistful. Or was he hearing what he wanted to hear?

Strange, a few minutes ago, he'd been thinking of ways to let her go. To tell her they were done. Now that she'd beaten him to the punch, he felt different. What the hell was happening to him, anyway?

Whatever it was, Nick told himself firmly, it was time to nip it in the bud. No way was he going to be tripping on his own heartstrings. Not over a woman he already knew to be an accomplished liar.

Besides, she hadn't come on this trip for him, he told himself sternly, but for what he could give her. She'd booked passage on his ship with the sole purpose of getting money out of him. Sure, it was for child support. But she still wanted money. So what made her different from any other woman he'd known?

"I'm attracted to you," she was saying, and it looked like admitting that was costing her, "but then I guess you already figured that out."

Was she blushing? Did women still do that?

"But I'm not going to let my hormones be in the driver's seat," she told him and met his gaze with a steely determination. "Pretty soon, you'll be back sailing the world with a brunette or a redhead on your arm and I'll be back in Seal Beach taking care of my sons."

The babies.

Hers? His?

He wasn't going there until he knew for sure. Instead,

he decided to turn the tables on her. Remind her just whose ship she was on. Remind her that he hadn't come to her, it had been the other way around.

"Don't get yourself tied up in knots over this, Jenna," he said, reaching out to chuck her under the chin with his fingertips. "It was one night. A blip on the radar screen."

She blinked at him.

"We had a good time," he said lightly, letting none of the tension he felt coiled inside show. "Now it's over. End of story."

He watched as his words slapped at her, and just for a minute he wished he could take them back. Yet as that feeling rushed over him, he wondered where it had come from.

"Okay, then," Jenna said, her voice nearly lost in the rush and swell of the sea below them, tumbling against the ship's hull. "So now we know where we stand."

"We do."

"Well, then," she said, forcing a smile that looked brittle, "maybe I should just fly home early. I can catch a flight out of Acapulco easily enough. I talked to my sister earlier and she's going a little nuts—"

He cut her off instantly. "Are the babies all right?"

She stopped, looked at him quizzically and said slowly, "Yes, of course. The boys are fine, but Maxie's not used to dealing with them twenty-four hours a day and they can be exhausting, so—"

"I'd rather you didn't leave yet," he blurted.

"Why not?"

Because he wasn't ready for her to be gone. But since admitting that even to himself was too lowering, he said, "I want you here until we get the results from the DNA test."

Her gaze dropped briefly, then lifted to meet his again. "You said we'd probably hear sometime today, anyway."

"Then there's no problem with you waiting."

"What's this really about, Nick?" she asked.

"Just what I said," he told her, taking her arm in a firm grip and turning her around. Heat bled up from the spot where his hand rested on her arm. He fought the urge to pull her into him, to dip his head and kiss the pulse beat at the base of her throat. To pull the hem of her shirt up so he could fill his hands with her breasts.

Damn, he was hard and hot and really irritated by that simple fact.

Leading her along the wide walkway, he started for his suite. "We've got unfinished business together, Jenna. And until it's done and over, you're staying."

"Maybe I should get another room."

"Worried you won't be able to control yourself?" he chided as he opened the door and allowed her to precede him into the suite.

"In your dreams," she said shortly, and tossed her purse onto the sofa.

"And yours," he said.

Jenna looked at him and felt herself weakening. It wasn't fair that this was so hard. Wasn't fair that her body wanted and her heart yearned even as her mind told her to back away. She had to leave the ship. Soon.

In the strained silence, a beep sounded from another room, and she glanced at Nick, a question in her eyes.

"Fax machine."

She nodded and as he walked off to get whatever had come in for him, Jenna headed for his bedroom. All she wanted to do was get the underwear she'd left in there the night before. And better to do it while he was occupied somewhere else.

Opening the door, she swung it wide just as Nick called out, "It's from the lab."

If he said anything else, she didn't hear him. Didn't even feel a spurt of pleasure, knowing that now he'd have no choice but to believe her about the fact that he was the father of her sons.

Instead Jenna's gaze was locked on his bed, and her brain short-circuited as she blankly stared at the very surprised, very *naked* redhead stretched out on top of Nick's bed.

Eight

"Jenna?" Nick's voice came from behind her, but she didn't turn.

"Hey!" The redhead's eyes were wide as she scrambled to cover herself—a little too late—with the black duvet. "I didn't know he already had company…."

Nick came up behind Jenna, and she actually felt him tense up. "Who the hell are you?" he demanded, pushing past Jenna to face the woman staring up at him through eyes shining with panic.

"Babe of the month?" Jenna asked curtly.

"Look," the redhead was saying from beneath the safety of the duvet, "I can see I made a mistake here and—"

"Oh," Jenna told her snidely, "don't leave on my

account," then she spun on her heel and marched down the long hall toward her own bedroom.

"Jenna, damn it, wait." Nick's voice was furious but she didn't care. Didn't want to hear his explanation. What could he possibly say? There was a naked woman in his bed. And he hadn't looked surprised, just angry. Which told Jenna everything she needed to know. This happened to him a *lot*.

That simple fact made one thing perfectly clear to Jenna.

It was so past time for her to leave.

God, she was an idiot. To even allow herself to *think* that she loved him. Was she a glutton for punishment?

She marched into her room on autopilot. Blindly she moved to the closet, grabbed her suitcase and tossed it onto the bed. Opening it up, she threw the lid back, then turned for the closet again. Scooping up an armful of her clothes, she carried them to the suitcase, dropped them in and was on her way back to the closet for a second load when Nick arrived.

He stalked right up to her, grabbed her arm and spun her around. "What the hell do you think you're doing?"

She wrenched herself free and gave him a glare that should have fried him on the spot. Jenna was furious and hurt and embarrassed. A dangerous combination. "That should be perfectly obvious, even to you. I'm leaving."

"Because of the redhead?"

"What's the matter, can't remember her name?"

"I've never even *met* her for God's sake," he shouted,

shoving one hand through his hair in obvious irritation, "how the hell should I know her damn name?"

"Stop swearing at me!" Jenna shouted right back. She felt as if every cell in her body was in a stranglehold. Her blood was racing, her mind was in a whirl of conflicting thoughts and emotions, and the only thing she knew for sure was she didn't belong here. Couldn't stay another minute. "I'm leaving and you can't stop me."

"Jenna, damn it, the results from the lab came in—"

Not exactly the way she'd imagined this conversation going, she told herself indignantly. Somehow she'd pictured her and Nick, reading the results together. In her mind, she'd watched as realization came over him. As he acknowledged that he was a father.

Of course, she hadn't pictured a naked redhead being part of the scene.

"Then you know I was telling you the truth. My work here is done." She grabbed up her sneakers, high heels and a pair of flats and tossed them into the suitcase on top of her clothes. Sure it was messy, but she was way past caring.

"We have to talk."

"Oh, we've said all we're going to say to each other," Jenna told him, skipping backward when he made a grab for her again. She didn't trust herself to keep her anger fired if he touched her. "Have your lawyers contact me," she snapped and marched into the connecting bathroom to gather up the toiletries she had scattered across the counter.

"Damn it," Nick said, his voice as tight as the tension coiled inside her. "I just found out I'm a *father*, for God's sake. I need a minute here. If you'll calm down, we can discuss this—"

"Shouldn't you be down the hall with Miss Ready-And-Willing?" Jenna inquired too sweetly as she pushed past him, her things in the crook of her arm.

He shook his head. "She's getting dressed and getting out," he said, grabbing Jenna's arm again to yank her around to face him.

God help her, her body still reacted to his hands on her. Despite everything, she felt the heat, the swell of passion rising inside to mingle with the fury swamping her, and Jenna was sure this wasn't a good thing. She had to get out.

But Nick only tightened his grip. "I didn't invite her. She bribed a maid."

She swallowed hard, lowered her gaze to his hands on her arms and said, "You're hurting me." He wasn't, but her statement was enough to make him release her.

"Jenna—"

"It's a wonder the woman had to bribe anyone. I'm sure the maids are used to letting naked women into your suite. Pretty much a revolving door around here, isn't it?"

"Nobody gets into my suite unless I approve it, which I didn't in this case," Nick added quickly. "And I hope for the maid's sake that it was a *good* bribe, because it just cost her her job."

"Oh, that's nice," Jenna said as she turned to zip her

suitcase closed. "Fire a maid because you're the horn-iest male on the face of the planet."

"Excuse me?"

Jenna straightened up, folded her arms across her chest and tapped the toe of her sandal against the floor as she glared up at him. "Everyone on this ship knows what a player you are, Nick. Probably wasn't a big surprise to the maid that a woman wanted into your suite and for all she knew, you *did* want her here."

He glared right back at her. "My life is my business."

"You're right it is." She grabbed the handle of her suitcase and slid it off the bed. Jenna didn't even care if she'd left something behind. She couldn't stay here a second longer. She had to get away from Nick, off this ship and back to the world that made sense. The world where she was wanted. Needed.

"And I don't owe you an explanation for anything," he pointed out unnecessarily.

"No, you don't. Just as you don't have to fire a maid because she assumed it was business as usual around here." Jenna shook her head, looked him up and down, then fixed her gaze on his. "But you do what you want to, Nick. You always do. Blame the maid. Someone who works hard for a living. Fire her. Make yourself feel better. Just don't expect me to hang around to watch."

"Damn it, Jenna, I'm not letting you walk out." He moved in closer and she felt the heat of his body reaching out for her. "I want to know about my sons. I want to talk about what we're going to do now."

Tightening her grip on the suitcase handle, Jenna

swung her hair back behind her shoulders and said softly, "What we're going to do now is go back to our lives. Contact your lawyer, set up child support. I'll send you pictures of the boys. I'll keep you informed of what's happening with them."

"It's not enough," he muttered, his voice low and deep and hard.

"It'll have to be, because it's all I can give you." Jenna walked past him, headed for the living room and the purse she'd left on a sofa. But she stopped in the doorway and turned for one last look at him.

Diffused sunlight speared through the bank of windows and made his dark hair shine. His eyes were shadowed and filled with emotions she couldn't read, and his tall, leanly muscled body was taut with a fury that was nearly tangible.

Everything in her ached for him.

But she'd just have to learn to live with disappointment.

"Goodbye, Nick."

Jenna was gone.

So was the redhead.

And he didn't fire the maid.

Nick hated like hell that Jenna had been right about that, but how could he fire some woman when everyone on the damn ship knew he had women coming and going all the time? Instead, he'd had Teresa demote the maid to the lower decks and instructed her to make it clear that if the woman ever took another bribe from a guest, she'd be out on her ass.

Sitting at the desk in his office, he turned his chair so that he faced the sprawl of the sea. He wasn't seeing the last of the day's sunlight splashing on the water like fistfuls of diamonds spread across its surface. He didn't notice the wash of brilliant reds and violets as sunset painted a mural across the sky. Instead his mind continued to present him with that last look he'd had of Jenna. Standing in the open doorway of her bedroom, suitcase in her hand, wearing an expression that was a combination of regret and disappointment.

"What right does she have to be disappointed in me? And why the hell do I care what she thinks?" he muttered. He'd meant to have her and let her go. It had been a good plan and that's exactly what had happened. He ought to be pleased. Instead, his brain continued to ask him just why Jenna had been so pissed about the redhead.

Was she being territorial?

Did she really care for him?

Did it matter?

Then he glanced down at the single sheet of paper he still held in his hand. The fax from the lab in San Pedro was clear and easy to read.

His DNA matched that of Jenna's twins.

Nick Falco was a father.

He was both proud and horrified.

"I have two sons," he said, needing to hear the words said aloud. He shook his head at the wonder of it and felt something in his chest squeeze tightly until it was almost impossible to draw a breath.

He was a *father.*

He had *family.*

Two tiny boys who weren't even aware of his existence were only alive because of *him.* Pushing up from his chair, he walked to the wide bank of glass separating him from the ocean beyond and leaned one hand on the cool surface of the window. Sons. Twins. He felt that twist of suppressed emotion again and murmured, "The question is, how do I handle it? What's the best way to manage this situation?"

Jenna had left, assuming that he'd keep his distance. Deal with her through the comforting buffer of an attorney. He scowled at the sea and felt a small but undeniable surge of anger begin to rise within him, twisting with that sense of pride and confusion until he nearly shook with the rush of emotions he wasn't used to experiencing.

He was a man who deliberately kept himself at a distance from most people. He liked having that comfort zone that prevented anyone from getting too close. Now, though, that was going to change. It had to change.

Jenna thought she knew him. Thought he'd be content to remain a stranger to his sons. Thought he'd go on with his life, putting her and Jacob and Cooper aside. Knowing her, she thought he'd be satisfied to be nothing more than a fat wallet to his sons.

"She's wrong," he muttered thickly, and his hand on the glass fisted. "I may not know anything about being a father, but those boys are *mine.* And I'll be damned if I let *anyone* keep me from them."

Turning around, he hit a button on the intercom and ground out, "Teresa?"

"Yes, boss?"

He folded the DNA report, tucked it into the breast pocket of his shirt and said, "Call the airport. Hire a private jet. I'm going back to California."

By the following morning, it was almost as if Jenna had never been gone. She'd stopped on the way home from the airport the night before to pick up the boys at Maxie's house. She hadn't been able to bear the thought of being away from them another minute. With the twins safely in their rooms and her suitcase unpacked, Jenna was almost able to convince herself that she'd never left. That the short-lived cruise hadn't happened. That she hadn't slept with Nick again. That she hadn't left him with a naked redhead in his bedroom.

The pain of that slid down deep inside, where she carefully buried it. After all, none of that had anything to do with reality. The cruise—Nick—had been a short jaunt to the other side of the fence. Now she was back where she belonged.

She'd been awake for hours already. The twins didn't take into consideration the fact that Mom hadn't gotten much sleep last night. They still wanted breakfast at six o'clock in the morning. Now she was sitting on the floor in the middle of her small living room, working while she watched her boys.

"I missed you guys," she said, looking over at her sons as they each sat in a little jumper seat. The slightest motion they made had the seat moving and shaking, which delighted them and brought on bright, toothless grins.

Jake waved one fist and bounced impatiently while Cooper stared at his mother as if half-afraid to take his eyes off her again for fear she might disappear.

"Your aunt Maxie said you were good boys," she said, talking to them as she always did. Folding the first load of laundry for the day, Jenna paused to inhale the soft, clean scent of their pajamas before stacking them one on top of the other. "So because I missed you so much and you were so good, how about we walk to the park this afternoon?"

This was what Jenna wanted out of her life, she thought. Routine. Her kids. Her small but cozy house. A world that was filled with, if not excitement, then lots of love. And if her heart hurt a little because Nick wasn't there and would never know what it was to be a part of his sons' lives, well, she figured she'd get over it. Eventually. Shouldn't take more than twenty or thirty years.

The doorbell had her looking up, frowning. Then she glanced at the twins. "You weren't expecting anyone, were you?"

Naturally, she didn't get an answer, so she grinned, pushed herself to her feet and stepped around them as she walked the short distance to her front door. Glancing over her shoulder, she gave the living room a quick look to make sure everything was in order.

The couch was old but comfortable, the two arm

chairs were flowered, with bright throw pillows tucked into their corners. The tables were small, and the rag rug on the scarred but polished wooden floors were handmade by her grandmother. Her home was just as she liked it. Cozy. Welcoming.

She was still smiling when she opened the front door to find Nick standing there. His dark hair was ruffled by the wind, his jeans were worn and faded, and the long-sleeved white shirt he wore tucked into those jeans was open at the throat. He looked way too good for her self-control. So she shifted her gaze briefly to the black SUV parked at the curb in front of her house. That explained *how* he'd gotten there. Now the only thing to figure out was *why* he was there.

Looking back up into his face, she watched as he pulled off his dark glasses, tucked an arm into the vee of his shirt and looked into her eyes. "Morning, Jenna."

Morning? "What?"

"Good to see you, too," he said, giving her a nod as he stepped past her into the house.

"Hey! You can't just—" Her gaze swept over him and landed on the black duffle bag he was carrying. "What are you doing here? Why're you here? How did you find me?"

He stopped just inside the living room, dropped his duffel bag to the floor and shoved both hands into the back pockets of his jeans. "I came to see my sons," he said tightly. "And trust me when I say it wasn't hard to find you."

"Nick…"

"And I brought you this." He pulled a small, sealed envelope out of his back pocket and handed it over. "It's from your friend Mary Curran. She was upset when she found out that you'd left the ship."

Jenna winced. She hadn't even thought of saying goodbye to the friend she'd made, and a twinge of guilt tugged at her.

"She said this is her telephone number and her e-mail address." He stared at her. "She wants you to keep in touch."

"I, uh, thanks." She took the envelope.

He looked at her, hard and cold. His pale eyes were icy and his jaw was clenched so tightly it was a wonder his teeth weren't powder. "Where are they?" he demanded.

Her mouth snapped closed, but she shot a look at the boys, jiggling in their bouncy seats. Nick followed her gaze and slowly turned. She watched as the expression on his face shifted, going from cool disinterest to uncertainty. Jenna couldn't remember ever seeing Nick Falco anything less than supremely confident.

Yet it appeared that meeting his children for the first time was enough to shake even his equilibrium.

Walking toward them slowly, he approached the twins as he would have a live grenade. Jenna held her breath as she watched him gingerly drop to his knees in front of the bouncy seats and let his gaze move from one baby boy to the other. His eyes held a world of emotions that she'd never thought to see. Usually he guarded what he was thinking as diligently as a pit bull on a short chain. But now…Jenna's heart ached a little in reaction to Nick's response to the babies.

"Which one is which?" he whispered, as if he didn't completely trust his voice.

"Um—" She walked a little closer, her sneakers squeaking a bit as she stepped off the rug onto the floor.

"No, wait," he said, never looking at her, never taking his gaze off the twins, "let me." Tentatively, Nick reached out one hand and gently cupped Jacob's face in his big palm. "This one's Jake, right?"

"Yes," she said, coming up beside him, looking down at the faces of her sons who were both looking at Nick in fascination. As usual, though, Jacob's mouth was open in a grin and Cooper had tipped his little head to one side as if he really needed to study the situation a bit longer before deciding how he felt about it.

"So then, you're Cooper," Nick said and with his free hand, stroked that baby's rounded cheek.

Jenna's breath hitched in her chest and tears gathered in her eyes. God, over the past several months, she'd imagined telling Nick about the boys, but she'd never allowed herself to think about him actually meeting them.

She'd never for a moment thought that he would be interested in seeing them. And now, watching his gentle care with her boys made her heart weep and every gentle emotion inside her come rushing to the surface. There was just something so tender, so poignant about this moment, that Jenna's throat felt too tight to let air pass. When she thought she could speak again without hearing her voice break, she said, "You really were listening when I told you about them."

"Of course," he acknowledged, still not looking at her, still not tearing his gaze from the two tiny boys who had him so enthralled. "They're just as you described them. They look so much alike, and yet, their personalities are so obvious when you're looking for the differences. And you were right about something else, too. They're beautiful."

"Yeah, they are," she said, her heart warming as it always did when someone complimented her children. "Nick," she asked a moment later, because this was definitely something she needed to know, "why have you come here?"

He stood up, faced her, then glanced again at his sons, a bemused expression on his face. "To see them. To talk to you. After you left, I did a lot of thinking. I was angry at you for leaving."

"I know. But I had to go."

He didn't address that. Instead he said, "I came here to tell you I'd come up with a plan for dealing with this situation. A way for each of us to win."

"Win?" she repeated. "What do you mean 'win'?"

Shifting his pale blue gaze back to hers, his features tightened, his mouth firming into a straight, grim line. A small thread of worry began to unspool inside of her, and Jenna had to fight to keep from grabbing up her kids and clutching them to her chest.

Only a moment ago she'd been touched by Nick's

first sight of his sons. Now the look on his face told her she wasn't going to be happy with his "plan."

"Look," he said, shaking his head, sparing another quick glance for the babies watching them through wide, interested eyes, "it came to me last night that there was an easy solution to all of this."

"I didn't come to you needing a solution. All I wanted from you is child support."

"Yeah, well, you'll get that." He waved one hand as if brushing aside something that didn't really matter. "But I want more."

That thread of worry thickened and became a ribbon that kept unwinding, spreading a dark chill through her bloodstream that nearly had her shivering as she asked, "How much more?"

"I'm getting to that," he said. "Like I said, I've been doing a lot of thinking since you left the ship. And finally, last night on the flight up here, it occurred to me that twins are a lot of work for any one parent."

What was he getting at? Why was he suddenly shifting his gaze from hers, avoiding looking at her directly? And why had she ever gone to him? "Yes, it is, but—"

"So my plan was simple," he said, interrupting her before she could really get going. "We split them up, each of us taking one of the twins."

"*What?*"

Nine

Nick couldn't blame her for the outrage.

She jumped in front of the babies and held her arms up and extended as if to fight him off should he try to grab the twins and run. "Are you insane? You can't split them up," she said, keeping her voice low and hard. "They aren't *puppies*. You don't get the pick of the litter. They're little boys, Nick. Twins. They need each other. They need *me*. And you can't take either of them away from me."

He'd already come to the same conclusion. All it had taken was one look at the boys, sitting in their little seats, so close that they could reach out and touch each other. But he hadn't known until he'd seen them.

"Relax," he said, lifting one hand to try to stop her

from taking off on another rant. "I said that's the plan I *did* have. Things have changed."

"You've been here ten seconds. What could have changed?" She was still defensive, standing in front of her sons like a knight of old. All she really needed was a battle-ax in her hands to complete the picture.

"I saw them," he said, and something in his voice must have reached her because her shoulders eased down from their rigid stance. "They're a unit. We can't split them up. I get that."

"Good." She blew out a breath. "That's good."

"I'm not finished," he told her, and watched as her back snapped straight as a board again. "I came here to see my sons, and now that I have, I'm not going anywhere."

She looked stunned, her mouth dropping open, her big, blue eyes going even wider than usual. "What do you mean?" Then, as she began to understand exactly what he meant, she shook her head fiercely. "You can't possibly think you're going to stay here."

This was turning out to be more fun than he'd thought it would be.

"Yeah, I am." Nick glanced around the small living room. You could have dropped two entire houses the size of hers into his suite on the ship, and yet there was something here that was lacking in his place, despite the luxury. Here, he told himself, she'd made a home. For her and their sons. A home he had no intention of leaving. At least not for a while. Not until he'd gotten to know his sons. Not until he'd come up with a way that he could be a part of their lives.

"That's crazy."

"Not at all," he said tightly, his gaze boring into hers. "They're my sons. I've already lost four months of their lives and I'm not going to lose any more."

"But Nick—"

He interrupted her quickly. "I won't be just a check to them, Jenna. And if that's what you were hoping for, sorry to disappoint."

She chewed at her bottom lip, folded her arms over her chest as if she were trying to hold herself together and finally said, "You can't stay here. There's no room. It's a two-bedroom cottage, Nick. One for the boys, one for me and you're *not* staying in my room, I guarantee that."

His body tightened and he thought he just might be able to change her mind on that front, eventually. But for now, "I'll bunk on the couch."

"But—"

"Look," Nick said. "It's simple. I stay here, get to know my kids. Or," he added, pulling out the big guns, "I sue you for sole custody. And which one of us do you think would win that battle? Your choice, Jenna. Which will it be?"

Her face paled, and just for a second Nick felt like a complete bastard. Then he remembered that he was fighting for the only family he had. His sons. And damned if he'd lose. Damned if he'd feel guilty for wanting to be a part of their lives however he had to manage it.

"You would do that?"

"In a heartbeat."

"You really are a callous jerk, aren't you?"

"I am whatever I have to be to get the job done," Nick told her.

"Congratulations, then. You win this round."

One of the babies began to cry, as if sensing the sudden tension in the room. Nick glanced down to see that it was Jacob, his tiny face scrunched up as fat tears ran down his little cheeks. An instant later, taking his cue from his brother, Cooper, too, let out a wail that was both heart wrenching and terrifying to Nick.

He threw a panicked look at Jenna, who only shook her head.

"You want a crash course in fatherhood, Nick?" She waved a hand at the boys, whose cries had now reached an ear-splitting range as they thrashed and kicked and waved their little arms furiously. "Here's lesson one. You made them cry. Now you make them stop."

"Jenna—"

Then, while he watched her dumbfounded, she scooped up the stack of freshly folded baby clothes and walked off down a short hallway to disappear into what he guessed was the boys' bedroom, leaving him alone with his frantic sons.

"Great," Nick muttered as he dropped to his knees in front of the twins. "This is just going great. Good job, Nick. Way to go."

As he dropped to his knees, jiggled the bouncy seats and pleaded with the boys to be quiet, he had the distinct feeling he was being watched. But if Jenna was standing in the shadows observing his performance, he didn't really want to know. So he concentrated on his sons and told himself that a man who could build a cruise ship line out of nothing should be able to soothe a couple of crying babies.

After all, how hard could it be?

By the end of the afternoon, Nick was on the ragged edge and Jenna was enjoying the show. He'd fed the boys, bathed them—which was entertainment enough that she wished she'd videotaped the whole thing—and now as he was trying to get them dressed. Jenna stood in the doorway to the nursery, silently watching with a delighted smile on her face.

"Come on, Cooper," Nick pleaded. "Just let me get this shirt on and then we'll—" He stopped, sniffed the air, then turned a horrified look on Jacob. "Did you?" He sniffed again. "You did, didn't you? And I just put that diaper on you."

Jenna slapped one hand over her mouth and watched Nick in a splash of sunlight slanting through the opened louvred blinds. The walls were a pale green and boasted a mural she'd painted herself while pregnant. There were trees and flowers and bunnies and puppies, painted in bright, primary colors, racing through the garden. A white dresser stood at one end of the room and an over-stuffed rocking chair was tucked into a corner.

And now there was Nick.

Staring down into the crib where he'd laid both boys for convenience sake, Nick shoved both hands through his hair—something he'd been doing a lot—and muttered something she didn't quite catch.

Still, she didn't offer to help.

He hadn't asked for any, and Jenna thought it was only fair that he get a real idea of what her days were like. If nothing else, it should convince him that he was *so* not ready to be a single parent to twin boys.

"Okay, Coop," he said with a tired sigh, "I'll get your shirt on in a minute. First, though, I've got to do something about your brother before we all asphyxiate."

Jenna chuckled, and Nick gave her a quick look. "Enjoying this, are you?"

"Is that wrong?" she asked, still grinning.

He scowled at her, then shook his head and wrinkled his nose. "Fine, fine. Big joke. But you have to admit, I'm not doing badly."

"I suppose," she conceded with a nod. "But smells to me as if you've got a little problem facing you at the moment."

"And I'll handle it," he said firmly, as though he was trying to convince himself, as well as her.

"Okay then, get to it."

He scrubbed one hand across his face, looked down into the crib and murmured, "How can someone so cute smell so bad?"

"Yet another universal mystery," she told him.

"Another?"

"Never mind," Jenna said, thinking back to her conversation with Maxie when Jenna was still on the ship. Before the redhead. Before she'd left in such a hurry.

Oh God. Jenna straightened up and closed her eyes. Maxie. Wait until *she* found out that Nick was here.

"You okay?" he asked.

Opening her eyes again, she looked at him, so out of place there in her sons' nursery, and told herself that this was just what he'd said their night together was. Nothing more than a blip on the radar. One small step outside the ordinary world. Once he'd made his point, got to know his sons a little, he'd be gone again and everything would go back to the way it was supposed to be.

Which was good, right?

"Jenna?"

"Huh? Oh. Yeah. I'm fine. Just…thinking."

He looked at her for a long second or two as if trying to figure out just what she'd been thinking. Thankfully, mind reading was *not* one of his skills.

"Right."

"So," Jenna said softly, "are you going to take care of Jake's little problem or do you need a rescue?"

He didn't look happy, but he also didn't look like he was going to beg off.

"No, I don't need a rescue. I said I could take care of them and I can." He took a breath, frowned again and reached into the crib.

Jenna heard the tear of the Velcro straps on the disposable diaper, then heard Nick groan out, "Oh my God."

Laughing, she turned around and left him to his sons.

Though it made her crazy, Jenna spent the rest of the day in her small garage, working on a gift basket that was to be delivered in two days. If Nick wanted to play at being a father, then she'd just let him see what it was like dealing with twin boys.

It felt strange to be right there at the house and still be so separate from the boys, but she had to make Nick see that he was in no way prepared to be a father. Had to make him see that taking her sons away from her would be a bad idea all the way around.

Just thinking about his threat sent cold chills up and down her spine, though. He was rich. He could afford the best lawyers in the country. He could hire nannies and bodyguards and buy whatever the court might think the boys would need.

"And where does that leave me?"

A single mom with a pitifully small bank account and an office in her garage. She'd have no chance at all if Nick really decided to fight her for their sons.

But why would he? That thought kept circling in her mind and she couldn't shake it. Was this all to punish her? Was it nothing more than a show of force? But why would he go to such lengths?

Shaking her head, she wrapped the completed basket with shrink-wrap cellophane, plugged in her travel-size hair dryer and focused the hot air on the clear plastic wrap. As she tucked and straightened and pulled, the gift basket began to take shape, and she smiled to herself despite the frantic racing in her mind.

When she was finished, she left the basket on her worktable where, in the morning, she'd affix a huge red bow to the top before packing it up to be delivered. For now, though, she was tired, hungry and very curious to see how Nick was doing with the boys.

She slipped into the kitchen through the connecting door and stopped for an appalled moment as she let her gaze sweep the small and usually tidy room. The red walls and white cabinets were pretty much all she recognized. There was spilled powdered formula strewn across the round tabletop, discarded bottles that hadn't been rinsed and a *tower* of dirty receiving blankets that Nick had apparently used to wipe up messes.

Shaking her head, she quietly walked into the living room, half-afraid of what she would find. There wasn't a sound in the house. No TV. No crying babies. Nothing.

Frowning, she moved farther into the room, noticing more empty baby bottles, and a torn bag of diapers spilled across a tabletop next to an open and drying-out box of baby wipes. Then she rounded the sofa and stopped dead. Nick was stretched out, fast asleep on her grandmother's rag rug and on either side of him lay a sleeping baby.

"Oh, my." Jenna simply stood there, transfixed by the sight of Nick and their sons taking a nap together. A single lamp threw a puddle of golden light across the three of them even as the last of the sunlight came through the front window. Nick's even breathing and the soft sighs and coos issuing from the twins were the only sounds in the room and Jenna etched this image into her mind so that years from now she could call up this mental picture and relive the moment.

There was just something so sweet, so *right* about the little scene. Nick and his sons. Together at last.

Her heart twisted painfully in her chest as love for all three of them swamped her. Oh, she was in so much trouble. Loving Nick was not a smart thing to do. She knew there was no future there for them. All he wanted was to be a part of her sons' lives—that didn't include getting close with their mother. So, what was she supposed to do? How could she love Nick when she knew that nothing good could come of it? And how could she keep her sons from him when she knew, deep down, that they would need a father as much as Nick would need them?

"Why does it have to be you who touches my heart?" she whispered, looking down at the man who'd invaded her life and changed her world.

And as she watched him, Nick's eyes slowly opened and his steady stare locked on her. "Do I?" he asked quietly.

Caught, there was no point in trying to deny what she'd already admitted aloud. She dropped to her knees. "You know you do."

Carefully, so as not to disturb the twins, Nick sat up, wincing a little at the stiffness in his back. But his gaze didn't waver. He continued to meet her eyes, and Jenna wished she could read what he was thinking. What he was feeling.

But as always, Nick's thoughts were his own, his emotions so completely controlled she didn't have a clue what was going on behind those pale blue eyes.

"Then why'd you leave the ship so fast?" Nick asked quietly.

"You know why." Just the memory of the naked red-head was enough to put a little steel back into her spine.

"I didn't even know her," he reminded her with just a touch of defensiveness in his voice.

"Doesn't matter," she said, lowering her voice quickly when Jacob began to stir. She hadn't meant to wake him up. Hadn't wanted to get into any of this right now. But since it had happened anyway, there was no point in trying to avoid it. "Nick, don't you see? The redhead was just a shining example of how different we are. She brought home to me how much out of my ele-ment I was on that ship. With you."

He reached out, skimmed his fingertips along her cheek and pushed her hair back behind her right ear. Jenna shivered at the contact, but took a breath and steadied herself. Want wasn't enough. A one-sided love wasn't enough. She needed more. Deserved more.

"I don't belong in the kind of life you lead, Nick. And neither do the boys."

"You could, though," he told her, his voice a hush of sound that seemed intimate, cajoling. "All three of you could. We could all live on the ship. You know there's plenty of room. The boys would have space to play. They'd see the world. Learn about different cultures, different languages."

Tempting, so tempting, just as he'd meant it to be. A reluctant smile curved her mouth, but she shook her head as she looked from him to the twins and back again. "They can't have a real life living on board a ship, Nick. They need a backyard. Parks. School. Friends—" She stopped, waved both hands and added, "A *dog*."

He tore his gaze from hers and looked at first one sleeping baby to the other before shifting his gaze back to hers. "We'll hire tutors. They can play with the passengers' kids. We could even have a dog if they want one. It could work, Jenna. We could make it work."

Though a part of her longed to believe him, she knew, deep down, that this wasn't about him wanting to be with her—finding a way to integrate her into his life—this was about him discovering his sons and wanting them with him.

"No, Nick," she whispered, shaking her head sadly. "It wouldn't be fair to them. Or us. You don't want me, you want your sons. And I understand that. Believe me I do."

He grabbed for her hand and smoothed the pad of his thumb across her knuckles. "It's not just the boys, Jenna. You and I…"

"Would never work out," she finished for him, despite the flash of heat sweeping from her hand, up her arm, to rocket around her chest like a pinball slapping against the tilt bar.

She wished it were different. Wished it were possible that he could love her as she did him. But Nick Falco simply wasn't the kind of man to commit to any one woman. Best that she remember that and keep her heart as safe as she could.

"You don't know that. We could try." His eyes were so filled with light, with hunger and the promise of something delicious that made Jenna wish with everything in her that she could take the risk.

But it wasn't only herself she had to worry about now. There were two other little hearts it was her job to protect. And she couldn't bring herself to take a chance that might bring her sons pain a few years down the road.

But instead of saying any of that, instead of arguing the point with him, she pulled her hand free of Nick's grasp and said softly, "Help me get the boys up to bed, okay?"

He drew up one leg and braced one arm across his knee. His gaze was locked on her, his features half in shadow, half in light. "This isn't over, Jenna."

As she bent over to scoop up Jacob, Jenna paused, looked into those pale blue eyes and said, "It has to be, Nick."

Ten

"Here?" Maxie repeated. "What do you mean he's here? Here in Seal Beach here?"

Jenna glanced back over her shoulder at her closed front door. She'd spotted Maxie pulling up out front and had made a beeline for the door to head her off at the pass, so to speak. "I mean he's *here* here. In the house here. With the boys here."

For three days now. She'd been able to avoid Maxie by putting her off with phone calls, claiming to be busy. But Jenna had known that sooner or later, her older sister would just drop by.

"Are you *nuts?*" Maxie asked. Her big, blue eyes went wide as saucers and her short, spiky, dark blond hair actually looked spikier somehow, as if it were actually standing on end more than usual. "What are you thinking, Jenna? Why would you invite him here?"

"I didn't invite him," Jenna argued, then shrugged. "He…came."

Maxie stopped, narrowed her eyes on Jenna and asked, "Are you sleeping with him?"

Disappointment and need tangled up together in the center of Jenna's chest. No, she wasn't sleeping with him, but she was dreaming of him every night, experiencing erotic mental imagery like she'd never known before. She was waking up every morning with her body aching and her soul empty.

But she was guessing her older sister didn't want to hear that, either, so instead, she just answered the question.

"No, Saint Maxie, defender of all morals," Jenna snapped, "I'm *not* sleeping with him. He's been on the couch the last couple of nights and—"

"Couple of nights?"

Jenna winced, then looked up and waved at her neighbor, who'd stopped dead-heading her roses to stare at Maxie in surprise. "Morning, Mrs. Logan."

The older woman nodded and went back to her gardening. Jenna shifted her gaze up and down the narrow street filled with forties-era bungalows. Trees lined the street, spreading thick shade across neatly cropped lawns. From down the street came the sound of a basketball being bounced, a dog barking maniacally and the muffled whir of skateboard wheels on asphalt. Just another summer day. And Jenna wondered just how many of her neighbors were enjoying Maxie's little rant. Shooting her sister a dark look, Jenna lifted both eyebrows and waited.

Maxie took the hint and lowered her voice. "Sorry, sorry. But I can't believe Nick Falco's been here for two nights and you didn't tell me."

Jenna smirked at her. "Gee, me, neither. Of course, I only kept it a secret because I thought you might not understand, but clearly I was wrong."

"Funny."

Jenna blew out a breath and hooked her arm through her sister's. No matter what else was going on in her life, Maxie and she were a team. They'd had only each other for the last five years, after their parents were killed in a car accident. And she wasn't going to lose her only sister in an argument over a man who didn't even *want* her.

"Max," she said, trying to keep her voice even and calm, despite the whirlwind of emotions she felt churning inside, "he's here to get to know the boys. His sons, remember? We're not together that way, and believe me when I say I'm being careful."

Maxie didn't look convinced, but then she wasn't exactly a trusting soul when it came to men. Not that Jenna could blame her or anything…not after she was so unceremoniously dumped by that jerk Darius Stone.

"This is a bad idea," Maxie said, as if she hadn't already made herself perfectly clear.

"He won't be here long."

"His kind don't need much time."

"Maxie…"

"You sure he's not staying?"

"Why would he?"

"I can think of at least three reasons off the top of my head," she countered. "Jacob, Cooper and oh, yeah, *you.* So I ask it again. Are you sure he's not staying for long?"

Hmm. No, she wasn't. In fact, Jenna would have thought that Nick would have had his baby fix by now and be all too glad to go back to his life. But so far he hadn't shown any signs of leaving.

Was it just the boys keeping him here?

Or did he feel something for her, too?

Oh God, she couldn't allow herself to start thinking that way. It was just setting herself up for more damage once he really did leave.

"Jenna—" Nick called to her from the front porch, then stopped when he saw Maxie and her talking and added, "Oh. Sorry."

No way to avoid this, Jenna thought dismally, already regretting putting her sister and her ex-lover in the same room together. But she forced a smile anyway. "It's okay, Nick. This is my sister, Maxie."

When neither of them spoke, Jenna gave Max a nudge with her elbow.

"Fine, fine," Max muttered, then raised her voice and said grudgingly, "Nice to meet you."

"Yeah. You, too."

"Well, isn't this special?" Jenna murmured, and wondered if she could get frostbite from the chill in the air between these two. "Come on in, Max," she urged, wanting her sister to see that she had nothing to worry about. That Nick wasn't interested in her and that she wasn't going to be pining away when he left. Surely, Jenna thought, she was a good enough actor to pull that off. "See the boys. Have some coffee."

Still looking at Nick, Maxie shook her head and said, "I don't know…"

"I went out for doughnuts earlier," Nick offered.

"Is he trying to bribe me?" Maxie whispered.

Jenna snorted a laugh. "For God's sake, Max, be nice." But as she followed her sister into the house, Jenna could only think that this must have been what it felt like to be dropped behind enemy lines with nothing more than a pocketknife.

Nick knew he should have left already.

Then he wouldn't have had to deal with Jenna's sister. Although, she'd finally come around enough that she hadn't looked as if she wanted to stab him to death with the spoon she used to stir her coffee.

The point was, though, with access to a private jet, he could catch up with the ship in Fort Lauderdale in time to enjoy the second half of the cruise to Italy. Then he wouldn't have to play nice with Jenna's sister—who clearly hated his guts. And he wouldn't be tormented by the desire he felt every waking moment around Jenna herself.

The last couple of nights he'd spent on her lumpy couch had been the longest of his life. He lay awake late into the night, imagining striding down the short hall to her bedroom, slipping into her bed and burying himself inside her. He woke up every morning so tight and hard he felt as if he might explode with the want and frustration riding him. And seeing her first thing in the morning, smelling the floral scent of her shampoo, watching her sigh over that first sip of coffee was another kind of torture.

She was here.

But she wasn't his.

Now Jenna was off to a packaging store, mailing out one of her gift baskets, and he was alone with his sons.

Nick walked into the boys' nursery to find them both wide awake, staring up at the mobiles hanging over their beds. The one over Jake's crib was made up of brightly colored animals, dancing now in the soft breeze coming in from the partially opened window. And over Cooper's bed hung a mobile made up of bright stars and smiling crescent moons.

He looked from one boy to the other, noting their similarities and their differences. Each of them had soft, wispy dark hair and each of them had a dimple—just like Nick's—in their left cheek. Both boys had pale blue eyes, though Cooper's were a little darker than his brother's.

And both of them had their tiny fists wrapped around his heart.

"How am I supposed to leave you?" he asked quietly. "How can I go back to my life, not knowing what you're doing? Not knowing if you've gotten a tooth or if you've started crawling. How can I not be here when you start to walk? Or when you fall down for the first time?"

Soft sunlight came through the louvered blinds on the

window and lay across the shining wood floor like gold bars. Outside somewhere on this cozy little street, a lawn-mower fired up and Jake jumped as though he'd been shot.

Instantly Nick moved to the crib, leaned over and laid one hand on his son's narrow chest. He felt the rapid-fire thud of a tiny heart beneath his palm, and a love so deep, so pure, so all encompassing, filled him to the point that he couldn't draw a breath.

He hadn't expected this. Hadn't thought to fall so helplessly in love with children he hadn't known existed two weeks ago. Hadn't thought that he'd enjoy getting up at the crack of dawn just so he could look down into wide eyes, eager to explore the morning. Hadn't thought that being here, with the boys, with their mother, could feel so…right.

Now that he knew the truth, though, the question was, what was he going to do about it?

Moving across the room to Cooper, he bent down, scooped his son up into his arms and cradled him against his chest. The warm, pliant weight of him and his thoughtful expression made Nick smile. He drew the tip of one finger along Cooper's cheek, and the infant boy turned his face into that now-familiar touch. Nick's heart twisted painfully in his chest as he stared down into those solemn blue eyes so much like his own.

"I promise you, I'll always be here when you need me." His voice was as quiet as a sigh, but Cooper seemed almost to understand as he gave his father one of his rare smiles. Nick swallowed hard, walked to where Jacob lay in his crib watching them and whispered, "I love you guys. Both of you. And I'm going to find a way to make this work.

When Jake kicked his little legs and swung his arms, it was almost a celebration. At least, that's what Nick told himself.

That night Jenna pulled on her nightshirt and made one last check on the twins before going to bed herself, as was her habit. Only, this time when she stepped into the room lit only by a bunny nightlight, she found Nick already there.

He wasn't wearing a shirt. Just a pair of jeans that lay low on his hips and clung to his legs like a lover's hands. He turned when she stepped into the room, and she felt the power of his gaze slam into her. In the dim light, even his pale eyes were shadowed, dark, but she didn't need to see those eyes to feel the power in them. Her skin started humming, her blood sizzling, but she made herself put one foot in front of the other, walking past Nick first to Cooper's crib, then Jacob's, smoothing each of the boys' hair, laying a gentle hand on their tummies as they slept.

And through it all, she felt Nick's gaze on her as surely as she would have a touch. Her breath came in shallow gasps and her stomach did a quick enough spin that she felt nearly dizzy. What was he doing in here? Why was he watching her as he was? What was he thinking?

Her hands were shaking as she turned to leave the

nursery with quiet steps. She got as far as the hallway when Nick's hand came down on her arm.

"Wait." His voice was hard and low, demanding.

She looked up at him, and here in the dark, where even the pale light from the plugged-in plastic bunny couldn't reach, Nick was no more than a tall, imposing figure moving in close to her.

"Nick—" Could he hear her heartbeat? Could he sense the fires he kindled inside her? Could he feel the heat pouring off her body in thick waves? "What are you doing?"

Heaven help her, she knew what he was doing. And more, she was glad of it. Just standing with him in the dark filled her with a sense of expectation that had her breath catching in her lungs.

"Don't talk," he whispered, moving in even closer, until their bodies were pressed together, until he'd edged her back, up against the wall. "Don't think." He lifted both hands and covered her breasts.

She sucked in air and let her head thunk back against the wall. Even through the thin cotton fabric of her nightgown, she felt the thrill of anticipation washing through her. His hands were hot and hard and strong. His thumbs moved across the tips of her nipples and the scrape of the fabric over her sensitive skin was another kind of sweet agony.

"Yes, Nick," she whispered, licking dry lips and huffing in breaths as if she'd just finished running a marathon. "No thinking. Only feeling. I want—"

"Me, too," he said, cutting her off so fast, she knew

instinctively that he was feeling the immediacy of the moment. "Have for days. Can't wait another minute. I need to be in you, Jenna. To feel your heat around me." He dropped his head to the curve of her neck and swept his tongue across the pulse point at the base of her throat.

She jerked in his arms, then lifted her hands until she could cup the back of his head and hold him there. While her fingers threaded through his thick, dark hair, he dropped one hand down the front of her body, skimming her curves, lifting the hem of her nightshirt. Then he was touching her bare skin and she arched into him as he slid his magical fingers beneath the elastic band of her panties.

He touched her core, slid his fingers into her heat and instantly, she exploded, rocking her hips with the force of an orgasm that crashed down on her with a splintering fury. Whimpering his name, she clung to him with a desperate grip until the last of the tremors slid through her. Then she was limp against him until he picked her up and walked to her bedroom.

Holding on to him, Jenna smoothed her hands over his skin, his broad back, his sculpted chest, and when he sucked in a gulp of air, she smiled in the dark, pleased to know she affected him as deeply as he did her.

In moments she was on her bed, staring up at him as he tore his jeans off and came to her. In the next instant he'd pulled her nightshirt up and off, and slid her white lace panties down the length of her legs and tossed them onto the floor.

Since the second he'd walked, unannounced, into her home, Jenna had wanted this. She'd lain awake at night hungering for him, and now that he was here, she had no intention of denying either of them. Though, for all she knew, this was his way of saying goodbye. He might be getting ready to leave, to go back to his world.

And if that was the case, then she wanted this one last night with him. Wanted to feel him over and around her. Wanted to look up into those pale eyes and know that at least for this moment, she was the most important thing in the world to him.

Tomorrow could take care of itself.

He moved in between her legs and stroked her now all-too-sensitive center. She moaned softly, spread her legs farther and rocked her hips in silent invitation. All she wanted was to feel the hard, strong slide of his body into hers. To hold him within her.

Then he was there, plunging deep, stealing her breath with the hard thrusts of his body. He laid claim to her in the most ancient and intimate way. And Jenna gave him everything she had. Her hands stroked up and down his spine. Her short nails clawed at his skin. Her legs wrapped themselves around his hips and urged him deeper, higher.

When he bent his head to kiss her, she parted her lips and met his tongue with her own in a tangle of need and want that was so beyond passion, beyond desire, that she felt the incredible sense that *this* is where she'd always been meant to be.

He tore his mouth from hers, looked down into her eyes and said on a groan, "Jenna…I need you."

"You have me," she told him and then arched her spine as a soul-shattering climax hit them both hard. Holding him tight, Jenna called out his name as wave after wave of sensation crashed, receded and slammed down onto them again and again. She felt his release as well as her own. She held him as his body trembled and shook with a power that was mind numbing.

It seemed the pleasure would never end.

It seemed they were destined to be joined together for the rest of time.

But finally, inevitably, the tantalizing pressure and delight faded and they lay together in a silence so profound, neither of them knew how to end it.

Nick was gone when she woke up.

Not gone gone. His duffle bag was still in one corner of the living room, so he hadn't gone back to the ship. He was just nowhere to be found in the house. That shouldn't have surprised her. After all, he'd avoided her the morning after their night together on board ship, as well. But somehow, disappointment welled inside her, and she wondered if he was deliberately distancing himself from her. To make the inevitable leaving easier.

With the sting of unshed tears filling her eyes, she slipped into her normal routine of taking care of the boys, and tried not to remember how it had felt to have Nick there, sharing all of this with her.

Once the twins were fed and dressed, Jenna decided to get out of the house herself. Damned if she'd sit around the house moping, waiting for Nick to return so that he could break her heart by telling her he was leaving. She had a life of her own and she was determined to live it.

Buckling the boys into their car seats, she then grabbed up a stuffed diaper bag and her purse and fired up the engine on her car.

"Don't you worry, guys," she said, looking into the rearview mirror at the mirrors she had positioned in front of their car seats so that she could see their faces, "we're going to be fine. Daddy has to go away, but Mommy's here. And I'm never going to leave you."

Those blasted tears burned her eyes again and she blinked frantically to clear them away. She wasn't going to cry. She'd had an incredible night with the man she loved and she wasn't going to regret it. Whatever happened, happened.

When her cell phone rang, she assumed it was Maxie until she glanced at the screen and didn't recognize the number. "Hello?"

"Jenna."

"Nick," she said, and tried not to sigh at the sound of his deep, dark voice murmuring in her ear.

"You at home?"

"Actually," she said, lifting her chin as if that could help her keep her voice light and carefree, "I'm in the car. I'm taking the boys to the mall and—"

"Perfect," he said quickly. "Have you got a pen?"

"Yes, I have a pen, but what is this—"

"Write this down."

Both of her eyebrows lifted at the order. But she reached into her purse for a pen and a memo pad she always carried. Behind her Jacob was starting to fuss, and pretty soon, she knew, Cooper would be joining in. "Nick," she asked, pen poised, "what's this about?"

"Just...I want to show you something and I need you and the boys to come here."

"Here where?"

"Here in San Pedro."

She nearly groaned. "San Pedro?"

"Jenna, just do this for me, okay?" He paused, then added, "Please."

Surprise flickered through her. She couldn't remember Nick *ever* saying please before. So when he gave her directions, she dutifully wrote them down. When he was finished, she frowned and said, "Okay, we'll come. Should be there in about a half hour."

"I'll be waiting."

He hung up before she could ask any more questions, and Jenna scowled at her cell phone before she set it down on the seat beside her. "Well, guys, we're off to meet your father." Cooper cooed. "No, I don't know what this is about, either," she told her son. "But knowing your daddy, it could be anything."

It turned out to be a house.

Cape Cod style, it looked distinctly out of place in Southern California, but it was the most beautiful house Jenna had ever seen. It was huge, and she was willing to bet that five of her cottages would have fit comfortably inside. But for all its size, it looked like a family home. There was a wide front lawn, and when she stepped out of the car in the driveway, she heard the sound of the ocean and knew the big house must be right on the sea.

"What's going on here?" she wondered aloud. But then Jacob's short, sharp cry caught her attention and she turned to get her sons out of their seats.

"Jenna!"

She looked up and watched as Nick ran down the front lawn to her. He looked excited, his pale eyes shining, his mouth turned into a grin so wide, his dimple dug deeply into his left cheek. Naturally, Jenna felt an involuntary tug of emotion at first sight of him, and she wondered if it would always be that way.

God, she hoped not.

"Let me help with the boys," he said after giving her a quick, hard, unexpected kiss that left her reeling a little.

"Um, sure." She watched as he rounded the back of her car, opened the other back door and began undoing the straps on Cooper's car seat. "Nick, what's going on? Where are we? Whose house is this?"

He shot her another breath-stealing grin and scooped Cooper up into his arms. "I'll tell you everything as soon as we get inside."

"Inside?" Finished with Jacob's seat straps, she picked him up, cuddled him close and closed the car door with a loud smack of sound.

"Yep," Nick said. "Inside. Go on ahead. I'll get the diaper bag and your purse."

She took a step, stopped and looked at him. Dappled shade from the massive oak tree in the front yard fell across his features. He was wearing a tight black T-shirt and those faded jeans he'd been wearing the night before when they— *Okay, don't go there,* she told herself. "I can't just go inside. I don't know who lives here and—"

"Fine," he said, coming around the hood of the car, her purse under his arm and the diaper bag slung over that shoulder, while he jiggled Cooper on the other. "We'll go together. All of us. Better that way, anyway."

"What are you talking about?"

"You'll see." He started for the house and she had little choice but to follow.

The brick walkway from the drive to the front door was lined with primroses in vibrant, primary shades of color. More flowerbeds followed the line of the house, with roses and tall spires of pastel-colored stocks scenting the air with a heady perfume.

Jenna kept expecting the owner of the house to come to the front door to welcome them, but no one did. And when she crossed the threshold, she understood why.

The house was empty.

Their footsteps echoed in the cavernous rooms as Nick led her through the living room, past a wide staircase, down a hall and then through the kitchen. Her head turned from side to side, taking it all in, delighting in the space, the lines of the house. Whoever had designed it had known what they were doing. The walls were the color of rich, heavy cream, and dark wood framed doorways and windows. The floors were pale oak and polished to a high shine. The rooms bled one into the other in a flow that cried out for a family's presence.

This house was made for the sound of children's laughter. As Jenna followed Nick through room after room, she felt that there was a sense of ease in the house. As if the building itself were taking a deep breath and relishing the feel of people within its walls again.

"Nick…" The kitchen was amazing, but she hardly had time to glance at it as he led her straight through the big room and out the back door.

"Come on, I want you to see this," he said, stepping back so that she could move onto the stone patio in front of him.

A cold ocean wind slapped at her, and Jenna realized she'd been right, the house did sit on a knoll above the sea. The stone patio gave way to a rolling lawn edged with trees and flowers that looked as she imagined an English cottage garden would. Beyond the lawn was a low-lying fence with a gate that led to steps that would take the lucky people who lived here right down to the beach.

As Jenna held Jacob close, she did a slow turn, taking it all in, feeling overwhelmed with the beauty of the place as she finally circled back to look out at the sea, glittering with golden sunlight.

Shaking her head, she glanced at Nick. "I don't understand, Nick. What's going on? Why are we here?"

"Do you like it?" he asked, letting his gaze shift around the yard as he dropped the diaper bag and her purse to the patio. "The house, I mean," he said, hitching Cooper a little higher on his chest. "Do you like it?"

She laughed, uncertainty jangling her nerves. "What's not to like?"

"Good. That's good," he said, coming to her side. "Because I bought it."

"You—*what?*"

Nick nearly laughed at the stunned expression on her face. God, this had been worth all of the secretive phone calls to real estate agents he'd been making. Worth getting up and leaving her that morning so that he could finalize the deal with the house's former owners.

This was going to work.

It had to work.

"Why would you do that?"

"For us," he said, and had the pleasure of watching her features go completely slack as she staggered unsteadily for a second.

"Us?"

"Yes, Jenna. Us." He reached out, cupped her cheek in his palm and was only mildly disappointed when she stepped back and away from him. He would convince her. He *had* to convince her. "I found a solution to our situation," he said, locking his gaze with hers, wanting her to see everything he was thinking, feeling, written in his eyes.

"Our situation?" She blinked, shook her head as if to clear away cobwebs and then stared at him again.

The wind was cold, but the sun was warm. Shade from the trees didn't reach the patio, and the sunlight dancing in her hair made him want to grab her and hold her close. But first they had to settle this. Once and for all.

"The boys," he said, starting out slowly, as he'd planned. "We both love them. We both want them. So it occurred to me that the solution was for us to get married. Then we both have them."

She took another step back, and, irritated that she hadn't jumped on his plan wholeheartedly, Nick talked faster. "It's not like we don't get along. And the sex is great. You have to admit there's real chemistry between us, Jenna. It would work. You know it would."

"No," she shook her head again and when Jacob picked up on her tension and began to cry, Nick moved in closer to her.

He talked even faster, hurrying to change her mind. Make her see what their future could be. "Don't say no till you think about it, Jenna. When you do, you'll see that I'm right. This is perfect. For all of us."

"No, Nick," she said, soothing Jacob even as she smiled sadly up at him. "It's not perfect. I know you love your sons, I do. And I'm glad of that. They'll need you as much as you need them. But you don't love *me*."

"Jenna…"

"No." She laughed shortly, looked around the back-yard, at the sea, and then finally she turned her gaze on Nick again. "It doesn't matter if we get along, or if the sex and chemistry between us is great. I can't marry a man who doesn't love me."

Damn it. She was shutting him down, and he couldn't even find it in himself to blame her. Panic warred with desperation inside him and it was a feeling Nick wasn't used to. He was *never* the guy scrambling to make things work. People cowtowed to *him*. It didn't go the other way.

Yet here he stood, in front of this one woman, and knew deep down inside him that the only shot he'd have with her was if he played his last card.

"Oh, for—" Nick reached out with his free arm, snaked it around her shoulders and dragged her in close to him. So close that their bodies and the bodies of their sons all seemed to be melded together into a unit. "Fine. We'll do it the hard way, then. Damn it Jenna, I *do* love you."

"What?" Her eyes held a world of confusion and pain and something that looked an awful lot like hope.

She hadn't even looked that surprised when he'd shown up at her house a few days ago. That gave him hope. If he could keep her off balance, he could still win this. And suddenly Nick knew that he'd never wanted to win more; that nothing in his life had been this important. This huge. He had to say the right things now. Force her to listen. To really hear him. And to take a chance.

Staring down into her eyes, he took a breath, and then took the plunge. The leap that he'd never thought to make. "Of course I love you. What am I, an idiot?" He stopped, paused, and said, "Don't answer that."

"Nick, you don't have to—"

"Yeah, I do," he said quickly, feeling his moment sliding by. He hadn't wanted to have to admit to how he felt. He'd thought for sure that she'd go for the marriage-for-the-sake-of-the-boys thing and then he could have had all he wanted without mortgaging his soul. But maybe this was how it was supposed to work. Maybe you couldn't *get* love until you were willing to *give* it.

"Look, I'm not proud of this, but I've been trying to hide from what I feel for you since that first night we met more than a year ago." His gaze moved over her face and his voice dropped to a low rush of words that he hoped to hell convinced her that what he was saying was true. "I took one look at you and fell. Never meant to. Didn't want to. But I didn't have a choice. You were there, in the moonlight and it was as if I'd been waiting for you my whole damn life."

"But you—"

"Yeah," he said, knowing what she was going to say. "I pulled away. I let you go. Hell, I told myself I *wanted* you to go. But that was a lie." Laughing harshly, he said, "All this time, I've been calling you a liar, when the truth is, I'm the liar here. I lied to you. I lied to myself. Because I didn't want to let myself be vulnerable to you."

"Nick—" She swallowed hard and a single tear rolled down her cheek. He caught it with the pad of his thumb.

"It would have been much easier on me," he admitted, "if you'd accepted that half-assed, marriage-of-convenience proposal. Then I wouldn't have had to acknowledge what I feel for you. Wouldn't have to take the chance that you'll throw this back in my face."

"I wouldn't do that—"

"Wouldn't blame you if you did," he told her. "But since you didn't go along with my original plan, then I have to tell you everything. I love you, Jenna. Madly. Completely. Desperately."

Fresh tears welled, making her eyes shine, and everything in him began to melt. What power she had over him. Over his heart. And yet he didn't care anymore about protecting himself.

All that mattered was her.

"You walk into a room and everything else fades away," he said softly. "You gave me my sons. You gave me a glimpse into a world that I want to be a part of."

Another tear joined the first and then another and another. In her arms, Jacob hiccupped, screwed up his little face and started to cry in earnest. Quickly, Nick took the boy from her and cradled him in his free arm. Looking down at his boys, then to her, he said, "Just so you know, I'm not prepared to lose, here. Nick Falco doesn't quit when he wants something as badly as I want you. I won't let you go. Not any of you."

He glanced behind him at the sprawling house, then shifted his gaze back to her again as he outlined his master plan. "We'll live here. You can do your gift baskets in the house instead of the garage. There's a great room upstairs that looks over the ocean. Lots of space. Lots of direct light. It'd be perfect for you and all of your supplies."

She opened her mouth to speak, but Nick kept going before she could.

"I figure until the boys are in school, we can live half the year here, half on board ship. It'll be good for 'em. And if they like the dog I bought them, we'll take her along on the ship, too."

"You bought a d—"

"Golden retriever puppy," Nick said. "She's little now, but she'll grow."

"I can't believe—"

The words kept coming, tumbling one after the other from his mouth as he fought to convince her, battled to show her how their lives could be if she'd only take a chance on him.

"Once they're in school, we can cruise during the summers. I can run the line from here and I have Teresa. I'll promote her," he said fiercely. "She can do the on-board stuff and stay in touch via fax."

"But Nick—"

"And I want more kids," he said, and had the pleasure of seeing her mouth snap shut. "I want to be there from the beginning. I want to see our child growing within you. I want to be in the delivery room to watch him— or her—take that first breath. I want in on all of it, Jenna. I want to be with you. With them," he said, glancing at the twins he held cradled against him.

The boys were starting to squirm and he knew how they felt. Nick's world was balanced on a razor's edge, and he figured that he had only one more thing to say. "I'm not going to let you say no, Jenna. We belong together, you and me. I know you love me. And damn it, I love you, too. If you don't believe me, I'll find a way to convince you. But you're not getting away from me. Not again. I won't be without you, Jenna. I can't do it. I won't go back to that empty life."

The only sound then was the snuffling noises the twins were making and the roar of the sea rushing into the cliffs behind them. Nick waited what felt like a lifetime as he watched her eyes.

Then finally she smiled, moved in close to him and wrapped both arms around him and their sons. "You really are an idiot if you think I'd ever let you get away from me again."

Nick laughed, loud and long, and felt a thousand pounds of dread and worry slide from his shoulders. "You'll marry me."

"I will."

"And have more babies."

"Yes." She smiled up at him, and her eyes shone with a happiness so rich, so full, it stole Nick's breath. "A dozen if you want."

"And sail the world with me," he said, dipping his head to claim a kiss.

"Always," she said, still smiling, still shining with an inner light that warmed Nick through. "I love you, Nick. I always have. We'll be happy here, in this wonderful house."

"We will," he assured her, stealing another kiss.

"But you're going to be housetraining that puppy," she teased.

"For you, my love," Nick whispered, feeling his heart become whole for the first time in his life, *"anything."*

* * * * *

BABY BUSINESS

BY
KATHERINE GARBERA

Katherine Garbera is a strong believer in happily-ever-after. She's written more than thirty-five books and has been nominated for *RT Book Reviews* career achievement awards in Series Fantasy and Series Adventure. Her books have appeared on the Waldenbooks bestseller list for series romance and on the *USA TODAY* extended bestseller list. You can visit her on the web at www.katherinegarbera.com.

This book is dedicated to Courtney and Lucas
for always making me laugh.

One

"You're a lifesaver," Cassidy Franzone said as she opened her front door.

At thirty-four weeks pregnant, she needed food when she wanted it. She was single and fine with that. She'd made the choice to have her baby on her own, but she hated going out in Charleston's August heat to pick up her favorite she-crab soup if she didn't have to.

Her father had put his employees at her disposal. If she needed anything, no matter what time of day it was, someone on the staff at Franzone Waste Management was available.

"Am I?"

The man standing in the doorway wasn't her father's employee. In fact, he was the father of her child.

Cassidy gaped at Donovan Tolley. He was still the most attractive man she'd ever seen. His thick hair—hair she'd loved to run her fingers through—lifted in the warm summer breeze. His designer clothes were tailored perfectly to his frame—not for vanity's sake, but because he liked quality.

"What are you doing here?" she asked. She hoped that she sounded nonchalant, as if the reason was not important, but she couldn't help but cover her stomach with one arm protectively. How had Donovan found out that she was pregnant? Or had he?

Maybe it was the fact that she was so hungry, or maybe it had just been so long—almost eight months, to be exact—since she'd seen him. But she felt a sting of tears in the back of her eyes as Donovan smiled at her.

"Can I come in? I don't want to talk to you in the doorway." He seemed a bit dazed. As he pushed his sunglasses up to the top of his head she saw in his eyes that he was busy processing her pregnancy.

"What do you want to talk about?" she asked. What if he didn't believe he was the father of her child? What exactly did he want? And why the hell was she still attracted to this man after he'd broken her heart and left her alone for almost eight months?

He eyed her belly and arched one eyebrow. "Your pregnancy, for starters."

She hadn't told Donovan that she was pregnant with his child, but then again he'd made his views on children quite clear when he'd made his rather businesslike marriage proposal to her. "I know everything I need to about how you feel about kids."

"I'm not so sure about that. Invite me in, Cassidy. I need to talk to you. And I'm not going away."

She hesitated. She would have shut the door on any other man, but then she wouldn't be pregnant with any other man's child. Donovan was the only man she'd ever loved. Still, she didn't need this kind of tension right now.

She was hungry, the baby was moving around and she wasn't exactly sure she wanted to send Donovan on his way. That wasn't like her. She'd always been very decisive, but lately she hadn't been herself.

She felt a bit faint, probably due to the heat. She made up her mind to send Donovan away. She'd deal with him after the baby was born, when she had her act together.

A late-model black-windowed Mercedes pulled into her driveway and Cassidy smiled. Finally her food was here.

"Got your soup, Ms. Cassidy."

"Thank you, Jimmy," she said as the young man

handed her a brown bag. He nodded at her as she took the bag and then he left.

Donovan smiled. "Crab Shack?"

She nodded. She always tried not to focus on the fact that the soup she loved so much came from the place where she and Donovan had eaten at least once a week while they'd been together. The Crab Shack was a famous Charleston institution.

"I'll keep you company while you eat," he said.

"I don't think so. We can talk later this week. I'll call your assistant."

"I'm not leaving, Cassidy."

"Are you going to force your way into my house?" she asked.

"No," he said, bracing one arm on the door frame and leaning in over her. "You're going to invite me in."

His cologne was one-of-a-kind, made for him by an exclusive perfumery in France, and at this moment she really hated that company because Donovan smelled so good. The scent reminded her of the many times she'd lain cuddled close to his side with her head on his chest.

"Cassidy, baby, please let me in," he said, leaning closer so that his words were more of a whisper.

Everything feminine inside of her went nuts. Her breasts felt fuller and her nipples tightened against the fabric of her bra. Her skin felt more sensitive, her lips dry. She wet them with her tongue and saw his eyes narrow as he watched her.

"Is there anything I can do to convince you to go away?"

"No. I've missed you, Cassidy, and leaving is the last thing I want to do."

She hated the little thrill she got when he said he'd missed her. She tried to be nonchalant when she stepped back so that he could enter her house.

Donovan closed the front door behind them and she hesitated in the foyer of her own home. She should have never let him back into her house. She wasn't going to be able to keep any kind of distance between them. Face-to-face with Donovan again, all she could think about was sex. About being back in his arms one last time. Her hormones had been going crazy throughout her pregnancy, and once again they came rushing to the fore. She wanted this man. She hadn't even tried dating in the last eight months, though a few brave guys had asked her out. She didn't want anyone but Donovan.

She led the way to the first floor screened-in porch. It overlooked the wooded area behind her house, and with its tall ceilings and the shade provided by the nearby oak and magnolia trees, it was a cool refuge from the heat.

"Can I get you a beer or tea?" she asked.

"Beer would be great," he said.

She set her soup on the table and went to the wet bar to get Donovan's beer. He liked Heineken, same as she did. Though she hadn't had a beer since she'd gotten pregnant, she still kept her refrigerator stocked for when her brothers and friends visited.

She grabbed a bottle of Pellegrino for herself and came back to the table. Donovan stood up and held her chair for her. The gentlemanly courtesy was one he had always performed, and she appreciated it. That was one of the things that had always set Donovan apart from other men. She thanked him and sat down.

Food suddenly became unimportant as she realized the man she loved was sitting there next to her. She had to clasp her hands in her lap to keep from reaching out to touch him. To keep from leaning across the table and making sure he was really there.

"How are you, Cassidy?" he asked.

"Good. I haven't had any complications from the pregnancy." She was twenty-eight years old and in great shape thanks to a lifetime of exercise and eating right. The baby was healthy, something that she sometimes fancied was due to the fact that she and Donovan had been so much in love when he'd been conceived. But she knew that was her imagination running away with her.

"I'm glad."

"Are you?" she asked, trying for sarcasm but guessing she'd sounded a bit pleased that he was concerned about her health.

"Yes." He leaned back in his chair. "Why didn't you tell me about the baby? I'm assuming the baby is mine."

She suspected he knew she wasn't interested in any other man. She hadn't hidden her feelings for him when they were together.

"Yes, it is yours. I didn't tell you because it didn't seem like the type of information you'd be interested in."

"What do you mean by that?"

"Just that if something doesn't involve Tolley-Patterson Manufacturing or any of your other business interests, you usually don't pay much attention to it."

"I paid attention to you," he said.

"When there wasn't a crisis at one of your companies, sure, you did pay attention to me."

But she had always been aware that his position as executive vice president at Tolley-Patterson, the company his family owned, was the most important thing in Donovan's life. He was also consumed by his other business interests, and with increasing his holdings. He co-owned a sporting goods company with his former college roommate, and he had an interest in an island resort on Tobago with a friend from his boarding-school days. For a while his constant focus on business hadn't mattered. But during the last few months, while they'd been apart, she'd come to realize she had sold herself short in their relationship.

Donovan had always been obsessed with proving there was more to him than just his trust fund. And she wasn't interested in competing for his attention again. Getting over Donovan had been hard. The hardest thing she'd ever gone through. She'd thought she wasn't going to recover at first, and when she'd gotten confirmation that she was pregnant with his child, she'd made up her mind that the baby was the reason she'd been brought into Donovan's life. His child would be the one on whom she'd pour all the love that he'd never really wanted from her.

But now he was back, and she had this tingly excitement in the pit of her stomach that made her hope he might be back for good.

And that scared her more than facing the future alone.

"What does that comment mean? I never ignored you when we were together."

Donovan was still trying to process the fact that Cassidy was having his baby. He couldn't believe his good fortune in finding her pregnant. He'd come here today to ask her to marry him again, to convince her that he'd changed his mind about family. And he had to do it without revealing the circumstances that had brought him to her doorstep today.

Donovan had forgotten how truly beautiful Cassidy was. Her skin was like porcelain, fine and pale, and her hair was rich and thick. He knew from experience how soft it felt against his skin. Her lips were full, and though she didn't have lipstick on, they were a perfect deep pink color—the exact same shade as her nipples. God, he wanted to forget about talking and just draw her into his arms and kiss her. How he'd missed her mouth….

His body hardened and he adjusted his legs, trying to quell his erection. He'd never thought of pregnant women as sensual before, but there was something about seeing Cassidy's lush body filled out with his child.

"Only because I knew that you needed to be at work twelve hours a day and on weekends…I didn't make a lot of demands on your time," she said.

It took a moment for her words to register, because he'd been watching her mouth and wondering…if he leaned over and kissed her, would she kiss him back?

But then the words registered and he realized that she probably wasn't in the mood to be kissed. She was busy focusing on all the reasons they were no longer together. And he needed to get her thinking about why they should be again.

If there was one thing that Donovan was good at, it was winning—and winning Cassidy over was his first priority. He was competitive, and his drive for success went much deeper than wanting to make money. God knew, with his trust fund he never needed to work a day in his life. And the investments he'd made in the ventures with his friends had paid off handsomely. But he wanted more. He wanted his birthright—the CEO position at Tolley-Patterson.

Looking at Cassidy with her beautiful hair curling around her face made him realize that he'd missed her far more than he'd realized. He wouldn't have come back on his own, without the incentive of needing a wife and child, but being here now, he knew that coming back was exactly what he'd needed to do. Her pregnancy simply made his objective that much easier to attain.

"I'm sorry," he said. And part of him really meant the words. Another part—the man who was always looking for a way to turn every situation to his advantage—knew that being humble would help him win Cassidy back. Knew that even though he'd hurt her, there was a tentative hope in her eyes.

"For?"

"Making you feel like you weren't first in my life," he said.

She fiddled with her food bag and drew out a foam container of what he suspected was she-crab soup.

"Don't play games with me, Donovan."

"I'm not."

"Yes, you are. You're a master game player and everything you do is for a specific purpose."

She knew him well. In fact, that was one reason he'd let the distance grow between them when she'd walked out on him. She knew him better than he wanted anyone to know him. But she was the key to what he needed, and he wasn't going to let her walk away again. This time, he was better able to make room for Cassidy in his life.

"What? No snappy comeback?" she asked.

"Sarcasm doesn't suit you."

She shrugged. "I'm pregnant. Most of the time that means I get a pass on things like that."

"Does it?"

"Yes."

"From who?"

"Everyone." She gave him a grin that was pure Cassidy for sexiness. She had a way of accepting her feminine appeal and knew its effect on everyone she met.

"Is there a man in your life?" he asked, abruptly realizing that she might have met someone after they'd broken up. Oh, he knew the baby was his. Not just because she'd confirmed it, but because he knew Cassidy. She'd said she loved him, and he knew that, to her, that meant more than just words.

"My dad and brothers," she said, looking down at the table, the joy she'd exhibited a moment earlier totally extinguished.

"I meant a boyfriend," he said.

"Yeah, right. I'm pregnant out to here with your baby, why the heck would I be dating someone else?" she said, looking up at him with those clear brown eyes of hers.

"How long are we going to be dealing with the sarcasm? I didn't know you were pregnant," he said.

"I didn't think you'd care."

"Well, I do. So you're not dating?" he asked one more time. He couldn't help the rush of satisfaction that swamped him when he realized she'd been alone for the months they'd been apart.

"No. It didn't seem fair to get involved with another man right now. What about you, are you dating anyone?"

"Would I be here if I was?" he asked. The truth was he'd buried himself even more in work after they'd parted. That was one reason he'd had an edge over his cousin Sam, his competition for the CEO position. Sam had been married for more than ten years now and divided his time between the office and home. Then their grandfather's will had evened things up between them.

"Why are you here?" Cassidy asked.

He scratched the back of his neck. He knew what

to say, but as he looked at her he began to calculate the consequences of what he was about to do. Lying to Cassidy wasn't something he did lightly. But if he told her the truth—that thanks to his grandfather's will, to take over as CEO of Tolley-Patterson, he needed to be married and have a child within a year as well as win the vote of the board—she'd tell him to hit the road.

"Donovan?"

"I missed you, Cassidy."

"I've been right here," she said.

"I wasn't sure you'd take me back."

"You want to date again?" she asked. "Once the baby is born that will be difficult."

"I don't want to date you, I want to marry you. The last eight months have made me realize how much I want you as my wife. I came here today prepared to tell you I've changed my mind about having a family."

He heard her breath catch in her throat and saw a sheen of tears in her eyes.

He pushed back from the table, standing up and walking over to her chair. He pulled it away from the table and turned her to face him. She looked up at him.

He leaned down so that their lips were almost touching. Framing her face with his hands, he suddenly knew that he really didn't want to screw this up. And not just because he wanted to beat Sam. He wanted to do this right because Cassidy was the key to a life that he'd never realized he might want until this moment.

"I want to marry you, Cassidy Franzone. I want to be a father to our child and have that family you dreamed we'd have together."

With Donovan so close to her, all Cassidy really wanted to do was kiss him and wrap her arms around him, feel his arms around her and maybe rest her head against his chest for a while. It was what she woke up in the middle of the night longing for, that touch of his.

But Donovan had been so adamant that he wasn't going to have a family, and this change, though eight months in the making, was drastic for him.

"Why? What made you change your mind?"

"I missed you," he said.

But he'd said that before. And missing her wasn't an explanation of why he'd changed his feelings about kids.

"That's not why you suddenly want a family." She was afraid to trust the sudden turnaround in his attitude.

He moved and dropped his hands from her face as he stood up. He grabbed his beer from the table and paced to the railing of the porch. Leaning one hip on the wooden railing, he tipped his head back and drained the bottle.

"What do you want me to say, Cassidy?"

She had no idea. Eight months ago when he'd proposed to her, she'd suspected she was pregnant—and she'd walked away when he'd made his opinion on kids and family clear. She'd walked away, because she knew that Donovan was the type of man who'd marry a woman he'd gotten pregnant—and that wasn't why she wanted to be married. She needed Donovan to marry her because he was in love with her. Because he couldn't live without her the way she couldn't live without him.

"I want to know why you changed your mind. You said kids were the major source of all arguments between married couples. You said that having a child ruined many of the great relationships you'd seen. You said—"

"Hell, I know what I said."

"And?"

"I've had a lot of time to think about you and me, Cassidy. The way we were with each other, the way we were both raised… I think we can have a family and not lose the essence of who we are as a couple."

He was saying things that she wanted to believe, things that she'd dreamed of him saying, and a part of her wanted to just say yes. But being alone had made her realize that being in love wasn't the be-all and end-all of a relationship. And she couldn't go through getting over him again.

"Are you proposing because you found out I'm pregnant? I don't want you to marry me because you feel obligated."

Donovan crossed the porch back to her. He set his beer bottle on the table and drew her to her feet. "Cassidy, I wouldn't insult either of us that way. I'm here because I need you. I was coming to see you today to beg you to take me back."

"Does it have anything to do with your grandfather's death?" she asked. "I was sorry to hear of his passing." She'd sent flowers and felt awful for not going to the service.

Donovan couldn't believe how close to the truth she'd come with that one innocent comment. "Losing Granddaddy did make me realize how quickly life can change, and I thought about how much he'd always wanted me to have children of my own while he could see them. I thought we had more time…"

Cassidy wrapped an arm around his shoulder and hugged him briefly then stepped back. "Did that make you realize there was more to life than work?"

Cassidy knew how hard it was for Donovan to talk about his emotions. But if she was going to take a chance on him again, on letting herself really love him and bring up a child with him, then she needed to know where he stood.

It wasn't just about her anymore. She rubbed a

hand over her stomach, thinking of her baby—their baby. She wanted the best for this child, and that meant two loving parents.

"I guess it did. I don't want to talk too much about it. Granddaddy and I butted heads a lot, and his heart attack was so sudden...."

Donovan and Maxwell Patterson had had what could kindly be called an adversarial relationship. "Did you get a chance to make peace with him?"

"No, not really. Our last words were spoken in anger. I walked out on him."

"I'm sure he knew you loved him."

Donovan shrugged as though it wasn't important but she knew that he'd always had a driving need to make his grandfather proud of him. To prove to the family that he was more than his sculptor father's son. To prove that he had the same blood in his veins as his grandfather did.

"That's why I need you. I need to have you by my side. You and our child. I don't want to get to the end of my days and find I have nothing but Tolley-Patterson to show for it. I want you to marry me, Cassidy."

Her heart melted. She still thought there had to be more to his change of heart, but she didn't care. He was offering her more than she'd ever expected him to. Donovan was the kind of man who honored his commitments. And with their baby on the way she knew that she could make their life everything she always dreamed it would be.

"Um…"

"What?"

"Getting married now, like this," she said, gesturing to her stomach, "isn't what I had in mind. I want to have a big wedding and all that."

"What are you saying?"

"Um…" What *was* she saying? She wanted their child to be born with Donovan's name. But a public wedding was out of the question until she delivered their child. "I think I'm saying let's get married in secret, with just our families present, and then after the baby is here we can have a big public commitment ceremony."

Donovan hadn't thought beyond getting Cassidy to agree to marry him. Married in secret didn't seem like a plan that would fulfill the conditions of his grandfather's will. His lawyer was working on finding a loophole, but Granddaddy had been a smart man—he'd made sure that his bizarre requirements for the next CEO of Tolley-Patterson were legally sound. It didn't matter that everyone who'd heard the will and read the new CEO description thought it was crazy. Legally Granddaddy had followed every rule.

"Why do you want to keep the marriage secret?"

Cassidy flushed and wrapped her arms around

her stomach. One hand rubbed the top of her baby bump. "I just don't want the world to think that you're marrying me for the child."

"Cassidy, that's silly. Who cares what the world thinks?"

"I do," she said quietly.

"Then, okay, we'll do it your way."

"Really?"

"Yes."

"Thank you."

"You're welcome," he said, drawing her into his arms. The exhalation of her breath on a sigh brushed against his neck as she wrapped her arms around his waist and melted against him. Because of her belly, the embrace was different from all the ones they'd shared in the past, but Donovan felt a new sense of rightness to having her in his arms.

No matter why he was back here with her, this was where he was meant to be. She tipped her head back and he looked down into her brown eyes.

He cupped her face in his hands and lowered his mouth to hers. She rose on tiptoe to meet him. He brushed his lips over hers once, twice, and then he felt her lips part and her tongue touch his lower lip.

He'd never forgotten Cassidy's kisses. She was the only woman he'd ever found who fit him perfectly physically. There had never been any awkwardness to their sex life. She tasted wonderful to him, and as he slipped his tongue into her mouth he realized just how much he'd missed the taste of her.

She held on to him as she tilted her head to give him deeper access to her mouth. He tunneled his fingers into her hair, caressing the sides of her neck with his thumbs. She moaned deep in her throat, and the sound made him groan and slide one hand down to her hips to draw her closer to him.

She shifted against him, and then he felt a nudge against his stomach. It knocked him off track. He pulled back and looked down at her belly. A bump moved under her maternity top.

"Uh…"

She smiled. "He gets active in the afternoon."

"He?"

"Yes. We're having a son."

"A son," he said. Thinking about the baby as the means to an end was different than this. My God, he was going to have a son. That rocked him more than finding Cassidy pregnant. He sat down in the chair that Cassidy had vacated. She stood there watching him.

"Are you okay?"

"Yes. I just didn't think about the baby beyond you being pregnant. You know?"

She smiled at him. "Yes, I do. It's one thing to be pregnant but another to picture the baby in the future, isn't it?"

"Yes, it is. So I want to do this as soon as possible."

"Do this? You mean get married?" she asked.

"Yes. I'll take care of getting all the paperwork in order."

"Okay. I want to have our ceremony at my parents' house on the beach."

"That's fine. You can make the arrangements. When is the baby due?"

"In less than two weeks."

"Then I think we should get married over the weekend."

"So soon?"

"We don't have a lot of time if we're going to be married when our son is born."

"Does that matter to you?"

"Yes," he said, realizing that it did matter. He wanted to do everything by the book so that when the lawyers looked at his marriage to Cassidy and the birth of their son, they'd have no questions. And he needed to be married to her before she had his child. His primitive instincts demanded that she have his name.

"I'll give my mom a call and see if they can host the ceremony this weekend. Adam is in New York, so I'll have to see if he can make it back."

"Will both of your brothers be there?" he asked, guessing that the Franzone boys weren't too happy with him.

"I hope so. Don't worry, they understood about me having the baby on my own."

Somehow Donovan doubted that. Her two brothers were older and superprotective. He'd done his best to avoid them since he and Cassidy had broken up.

The late-afternoon sun spilled onto the porch, lighting the deep dark sheen of her hair and making him catch his breath. She was truly the most beautiful woman in the world. And he couldn't believe how easily this had all gone.

But then, this was Cassidy, and she'd always made his life brighter just by being near him. He would never admit it out loud, but maybe Granddaddy had done him a favor when he'd added that clause to the CEO requirements.

As he listened to her speaking with her mother, he realized that she was hopeful about their marriage. He made a vow at that moment to never let her find out why he'd come back. He'd do whatever it took to protect Cassidy from learning that he'd returned to her only to win the CEO position at Tolley-Patterson.

Two

Dwelling on details wasn't something that Cassidy was good at, and she knew it was one of the areas where Donovan and she weren't the same. He kept talking about all of the things that had to be done, but it was the first week in August and she was bigger than a beached whale—and about as comfortable as one, as well.

"Are you listening to me?" Donovan asked.

He'd coaxed her out of her house and to the country club where both of their families were members. They were sitting in a secluded alcove overlooking the ocean and she could feel the warm breeze stirring over the veranda.

"No."

"Cassidy, we don't have much time and I want everything taken care of before you go into labor."

"I don't understand what the rush is," she said, a part of her not believing that Donovan was back in her life. But here he was, and he was taking over the way he had before.

And she wasn't too sure she wanted to let him. The last time, she'd been more than happy for him to take the lead, but she was older and wiser—and crankier, she thought. She didn't want to talk about what kind of life insurance policy they should have for themselves to protect the baby if they died.

She didn't want to think about anything like that.

"We need to talk about guardians, as well. I think it would be best if the child went with my family."

"What do you mean, best? I've already asked Adam to be the guardian." Her oldest brother was very responsible and she knew that Adam would keep her child safe.

"You shouldn't have done that without consulting me first."

"Um…you weren't in my life, remember?"

"Again with the sarcasm."

"Yeah, I kind of like it."

"I don't."

"Then stop trying to run my life. I said I'd marry

you, but I'm not going to let you take complete control of everything."

"Cassidy…"

"Yes?"

"I'm not asking you to let me control your life."

"You're not?"

He leaned across the table. There was a glint in his eyes that was distinctly sexual and she had to fight not to smile. This was the Donovan she remembered, able to turn any situation into something fun and sexy.

"No, I'm not…I'm telling you."

She leaned closer to him. Her belly rested against the lip of the wooden surface. She reached out and traced his lower lip, and his mouth opened. She shifted farther in her chair and briefly pressed her lips to his. "You have to remember one thing, Donovan Tolley."

"And that is?" He brushed his mouth against hers. The soft kiss might have looked sweet and innocent, but a flood of hormones rushed through her body. Even though she was very pregnant, she really wanted this man.

"You aren't the boss outside of Tolley-Patterson."

He stroked a finger down the side of her neck, tracing the bead of sweat that had just taken the same path. "Once we're married I will be."

"How do you figure?" she asked, trying to ignore the way his finger felt as he stroked her skin just above the base of her neck. Her pulse was beating wildly. She had no idea where this conversation was going; she only knew that this was what she had missed. Having Donovan in her life meant she wasn't alone. And she could just be herself, no matter how crazy or silly she might seem to someone else.

"I'm going to insist that our vows have the word *obey* in them."

"I have no problem with that," she said. "I've always wanted you to obey me."

He threw his head back and laughed, drawing the attention of the other people on the veranda. Cassidy smiled at him and leaned back in her seat, taking a sip of the refreshingly cool lemonade she'd ordered.

Donovan's BlackBerry twittered and he pulled it from his pocket, glanced at the screen and then up at her. "I have to make a quick call. Will you be okay by yourself?"

She nodded. He got up and left the table, and she glanced around. Sitting alone at a table in a restaurant always made her feel exposed, something that she didn't like. She took a sip of her water.

"Cassidy?"

She turned to see her best friend, Emma Graham, and Emma's fiancé, Paul Preston. "Emma! How are you?"

"Good. Are you here alone?"

"No. I'm with Donovan."

Emma raised both eyebrows and told Paul she'd

meet him at their table. Emma wasn't a subtle person, and Cassidy immediately knew her best friend was concerned.

"What's going on?" Emma asked, sitting down in Donovan's seat. "The man left you alone and pregnant. I can't believe he'd have the gall to come back to you now."

"You know he didn't know I was pregnant."

"Okay, I'll give him that. What does he want?"

"To marry me."

Emma's eyes widened. "Are you going to?" she asked.

For the first time, Cassidy felt a twinge about how easily she'd capitulated. But she couldn't have done anything else. Surely Emma understood—she was getting married as well. Cassidy wanted a partner—a husband—in her life. "Yes. I think so. I mean…"

"You still think you love him."

"Who's to say that I don't love him?"

Emma shrugged one delicate shoulder. "No one but you. Are we happy about this?"

Cassidy thought about it. "I don't know yet. I was going to call you in the morning."

"I've got an early flight to New York for a meeting. I can talk until eight tonight and then again after three tomorrow. I was going to stop by your place later today anyway."

They had grown up together and attended the

same boarding school in Connecticut. Emma was like the sister Cassidy had never had and had always wanted. "Did you tell him about the baby, is that why he came back?"

"No. He just showed up."

"Why?"

"Um, he missed me," she said to her friend, feeling sheepish and suddenly wondering what Emma would say.

"And you believe that?" Emma asked.

"I—"

"Yes, Emma, she does believe me, because I told her that letting her walk out of my life was the biggest mistake I'd ever made."

"It's about time you realized it," Emma said. "Hurt her again and you'll deal with me."

Donovan nodded as Emma gave Cassidy a hug and then walked away. The threat should have seemed silly coming from the petite brunette, but Donovan knew Emma Graham was more than capable of backing up her words.

"Sorry about that," Cassidy said as he sat back down.

"It's okay. She cares for you and wants the best for you."

"Yes, she does."

Cassidy took a sip of her lemonade and glanced

toward the ocean. Donovan realized that getting her agreement to the marriage wasn't enough. He needed to…ah, hell, he needed to make some promises that would alleviate Cassidy's fears that he was going to hurt her again.

"I care, too," he said, realizing as the words left his mouth how lame they sounded. Lame-ass comments like that were exactly why he didn't talk about his emotions. He was much better keeping things light or talking about business.

"I'd suspected as much, since you asked me to marry you."

"See, you are a smart girl."

"Don't be condescending."

"I wasn't. You're one of the smartest women I know. It's what drew me to you the first time."

"Um…I thought that was my legs."

It had been everything about her. Her long legs in that impossibly short micromini she'd had on. Her long, dark curly hair hanging down her back in silky waves. But, to tell the truth, it had been her laughter that had first caught his attention. It was deep and uninhibited. He'd found himself distracted at the charity event. Instead of conducting business as he usually did at social functions, he'd followed her and joined her group just to hear that laugh again. And her intelligence was quickly evident as she debated and discussed myriad current events.

"Your legs were part of it," he said. He'd always been a leg man.

"I was drawn to your eyes."

"My eyes?" he asked, wondering what she saw in them.

"Every time you looked at me, there was this intensity that made me feel like I was the only person in the room that night."

"You were the only one I saw," he admitted.

"Yeah, until Sam entered and you remembered that he's your rival."

"That's not completely true." But it was partially true. He and Sam had always been in competition with each other. They'd been born a week apart and Donovan was the younger of the two of them. Every summer they'd been sent to live with their grandfather, and the old man had always challenged the both of them. Donovan had learned early on that the key to Granddaddy's praise was winning.

"Yes, it is. You even told me you'd do anything to beat him to the vice presidency, and you did it."

"That's right. You said you liked my ambition," he said.

"Did I?"

He nodded, wishing he knew what she was thinking at this moment. Because he had a feeling she was recalling the other things about him, the things she didn't like. Or had merely tolerated.

Part of the reason he'd let things lie between them was that she made him vulnerable, and only a man without any weaknesses could fully protect himself. Because then he had nothing for his enemies to attack.

He knew that sounded melodramatic considering he was an executive, but the modern-day business world was just as fierce as the ancient fiefdoms that had been defended by nobles and warriors. And Donovan had always known he was a warrior. The need to win was strongly bred into him.

"I like you when you're happy, and competing does that for you."

"You do that for me, too."

She tipped her head to the side. "Really?"

"Mmm, hmm. Want to get out of here and go for a walk on the beach?"

"No. Sorry, but my feet are swollen. I know that sounds totally unromantic, but I'm not up to a long walk on the beach until it's cooler."

"How about going out on the yacht? You can sit on the deck and feel the ocean breeze in your hair."

She hesitated.

"What?"

"I can't believe that you're back in my life and going on about everything as if nothing has changed. As if the last eight months never happened…but they did, and I…I'm not sure if I can trust you the way I did before."

Donovan rubbed his neck and looked away. What could he say to her? He needed Cassidy and their child. And he needed them now. He didn't have time to seduce her or convince her that he was the man she wanted in her life.

He put his sunglasses on and stood up. "I can't just stand around and pretend we have all the time in the world to reconnect."

"Because of the baby?" she asked.

There was something in her tone and a kind of worry in her eyes that told him he had to say the right thing at this moment. Dammit, he sucked at saying the right thing.

"Not just because of the baby, Cassidy. Because you and I have lost eight months and we have only a short time to find *us* again before we are going to have our child."

Tears glimmered in her eyes and he shook his head. "You know I stink at saying the right thing."

She held his gaze. "Sometimes you say exactly the right thing."

"Don't bet on it happening too often."

She chuckled and gave him a weak grin. She looked tired and so achingly beautiful that he wanted to just pull her into his arms and hold her forever. Never mind the warning flashing at the back of his mind that he had a meeting with the board of directors to prepare for.

"Come out on the yacht, just for an hour," he said.

* * *

Cassidy loved being out on the ocean. The wind was cooler out here. Donovan had seated her on the padded bench and gone to make arrangements with the captain of the yacht. He hadn't come back since they'd left the dock.

She didn't mind, though; it gave her time to regroup. She put one hand low on her belly and felt the baby's foot resting against the outer wall of her stomach. She was overwhelmed by Donovan and everything that he was doing right now. A part of her knew that this was his way of ensuring she married him. That he would do whatever he had to in this week leading up to the wedding. That was the way he'd been when they'd first started dating. He was really good at making her feel like his top priority when he wanted to.

Had she trusted him too much?

Her cell phone rang and she glanced at the caller ID. Adam. She didn't answer it. She wasn't up to a lecture from her oldest brother at this moment, and that was exactly what she'd get from him. She guessed that their mother had put the word out to the family that she and Donovan were back together and getting married next weekend.

She had a feeling that her brothers weren't going to be very welcoming to Donovan.

Her phone beeped to let her know she had a voice mail. She would listen to it later.

"Who was that?"

"Adam."

"You didn't answer it?"

"I'm not really up to another demanding male telling me what he thinks is best for me."

"Demanding male? Is that how you see me?" Donovan asked.

"Yes. You've been bullying me all afternoon."

"It's because I do know best," he said, handing her a glass of sparkling water with a twist of lime.

She took a sip and watched him through narrowed eyes. She was glad that the sun was still drifting in the sky, because it gave her an excuse to keep her sunglasses on.

"You don't know me these days," she said. "How can you know what's best?"

"I do know you, Cassidy. I know that you are loving and caring. And that you've always wanted a family, and that despite having a career you love, work has never come first for you."

That was very true. Her job as curator at a small museum in Charleston was nice, but it wasn't anything that could compare with being a mom. She was going to stay on at her position in a part-time capacity once her son was born.

She had never tried to pretend that family and relationships weren't important to her. Her father and Adam were so consumed with their jobs that she'd been soured on that kind of career when she was a young girl. There had to be more to life than work, in her opinion.

"But you don't feel that way, do you? Or is that something else that's changed since we've been apart?"

"No. I haven't changed my focus. But I have broadened it to include more than just Tolley-Patterson."

"Like what? I know about your other business interests."

"Of course I still have those. I've also invested in Gil's team for the America's Cup. He has a new design that's going to revolutionize yacht racing."

"That's still an investment. How have you changed to put relationships and people first?"

"Gil is one of my oldest friends."

"I've never met him," she said. She had noticed that most of Donovan's friends didn't contact him unless they needed money. To be fair, he didn't exactly encourage anyone to stay close to him. He was a bit of a loner, despite his social connections and the parties he frequented. She'd realized early on that he was pretty much all about business.

"We'll invite him to our public wedding," he said.

"Fine, but you still haven't convinced me that you know what's best for *me*."

"I don't have to convince you with words," he said. "I'm going to show you with actions."

She raised her eyebrows. "How?"

He rubbed a hand through his hair. "You'll have to wait and see."

"I will?"

"Yes." He paused, and she braced herself, guessing she wouldn't like what was coming next. "I called my parents and they're both home this evening. When we get back to shore I think we should drop by and tell them about the wedding."

Cassidy tried to keep her face expressionless.

"It won't be bad."

"Your mom doesn't like me. She thinks my family are white trash."

"That's not true. She asked about you after we broke up."

"Really?"

"Yes. And we can't be married without my parents there. They would be disappointed."

Cassidy doubted that. But family was important and Donovan's parents would be her baby's grandparents. Maybe knowing that she was pregnant with Donovan's baby would make Donovan's mother like her better.

Not that being liked was *too* important to Cassidy, but she hated the fact that Donovan's family always acted so superior simply because they'd been in Charleston forever.

She gritted her teeth and mentally prepared herself to face Donovan's mother.

Three

Donovan's family had lived in the same house for more than six generations. The 1858 mansion was registered as a historical landmark. The first Tolley family had moved to Charleston just after the Civil War. They traced their fortune back to those days, as well.

His mother was a member of the Junior League and the Charleston Preservation Society, and she sat on the board for directors of Tolley-Patterson. She prided herself on the work she did with that group. She was the kind of woman who never had a hair out of place, and family image was very important to her.

"You're getting *married?*" she asked as she and

Donovan sat in the parlor. She had a martini in one hand and looked every inch the genteel Southern lady that she was.

Cassidy was outside walking through the lamplit gardens with his father. His parents had both been shocked to see a pregnant Cassidy, and had covered their reaction only so-so. Donovan had been grateful when his usually withdrawn father had jumped up and asked to show his soon-to-be daughter-in-law his latest sculpture.

"Yes."

"I thought you broke up."

"We did, but now we're back together and getting married."

"Is this because of your grandfather's will? Even though she's pregnant, it might not be your child. Donovan, darling, there are a lot of women more suited to your social station that you could marry."

"Cassidy *is* suited to our station, Mother. And she's the one I chose."

"What about the baby?"

"Mother."

"Yes?"

"Stop it. I need you to just be happy for me and go along with this."

"I'll try, dear. It's just…I'm a little young to be a grandmother."

"And everyone will say that, you know that."

"Do you know if it's a boy or a girl?"

"A boy."

His mother took another sip of her martini. He couldn't read her thoughts. But she did smile for a second.

"Will her family be at the wedding? Surely you aren't going to have a big wedding with the pregnancy so far along."

"No, Mrs. Tolley, we aren't going to have a big wedding. Just an intimate ceremony at my parents' house. And we hope you'll both be there."

Donovan glanced at Cassidy to gauge her mood, but her face looked serene. She smiled politely at his mom. He had never thought before about the kind of attitude that Cassidy must have to endure from the oldest established families in Charleston. Her family, though wealthier than many, had accrued their fortune in the last twenty years and didn't have the kind of pedigree that the women in the Junior League approved of.

"I heard your parents were doing some remodeling," his mother said. "Would you consider having the ceremony here?"

Cassidy glanced at him and he shrugged. Everyone had heard about the bright pink stucco that been used to repaint the Franzone mansion. Two weeks worth of editorials on the eyesore that their mansion had become had ensured that.

The Franzones were in the middle of a lengthy

battle with their contractor to get him to repaint the house. The color was so bright and gaudy that the neighbors had complained to city hall in hopes of forcing the Franzones to do something immediately, instead of waiting for legal settlement.

"Thank you for that kind offer, but my mom has already started making arrangements."

"Very well. When is the ceremony going to be?"

Donovan knew from his mother's tone that she wasn't happy, but he didn't care. He needed Cassidy to be his wife. And his mother was never going to be happy to be related by marriage to the Franzones.

"This Saturday, Mother," Donovan said. He walked to Cassidy's side and wrapped his arm around her, pulling her close to him.

"Where is your father?"

"He went back to his studio," Cassidy answered. "He showed me the sculpture he's working on for the Myerson Museum."

"Did he?" Donovan and his father hardly had what anyone would call a close relationship, but he'd hoped that today, since he had come over to announce his engagement, his father would leave his studio for more than an hour and spend some time with him. But that wasn't the type of man his father was, and Donovan was old enough to accept that.

His parents had never had a close relationship. They'd married because his grandfather had wanted to merge Tolley Industries and Patterson Manufacturing. He'd always been aware that his parents didn't have a love match. His father's M.O. was to retreat to his studio whenever possible.

"Yes, he did. It's still rough, but you can see that it'll be breathtaking when it's done."

"I'm sure it will," Donovan said. "Mother, would you like to join us for dinner?"

"No, thank you, Donovan. I have a bridge game tonight."

"We will see you Saturday, then? At the Franzones'?" he asked.

"Of course. What time on Saturday?" she asked.

"Cassidy?"

She pulled her BlackBerry phone out and pressed a few buttons. "Six-thirty, Mrs. Tolley. There will be a dinner afterward."

"Do you need me to do anything to help?"

"No, thank you. We've got it all taken care of."

They said their goodbyes and were outside a few minutes later. Cassidy let out a breath.

"What?"

"Nothing."

"Cassidy, I know something's on your mind."

"Do I really need to tell you how snobby your mother is? She'll probably have a fit when she realizes that I've asked Emma to be one of the witnesses for the ceremony."

"Emma's not family."

"I don't have any sisters, and you know she's like one to me." She smiled shyly. "Do you want me to ask one of my brothers to be the best man?"

He stared at her. He hadn't thought about who should be his witness. "Which one?"

"Adam makes the most sense. You've met him."

He and Adam Franzone didn't get along. From the very beginning of his relationship with Cassidy, Adam had been telling him he wasn't good enough for her.

He didn't want her brother to stand up with him, but if it meant keeping Cassidy happy, he guessed he could do it. He shrugged. "Adam will do."

Donovan was silent as they drove away from his parents' house. Cassidy wondered if she was making the biggest mistake of her life. She'd been seeing Donovan as she wanted him to be. Seeing him with his mother, so arrogant and very much the wealthy son who'd always gotten his way...

"What are you thinking?" he asked.

"Nothing," she said. There were some doubts that she couldn't shake. She was waiting for the other shoe to drop, and that was exactly why she couldn't shake the panicked feeling deep inside of her.

"So it's something you don't want to share with me," he said, his voice a deep rumble in the cockpit of his sports car.

"How do you know I'm thinking anything at all?" Cassidy asked.

"Baby, you always have something going on in your head. Is it about work?"

"No. Lately I've been working with an artist, Sandra Paulo, who isn't coming in until a month after the baby is born. And she's been very cooperative. She shipped all of her paintings early so I'd be able to plan the display before I go out on maternity leave."

"Well if it's not the job, is it family?"

"Whose?"

"Mine or yours," he said.

"Not really. I mean, your mom *is* a bit of snob—that tone in her voice when she talked about the ceremony being held at my parents' place was a bit obvious."

"She's just used to things being a certain way."

"I imagine she is. You know your family is too caught up in pedigree."

Donovan shrugged. "So that's what you were thinking about? I can't change my mother's attitude."

"I know, it's a part of who she is. It really doesn't bother me at all. I only mentioned it because you brought the subject up."

"I didn't bring it up. I asked what was on your mind, and you still haven't told me."

"That's because it's a nice day and I don't want to start an argument."

Donovan glanced over at her and arched one eyebrow at her. "I won't argue with you, Cassidy."

"I know that. You get quiet and clam up and act like nothing is wrong."

"I sound like a sulky two-year-old."

She forced herself not to smile. "Well…if the shoe fits."

He reached over and tickled her thigh, making her squirm in her seat. Laughing put too much pressure on her bladder.

"Stop, Donovan."

"Not until you take that back."

"Okay, I take it back," she said. He stopped tickling her, caressing the inside of her thigh before he removed his hand.

"You're so incredibly sexy," he said, his voice deepening with lust.

"I'm not sexy at all. I'm almost nine months pregnant. Big as a whale."

He pulled off the road under a streetlamp. "Cassidy, look at me."

She faced him. She'd never really had body issues, but the bigger her stomach had gotten and the skinnier her friends had stayed, the more conscious she'd become of her size. Being alone all these months hadn't helped, either.

He leaned over her and released her seat belt and

then his own. He drew her into his arms and held her close.

"You are the only woman in the world who is always beautiful to me. First thing in the morning, after a workout, sunburned and swollen." He tipped her head back and leaned in to kiss her. "You've always been beautiful to me, but never more so than now. You are carrying my child."

He pulled back and put his hand on her belly. "I thought my life was meant to follow one path. Business has always been my focus. But when our baby kicked against me the other night…it was like an awakening for me."

"Awakening how?" she asked. This was what she wanted to understand. This was what she needed to know. Was Donovan really back because he'd had a change of heart and needed her the way she needed him? This moment could change everything. Put her doubts to rest for good.

"It made me realize that our futures—my future and yours—were intertwined. And it made me see that I had a chance to leave behind a legacy outside of Tolley-Patterson."

Cassidy started to ask another question, but he stopped her with his mouth. The kiss was soft but not tentative. It felt like a promise to her. The promise of a life that they would build together with their child.

He sucked her bottom lip between his teeth and

nibbled on her. She shifted in his arms, trying to get closer to him, but the close confines of the car made it impossible.

He groaned, his hands skimming up her belly to brush over her breasts. They were sensitive and his touch on them made her squirm as a pulse of desire speared through her body.

"Donovan," she said, holding tight to his shoulders when he would have pulled back.

"Baby," he said. "God, I want you."

"I want you, too," she said, thinking of all the vivid sexual dreams she'd had of him during her pregnancy.

He kissed her again and this time there was nothing soft or tentative about it. He was reclaiming her, and she knew that if they weren't in the front seat of his sports car this encounter wouldn't end until he was buried deep inside her body. But instead he gentled the embrace with some light kisses and eventually put her back in her seat, fastening her seat belt.

"Don't worry about us, Cassidy. We are solid this time. I'm not going to let you go."

As he pulled back out into traffic, she smiled, believing in Donovan and the future they'd have together.

Donovan dropped off Cassidy at her place and turned to leave. He had a meeting with his directors first thing in the morning and he still had a few hours preparation ahead. Something made him look back. Cassidy fingered her swollen lower lip as she stood in her doorway watching him. As their eyes met, he knew the promise he made to her in the car would be kept.

So that wasn't the reason for the churning in his gut. No, that was due to the fact that he knew the reason he'd made those promises wasn't because of his faith in their love but because he wouldn't be able to become CEO of Tolley-Patterson without Cassidy by his side.

He never lost focus, but right now he was torn. He wanted to stay with Cassidy even though he had reports to analyze.

He shook his head and got into the car. The job—his career at Tolley-Patterson—was the most important thing in his life. Winning the last challenge that Granddaddy had put before him and Sam was what he needed.

He glanced in the rearview mirror and saw Cassidy lean heavily against the doorjamb and knew he'd disappointed her.

Instead of going back, he hit the car phone button. "Call Marcus Ware."

"Calling Marcus," the car speaker responded.

Marcus answered on the third ring, exactly as Donovan expected of his right-hand man. Marcus had the same hungry ambition that Donovan did.

The other man lived for Tolley-Patterson and the deals they both made.

"Catch me up on where we stand with the West Coast production problem," Donovan said without exchanging pleasantries.

"Not good. Someone needs to go out there and take care of the problem. Jose's been trying to negotiate with the workers, but he's made little headway."

The last thing he needed right now was a trip to the West Coast. It was Wednesday, and he and Cassidy were getting married on Saturday. "Marcus, I'm getting married this weekend."

"I know, sir."

He'd informed his second in command of the marriage to make sure that he covered all the bases for the terms of the will. He'd instructed Marcus not to mention it to anyone yet. "I need this problem fixed tomorrow."

"That's why I'm booked on the next flight to San Francisco. I'm not going to leave the table until we have this dispute resolved."

"Call me when it's taken care of."

"I will."

He disconnected the call. Donovan knew that Marcus was ambitious; in fact, the younger man reminded him a lot of himself, which was one reason he'd hired him. He had brought Marcus up the ranks with him each time he'd been promoted, and if

Marcus got the West Coast operation back online tomorrow, Donovan intended to promote the man to his position when he became CEO.

And there was little doubt he'd be CEO with Cassidy already pregnant. Every detail was falling into place. So why then did he have this hollow feeling inside?

His cell phone rang and he glanced at the caller ID before answering it. "Hello, Sam. What's up?"

"My mother just called... So you're back with Cassidy Franzone." It was a statement, not a question.

"I am."

"You know that most of the board don't approve of her family."

"Granddaddy's will just said the CEO must be married and have an heir. It said nothing about the type of family she had to come from."

There was silence on the line.

"But I think everyone assumes you'll marry someone from Old Charleston."

"Then they don't know me very well, do they?" He deliberately didn't tell Sam that the wedding was already planned. No need to tip off the competition.

"No, they don't. But I do," Sam said. "You sound confident."

"I'm the best man to take control of the company, and at the end of the day everyone is more interested in making money than social connections."

Sam cleared his throat. "You aren't the best man for the helm, Donovan."

"You think you are?"

"I know I am, because I know that to be successful in business you have to have a life outside of the office. You have to see the world in which we sell our products."

Donovan disagreed, but then Sam had lost his competitive edge four years ago when he'd married Marilyn. Since then Sam had become strictly a nine-to-five man, getting home to his wife every night. Donovan knew that a lot of people believed in balance, but he thought that theory was full of crap.

"Well, we'll see what the board decides in January when they meet."

"Yes, we will. Good luck," Sam said, hanging up.

Donovan continued driving, needing some time to figure out if there was value to anything Sam had said. He'd kept the news about Cassidy's pregnancy to himself and he wondered if his mother had, too. She probably hadn't said anything about it to her sister, Sam's mother, because his marrying his pregnant girlfriend wasn't exactly something she'd brag about.

For the first time in years, Donovan thought about his dreams and he realized that home and family had never been part of them. And with Granddaddy dead, he didn't know what he was searching for anymore. The old man's approval was always going to be just out of reach.

Four

"I don't like the way he's come back into your life," Adam said.

It was the same argument she'd heard many times since she'd called her brothers to tell them she and Donovan were getting married. At least her mother was thrilled for her. Her father had been out of town on business at the time and had sent her a text note to say that he hoped the house would be repainted by the wedding day. She tried to pretend it didn't matter that her father was more concerned about business than her, but deep inside it did.

"You promised you wouldn't start anything today."

"I'm not starting anything, Cassie," Adam said, sitting down next to her on the settee and putting his arm around her. "I just don't want to see you hurt again."

"I'm not going to be hurt again. Raising my baby with his father is what I've wanted since I found out I was pregnant."

"I don't understand why he left in the first place," her other brother, Lucas, said as he joined them. "And now he's back."

Eight months ago, she hadn't told her family that Donovan didn't want kids. She'd kept that to herself because it had been such a deep blow. Now she realized that they must have guessed anyway from the way the relationship had ended.

"It wasn't about the baby," she said.

"Of course not," Lucas said. "It was about him not being ready to be a father."

Lucas was married and had three sons. He had been a father since he was twenty-one and at thirty he felt that he was an expert on what men should do in family situations. Adam was three years older than Lucas and married to his job.

Her brothers had a lot in common with Donovan in that they seemed to exemplify the fact that men could be either family oriented or workaholics. Especially if their work involved a family business.

"Could be. Not every man is like you. Just

because he needed time to consider everything doesn't mean anything."

"Having a wife and kids isn't an easy thing for some men," Adam said. "I couldn't do it. The job comes first for me the way it does with Dad."

Lucas nodded. Cassidy remembered every event their father had attended for them when they were growing up. Because there had only been two events—Adam's graduation from prep school and Lucas's college graduation. Their father had always put business first.

She put her head in her hands. The things that Donovan had said since coming back into her life made her believe that he was truly a changed man. That he was really going to be in her life and their child's.

Could she do what her own mother had? Could she watch her children's disappointed faces as their father once again missed out on an important school function?

"I need to talk to Donovan."

"Now? Why? Are you having second thoughts? We'll go and tell him the ceremony is off," Adam said, standing up and heading for the door.

"Adam, no. I just want to talk to him."

"Beth had the jitters on our wedding day," Lucas said. "Of course, our situation wasn't that different from yours."

Lucas's wife had been pregnant at their wedding—not as far along as Cassidy was, but pregnant all the same. "Are you happy, Lucas?"

"You know I am. But it was a struggle at first."

Lucas came over and hugged her close. "He wouldn't have asked you to marry him if he didn't want to make the relationship with you and your baby work."

She nodded. Lucas was always the sensible one. He'd made family his number-one priority, working a low-stress job so he could coach his kids' Little League team and be at every school event.

"Can you guys leave me alone for a few minutes?"

Lucas gave her another hug and then nodded. "Let's go."

Both her brothers left the room. Cassidy went to the French doors that led out to the garden, which had a beautiful white gazebo in the middle that overlooked the ocean. Chairs were set up for the few guests, and flowers decorated the white lattice around the sides of the gazebo.

The backyard looked fairy-tale perfect. Like something out of *Bride's* magazine—if you ignored the fact that the house in the background was bright pink. And Cassidy wanted to believe in the picture-perfect image. But she was a realist. Picture-perfect was just an image, not reality.

Not knowing exactly where Donovan was at this moment, she went to the house phone and dialed his cell number. While the phone rang, she tried to think of what she'd say, how she'd word her questions. The words eluded her.

"This is Donovan."

"Hey, it's me."

"Hello, baby. Is everything okay?"

There was caring and concern in his voice, bringing up her usual dichotomy of feelings toward Donovan. He was like this sometimes, and then she remembered the way he'd kissed her with all that passion and left her on her own doorstep.

Did he have a switch inside that he turned on and off when it came to her? How would having a father who did that affect their child?

"Cassidy?"

"I have to ask you something. I'm not even sure what I want you to say, but it's important, okay?"

"Sure. Go ahead."

"What kind of a father are you going to be? I mean, are you going to always be at work when our son has a school event, or will you take time off for him?"

"Just a second." She heard the scrape of a chair and then the ringing of his footsteps on a hardwood floor. He must be in her father's study. A second later she heard a door close, and then he said, "I don't know."

"Oh."

"Cassidy, less than a week ago I found out I was going to be a father. I came to your house that night planning to ask you to be my wife, but beyond that I haven't had time to think about our son."

"But just thinking about it now, what's your gut reaction?"

She heard him take a deep breath. "My gut is to tell you what I know you want to hear. But lying to you, Cassidy, isn't something I want to do. I have no idea what kind of father I'll be. I do know that I want to know our son and be a part of his life, but work has always been my focus… I can't promise to change that, but I can promise I will try."

She held the handset loosely and thought about what he'd said. "I'm not going to let you fail at this, Donovan. My dad…he wasn't there for us growing up. Now he's trying, but it feels like guilt. I'm going to insist you be a part of your son's life."

"Good," he said. "We'll make this life of ours work…together."

Donovan glanced over the small crowd of people gathered in back of the Franzones' gaudy pink mansion to celebrate his marriage to Cassidy. Tony Franzone was standing off to one side talking on his cell phone. The man was a better father than Cassidy realized—he'd come over to Donovan earlier and told him in no uncertain terms that if Donovan made his daughter cry again he'd put a hurt on him. The man had actually said that.

Donovan understood the sentiment that went behind it. He searched the crowd for his own parents and found them sitting alone, not talking to each other but each staring at the people around them. He saw his mother shudder when she took in the Franzone mansion.

His extended family had never been close-knit, and he didn't think they ever would be. He told himself it didn't matter that family had no place in his life and they'd never been particularly close, but a part of him was disappointed that more of his relatives weren't here.

Of course, he hadn't invited that many of them. He'd needed to keep the marriage quiet until he was ready to talk to the board.

Marcus had resolved the West Coast matter on Thursday and was back in the office Friday. Donovan had gotten a late-night call from his uncle Brandt congratulating him on taking care of the mess. Brandt had hinted that marriage was the only thing keeping Donovan from the CEO position. Donovan had almost told his uncle about the wedding, but had decided discretion was still wise at this point.

Donovan steeled himself as Adam Franzone approached.

"You sure about marrying my sister?" Adam asked as he came to stand in place next to Donovan at the stairs of the gazebo.

"As sure as any man can be," Donovan said.

"Hurt her again and I'll make sure you regret it for the rest of your life."

"I didn't hurt her on purpose eight months ago. I proposed to her, and she turned me down."

"She turned you down?" Adam asked.

"Yes, she did." He knew now that she had done it because of what he'd said about not wanting a family. From what Adam said, he must have hurt her. "I'll take care of Cassidy."

"Make sure you do."

"Are you threatening me?" He knew he'd do the same if he were Cassidy's brother and some other man had abandoned her. It was a sobering thought, and for the first time he was forced to look outside of himself.

"Yes," Adam said, totally unashamed of himself. "I should have done it the first time you dated her. I knew you were the kind of man who always put himself first."

"The same can be said of any successful businessman. And that's what women want, Adam. Success."

"They also want a guy to be able to balance that with family time."

"I don't see a ring on your finger. What makes you an expert?"

"The fact that I don't have a ring. I've spent my entire life avoiding the situation you're in because for me work always comes first."

Donovan knew it did for him, too. Always had. That was why he'd let Cassidy go. Because he'd known she could interfere with his success.

Donovan didn't want to have this discussion with Adam. The pressure he was under at work to make sure that every aspect of his division was running smoothly was tremendous.

"If it were any other woman, I'd walk away," Donovan said, realizing the words for the truth they were. It didn't matter that he'd had Granddaddy's will as an excuse to get back to her side. He'd wanted Cassidy for a long time. And now that he had her back where she belonged—in his life—he wasn't going to let her go.

The music started and Donovan saw Emma walking up the aisle. And then, Cassidy. She looked so lovely that for a second his breath caught in his throat. He was humbled by the fact that she was marrying him and having his baby.

Humbled by the fact that this woman was now going to be his. When she got to his side and he took her hand in his, he saw the joy on her face and knew he never wanted to disappoint her.

She could never know that he had come back into her life because of a will. That he was marrying her not only for herself but also because his job demanded it.

The lie of omission weighed on him. He would have to balance it with his actions. He was marrying her, and that was ultimately what she'd always wanted. And he would do his damnedest to be a good husband and father. But part of him—the man who was her lover—knew that Cassidy was never going to see a lie as balanced out by anything.

As he took her small hand in his and turned to face the pastor, he vowed to himself that he'd make their life together so fulfilling that, if she ever found out the real reason he'd come back to her, it wouldn't matter.

As the pastor led them through the ceremony, he felt the noose tighten. He heard words he'd heard a hundred times before in other ceremonies, but this time they sank in. This time they resonated throughout his body. His hand tightened in Cassidy's, and she looked up at him.

"You okay?" she mouthed.

He nodded. But was he? Marriage wasn't something to be entered into lightly. And this was the worst possible time for him to be having this thought, but maybe marrying Cassidy wasn't the only solution.

Then the pastor asked if he took Cassidy to be his, and the panic and the uncertainty left. Cassidy was already his, and this ceremony today would do nothing but affirm that to the world.

"I do," he said.

Cassidy smiled up at him, and that was it. That moment of panic retreated to a place where he would never have to think about it again. He wasn't a man who looked back and lamented the choices he'd made. He was a man who looked forward and shaped his own destiny, and this moment, with this woman, was where he was meant to be.

The rest of the ceremony passed in a blur and before he knew it, the pastor was telling him he could kiss his new wife.

He pulled Cassidy into his arms, felt the bump of her belly against his stomach. As he lowered his head to hers, she came up on her tiptoes, meeting his lips. He stroked her mouth with his tongue before pushing inside. She held on to his shoulders and he bent her back over his arm, kissing her and claiming her…Cassidy Franzone—no, Cassidy Tolley. His wife, his woman, the mother of his child.

"Cassidy, do you have a minute?"

"Sure, what's up?"

"I just heard something… I don't want to make waves on your wedding day, but—"

"Emma, just say it. Whatever it is."

"Um…there's something weird going on with Tolley-Patterson."

"Like what?"

"I don't have the details, but one of the attorneys at my father's firm, Jacob Eldred, handled Maxwell Patterson's will. I was talking with some of the firm's associates at a cocktail gathering the other night, and when I mentioned I was attending your wedding, they said something about Maxwell's will."

"His grandfather's will?"

"I couldn't ask more. I started to, and then they realized that they shouldn't be talking to me about the matter, so I asked my father, but you know how he is."

Cassidy sat down and Emma sat next to her, holding her hand. "I…I don't know what to think."

"I know, Cassidy. It may just be business, but I was thinking about how he came back to you out of the blue…."

"I don't think our marriage has anything to do with his job. His grandfather liked the fact that Donovan was single."

"You're right. I just wanted to mention it."

"Mention what?" Donovan asked, coming up behind them.

"Nothing, Donovan. Just a comment I'd heard about you and your grandfather's will."

Cassidy wasn't sure, but it almost looked as if Donovan's face went white. "Like what?"

"Nothing specific, just that it was a bit strange."

"Well it's one of those old-time Southern wills. Nothing either of you has to worry about."

Emma and Donovan had never been great friends. She wished they'd find a way to get along, but it wasn't a main concern of hers. They didn't have to be best friends for her to continue her relationship with each of them.

"Of course it isn't. That's business and this is personal," she said to Donovan. Donovan reached for her hand and she gave it to him. He drew her to her feet. "Did you need me for something?"

"I wanted to dance with you," he said. "Will you excuse us, Emma?"

Her friend nodded, but Cassidy sensed that it wasn't over. There was more to what Emma had been saying, and she'd talk to Donovan about it later. Tonight, she wanted to enjoy their party. To hang on to the illusion that he was her Prince Charming and she was embarking on happily-ever-after with him.

The band started to play "Do You Remember" by Jack Johnson, and Cassidy tipped her head back. "Did you request this?"

"I did. I couldn't think of a better song to be our first as husband and wife."

She'd always liked the song. It had a feeling of

permanence to it. A feeling that the couple would be together forever. And she'd always wanted that for her and Donovan.

"I didn't think you'd remember I liked this song."

"I remember everything about you, Cassidy."

Sometimes, when he said things like that, she knew that her doubts about him were groundless. He drew her closer and sang along with the lead singer. His voice made her feel good deep inside.

She loved being in his arms. She'd missed that so much. She sighed and snuggled closer to him. His hands smoothed down her back and he shifted a bit to pull her even closer.

"Baby, you okay?"

"Yes. I've missed your arms around me."

"Me, too," he said. "We'll never sleep apart again."

She liked the sound of that. But she knew he traveled for business and doubted the words were the absolute truth.

She'd thought that getting married today would ease some of the doubts she'd been carrying inside, but instead she realized that more were being generated.

"Don't you want that?" he asked.

"Yes. I've missed sleeping next to you."

"I'm hearing some hesitation in your voice."

"There isn't any. I was just thinking how our lives sometimes don't follow the path we want for them."

"Even me?"

"Especially you."

"What can I do to alleviate those fears?"

She shrugged. "I don't know. I worry about a lot of things lately."

"What did Emma say to you?" he asked as the band switched gears to play an old Dean Martin song, "Return to Me." She suspected one of her brothers had requested it, since it was her parents' wedding song.

"Something about your grandfather's will."

"What about it?"

"Just that it was a bit strange," she said. "Don't my mom and dad look sweet?"

"Your mom does."

"Dad's not that bad. I'm just glad he was able to make it today. They were having some problems with the workers' union."

"Your dad's a tough guy, and he doesn't look sweet at all. I'm glad he made it today, as well."

"With Mom, he always seems different."

"He loves her," Donovan said. "That's why he's different."

"Yes, he does. Even when Dad disappointed us, he would never disappoint Mom."

"That's not a bad thing, Cassidy. He probably did what he could to be a good father to you."

"I know. I'm not complaining. It's just that if he'd

been the way he is with Mom with me and the boys…"

She didn't know that it would have made a difference. But she thought about Adam and how he was sure he couldn't be a father and an executive, and then she thought about how Donovan was going to be both.

Donovan was a man who never let anyone get the better of him. Not her, not his cousin, not a business rival. What kind of father was he going to be? Someday, were they going to be dancing together at their child's wedding, or would they be divorced… two strangers standing across the dance floor, remembering this moment when they were young?

"Cassidy?"

"Hmm?"

"Don't worry about anything. We're together now, and that's all that matters."

She wished she could believe him, but a part of her feared that just being together was never going to be enough for her.

Five

Cassidy had envisioned her wedding night many times when she'd been younger. Now, looking at herself in the mirror of the bathroom dressed in a maternity negligee, she felt…scared. She'd made love with Donovan many times, but he hadn't seen her body since she'd been pregnant.

And she wasn't even sure that she could make love to him now. Her stomach felt tight, and she couldn't stand still. Probably because of worry over what Emma had said to her. What did she really know about why Donovan had come back?

Only what he'd told her.

Did she trust him? Heck, she already knew that

she did trust him, now she just had to let go of the past and her fears and simply enjoy being with him.

He knocked on the door. "Are you almost done in there?"

"Yes. Just washing my face," she said, turning on the water to give her lie credence.

She heard the door open behind her and leaned down to cup her hands under the water, but then she froze. Donovan had removed his shirt and had on only his dress trousers. They hung low on his hips.

He looked incredibly sexy and she wanted nothing more than to get closer to him. To wrap her arms around his lean waist and rest her head against his chest and pretend that all the things she was worried about didn't exist.

"Why are you hiding out in here?"

"I'm not hiding. I just want… Okay, I am hiding. You haven't seen me all pregnant before. And this is our wedding night, which is supposed to be romantic, and I'm not sure I feel romantic at all."

"That's fine. Just come out and let me hold you," Donovan said.

He opened his arms and she stepped into them. The baby kicked as he drew her close, and Donovan's hand moved to her stomach, resting on the spot where the baby's foot had just been.

Donovan lifted her into his arms and carried her out of the bathroom and across the luxurious hotel suite to the king-size bed. He set her gently in the center of the bed.

He followed her down, lying next to her on his side. He propped his head up on his hand and stared down at her with a look of concentration.

"You seem very serious."

"I'm lying here with my wife…."

Her husband. She hadn't really let herself believe it, no matter how many plans they made, because a part of her hadn't been sure they'd get to the altar. Being married quietly with just family in attendance had sounded good when she'd insisted upon it, but now it made their relationship seem like a secret. That, and the fact that he hadn't wanted to put an announcement in the newspaper about the marriage.

"You're thinking way too much," he said, leaning down to trace her brow with one fingertip.

"Donovan—"

His mouth on her neck made her stop. She didn't want to have a heavy conversation tonight. She wanted just to lie in his arms.

She put her hands on the back of his head, felt the silky strands of his hair against her skin. His breath was warm against her, his mouth a hot brand as he kissed her neck.

She shifted onto her side and into his body. With a hand on her hip he pulled her closer and raised the fabric of her nightgown up over her legs.

"Lift up."

She shifted her hips and he drew the nightgown over her head. And she was lying there completely bare except for her panties. He traced a path from her neck down over her breasts, which were bigger now than they had ever been before. Her nipple beaded as he drew his finger around the full globe of one breast.

He bent to capture the tip of her breast in his mouth. He sucked her in deep, his teeth lightly scraping against her sensitive flesh. His other hand played at her other breast, arousing her, making her arch against him in need.

He lifted his head. The tips of her breasts were damp from his mouth, and very tight. He brushed his chest over them.

"Is this okay?"

"Yes," she said, feeling cherished by the gentle way he was touching her.

"I want you, Cassidy."

She slid her hand down his body and wrapped her fingers around his erection. "I know."

"You are so damned sexy. I've been thinking of this moment all day."

"Have you?"

"Mmm, hmm," he said, his mouth on her breast again. He kissed his way lower, following the mound of her stomach. He paused, whispering something soft that she couldn't hear.

He shifted on the bed, kneeling between her legs, and caressed her body from her neck, down her sternum to the very center of her.

"Do you want me?"

"Yes," she said, shifting her legs on the bed.

He drew her flesh into his mouth, sucking carefully on her. His hands held her thighs open, his fingers lightly caressing her legs as he pushed her legs farther apart until he could reach her dewy core. He pushed one finger into her body and drew out some of her moisture, then lifted his head and looked up her body.

She watched as he lifted his fingers to his mouth. "I've missed your taste."

Donovan had always been an earthy lover, and she hadn't realized how much she'd missed their lovemaking until this moment.

He lowered his head again, hungry for more of her. He feasted on her body, carefully tasting the flesh between her legs. He used his teeth, tongue and fingers to bring her to the brink of climax but held her there, wanting to draw out the moment of completion until she was begging him for it.

Her hands left her body, grasped his head as she thrust her hips up toward his face. But he pulled back so that she didn't get the contact she craved.

"Donovan, please."

He scraped his teeth gently over her and she

screamed as her orgasm rocked through her body. He kept his mouth on her until her body stopped shuddering and then slid up her.

He wrapped his body around hers. "That will have to do until after you have my baby. But you know that I've claimed you as my wife."

"Claimed me?"

"Yes. I don't want there to be any doubts. You are mine, Cassidy Tolley, and I don't give up anything that is mine."

Donovan woke aroused. He wanted to make love to Cass, and as she shifted against him he thought she was feeling the same way. He pulled her more fully against him and she turned her head into his shoulder, moaning softly.

He leaned down to find her lips. They parted under his and he kissed her. He knew he couldn't pull her under his body as he would have in the past. He skimmed his hands down her curves. Her hands tightened on his shoulders and her eyes opened.

"Hey, baby."

"Hey, you," she said, shifting in his arms and kissing him lightly.

He leaned in to kiss her again when she drew back. And groaned this time. "Donovan?"

"Yes."

"I think my water just broke."

"What the hell?!" He jumped out of bed, glancing around for his pants. He found them on the back of the chair. He wasn't completely unprepared for this. He'd had his assistant get him a couple of books on pregnancy, and he knew the layout of the hospital where Cassidy was expected to give birth…in two more weeks. He was even scheduled to attend his first childbirth class with Cassidy next week.

"Did it?"

She glanced down at the bed. "Um…yes."

He kept cool but inside he was panicking. What was he supposed to do with a pregnant woman? "Okay, let's get you dressed and we'll head out."

"Donovan?"

"Yes, baby?"

"I'm scared."

"Don't be. I'm here and I'll make sure everything goes exactly the way it's supposed to." He knew then that he couldn't give in to the uncertainty that swirled around him. He had to be the one to take control and present a calm front for her.

She smiled at him and he felt the burden he'd taken from her. He was scared, too, because he didn't want anything to go wrong. He needed Cassidy, and not just because he wanted to beat Sam in their quest for the CEO position.

He grabbed clean clothes for her from her overnight bag and called her doctor while she changed in the bathroom. He finished dressing and got his wallet. He also called the valet desk and had them bring his car around.

The door opened and Cassidy stepped out looking a bit dazed and scared. He didn't think of anything but Cassidy and the baby. Didn't think of anything but taking care of her.

This was a first for him, putting someone else completely before himself. He'd analyze that later. But for now, as they were riding in the elevator, he just wrapped his arm around her and held her close.

"I was so sure I could do this on my own," she said.

"You could have. Your mom would have been here with you, or Emma."

"That's true, but I was just thinking that having you here is exactly what I need. With you I can really relax and know that you'll take care of everything."

He really was a bastard for having walked out of her life the way he had and for only coming back for himself. There was so much he hadn't realized he was doing to her.

His car was waiting when they got downstairs and Cassidy started having some serious contractions while he drove them to the hospital. The decision to have their wedding night in Charleston instead of somewhere else outside the city had been a good one.

"Did you call my parents?"

"Not yet."

She pulled her phone from her pocket and dialed their number. He half listened to her conversation, thinking about the fact that this was his life now. This woman and the child about to be born.

He wasn't sure he was ready for his life to change this drastically.

He pulled into the parking lot at the hospital and got Cassidy out of the car and into the reception area. He pushed aside everything but Cassidy and the baby. He took control in the waiting area, got the nurses to see to Cassidy. He signed paperwork and talked to the doctor on call. Then there was nothing else to do.

He paced around the private room. It was nice enough, he supposed, with walls painted in neutral, soothing colors.

"Stop pacing," Cassidy said.

"Sorry. After all the stuff we had to do to get here, just standing around waiting for the monitor to do something…"

"Is making you crazy?"

"Pretty much. The next thing that should happen is your contractions getting more intensive. I'll help you manage them."

"You will? How?"

"By managing…distracting you," he said.

"I'm not exactly looking forward to this part," Cassidy said.

"What did you think when you found out you were pregnant?" he asked.

"Well, at first I was excited."

"When did you find out?" he asked. Everything had been going so fast since he'd walked back into her life that he hadn't had a chance to really talk to Cassidy about the baby. He'd been at the office as much as possible, shoring up his position with the board. Making sure that they knew he was the only man for the CEO position.

"The day you asked me to marry you," she said.

He crossed his arms over his chest. "Why did you turn me down? I mean, you knew about the baby, right?"

She closed her eyes for a second, and he checked the monitor and saw that she'd just had a contraction. "Sorry about missing that."

He went back to her side and took her hand in his. He kept one eye on the monitor. "Tell me why you didn't just marry me when I asked you to. Was it only because of what I said about children and family?"

"Yes. I didn't want you to feel trapped. I could have mentioned I was pregnant, and I know you, Donovan, you would have done the right thing."

He wasn't too sure about that. As much as he prided himself on being an upstanding man, a real

gentleman when it came to women, he'd also seen
what kids did to a man and his career. Relationships
that had once been solid often folded under the pres-
sures that a man inherited when he became a father.

"What's wrong about that?" he asked, truly not
understanding what she was saying. He only knew
that if she backed out of being married to him now,
he didn't know what he'd do.

"I wanted you to marry me for me."

Cassidy didn't want to have a conversation about
herself right now. The baby and marriage weren't
exactly topics that she wanted to discuss during labor.
She was interested in finding out what was going on
with his cousin and Tolley-Patterson, but right now she
didn't think she was up to an in-depth conversation.

Right now, she was figuring out that moderate
pain wasn't as moderate as the books described—or
maybe she was wimpier than the average woman.
Hell, she didn't care. The sensation in her abdomen
was getting more intense and Donovan was standing
over her, looking like a man who wanted to discuss
the weight of the world.

"Baby," he said in a very low tone, and she felt a
sting of tears in her eyes.

She turned away so he wouldn't see. He sounded
as though he really cared. The man who could never
and probably would never tell her how he felt had a

voice that could melt her heart sometimes. She hated her weakness for tears. Especially now, when she was trying not to let him see how much pain she was in.

"I was speaking hypothetically. I was a man who arrogantly thought he knew what he felt about children."

"And you didn't?" she asked. Because Donovan was the kind of man who knew how he stood on every topic. She appreciated that he wanted to make her feel better and was trying to say something that would, but she saw through his words to the truth underneath.

And that truth was exactly what she'd feared. That Donovan would have married her and in fact probably *had* married her because she was pregnant with his child.

"Well, let's just say that I didn't anticipate anything to do with you and me and this child."

"What does that mean?" she asked, feeling her stomach start to tighten.

"You've got another contraction coming," he said, holding her hand solidly in his.

She gripped his hand.

"I just… Listen, Cassidy," he said once her pain subsided. He sank down on the bed next to her hip and took her hand in both of his. "My life was on a certain track, you know? Working my way to the top and proving to Granddaddy that I was his logical successor was always my focus."

He was trying to tell her something, but she had no idea what. There was too much going on inside her as her body prepared to give birth. She appreciated that Donovan was finally opening up to her but now was seriously not the time.

"I know. You've always been focused on your job," she said.

Her belly started to tighten again and she clamped down on his hand, her nails digging into his skin. "God this hurts."

Donovan held her hand through the long contraction and then stood up. "I'll take care of this."

She was amazed at how quickly he got the floor nurse into her room to take care of the pain. The technician who was supposed to be administering her epidural arrived and in a very short time she was resting comfortably. Donovan was commanding and in charge, making sure the hospital staff took care of her every need.

Her mother and Emma arrived. The women swarmed around the bed to ask if she was okay. Her father stood in the hallway, cell phone attached to his ear. She could hardly believe he'd come at this hour.

"I'll leave you alone with your girls for a little while. Have them call me on my cell if you need me." Donovan kissed her forehead.

She nodded, guessing he was uncomfortable and

probably needed his space. But the last thing she wanted at this moment was for him to leave. She was scared that something would go wrong with the labor or that Donovan wouldn't get back in time to be by her side when she delivered.

"Where are you going?"

"Just down the hall. I want to call my parents," Donovan said.

"You'll be close by?" she asked.

"Yes," he assured her. Leaning down, he brushed the bangs off her forehead. "Emma?"

"Yes."

"You come and get me the moment anything changes in here. I want to be by her side."

Again she felt that melting deep inside. That certainty that Donovan had the same deep emotions for her as she did for him.

"If she wants you, I'll come and get you," Emma said.

Donovan kissed Cassidy again and left the room. Her mom and Emma both stood there for a second.

"Tonight?" Emma asked, a grin teasing her features. "On your wedding night you go into labor…that has to be the best wedding-night story ever."

"I don't know about best, but certainly the strangest."

"Oh, no, not the strangest," her mom said. "Cousin Dorothy's husband had an allergic reaction to the silk of her negligee and his entire body was covered in hives. He had to be rushed to the E.R."

Cassidy laughed at the story and once she started she found she couldn't stop. Soon her laughter changed to tears and she was crying.

Emma held her left hand and her mother leaned down to hug her from the right side. "Everything is going to be okay."

"Promise?"

"Yes. Childbirth is the greatest experience a woman can have."

"Greatest?"

"Cassidy, you are taking part in a miracle. You are going to be holding your son in a few hours and all of this will be forgotten."

Cassidy liked the sound of that. But then, her mother had always known how to say the right thing at the right time. She held tightly to Emma's hand and realized that as much as she appreciated her mother and her best friend being with her, she really needed Donovan.

She was afraid to ask Emma to go get him. Didn't want to seem too needy on this night, especially after she'd told him she hadn't wanted to be married for their child.

But when the door to her room opened a while later and Donovan poked his head in, she felt relieved. "Do you need anything?" he asked.

"You," she said.

Six

Cassidy woke from a sound sleep in a panic. Nearly three weeks had passed since she'd given birth and returned to her new home with Donovan and their baby boy. She glanced at the clock, and that only intensified her feelings. It was nearly 9:00 a.m. And Donovan Junior, or Van, as they'd decided to call him, hadn't woken her. She jumped out of bed and grabbed her robe on the way out the door.

She ran over the marble floor to the nursery door, which was closed. Who had closed the door? Her son wasn't even a month old, no way was she going to close the door to his room at night.

She pushed it open and stopped still in her tracks.

Van's crib was empty, and on the changing table were his pajamas. But no baby.

She walked back out to the hallway and made her way down the stairs. Hearing the sound of Donovan talking, she went to his home office and stood on the threshold, peering inside.

Van was in Donovan's arms, dressed in a pair of khaki pants and an oxford cloth shirt. He looked like a mini Donovan in his work-casual attire. Except that her son was drooling a bit as he slept.

The sight of the two of them, her two men together, made her heart stop. She just stared at them. And felt all the worries she'd had since her Donovan had come back into her life fade. Seeing him holding their son was all she'd ever wanted.

He looked perfectly at home with Van. Donovan had the baby cradled on his shoulder while he paced the room, talking to the speakerphone.

"Joseph has asked for a special board session to discuss Van."

"He can convene the board as often as he wants. Until the official board meeting, no changes can be made," Donovan said.

"He's positioning himself for the official meeting. There is only three months until the vote. And I have to tell you, what I'm hearing doesn't look good for you."

"Let me worry about my position, Sam. I've

heard the same things about you. Marcella isn't too happy with the way you've been handling the Canadian Group."

"You barely pulled the West Coast office through the latest mess."

"But I did. And that's what the board is looking for."

"You know, Granddaddy isn't here to set us against each other anymore."

"He left us one last challenge, Sam."

"And you think you won?"

"I know I did," Donovan said. Turning around, he paused as his eyes met Cassidy's.

She took another step into the room.

"I'll call you back, Sam."

He leaned down and hit a button on the phone.

"What was he talking about? Why does the board need to talk about Van?"

"It's nothing for you to worry about. Did you enjoy sleeping in this morning?"

"Yes," she said. "Though I did panic a bit when I woke up so late and couldn't find him."

"You have lunch today with Emma and Paul, so I figured the little man and I could spend all day together."

"That's very thoughtful," she said. She walked over to Donovan and kissed Van on his head. She hadn't known it was possible to love another being as much as she loved her son. Having him put everything in perspective. There was nothing in the world that was as important as taking care of him. She'd been disappointed when breastfeeding hadn't worked out for them, even though it gave Donovan more ways to help with his care.

"Are you sure you'll be okay with him?"

"Yes," he said. His cell phone rang and he glanced at the caller ID before turning back to her.

"Do you need to get that?"

He shook his head.

"Good. I've been wanting to talk to you about Sam and Tolley-Patterson… Emma heard some rumors about an odd stipulation in your grandfather's will."

"That's confidential information."

"She didn't know the details, just had heard a comment at a cocktail party her parents had." Cassidy had tried to bring up the will a few times, but she'd been tired from giving birth and taking care of her son. She hadn't really had time to investigate it further until now.

"From who?"

"Lawyers at her father's firm," Cassidy said. "Emma mentioned it because…"

"She was hoping to stir something up between the two of us," Donovan said.

"True, and I trust you, sweetheart. I'm just worried Sam might be putting together something shady.

And what I heard just now makes me even leerier of him."

Donovan hugged her to his side with his free arm. He kissed her. "Don't worry, baby. I've got everything I need right here."

"Really?" She was afraid to believe him when he said things like that. She knew that his life was business and everything else came second.

"Yes."

She tipped her head back and leaned up on her tiptoes to kiss him, but he dropped his arm and stepped away and she stood there awkwardly for a second. Donovan and she hadn't been out together since they were married, and he worked long hours. In fact, this moment was the most waking time she'd spent with her husband since they'd left the hospital.

She wasn't sure what was going on in his mind. Did he regret marrying her? They could have just as easily had Van and raised him without being married or even living together.

"What?"

"Nothing."

"Not nothing. You were staring at me like you wanted to say something."

She did, but how was she going to ask him if he no longer found her attractive since she'd given birth? How was she going to bring up the fact that she needed more one-on-one time with him?

"Just wanted to follow up on our plans for today. Are you sure that you can take Van this morning?"

"Yes, I can."

She stared at Donovan and realized that the love she'd always felt for him was getting stronger. She wanted him to be the husband she'd always fantasized about, and he was doing some things that made her believe he was that man. But then there were times like just now, when he'd pulled back from her, that let her know this wasn't a fantasy happy-ever-after marriage, but one based on necessity and reality.

Donovan wasn't the type of man who'd ever cared to be domestic, and carrying Van into the office didn't change his mind. The secretaries all cooed over the baby and the other men stood kind of awkwardly to one side while he set the baby in his car seat on the boardroom table.

"Never too early to start training the future generations," Marcus said as he entered the room.

Donovan laughed. "That was my granddaddy's creed. My earliest memories are of Sam and I playing on the floor of the executive offices."

"And now you're passing it on… I never saw you as the kind who'd bring a kid to work."

Donovan hadn't, either. He still wasn't one hundred percent certain of himself as a father or in the father role. But being in the office energized him, raised his confidence. Here he made no missteps. Here he knew exactly what he was supposed to do and how to do it.

As opposed to at home with Cassidy, where he was stymied by his own desire for her. It was all he could do not to make love to his wife. He knew she needed time for her body to recover from giving birth, but he was constantly aroused when he was around her.

This morning he'd woken up with a hard-on and had started to caress her when Van had cried out, stopping Donovan from making love to his wife.

"Let's get on with this meeting. I'm not sure how long Van's going to sleep."

"Don't you have a nanny or something?"

"Not yet. Cassidy is still interviewing them." Donovan didn't see how that was Marcus's business. He had the right to have his son with him in the office.

Marcus raised one eyebrow and shook his head. "This is why I always keep things casual."

"Why?"

"Look at you," he said, gesturing to Van's car seat, which Donovan had positioned directly next to him. "Your attention is divided now."

Donovan didn't like the way that sounded and glanced protectively at Van. Van was the future…his future. And he wanted his son to know from the start that he loved and cherished him. It was important to Donovan that Van feel comfortable in the offices of Tolley-Patterson and not as if he had to compete for the right to be there. "Have a seat, Marcus."

"Yes, sir." Marcus sat down as the rest of the staff started filing in.

Donovan moved Van's car seat to the credenza that sat against one wall, close enough so he could see his son but far enough away that the meeting wouldn't disturb the baby.

He brought the meeting to order, but his mind was only half on business. The other part was on Van. The baby had simply been a tool to beating Sam to the final prize his grandfather had dangled in front of both cousins. But now, as he watched his boy sleeping, he realized that the baby was so much more to him. Everything.

Marcus had been right on the money when he'd said that Donovan had changed. How had that happened? It seemed as if he'd become a different man. How could a few short weeks change a man's life?

"Donovan?"

"Yes?"

"We were discussing the budget for the next quarter... Do you think we're going to need an increase in labor on the West Coast?"

Donovan pulled himself back into the meeting, pushing little Van to the side of his awareness, but it was hard. And as he tried to focus on the business at hand, he realized it wasn't just Van who was on his mind, but also Cassidy. He remembered her earlier kiss and how he'd gotten hard just from holding her. He could hardly think from wanting her.

He knew they still had a few more weeks before he could make proper love to her. And yet his body didn't seem to care. He wanted her. He needed to seal the bond of their new life together by thrusting into her sexy body and making them physically one.

He hardened thinking about the way her mouth had felt under his and her warm body had felt pressed against his side.

Was that why he was distracted? Because he hadn't been able to make love to his wife? He scrubbed a hand over the back of his neck, trying to release the tension he felt. But cold showers weren't working, and a quick massage wasn't getting the job done.

The only thing that would take care of his problems was Cassidy.

He suspected that this was what Marcus had been referring to. The need he felt to be with her every minute of the day. The way she was infiltrating this meeting without even being in the room with him.

The meeting adjourned thirty minutes later and Donovan picked up Van and went toward his office.

"Theo is waiting in your office," Karin said when he reached the outer office.

"Was he on my calendar for today?"

"No, but he wouldn't take no for an answer. He said it was highly urgent, regarding the upcoming board meeting."

"Okay. Anything else?"

"A few messages, I left them on your voice mail. And Sam wants five minutes of your time to discuss Canada."

"I talked to him at home this morning. When did he call?"

"Twenty minutes ago."

"Very well. When Theo leaves I'll call him."

"Do you want me to keep Van while you meet with Theo?"

Donovan set the baby seat on the edge of Karin's desk and set the diaper bag next to it. "Do you mind?"

"Not at all. My kiddos are all teens now, I miss little ones."

He left Van with Karin and entered his office. There was a sculpture in the corner that his father had made for him when he'd gotten the promotion to executive vice president. The desk that he used had been his great-grandfather's.

"Afternoon, Uncle Theo."

Theo was currently serving as interim CEO until the next board meeting when either Sam or he would take over that position. Theo was a bit of a cold fish and had at one time wanted to be appointed CEO, but he had given up that aspiration when Granddaddy had announced that either Donovan or Sam would be his successor.

"I'm not here for chitchat, Donovan."

"Why are you here?" he asked as he took a seat in the leather executive chair. He saw the picture of himself, Cassidy and Donovan that Emma had taken of the three of them in the hospital. Cassidy looked radiant as she looked down at their son and Donovan's stomach knotted thinking about how happy she looked.

In that picture they looked perfect, like a couple who'd finally made their lives complete by bringing a child into the world. Only Donovan knew the truth—that their life together was based on a lie.

"The board isn't pleased with your engagement to Cassidy."

"Engagement?" he asked. Surely his mother had told the other members of the board by now that he and Cassidy were married. She'd never kept anything from the board before. And even though he'd told her he wouldn't be announcing the marriage yet, he hadn't specifically asked her to keep it quiet.

"Yes. We understand that you want to marry her

for Van's sake, but we strongly recommend you end all relations with Cassidy Franzone and find a proper woman to marry."

Cassidy enjoyed her lunch with Emma and Paul, but seeing them together underscored the distance between her and Donovan. She knew there was something missing from their relationship.

"So how's motherhood?" Emma asked when Paul went to get the car and they were both alone.

"Good. Tiring, but good."

"How's marriage?"

"Um…"

"Not good? What's up?"

"Nothing really. It's just that I don't see Donovan at all. And when he is home, I'm exhausted."

"That's to be expected, given how suddenly you two married. What about at night in bed?"

She looked at her friend. Only the fact that Emma was the sister of her heart allowed her to even think of sharing.

"I'm usually asleep by the time he comes in, and if I'm not he just rolls over on his side."

"He might be afraid to touch you since you had Van. A lot of guys don't really know when it's okay to do that."

"This is Donovan we're talking about. He knows everything about…well, everything."

Emma pulled her compact and lipstick from her purse and touched up her lips. "I don't know what to say. Have you talked to him about it?"

"No." When she and Donovan had first started dating, he'd told her how much he loved her body, that her slim figure was one of the first things he'd noticed about her. Now she was afraid that her post-pregnancy belly was a huge turnoff for him. As soon as her doctor had OK'd it, she started doing sit-ups like a Marine going through boot camp, but her stomach had a little saggy bit that remained.

"That's what I'd do."

"Would you really, Emma? You wouldn't just let things ride to kind of keep the peace?" Cassidy asked her friend.

"Are you kidding me? There is never peace between Paul and I. We're always on about something."

Cassidy knew that. Emma's personality was a bit fierce and she didn't hesitate to speak her mind no matter what the circumstances. "What if you were afraid that you'd be bringing up something that would make Paul leave you?"

Emma nibbled on her lower lip. "Honestly, Cassidy?"

Cassidy nodded as she pulled her sunglasses from her Coach handbag. She hid her eyes behind the overlarge Gucci glasses.

"I'd do it. I'd probably be bitchy about it the whole time, though. I hate feeling unsure, you know?"

"Yes, I do. This entire relationship with Donovan has gone from nothing to everything in such a short span of time, I don't think I've had a chance to adjust." She hated how much she worried about everything with Donovan. Before, she'd known that she could make things right between them in bed, and now…that simply wasn't the case.

"He might be feeling the same way. I mean, he came back to you to try again, not expecting to have a baby and a wife so quickly. How is he adjusting to fatherhood?"

"I'm not sure. This morning he took care of Van so I could sleep in, and he does spend at least a half hour every morning with Van, talking to him and walking him around the house while I get ready."

"What does he say?"

Cassidy didn't know. She felt as if she was intruding and wanted to let Donovan have some alone time with their son. She knew the things she talked to Van about were personal. Things that were full of her love for her baby. And sometimes she talked to him about her dreams for him.

"Do you know?" Emma prodded her.

"Not really. But he does seem to be making time

for Van. I mean, he's a busy executive and that's not going to change, but when I need him he's there."

Emma gave her a one-armed hug. "He's different than I thought he would be at this point. I don't know what happened when ya'll were apart, but he's not the same guy he was before."

That was what she kept telling herself. And a part of her was afraid to believe it. She wanted this new beginning to be what led them to happily-ever-after. But she knew she was steeling herself for the possibility that it might not work out. And that attitude was coloring everything, making it so much harder to just be happy in the moment.

Maybe because she was afraid to let herself believe in those dreams that she'd held for so long.

Paul pulled up but was on his cell phone so Emma gestured that she'd be another minute. "He talks so loudly when he's on that thing."

Cassidy laughed at that. Paul did talk loudly on his cell.

"Did you ask Donovan about Maxwell's will?" Emma asked.

"Yes. He said it wasn't a big deal. He's already aware of whatever it was that Sam was talking about."

"That's all he said?"

"Yes. Why, did you hear anything else?"

"No. I asked my father about it, but he said it was none of my business."

"Well he's right."

"He isn't. If it concerns Donovan then it concerns you and we're best friends."

"Uh-huh. Did that change your dad's opinion?"

"Absolutely not. But he can be a bit of a stickler when it comes to rules. Remember that time he went ballistic when we took his Mercedes for a test-drive?"

Cassidy did indeed remember the incident, which had happened when they'd both been thirteen. Emma's older brother, Eric, had been bragging about his abilities behind the wheel and Emma had had to prove she could drive as well as he did. To be fair, Emma was at least as good a driver as Eric. Unfortunately her father didn't care about that, he cared only that thirteen-year-olds weren't supposed to be behind the wheel.

They parted ways when Paul got off the phone. Cassidy left, wondering if she had let her reunion with Donovan change something essential inside of her. She'd never been a coward before this. From the moment she'd met Donovan she'd known she wanted to be his wife—why would she let anything intrude on her happiness now that she was?

She needed to take some action. No more waiting for Donovan to make the first move. Tonight, when he came home from work and Van was in bed, she was going to seduce her husband.

Seven

Donovan drove home with Van buckled in the backseat of his Porsche Cayenne. He'd bought the SUV the day after they'd brought Van home from the hospital. The Cayenne had the engine power he was used to in his Porsche 911, but the safety and room needed for an infant.

He hadn't met with Sam or anyone else after Theo had left. His family made the Machiavellis look like inhabitants of *Mr. Rogers' Neighborhood*. He was angry and frustrated and ready to take on the entire board. This mess was getting out of hand. Granddaddy had started this fiasco with his ridiculous will and the way he'd always pitted his sons and grand-sons against each other.

He dialed his parents' number and got their house-keeper, Maria, who informed him that his mother was out for the evening with her bridge club and that his father was in his studio.

Without thinking twice Donovan drove to his parents' house. He needed to talk to his father. He took Van out of the car seat when they got there and found that the baby needed his diaper changed. Donovan took care of it and then carried the baby around the back of the mansion he'd grown up in to his father's studio.

He knocked on the door but then opened it and entered, knowing his father never answered the door. His dad held up one hand in a gesture that Donovan knew meant he'd be a minute.

So he took Van on a walk around his father's studio, showing his son the pictures that had been taken of his father at different exhibits.

"What can I do for you?" his dad asked.

"I'm not sure. Uncle Theo visited me today and warned me against marrying Cassidy…. Dad, what's up? I thought for sure Mom would have mentioned the wedding to more of the family."

His dad wiped his hands on the front of his shirt and then walked over to where Donovan stood.

"I have no idea. Your mother votes my shares and

has the active seat on the board. I haven't said anything to anyone because I've been in the studio. I have a show in three months and really don't have time for any of the Tolley-Patterson business."

It was a familiar scenario. Donovan had never really had any of his father's attention or his father's time. Sculpting came first for his father, and then family.

He looked down at little Van sleeping so quietly in his arms.

"I remember when you were that size," his dad said, gesturing to Van. "I used to keep you in here with me during the day."

He didn't remember that. "Really?"

"Well your mother was still an active executive at the company so it made sense for me to keep you. I had a playpen for you over in that corner."

His father turned to look in the direction he'd indicated and Donovan stood there awkwardly, realizing that he and his father had never been close so he'd never considered that he might have had dreams for him to be an artist. He thought of it now only because he knew he wanted Van to follow in *his* footsteps and one day take over running the family company.

"I need to talk to Mom about this. Will you ask her to call me when she gets home?"

"Yes. What did Theo say?"

"That I needed to marry a proper girl. One from the right sort of family."

His dad chuffed. "Sometimes I think the Tolleys forget that they were carpetbaggers."

"Dad, watch out, that kind of talk will get you disinherited."

"Wouldn't be the first time that I was threatened with that. That might not be a bad thing. Always remember that you aren't a clone of your grandfather."

"I know that."

"Do you? I think you've always wanted to be better than he was, but you know he took the company from a nearly bankrupt run-down business to where it is today. He carved his own path, Donovan, and I think a part of you has always hungered to do the same."

"Did he want you to do that, too?"

"We had a big argument about it when I decided to go to the Art Institute of Chicago instead of Harvard. He said that I was letting him down by not following in his footsteps…called me weak."

"That sounds like Granddaddy. He never could understand anything that happened outside the walls of Tolley-Patterson."

"I told him I wasn't his clone and I couldn't follow his path. I needed to follow my own."

Donovan's family didn't just live in Charleston, they were steeped in the history of this town. He'd grown up surrounded by his past the same way his dad had. But instead of shunning what was all around him, Donovan had embraced it.

Today, though, he'd seen another side of being a Tolley, and he acknowledged that Uncle Theo and the board might never come around to accepting Cassidy.

He left his father's studio with nothing resolved and more questions in his own mind. Had he been just as guilty as Uncle Theo and the board of discriminating against Cassidy and her family and friends? He had kept their marriage quiet so that he could use her and Van to the best advantage when it came to beating Sam.

He sat in the front seat of the Cayenne and glanced over his shoulder into the backseat. Van was awake and waving his fist in front of his face.

"What do you think, buddy?" he asked the baby. "Should I tell the board to go to hell?"

The baby cooed and looked up at him with eyes that were shaped like Cassidy's. He knew he had his answer. The thing was, he didn't know if he could let go of the goals that had been a driving force in his life for so long. Could he give up beating Sam and taking over as CEO for Cassidy?

Not that she would ask him to. But if his family wouldn't accept her, he couldn't allow anyone to treat her with disdain. All she'd ever done was love him and give him a son.

He leaned over to brush the drool off Van's lower lip with his thumb and realized that his life had already changed, whether he wanted to admit it or not.

Cassidy was ready for Donovan that night. She'd gone to the salon to get her legs waxed. She'd taken a long bath and taken time with her appearance. She'd gone shopping after she'd left Emma and purchased a new wardrobe that fit her postpregnancy body.

She'd even cut her hair and had it highlighted. She looked more like her old self than she had in a long time. She *felt* more like her old self. She glanced in the mirror and saw the flirty woman she used to be.

Cassidy gave the housekeeper the night off and was prepared to fix a simple supper of grilled salmon and watercress salad whenever Donovan got home. She even had a shaker and ingredients ready to make martinis as soon as he walked in the door.

She heard his car in the back driveway and realized she was standing around, staring at the back door as if she were waiting for him. Which she was, but he didn't need to know that.

But she had no idea where she should go. She didn't watch TV and the study was on the other side of the house. Dammit. Why hadn't she planned this part better?

She went into the living room to the wet bar and started mixing the drinks.

"Cassidy, we're home. Where's Mrs. Winters?"

She went over to Donovan and gave him a kiss on the cheek before taking Van from him. "I gave her the night off. I thought it would be nice to have a family night."

"Sounds good. We need to talk anyway."

"About what?"

"My family… What were you making here?"

"Gin martinis."

"I'll do that. Are we doing dinner?"

"Yes. Salmon steaks on the grill and salad."

He grinned at her and she felt the groove she'd been searching for between them. "I'm going to go change Van out of his work clothes."

"I'll come with you. I need a change, too. Is the baby too small for the pool?"

"To be honest I have no idea. I think he'll be fine as long as we hold him."

They walked up the curving staircase in the front of the house. Donovan touched her shoulder and then caught a strand of her hair. She turned and looked at him eye to eye since she was a step higher than he was.

"I like your hair."

"Thank you," she said, her voice sounding a little hoarse to her own ears.

"God, Cassidy, you are so gorgeous." His mouth found hers and he kissed her the way she'd been longing for him to. His lips moved over hers with surety, his tongue teasing first her lips and then brushing over the seam of her mouth and thrusting inside. He tasted faintly of mint and something that she associated only with Donovan.

She leaned toward him, wanting to feel his chest pressing against her breasts, but instead felt Van's little hand on the bottom of her neck. She pulled back and stared at her husband for a long moment, remembering the orgasm she'd had on their wedding night. Man, that felt like a lifetime ago.

Donovan kissed the baby's hand and then walked around her on the stairs and continued up toward the master suite. "He was good for me today. Slept through two meetings and flirted with all the secretaries."

"Then he's a lot like his father."

"Funny. You don't get to the executive office by sleeping through meetings."

"But flirting helps?" she asked, teasing him, trying to find some kind of lightness to take her mind off of the physical ache she felt. Oh, how she wanted him.

"It doesn't hurt."

They entered the master suite and Donovan went into his closet, to change, she supposed. She laid

Van on the center of their king-size bed. She took off his khaki pants and button-down shirt and then checked his diaper, which was dry.

The baby lay on his back cooing and chewing on his fingers until she handed him a little plastic pretzel chew toy. She wanted to go change but didn't feel safe turning her back for even a second while the baby was up on the high bed.

She took the bolster pillow from the head of the bed and put that on one side of Van and then used the other pillows to create a barricade around the baby. He wasn't crawling yet so he should be fine, she thought.

Her bathing suit was in the dresser in this room. She grabbed it quickly and then went back to the side of the bed. Van had fallen asleep in the midst of the pillows, the toy on his chest. She watched him as she got changed next to the bed.

Instead of the daring bikini she used to wear, she donned a new tankini, and when she caught a glimpse of herself in the mirror she thought she looked pretty good.

She turned back to Van, leaning over him to adjust one of the pillows. She felt Donovan's breath on the back of her neck a second before she felt his lips on her skin.

He nibbled down the length of her neck. She shivered under his touch as his hands found her waist and he drew her back against his body. His chest was bare and felt wonderful as he wrapped his arms around her and pulled her fully against his body.

"Can we make love?" he asked. "Because I'm aching to be inside you."

"I can't take you," she said. "Not yet. But in a few more weeks I can."

"Then we'll have to do something else, because I can't keep my hands off you for another day."

Cassidy turned in his arms. "I want you, too."

"I know."

She arched one eyebrow at him. "How?"

"Your pheromones have been making me crazy since I walked in the door."

She started to respond but he kissed her mouth, cutting off her words and making it impossible to do anything but kiss him back.

Donovan couldn't keep his eyes or his hands off Cassidy as they prepared and ate dinner. Van was sleeping happily in his portable crib and for a moment Donovan felt that everything in his life was perfect. There was none of the intense competitive need to be better than anyone. To keep reaching for that elusive whatever that was always missing in his life.

Instead, as he looked across the table at Cassidy sipping her pinot grigio and wearing that bathing suit, he felt something close to contentment. And that scared him as nothing else could. Content men weren't hungry or successful. Content men sat on the sidelines while others made things happen, and Donovan knew he could never be the kind of guy who did that.

He wanted Cassidy, wanted this peace she brought to him and his life, and yet he knew that this was false. That there was no way they were going to have this moment for too much longer. His job was going to come between them.

She had her iPod plugged in to the Bose speaker system that surrounded the pool and the songs that were playing were romantic. After holding her and kissing her earlier, he wanted nothing more than to make love to her.

But he needed to talk to Cassidy. Needed to tell her that most of his family didn't know they were married. He needed to come clean about what had been going on.

Part of him didn't want to. That was work related and shouldn't be something for her to worry about. This marriage was what she'd wanted. And he was going to make everything at Tolley-Patterson work out.

"You're staring at me."

"Am I?" he asked.

She nodded. "Why?"

"Because I want to."

She arched her eyebrows at him. "Why do you want to?"

One thing that had always drawn him to her was the way that her eyes sparkled when she laughed or teased. It wasn't even just when she teased him. He found her joy of life attractive no matter whom she was teasing.

"I'm surprised someone with your upbringing would do something as rude as staring."

"Well I'm a rebel."

"I've always liked that about you."

"What else do you like about me?"

"Your butt."

That surprised him and he leaned back in his chair. "I like yours, too."

"I know," she said, mimicking him from earlier.

The music changed and "Brown-Eyed Girl" by Van Morrison came on. Donovan was pushing back his chair as Cassidy got to her feet. "This is my song."

He knew that. It was always Cassidy's song. With her vibrant brown eyes and her shorter hair dancing around her shoulders, she started to move to the song. And he knew that, no matter what he'd been telling himself, this brown-eyed girl was important to him. At least as important as Tolley-Patterson.

He took her hand in his and drew her into his arms. She sang a bit off-key as they danced around the pool. Her limbs were silky and cool against his as he held her.

She tipped her head back. "I've been afraid of being myself with you."

"How do you mean?"

"Our marriage felt like it was so rushed, and I'm still not entirely sure why you came back when you did…." She pulled out of his arms. "I guess that part of me didn't want to rock the boat."

"I can understand that. I've been doing the same thing. Just working and keeping to my old routines."

"That's it exactly, but because I'm not working I've been sitting at home stewing and going a bit crazy because I couldn't figure out what was going on with you."

"And now you have me figured out?" he asked, sliding his hands up and down her back. It never ceased to amaze him how small she was or how right she felt in his arms.

"Not you. I figured *me* out. I was lost for so long, not sure what I was going to do, just waiting for Van to be born so I could figure out my next move. But now he's here and you're here, and I had to get here, too."

Listening to her talk made him feel like a bastard. He was here not because of any great philosophical development but because he needed her. "I didn't journey to you like that."

"It doesn't matter. This isn't about you really."

"Should I be offended?"

She shrugged. "If you want to be."

"Nah. Tell me more about being afraid to be you," he said. The music changed to Jamiroquai's "Virtual Insanity." And as Cassidy danced around him, he realized that she was a bit buzzed. She smiled at him each time she turned to face him.

"I think I didn't know if you could still want me, because I'd changed so much as a woman."

"In what way? By being a mother?"

"No. I mean my body. I've put on some weight and I'm never going to have that flat stomach I used to have."

He pulled her to a stop. "I love your body, Cassidy. Flat stomachs don't attract me—you do."

She tilted her head to the side and eyed him with that level stare of hers. The one that he was sure could see straight into his soul. "Really? The first thing you complimented me on was my slim figure."

"That's only because I thought I'd sound ridiculous if I told you that I loved your laugh and the way you smile when you're teasing."

She quieted and got really serious. "Do you mean that?"

"I don't say things I don't mean."

She wrapped her arms around him and squeezed him so tightly that he felt it all the way to his soul.

"Being married to you has made me so incredibly happy."

She rested her head on his shoulder and he held her loosely because he desperately wanted to clutch her to him. And men who were afraid to lose what they held were a liability. They stopped looking to the future and only looked to the present, his Granddaddy used to say. Those kind of men were the kind that life left behind.

<u>Eight</u>

Cassidy was seated at her vanity table when he came into their bedroom from putting Van down in his crib. He set the baby monitor on his nightstand and tried to calm his raging libido. Traditional sex was out of the question; she'd said she couldn't for a few more weeks. But he wanted to make love to her tonight. To seduce her with his lips and hands and give her the concrete reassurances that he still found her attractive.

"Thanks for tucking Van in."

"You're welcome," he said, watching her in the mirror. He walked over to her and put his hands on her shoulders. Her skin was smooth to the touch—

he never got over how soft she was. She smelled sweetly of flowers.

He leaned in low to brush his lips over her shoulder. Her nightgown had spaghetti straps and he kissed his way toward her neck, moving that thin strip of fabric out of his way so that he dropped kisses on every inch of her flesh.

"Donovan," she said his name on a sigh.

"Yes, baby?" he asked.

She turned on the stool and twined her arms around his shoulders, drawing his mouth to hers. Take it slow, he told himself. But slow wasn't in his programming with this woman. She was pure feminine temptation. He lifted her from the padded bench she sat on and set her down on the vanity counter. He slid his hands down her back, finding the hem of her nightgown and pulling it up until he caressed between her legs. She was creamy with desire, and hot.

She moaned deep in her throat and he hardened painfully. He thrust against her, rubbing their groins together until he thought he was going to explode.

He slid the straps of her nightgown down her arms until he could see the tops of her breasts and the barest hint of the rosy flesh of her nipples. He lowered his head, using his teeth to pull the loosened fabric away from her skin.

Her nipples stood out against the cool air in the

room. He ran the tip of one fingertip around her aroused flesh. She trembled in his arms.

Lowering his head he took one of her nipples in his mouth and suckled her. She held him to her with a strength that surprised him. But shouldn't have.

Her fingers drifted down his back and then slid under the T-shirt he'd put on to sleep in. She tangled her fingers in the hair on his chest and tugged, spreading her fingers out to dig her nails lightly into his pecs.

He liked the light teasing of her fingernails. She shifted back away from him, and he kept his hands on her breasts. His fingers worked over her nipples as she pushed the shirt up to his armpits. He let go of her for a minute to rip the shirt off and toss it across the room. He growled deep in his throat when she leaned forward to brush kisses against his chest.

She bit and nibbled and made him feel like her plaything. He wanted to sit back and let her have her way with him. But there was no room here. No time for seduction or extended lovemaking.

He pulled her to him and lifted her slightly so that her nipples brushed his chest. Holding her carefully he rubbed against her. Blood roared in his ears. He was so hard, so full right now that he needed to be inside of her body. But tonight he'd have to focus on other things.

Impatient with the fabric of her nightgown, he

shoved it up and out of his way. He caressed her creamy thighs. She was so soft. She moaned as he neared her center and then sighed when he brushed his fingertips across the humid opening of her body.

She was warm and wet. He slipped one finger into her body, felt the walls tighten around him and hesitated for a second, looking down into her heavy-lidded eyes. She bit down on her lower lip and he felt the minute movements of her hips as she tried to move his touch where she needed it.

He was beyond teasing her or prolonging anything. He plunged two fingers into her humid body. She squirmed against him.

He needed to taste her *now*.

He dropped to his knees in front of her, kicking the vanity chair out of his way.

"What are you doing?" she asked, looking down at him.

"Taking care of you," he said.

She murmured something he didn't catch as he lowered his head and touched his tongue to her center. Her thighs flexed around his head and he thrust his fingers in and out of her warm body. Her hands tangled in his hair as he caught her sweet flesh lightly between his teeth and nibbled on her.

He guided her hands to the cool surface at the rounded edge of the table. "Hold on."

"Yessss…" she said. And then he heard those little

sounds she made right before she came. He felt her body tighten around his fingers and was careful to keep the pressure on until he felt her shake and tremble around him.

He stood up and braced his hands on the vanity, trying to catch his breath.

She reached for him and he pulled away.

"Donovan?"

"Don't touch me, baby. I want you too badly right now."

She reached between their bodies and took him in her hand. "Let me—"

"Not tonight," he said. "This night is for you. I wanted you to sleep in my arms knowing how much I want you and how attractive you are to me."

"Thank you," she said.

"You're welcome, baby."

Cassidy never felt as wanted as she did that night in Donovan's arms. He brought her to orgasm after orgasm, and only took pleasure for himself when Cassidy finally insisted that she needed to enjoy the sensuality of his body as well. She fell into an exhausted sleep wrapped in his arms. Cuddled up against his side with his body pressed to hers she found a strength and peace that came from him.

But that peace faded at breakfast when she read

an article in the business pages about her son's birth in which she was named as Donovan's former girl-friend. She read the article twice and learned a little more about the situation that Donovan was facing at work. The reporter speculated that either Sam Pat-terson or Donovan Tolley would be appointed CEO of Tolley-Patterson at the next board meeting in January.

Cassidy finished her juice while she waited for him to come down from getting ready for work.

She heard the phone ring and a moment later Mrs. Winters came in with the cordless phone. "It's your mother."

"Thank you," Cassidy said, waiting until Mrs. Winters left the room before she lifted the phone. "Hi, Mom."

"Did you see this morning's paper?" her mother asked. It was noisy at her parents' house. Loud music and the sound of her mother's treadmill vied for dominance.

"Just now."

"What's going on? Why does this article make it sound as if you and Donovan aren't married?"

"I don't know, Mom. Donovan's still upstairs getting ready."

"Your father is outraged.... I think Adam is going to call the editor of the paper."

"Don't let him do that, Mom."

"Why not?"

"Because I wanted to keep the marriage quiet."

"Cassidy…"

"I needed time to adjust to everything and I didn't want there to be any speculation that Donovan married me because I was pregnant."

"Who cares what anyone has to say?" her mother said.

"Donovan's family."

"They're too full of themselves. It shouldn't matter to you what they think."

"I know, Mom."

Her phone beeped, letting her know there was another call waiting. She promised to call her mother back as she switched over to the other call.

"Hey, girl, brace yourself before you open up the paper this morning," Emma said.

"I've already seen it." She really should have thought through the consequences of keeping her marriage to Donovan secret. She'd just wanted a quiet ceremony and time for them all to adjust to being a family. How weird was it going to be for Donovan when he realized that his uncle had lied to protect their secret? She knew that honesty was one of the cornerstones of Tolley-Patterson. They had a public mission statement that reiterated that value.

"Okay. So what's up?"

"Um… Remember how I wasn't sure if Donovan was being real with me when he came back and proposed?"

"Yes."

"Well, I asked him to keep quiet about us. I just didn't want Charleston society to see our wedding as him marrying me for the baby."

"Why not?"

Cassidy wrapped one arm around her waist. "In case he changed his mind."

"Oh, Cassidy."

"I know. This is a mess."

"What's a mess?" Donovan asked. "Van?"

He entered the breakfast room and kissed her on the head. "You okay?"

"Emma, I'll call you back."

She hung up the phone as Donovan poured himself a cup of coffee. How was he going to react to the article? From their time dating, she knew he hated for any personal information to make its way into articles about him.

"There's an article about you and Van in today's paper."

"Just me and Van?" he asked, reaching for the newspaper. She handed him the Business section.

"Yes. It mentions me as your former girlfriend."

"Who mentioned you that way?" he asked, flipping to the article.

"Theo Tolley," Cassidy said. She'd only met

Donovan's uncle once, and from the article she'd learned that he was the interim CEO until the next board meeting.

"Dammit. It's not the way it might seem to you."

"What's not? Your parents were at the wedding, right? I mean, I know I wanted to keep it quiet, but I didn't mean that you had to pretend that we weren't even together."

Donovan skimmed the article and then turned away.

"I'm not pretending we aren't together," he said.

"It's okay," she said. "I suggested we keep things quiet. I just had no idea how it would feel to read something like this. It makes me feel like I'm not even a part of our son's life."

"There's a news van in front of the house," Mrs. Winters said, entering the kitchen.

Cassidy didn't like the sound of that. "Where?"

"At the edge of the property."

Cassidy had a feeling that more than the business journalists were interested in their story. For a society as staid and steeped in tradition and history as Charleston's was, this was a scandal. Especially since Donovan's family and hers were like oil and water.

"This is crazy." The last thing she wanted was to have to deal with the media today. Last night had felt like a real beginning in her relationship with Donovan.

"I agree," Donovan said. "This is a huge mess."

"Yes, it is. This goes way beyond an article in the business pages. If anyone does a records search, they're going to know that we *are* married, and then your uncle is going to look foolish. I'm not sure what to do. I should call my father and tell him what's going on."

"Cassidy…"

"I'm sure you'll have a plan for this. But talking to the reporters is something my father is used to doing. He can help."

"Your father can't comment on this. You aren't to say anything to the media. In fact, no one in your family is."

"You're kidding, right?"

"No, I'm not. Call your folks right now, tell them to say nothing."

"Donovan."

"What?" he asked, impatiently. She knew he'd probably already moved on to the next order of business in his head, but no way was she going to call her parents and tell them what to do.

"We have a problem. I don't take orders, and neither does my family."

"Until we have this sorted out, you both do," he said, walking away.

Donovan's first call was to an old college roommate, Jamie, who worked for the local NBC affiliate in Charleston.

"You are one hot story right now," Jamie said. "The stipulations of your grandfather's will were just leaked."

Donovan stilled. "By who?" he asked, his legendary cold, calm reaction coming to the fore. He automatically prioritized the situation and knew getting the media off his back was number one. Talking to Cassidy…oh, man, that was going to take more time.

"I don't know. I just wanted to give you the heads-up."

"Thanks, Jamie."

"You're welcome. I don't suppose you have a comment…"

"Not right now."

He hung up and called his uncle. Theo was on voice mail, and who could blame the man. His grandfather's will wasn't the first to have the kind of stipulation it did, but no one on the board wanted the media or the world to know about it.

"What is going on?" Cassidy said as she entered his study.

She held Van in her arms, and she looked upset.

Cassidy took a deep breath and released it slowly. Donovan watched her and realized for the first time that his priorities were wrong. He didn't care what the board did or what the media knew. He needed to make this right for Cassidy.

"I think it'd be better for me to handle this," she

said. "I can say that I wasn't ready to talk to the press since I just gave birth and that your family, out of concern for me, kept quiet." She gazed at him. "What do you think?"

He was speechless. That Cassidy would take the blame for something that wasn't even her fault was beyond his comprehension. He had to act. He hadn't anticipated Theo going after Cassidy in such a public way. Donovan was going to have to go in front of the entire board to get to the bottom of this.

Judging by his mention of Cassidy in the paper, Theo was up to something, and the power play wasn't one that Donovan was going to respond to.

"I think that you're extremely generous, but you should let me take care of this," he said.

"Well, I think we should handle it together. I'm going to issue a statement so that it doesn't seem as if I'm ignoring the media."

Donovan didn't want the story to go any further than it already had. He needed to get Marcus on the phone and have his team meet him at the office. It didn't matter that it was a Saturday.

"No. You will not do anything of the kind," he said. He pulled his cell phone from his pocket and sent a text message to his staff. He looked back up to see Cassidy glaring at him.

"What?" he asked, distracted.

"Did you just tell me what to do? *Again?*"

"Yes, I did. And I'm going to continue doing it."

"Excuse me?" Cassidy asked.

"You heard me."

"You are acting like a…"

"Jerk? I know. But you aren't prepared to deal with reporters shouting questions at you. And you're too old to have your father do it. I'll take care of it for us. This mess—"

"Mess? Do you mean our marriage and our son?"

Cassidy was on the verge of breaking down. He saw it in her eyes and in the almost desperate way she was holding their son close to her.

"No, of course not. You and Van are the best things to ever happen to me."

The words were meant to bring her solace, but they resonated with him, as well. He did need Cassidy and his son.

The doorbell rang but Donovan ignored it. "I think it would be best if you and Van kept a low profile until I talk to my people. Please."

"Fine," Cassidy said shortly.

Mrs. Winters knocked on the study door. "Sam Patterson is here."

The last thing he wanted was to have Sam here, but in light of the will being made public, the two of them would have to address the stipulation together.

"I'll be with him in a minute. Ask him to wait in the conservatory."

"No," Cassidy said. "Show him in here. I'll go upstairs and leave you both to it."

There was too much left unresolved between the two of them. He hadn't come close to explaining anything to her, and it was only a matter of time until she found out the entire truth.

"Cassidy?"

"Yes?"

"There's something I have to tell you—"

Sam entered the room without knocking. He gave Cassidy a vague smile and turned to Donovan. "We need to talk."

"Not now," Donovan said.

"Yes, now. You and Cassidy can finish your conversation later. Tolley-Patterson comes first."

"Not today."

"Really? Well then, our conversation will be short," Sam said. "I guess this means I'll be the new CEO."

"No, it doesn't," Cassidy said. She turned to Donovan. "Talk to your cousin. We can finish our discussion later."

Cassidy walked away, and as he watched her go, he began to understand just how much he loved her. *Loved* her.

Nine

"Oh my God. You aren't going to believe it, but Donovan needed you and your baby." Emma burst into the sunroom.

"What are you talking about?"

"That's the weird will thing. The thing I told you I heard at the cocktail party? Maxwell's will said that either Sam or Donovan would be his successor and left them both some very challenging business objectives to accomplish."

"Of course he did. That was what he always did with those two," Cassidy said. "And it makes sense that either Sam or Donovan take over. They're both young and have the drive and experience to take the company to the next level."

"I'm not arguing that. But there was one more thing in the will…the reason why there are news vans outside your door."

Cassidy waited. She felt a trickle of apprehension, because there *was* something that Donovan hadn't told her. Some secret he'd been keeping.

"They each have to be married and produce an heir before they can be appointed CEO!"

Cassidy was glad she was sitting down. She felt faint and her stomach knotted. She thought about the new bonds she and Donovan had forged last night, and she realized that he had just been playing his part. Doing what he thought he needed to do to keep her happy.

She had feared being married for her child, but had believed that he'd only do that out of a sense of responsibility. She'd had no idea that he'd stoop this low. She knew that his company meant everything to him, but he should never have married her without revealing this.

"Cassidy? Are you okay?"

"Yes, I'm fine," she said, but she knew that wasn't true. And yet it was. Because she'd loved Donovan Tolley from the moment she'd met him and he'd smiled at her. She'd loved him even though he always put his job and career in front of her. She'd loved him even though he'd left her alone all those months.

And finally, she thought, she didn't love him anymore.

Well, that wasn't true. She still loved him, but she finally had the proof she needed that *he* didn't love *her*. That he wasn't ever going to love her the way she wanted him to.

"I'm sorry," Emma said.

"What for?"

"Being the one to tell you. But I couldn't let you find out from some nosy reporter."

"Thanks, Emma. I did need to know this. What am I going to do?"

"Take Van and leave. Let Donovan know that he doesn't have a wife or heir as far as you're concerned. Get him back for what he's done to you."

"Emma…I can't do that."

"Why not? He obviously didn't care about hurting you."

Was that true? She didn't know, and right now she really couldn't figure it out. She only knew that she hurt so much she couldn't think of what to do next. She needed some space.

Her cell phone rang and she glanced at the caller ID. It was her mom.

"Are you going to answer that?"

"Not now," Cassidy said, hitting the ignore button

on the phone. She put it on the table and then reached for Van, pulling him into her arms. She tucked him to her and let the love she felt for him soothe her. But it didn't, completely. When she looked into his eyes, she was struck by how much he was a part of both Donovan and her.

That he was a part of the lies that she'd been telling herself for so long.

Emma was staring at her, and Cassidy knew she needed to do something. "Thanks for telling me everything. I'm going to…"

Do what? She wanted in that instant to make Donovan feel the same kind of pain she was experiencing. Because the more she thought about that article she'd read, the more she began to suspect that he'd deliberately kept quiet about their marriage, possibly to use it to his advantage when the time came.

"I'm not leaving you. We'll fix this. I think the first thing to do is—"

"Nothing," Cassidy said. "I want to see what Donovan's going to do next. I mean, he's had a plan all along and I want to wait until he gets to his final move."

"And then tell him it's all over?"

Cassidy thought about that. Essentially, they *were* all over. This was the kind of blow to a relationship that she couldn't fix. The only thing that would fix it would be for Donovan to love her more than he did his job. More than he did the one thing he'd always turned to and found solace in.

Her anger mellowed as she realized they were both trapped in this thing together, because Donovan couldn't change the man he was. And she didn't want to stop loving him. The only way they'd both be happy was if that happened.

Because Donovan was never going to love her, and she wasn't going to be able to endure the humiliation of knowing that he'd come back into her life and married her simply to beat his cousin to the finish line.

Emma watched her and Cassidy realized she had to start detaching herself from her emotions. It was time for her to seriously move on. Or at least create the illusion that she had.

Deep inside, where she kept those dreams of happily-ever-after alive, she wept, but on the outside she simply smiled and stood up with her son in her arms.

"Let's go out," she said to Emma. She wasn't about to hide.

Sam paced around Donovan's office. He'd always seen his cousin as an adversary, and nothing in either of their lives had ever really changed that. The few times they had worked together, they'd both done so in their own way and with their own agenda.

This situation was no different. They were never going to be friends. But when it came to Tolley-Patterson, he knew that they both would do anything to make sure the company prospered and its profits continued to grow.

"We need to find the leak. This kind of press leaves us vulnerable and the investors aren't going to be too happy with the fact that a wife and child are the main requirements for their new CEO."

"Indeed," Sam said. "I've got Kyle from my team using his contacts to try to locate the source of the leak."

Donovan nodded. He was going to check with Jamie later to see if he'd found out anything more on the media side.

"I'm going to ask Theo and the rest of the board to address this. I already sent a message to Franklin in PR. I had asked him to draft a press release in case this situation arose," Donovan said.

"Why did you do that?"

"Granddaddy's will was too sensational for someone not to talk about it. Cassidy's friend Emma already had heard some rumblings, so it was only a matter of time."

"You should have kept me in the loop on this."

Donovan shrugged. He probably should have, but the will had been one of the things that he and Sam had never seen eye to eye on. If they'd both protested it, they could have gone to the board and had it thrown out. But Sam had steadfastly refused to do that.

"It's too late now. Franklin will issue an official statement from the company, and I think you and I should say 'no comment.'"

"I've asked the board to schedule an emergency meeting for tomorrow afternoon to give everyone time to get into town. I think we should both be prepared to make an argument for a new CEO appointment. Theo isn't equipped to deal with this, and I think our investors are going to need some reassurance," Sam said.

"I agree. I've got two of my guys monitoring our competition to ensure we know what they're doing."

Sam cocked an eyebrow at Donovan. "I guess we're working together on this."

"Seems like it."

"Did you ever wonder why Granddad always set us against each other?" Sam asked.

"Not really. I imagine you and I were always competing. I can't remember a time when we weren't."

In college, he'd gone to Harvard and Sam to Yale. They'd both interned at Fortune 500 companies, Sam at a company owned by one of Maxwell's cronies, Donovan at another one. For every major moment in his life, Donovan realized he'd basically been alone.

He was simply better by himself than working

with others. And that was part of what made him leery of this current situation with Sam and the company.

"I don't know if I can work with you on this," Sam said. "My instinct is to go to the media and do my own thing."

"But that wouldn't be best for Tolley-Patterson," Donovan said.

"No, it wouldn't," Sam said a bit ruefully. "Do you ever wish we were just two normal guys?"

"Hell no."

Sam laughed. "I wonder if Granddaddy had any idea that our path to the chairmanship would go this way."

"Who knows? The old man was good at thinking through every variable. But I don't think he could have predicted what happened with Cassidy and me."

Sam leaned back in his chair. "I'm not so sure about that."

"What do you mean?"

"Just that one look at Cassidy and everyone could tell she loved you. And I think Granddaddy always wanted that for you."

Donovan wasn't sure what Sam was getting at, but he didn't want to discuss Cassidy or how she felt about him with his cousin.

Donovan took control of the discussion and soon had the feeling that even Sam knew he was the right choice to lead the company. They spent the rest of the day in his home office on the phone with the board and different investors, working together to assuage them.

"Thanks for all your hard work today, Sam," Donovan said as his cousin prepared to go.

"You don't have to thank me. It's my company, too."

"True, but after today I think we both know that I'll be taking the helm."

"How do you figure?"

"You heard Theo say that they refused to waive the stipulations from the will. And with the board all meeting tomorrow, I'm going to push for a vote for the new chairman. Clearly I'm the best candidate."

Sam got to his feet. "Keep telling yourself that. If I ask the board to postpone the vote or to consider the fact that my wife may now be pregnant…"

"Whatever you do, I think we both know that waiting isn't the best course of action. We need to take the stand as a company that we have a bigger story than Granddaddy's will, and the only thing bigger than that is a new CEO. And I'm the most logical choice," Donovan said. He opened the door to his office to show Sam out.

"Don't bother," Sam said. "I know the way."

Cassidy collided with Sam on his way out the door. She had Van strapped to her chest in a baby carrier and her arms were laden with packages from her and Emma's shopping trip.

He steadied them both and glared at Van. "I hope you know what you've gotten yourself into."

"What do you mean?"

"By having a child with a man who lives only for the company."

Cassidy wasn't sure what had happened, but she'd never seen Sam so hot under the collar before. Though she wasn't happy with Donovan right now, she wasn't going to talk trash about him with his rival.

"Donovan always does what he thinks is best for Tolley-Patterson because he wants what's best for his family."

Sam's eyes narrowed. "I can't believe you're defending him. You know he used you."

"How do you figure?"

"He came back to you to beat me. How does that make you feel? You're nothing more than a brood-mare to an egomaniac."

He wasn't telling Cassidy anything she hadn't already figured out for herself. And though she was angry with Donovan for his actions, she wasn't about to condemn him.

"You're nothing but a bitter man who's afraid to admit that he isn't as good as the competition," Cassidy said, desperately trying to hold on to her composure. Sam had just vocalized everything that she'd been thinking for a long time.

She believed, just as Sam did, that Donovan had been using her. Probably from the very beginning when they'd dated over a year ago. Long before Van had been conceived and his grandfather's will had demanded an heir.

Even her realization that Donovan probably couldn't help being the way he was didn't change the fact that he'd lied to her. That he'd made her believe that he'd come back to her because of a change of heart. But she'd begun to comprehend that maybe she hadn't really loved him as well as she thought if she hadn't understood that his love and focus was always going to be on work. She *knew* that. She had known that forever.

"I feel sorry for you," Cassidy said at last, running her hands over the back of her sweet, sleeping baby. No matter why she and Donovan had come together, she had Van, and that counted for a lot in her book.

"Why?"

"Because you're so busy looking at Donovan and blaming him for your failures that you haven't looked at yourself. You're the only one who can control your actions."

"I could say the same of you."

"How so?" she asked, setting down her packages so she could remove Van from the carrier.

"You see him as you want him to be and not as he really is," Sam said. "Turn around and I'll unhook the carrier for you."

Sam's entire demeanor changed and suddenly he was the rather mild-mannered man she'd met a few times before. It was odd to think that he was the competition for Donovan, because personalitywise the two men were polar opposites. Sam was more easygoing and inclusive…more of a team player than Donovan would ever be.

Donovan was a loner. And that was something she should have realized a long time ago.

"I don't know if I trust you with my back turned."

"Look," Sam said. "I'm sorry I attacked you like I did. Seeing your son…he reminded me of a conversation I had with Granddaddy last Christmas."

"What did he say?"

Sam shook his head. "That we had to remember Tolley-Patterson was looking to the future. That we weren't going to be the last generation to run our family's company."

"Maybe that's why he was so determined that his next CEO produce an heir," Cassidy said. It seemed to her that Maxwell Patterson had wanted to control his grandsons for as long as he could.

"Perhaps. I *am* sorry for what I said. It seems as if you do know what you're getting into with Donovan."

She smiled and tried to appear confident. But she wasn't sure she'd pulled it off. Because to be honest, she had no idea what to expect from Donovan. "I guess."

"The rest of the family isn't going to accept your marriage, Cassidy."

"Why not?"

"Uncle Theo's quote in the business section… Did you see that?"

"Yes, I did."

"Well, he knows you and Donovan are back together. He's trying to push the two of you apart."

"Why?"

Sam shook his head. "I can honestly say that it has nothing to do with you."

"Who does it have to do with? Van? I'm not going to let your uncle or Tolley-Patterson be the focus of his life. I don't want him to grow up like that."

Sam smiled at her. "I can see that Donovan chose the right woman to be the mother of his children."

It was such a change from where Sam had been before that she almost didn't trust him. "Thanks, I think."

"Do you need a hand with your bags?" he asked.

"No, thanks."

"Good night then," Sam said, and he walked down to his Mercedes and drove away.

Cassidy watched him go, wondering desperately what she was going to do about both the mess that was her marriage and her son's future.

Ten

Donovan didn't leave his office until well after midnight. Even though he hadn't spoken to Cassidy, he knew she was aware that he'd married her to fulfill the requirements of his grandfather's will. Her lack of contact spoke volumes. He rubbed a hand over his eyes. They felt gritty and his back ached from sitting in one position for too long.

The house was quiet and air-conditioned cold as he walked up the grand staircase to the second-floor landing. One of his father's sculptures was displayed there. This one was of him, from when he'd been in his first year of college. The cold marble seemed startlingly like him. The eyes were vacuous, though, something he'd never noticed in his own.

Seeing himself in stone like this always made him strive harder. Work harder. His grandfather used to say that the boy in that sculpture had so much potential and fire to change the world. And Donovan was reminded of those words each time he walked past it.

But he was fifteen years older and he'd changed. He'd had to change. Hadn't he?

He entered the master suite and found it empty and quiet. He stood in the doorway feeling the hollowness of his victory. His long hours in the office this last week had assured that victory. Tomorrow there would be a public announcement officially declaring him the new CEO of Tolley-Patterson.

And he was all alone.

He strode to his nightstand and reached for the fine quality embossed note card that had Cassidy's monogram on the front. Not the one from when she'd been a Franzone, but the new one that reflected her married name.

He opened the card and traced his finger over her signature. It was flowery and pretty, very feminine and reflective of the woman she was.

Donovan,

I hated to leave without saying anything but I couldn't wait around for you. I need to get away so I can think about everything that's happened. I think I made a mistake in marrying you so quickly, without understanding exactly what your needs were.

Van and I are moving back into my house so I can have space to figure this out. I know you'll be busy with the company and your new role. Somehow, without even asking, I know you will be the new CEO.

I pray it's everything you hoped it would be.
Love, Cassidy

He tossed the note on the bed and left the bedroom. The house was a monument to his success. He had every "thing" anyone could possibly want. And for what?

He shook it off. Cassidy was just a woman. He'd lived just fine without her for the eight months they were apart. He went downstairs to the wet bar and poured himself a stiff drink.

He heard a sound behind him on the marble floor and turned to see a shadow in the doorway.

"Cassidy?"

She stepped into the room.

"I thought you'd gone."

"I did."

She wore a pair of faded jeans and a scoop-neck, sleeveless top. She looked tired. Her eyes were red, and he suspected that she had been crying. *He had made her cry.* He tried to think how he could make it better for her. She'd come back, so that had to mean that she didn't really want to be apart from him.

"Where's Van?"

"With my parents. I needed to talk to you. I want to make sure you understand why I left."

"I run a multimillion-dollar company. I think I can figure it out," he said, not really up to discussing all the things that were wrong with him when it came to relationships.

"You can be a real bastard."

"I know," he said, rubbing the back of his neck. "Listen, I didn't mean it that way. You know how I am. I'm not the kind of guy who talks about his emotions…."

He trailed off, hoping that she'd rescue him. That she'd give him a pass the way she had so often before. But she didn't.

"I do know how you are."

"Then why are you surprised?"

"Because…listen, I can't explain it any better than to just say I love you. And I think in loving you I made you into the hero I needed you to be. I have always been drawn to men who are driven, and you are that in spades."

"So what's the problem?"

"I thought you were different from my dad. That you had all of his strengths and none of his weaknesses."

"I've never talked on the phone all through a dinner with you."

"Donovan…do you care about this relationship, or do you want me to just walk out the door?"

It would be so much easier to have a clean break with Cassidy. She complicated things, complicated his life endlessly because she made him want to be that white knight she thought he was.

But he wasn't naive and never had been. He couldn't be the man she wanted him to be. His life was this empty house. His life was Tolley-Patterson.

"Donovan?"

"Yes?"

"What are you thinking?"

"About letting you go," he said honestly.

"That's funny," Cassidy said, feeling calm for once. No tears burned in her eyes. She felt nothing but a sense of unreality. "I think you probably already let me go…almost a year ago."

He shook his head and walked to her. He looked so tired and drained, and she wanted nothing more than to open her arms and offer him the comfort of a hug. But this was the man who kept breaking her heart, and solace wasn't something she should even be thinking of giving him anymore.

Yet to quit loving him was hard. She couldn't just fall out of love with him in less than one week. She couldn't stop the emotions that had been there from the moment their hands had touched. But she was determined to let him go. Determined to make a new start for herself. One where Donovan was nothing more than her baby's father.

"Baby, I have been holding on to you in ways you can't even imagine," he said.

The words sounded true, but she had learned during their brief marriage that Donovan wasn't above manipulating the truth.

"It feels to me more like you're pushing me away. You lied to me, Donovan. Flat-out lied when I asked you why you came back."

She'd come back for closure. Writing a note to him and leaving the way she had had left her feeling as if…oh, God, as if maybe there was still a chance for the two of them. The only way she was going to be able to move on was through some sort of final conflict.

"What did you want me to say, Cassidy? That I needed a wife and a baby for the company?" he asked, sarcasm dripping from every word.

"Well it would have been the truth." She wasn't about to take the blame for this. He had lied to her, and he had planned to keep on lying to her.

"You were happy to believe I was back for you."

"I was happy to believe that, because I wanted it so much. But I think maybe I was lying to myself. Listen, I just came back tonight because I didn't want things to end the way they did last time." She thought about telling him about her other stop that day—at his parents' house—and decided against it.

"I'm not sure what you mean," he said. "There isn't any reason for our marriage to be over…but that's what your note meant, right?"

"Yes. Our marriage *is* over." It was mainly pride talking, but she didn't care. She was tired of loving Donovan too much and him caring for her too little. She was never going to be able to compete with Tolley-Patterson. She was never going to be able to challenge him and fill his life the way that company did. She was never going to be anything more to him than the mother of his son.

"Why?" he asked.

He seemed perplexed, and frankly she didn't understand it. He had to see that she was more than a cog in the wheel of his plans for the future.

"What do you mean, why? Honestly, I think you can see why we can't stay married."

She wanted to say because he'd hurt her when he'd lied to her, but it was more than that. Tonight, as she'd tucked Van into his crib at her parents' house and seen the picture her parents had placed over his crib of her and Donovan holding the baby in the hospital—she'd wanted desperately for the emotions she felt to be real on both sides.

"No, I can't, Cassidy. Nothing's changed."

"Everything's changed."

He came over to her and took her hand in his, lacing his fingers with hers. She noticed the way their wedding rings nestled together.

"I married you, and we had Van together. My grandfather's will was in place before he was born."

"I didn't know that that was why you married me."

"Haven't you been happy?" he asked.

She *had* been happy. Had been finding her way in this new role. She still had to go back to her job, and they'd never made a public announcement of their marriage, but she'd been happy with Donovan.

"Well, yes, but…" How to explain? "I kept hoping you'd come back, and then you did. I set myself up for it."

"Set yourself up for what?"

She swallowed hard, hating to admit once again that she'd wanted to be wanted, to feel special, for herself. To be the one thing that he hadn't been able to live without.

"For you. I set myself up to be totally vulnerable to you. And that's what makes me mad. I made everything so easy for you."

Donovan cursed and dropped her hand, pacing

away from her. She watched his back, watched him walk away, though he didn't go too far. She made herself watch that view and remember it. He had walked away from her, and from her love.

"Nothing about this has been easy, Cassidy. Lying to you didn't sit right with me, but as long as you seemed happy I told myself that the ends justified the means."

"Of course you would say that. You've never needed me the way I need you."

Silence built between them, and she realized how much she'd hoped he would argue with her about this. Hoped that he'd suddenly confess to loving her and needing her. And the last of her dreams around Donovan Tolley died.

She pivoted on her heel and walked toward the door.

"Cassidy, wait," he said.

She stopped where she was but didn't turn around. The numbness she'd wrapped herself in when she'd come back to this house was fading, leaving behind the kind of aching pain that she'd experienced only one other time…when he'd let her down before.

"How can I fix this?" he asked.

That he'd asked made her feel marginally better. That he couldn't figure out what she needed from him negated those good feelings. No one wanted to

have to tell someone that they needed to be loved.
That they needed to be first in their life.

"I don't think you can."

There were a few moments in a person's life
that defined him, and Donovan knew this moment
with Cassidy was one. This would determine for
the rest of his life what the balance of their relationship would be. And he had only to think about
that feeling he'd had when he'd walked into the
empty master suite to know that losing her now
wasn't an option.

"*Can't* isn't in my vocabulary," he said.

She glanced back at him, that long curly hair of
hers swinging around her shoulders. "What are you
trying to say?"

He didn't blame her. He'd used evasion and half-
truth for so long. They'd become his standard way
of communicating with everyone. It was simply
easier to play his cards close to his chest. He could
protect himself and use the knowledge he collected
to his advantage.

And the knowledge he'd collected about Cassidy
was simple and straightforward. She needed some
kind of emotional reciprocity. And it was about time
that he delivered it.

But laying bare his soul…

"That we aren't done talking yet. Don't walk

away while there are still things to be said." No response. "Please."

She turned to face him, arms crossed. "I'm listening."

"Let's go outside. I'm tired of being in the house."

She nodded and followed him out onto the patio. The soothing sound of the waterfall in the pool area eased the tension that was riding him.

He didn't lose. He wasn't going to lose Cassidy. He just had to do the right thing. He'd always been able to fix things that way.

This was no different. He was going to win Cassidy back. He'd come back from worse situations. It wouldn't be the first time that he'd been down like this. She wouldn't have come back tonight if she hadn't wanted to.

"I know that I haven't exactly been your knight in shining armor, but I can change that. This stuff with Granddaddy's will was making me a bit crazy, and I had to focus on that and outplaying Sam. But that's behind me now, and I want to make you and Van the focus of my life."

Cassidy watched him and he didn't even kid himself that he had any idea what she was thinking. But he did know that she was no longer walking away. It eased the ache that he'd felt when he'd stared at her back.

"You're talking about starting over?"

"If that's what you want. I'd prefer to start from here," he said, meaning it. "We've had some good times, haven't we?"

"Yes, we have. But I can't—"

"What?"

"Listen, I want this to work. I mean, I love you, Donovan, but you have been a jerk about certain things in our relationship, and I'm not about to put up with it anymore."

"Fair enough. You tell me what you want me to change and I'll change it."

"It's not that easy."

"Why not? That's what makes the most successful relationships work."

"What relationships?"

"Business partnerships, mergers."

He felt her go quiet. She stopped leaning toward him and even though she didn't turn away he felt exactly as he had earlier when she'd walked away.

"Mergers? Was this a hostile takeover, or a friendly acquisition?"

"A friendly merger," he said, drawing her into his arms.

She held herself stiff and he realized that the situation was slipping away from him again. Was it time to pull back and regroup? Hell, he'd never done that and wasn't about to now.

He leaned down to kiss her but she put her arm

between them. "This will change nothing. Physical compatibility isn't the issue between us."

"Prove it."

"*Prove* it? You're supposed to be the one giving ground and wooing me back."

"Am I?"

"Yes," she said. "And frankly, I'm not that impressed right now."

He pulled her back into his arms and didn't hesitate to take her mouth. He kissed her slowly and deeply, reminding her with passion of the bond they shared. Reminding her that it was deeper and stronger than anything she'd experienced before. Than anything *he'd* experienced before.

He wasn't going to accept defeat. He swept his hands down her back to the curve of her hips, holding her tightly to him. Dominating her with the passion that had always been so much a part of their relationship.

She moaned, a sweet sound that he swallowed. She tipped her head to the side, allowing him access to her mouth. She held his shoulders, undulating against him. He wanted more of her and hardened in a rush. Making love to Cassidy was an addiction.

He brought his hand between them, cupping the full globe of one breast. She shivered in his arms as he brushed his thumb over her nipple.

He lifted his head so that their eyes met. Slowly he raised the hand between them and unbuttoned her blouse. She arched her shoulders and let him push the blouse off. She reached for the front clasp of her bra, opening it and baring herself to him.

He pushed back a little to see her. Her breasts were bare, nipples distended and begging for his mouth. He lowered his head and suckled.

He held her with a hand on the small of her back and buried the other in her hair. She arched over his arm, and her breasts thrust up at him. Nothing compared to the way she made him feel.

Her eyes were closed, her hips moving subtly against him, and when he blew on her nipples, goose-flesh spread down her body.

He loved the way she reacted to him. Her nipples were so sensitive he was pretty sure he could bring her to orgasm just by touching her there. He kept kissing and caressing, gently pinching her nipples until her hands clenched in his hair and she rocked her hips harder against his length. He thrust against her and bit down carefully on one tender, aroused nipple. She cried his name, and he hurriedly covered her mouth with his, wanting to feel every bit of her passion, rocking her until she quieted in his arms.

He held her close. Her bare breasts brushed his chest. He was so hard he thought he'd die if he didn't get inside her. Yet this was the perfect moment. Because he knew that he'd turned a corner, and that Cassidy was the one negotiation that he couldn't bear to lose.

Oh, hell, he loved her.

Eleven

Cassidy got out of bed late in the morning. The room was empty and it was clear that Donovan was gone. She dressed in last night's clothing, since she'd packed all of her other clothes the day before. She heard Mrs. Winters in the kitchen and smelled the enticing aroma of coffee wafting through the house.

She felt small and alone, ashamed that she'd let herself fall once again for Donovan's silver-tongued charm.

She was in the foyer when Mrs. Winters came out of the study. "Good morning, Mrs. Tolley."

"Morning."

"Mr. Tolley left this for you."

"Thank you." She took the small, oblong-shaped box and put it in her purse. She'd received enough jewelry in her life to recognize the box for what it was. And it felt like a bribe. She needed to get out of this house and back to her own.

She walked out of the house. There was a News 4 Van parked at the end of the circular driveway. As she approached her car, a reporter and cameraman scrambled toward her. She hated this part of being an heiress and a magnet for news.

Deciding she wasn't going to talk to anyone, she got into her car and put on her dark glasses. They ran toward her, but she waved them off and drove away.

But she had no idea where to go. Her parents' house, she imagined, was the best place. She called her mom to let her know she'd be there soon to pick up Van. She could collect her son and then plan a trip out of town for a few months. Until the local media had something better to report on than her and her Donovan.

When she pulled into her parents' house, her older brother, Adam, was standing in the portico.

"What are you doing here?"

"Waiting for you."

She stared at him, nonplussed. "How'd you know I'd be here?"

"I was with Mom when you called. I thought we should talk," he said, taking her arm and leading her to the back gardens.

"About?"

"Tolley-Patterson. It seems that the stipulation of marriage wasn't the only thing in that will of Maxwell Patterson's. He also left it up to the board of directors to approve Donovan's choice of wife."

"That's ridiculous."

"Exactly. I don't know what's going on today, but according to what I've been able to piece together, Donovan called for an emergency meeting to force the board to make a decision on the CEO."

"Why are you telling me this?"

"Because I have a man on the inside—"

"You sound like a secret agent, Adam. What does that mean?"

"A guy who works for Tolley-Patterson is keeping me abreast of what's happening in the meeting."

"Why would he do that?"

"I asked him to."

"Oh." No further explanation seemed to be forthcoming. "What did he say?"

"That the board will only accept Donovan as CEO if he doesn't marry you."

She heard the words as if from a distance and realized what they meant. Donovan had to choose between her and that position he'd always craved. Her and the last chance he had to prove himself to his grandfather over Sam.

"Thanks for letting me know."

"Cassidy?"

"Yes?"

"Mom and Dad have suggested having your marriage annulled quietly so that you don't have to go through the humiliation of a divorce."

She nodded. "Are they waiting for me?"

"Yes."

"I'm not going to let them take over. I need to do things in my own time."

"What will you do?"

"Talk to Donovan. Who's your source?"

Adam turned away from her. "I don't think I should say."

"I think you better. Is he reliable?"

Adam faced her again, taking off his sunglasses. There was a seriousness in her brother's eyes that she was used to seeing, but she also noticed that he seemed angry. She knew it was on her behalf, and she realized how deeply she was loved by her family.

"Very reliable."

"Who?"

"Sam Patterson."

"*Sam?* He hates Donovan! Adam, I wouldn't trust anything that he said. He's always working an angle."

"Hell, I know that. That's why I contacted him. I wanted to know more about what was going on."

"Why would he talk to you?"

"I have no idea."

"Liar."

"Liar?"

"Yes. You wouldn't make a deal with a man you didn't trust and there has to be more to this than Sam keeping you in the loop out of the goodness of his heart."

Adam looked uncomfortable for a moment before he put his sunglasses back on. "You're right. There is. I'm helping Sam with a contract he's working on in Canada using some of our contacts."

He didn't elaborate, which just made her mad. She was sick of the men in her life. Just plain sick of them and the way that everything in their worlds revolved around business.

"Did he say when we'd know what the board decides?"

"We should know soon. They're due for a lunch break in a few minutes."

Theo's power play was going to net Donovan the results he wanted. Donovan had no doubt about that. The board of directors had been unmoved by Theo's presentation, he suspected.

"What are you going to do?" Sam asked him as they both stood outside the boardroom. They'd been asked to leave while the board had a final vote.

"About what?"

"If they insist that you not marry Cassidy."

"Sam, I'm already married to her, so there's little the board can do. Even they can't insist I get a divorce."

"You're *married?* I thought she was just living with you."

"Do you honestly think I wouldn't marry her?"

"Well…yes. We all believed—"

"All? Who else? Theo? Have you been in league with him?"

"No. Theo has his own issues because Grand-daddy left him out of the running for successor."

Donovan agreed. Maxwell Patterson had left them all with a heck of a mess. The company wasn't in the best financial shape, but with him and Sam working as they had for the last few months, Tolley-Patterson was finally on the right track.

"If not Theo, then who?"

"Um…Adam Franzone."

"Then you must have known I was married to Cassidy," Donovan said.

"No, I didn't. Adam and I have a very limited agreement—I'm keeping him informed about what's going on in the board meeting today, and he's using his contacts to get us the land we need in Canada for our new facility."

Donovan was surprised that Sam had thought to use Adam for help in the land acquisition, which had been progressing very slowly. "Did you go to him?"

"No. Adam came to me."

Donovan realized that after all the years he'd spent competing with his cousin, he really didn't know the man. He had always just looked at Sam's weaknesses and tried to exploit them. But now he saw a glimpse of a future.

"I'm not going to leave Cassidy. I've just figured out how to get her back into my life. The board is going to have to accept some kind of compromise. I suggest you and I go in there united."

"What do you have in mind?" Sam asked.

"A joint venture. Granddaddy knew you and I were the future, and I'm not sure that he didn't mean for us to somehow work out an agreement."

Sam laughed. "He didn't. He set us against each other because we both respond to a challenge."

"True. So can you do it?"

"If you can convince the board? Then, yes, I'll go for it."

"If the board doesn't meet my terms, I'm walking. I've given this company everything, and to have them tell me who I can marry is going too far."

Donovan had thought about it good and hard before he'd come to the office today. Leaving Cassidy behind in bed had been difficult. He'd wanted to be there when she woke so he could make sure she understood that he wasn't letting her walk out of his life.

"They won't respond to a threat," Sam said.

"They will respond to the bottom line. You and I have already impacted revenues in ways that Theo never could and won't be able to. He's too stuck in the old way of doing business."

"Right. Do you have documentation to back up the figures?"

"I do," Donovan said. He took out his Black-Berry and sent a quick text to Marcus. Then he sent another note to Cassidy. Just a quick one to tell her that he needed to see her as soon as he was done with this meeting.

Because if this morning had done one thing, it had reinforced to him how much he loved her—and he needed to tell her that.

"We're ready for you both now," Theo said from the doorway.

"I need a word with Donovan." His mother stood behind his uncle.

"Fine. We can wait five minutes," Theo said.

His mother began walking down the hall toward his office. "Mom?"

She turned. "We can't talk in the hallway."

He nodded and followed her past Karin, his assistant, who glanced up, arching her eyebrows at him. He signaled her to hold his calls.

His mother walked over to the window overlooking downtown Charleston and crossed her arms.

"What is it?" he asked.

"I owe you and Cassidy an apology."

Okay. *That* he hadn't expected. "Why?"

"For hiding your marriage from the board and Sam. I know that you meant to hide it from the public just temporarily until Van was born, but I kept hoping that the marriage would fall apart."

"It isn't going to," Donovan said. "Her family isn't as bad as you make them out to be."

"I know. That's why I'm apologizing. I told the board that you two are married and that the marriage is a solid match."

"Did that sway them?" he asked, aware that his mother had in her own way gone to bat for him. And he appreciated it more than he'd thought he would.

She shrugged. "It was a written vote, not vocal, so I have no idea of the outcome."

"Thanks, Mom. What changed your mind about Cassidy and the Franzones?"

"Cassidy did. She brought Van by to visit us yesterday. She was very frank with your father and I about the lies you'd told her and how that made her feel. She said she had no idea how much longer your marriage would last, but she wanted Van to know his grandparents."

Donovan wasn't surprised. Cassidy was kinder than he deserved. And if she had any idea of the things his mother had done, apparently that hadn't stopped Cassidy from doing the right thing.

"That girl is a keeper, Donovan," his mother said.

He agreed with his mother, which didn't happen that often.

As his mother left and he prepared to go to the boardroom, his BlackBerry vibrated. He glanced at the screen to see a message from Cassidy, informing him that she was aware that he had to divorce her to become CEO. He stared at the words, wondering how she knew what had happened in the boardroom.

He dialed her number and got her voice mail. He left a message, but had the feeling that Cassidy wasn't interested in listening to anything he had to say.

Cassidy and Van were having a quiet evening at home. Well, at her home. She hadn't been able to go back to the mansion she shared with Donovan. She also wanted to be away from her family, as they were acting as though they had a right to make decisions in her life. She'd set them straight and told Adam to mind his own business.

The doorbell rang just before seven and she opened the door to find Jimmy standing there.

"What are you doing here?"

"Delivery again."

"I don't need any soup."

"It's not soup."

He handed her a padded envelope and gave her a

smile before he walked back to his car. She closed the door and stared bemusedly at the envelope in her hand. It had her name written on it in very distinctive handwriting—Donovan's.

She wasn't ready to deal with anything else from him right now. The jewelry box sat on the table in the foyer, still unopened. She tossed the envelope next to it and walked back to the family room, where Van was sleeping in his playpen.

Ten minutes later her cell phone rang and she checked the caller ID before answering it. "Hey, Emma."

"Hey, girl. Did you open the envelope?"

"Which one?"

"The one Jimmy delivered."

"No, and how do you know about it?"

"Because I'm coming over to babysit."

"I don't want to talk to Donovan."

"Trust me, on this you're going to want to at least give him a chance to explain."

"I've already given him three chances with my heart, and each time he's let me down."

"I know. If you didn't love him then I'd say to ignore him, but you do, so give him a chance to explain and make things up to you."

"What does he have planned?"

"I don't know. Open the envelope. I'm going to be there in fifteen minutes."

Cassidy hung up and went back to the foyer. She brought the envelope and jewelry box into the living room and sat down where she could see Van.

She opened the envelope first and inside found an invitation requesting her presence at the yacht club tonight at nine.

She shook her head. Romance and romantic gestures weren't going to win her over. But a part of her…okay, all of her, wanted her relationship with Donovan to work. As hurt as she was by his actions, she still hadn't had time to fall out of love with him. She didn't know if she'd ever be able to.

She opened the jewelry box and found inside a platinum charm bracelet. There was only one charm on it. A photo of her, Van and Donovan, a small version of the photo that hung by Van's crib at her parents' house. On the back of the charm was a small engraving that read, This is my world.

She felt a sting of tears as she read it. She wasn't sure what Donovan had in mind for later this evening, but she knew now she was going to go and hear him out. She owed it to the both of them to give their relationship one last chance.

She took the baby monitor down the hall to her bedroom and got changed out of her jeans and shirt into a cocktail-length sundress. She put her makeup on with a steady hand and touched up her curls.

When Emma arrived a few minutes later, she was

almost ready to go. She put on her wedding rings and her charm bracelet.

"I'm going to take Van to my place for the night," Emma said.

"Emma…"

"If you need to come and get him before morning, don't worry. But I have the feeling you're going to be otherwise occupied."

She bit her lower lip. She needed more than another sexy night in Donovan's arms. But she had no idea if he could give her anything more. Romance was fine, but she needed his heart. She really needed him to be the man she'd always believed him to be.

A limo arrived just after Emma, and she hugged her friend and dropped a kiss on Van's head as she left.

In the backseat of the limo she found another envelope. She opened it, and a piece of vellum paper dropped out. On the paper was a poem written by Christopher Brennan called "Because She Would Ask Me Why I Loved Her."

The poem was beautiful and sweet, and the scrawled *I love you* at the bottom made her heart beat a little faster. She wanted to believe that Donovan was making this gesture because he loved her, but a part of her—the part jaded by his betrayals—feared he was going to ask her to remain his secret wife.

Twelve

Donovan was waiting on the dock when the limo pulled up. He had spent the evening making sure every detail was in place. For once, he was nervous, but not because he was afraid of the outcome. He'd always been a winner, and there was no way he'd settle for anything less than complete victory with Cassidy tonight.

"Good evening, Cassidy," he said as he took her hand and helped her out of the back of the car.

"Donovan."

The night sky was filled with stars and a warm tropical breeze stirred off the water. "Thank you for joining me."

"You're welcome. I'll admit I came only because I want to hear what you have to say."

"Did you read my notes?"

"I did."

"And?"

She hesitated.

"I love you, Cassidy."

"Did you lose your job today?" she asked.

Not exactly the response he'd been looking for.

"What does that have to do with anything?"

"Adam said—"

"Adam doesn't know everything."

"No, but I thought Sam did."

Donovan shook his head. "Let's go onto my yacht. I'll tell you all about the day if you want."

She followed him onto the yacht. His chef had prepared some hors d'oeuvres and they were set out near the stern.

"My uncle and the board gave me an ultimatum, which you obviously heard about—leave you, or forfeit the chairmanship. I declined their offer and countered with a joint chairmanship.

"Sam and I have really made a difference in the company bottom line, and we decided we both should be at the helm."

"And they didn't go for it," she said.

"Why are you so sure that they said no?"

"Why else would you be trying so hard to hold on

to me unless you lost the company? That was your number one priority."

He shook his head, regretting the fact that he'd let her down and made her feel as if she didn't mean as much to him as his job did. He'd wanted his grandfather's respect, had craved a chance to make his mark in the world, but over the short course of his marriage, he had realized that being a husband and father was the one thing that mattered most.

"They took our offer. Sam and I are co-CEOs. I'm telling you how I feel about you because, when I thought I was going to lose everything, I didn't feel devastated."

"You didn't?" she asked.

He shook his head and drew her into his arms. "Instead, I thought about you and Van and the family we were starting, and I looked at my relatives who sit on the board. Even though they also represent the investors in the company, I knew that family was the most important thing.

"That *you* were the most important thing in my life," he said, leaning down to kiss her. "You and Van.

"I love you, Cassidy Franzone Tolley. And I want to marry you again in front of the world so that everyone knows you are mine."

Cassidy was crying, but she was also smiling— the brightest smile he'd ever seen. "I love you, too, Donovan."

"Will you marry me again?"

"No," she said, and his heart nearly stopped. "I don't need a ceremony in front of the world."

He let out a breath, overwhelmed by his love for this woman. "What do you need?"

"You," she said.

* * * * *

BABY ON THE BILLIONAIRE'S DOORSTEP

BY
EMILY McKAY

Emily Mckay has wanted to write romantic novels since she read her first romance when she was eleven. Now that she's all grown up, she still thinks it's the best job in the world!

Despite all the books she read during those formative years, she did not grow up to marry a Greek shipping tycoon, but rather her college sweetheart, who turned out to be the perfect romance hero. They live in Texas with their little girl, two big dogs and one beleaguered cat.

When she's not writing (or reading), she likes to garden, bake and hear from fans. You can contact her at emily@emilymckay.com.

To my partner in crime, Robyn DeHart. My dear friend,
without your help I'd be unable to write a book.
Without your friendship, I probably wouldn't want to.

One

As the taxi pulled to a stop in front of the sprawling monstrosity his brother called home, Dex Messina pinched the bridge of his nose. Man, he was tired.

He was getting too old for this. He'd just spent a week in Antwerp working sixteen-hour days getting ready for the opening of Messina Diamonds' new diamond-cutting branch. On top of that, the seventeen-hour flight from Belgium—complete with a six-hour delay in New York—had taken its toll.

"This the place?" the cabbie asked from the front seat.

"Home sweet home."

Since the renovations on his own urban loft had hit yet another snag, Dex was living with his brother, Derek, a situation that suited neither of them and had been going on far too long. Only the amount of time Dex spent out of the country and the fact that he stayed in the detached guesthouse made it bearable.

Dex handed the driver a fifty, pulled his bag from the seat beside him and climbed out of the car. He swung the rugged canvas duffel over his shoulder and walked up the curved path. The towering oaks and clusters of shrubbery were perfectly manicured to hide the house from the road while creating the impression one had left the exclusive Dallas neighborhood of Highland Park altogether.

Ivy crept up the far corner of the building. A low stone retaining wall crumbled at one end. Both gave the impression of gently declining nobility.

Everything in Derek's life was like that. Perfect. Controlled. Pretentious.

It set Dex's teeth on edge. Made him want to take his motorcycle out of storage and pop some wheelies on his brother's plush green lawn.

Not that he would. He was a respectable contributor to the family business these days. A damn pillar of society.

Why he even—

Dex stopped short just shy of the mahogany double doors.

"What the—"

He stared for a long moment at the object blocking his path before he convinced himself he wasn't hallucinating.

It was an infant car seat.

Next to the car seat sat a bag decorated with smiling cartoon bears. Far more disturbing than the car seat itself was what appeared to be in it. A pile of blankets, out of the top of which rose a tiny pink stocking cap.

Dex crouched down to get a closer look, then thought better of it. Instead, he yanked his cell phone out of his pocket and dialed his brother's number.

"Derek here."

"You at home?"

"Yes. Don't tell me you missed your flight. I need you in the office to—"

"No. I'm at the front door. You might want to join me."

"Then why are you calling me?" A note of frustration crept into Derek's voice.

Dex was too shocked to be annoyed by it. "Just get your butt down here."

He flipped his phone closed. Sitting back on his heels, he rubbed his hand along his jaw, staring at the car seat and its bundle of…joy or whatever.

Five minutes later Derek swung open the front door. He had clearly been working. He'd lost his jacket and tie and the sleeves of his white dress shirt were rolled up. "This better be good."

Dex said nothing but looked up at his brother with a quirked eyebrow, waiting for Derek's reaction. If he hadn't been so completely thrown for a loop himself, the situation might have been amusing.

Derek looked down at the car seat. "Is this some kind of joke?"

"If it is, I'm not in on it."

"You didn't bring this thing home with you?"

Dex chuckled despite himself. "No. I didn't bring home a baby from Antwerp. I'm guessing that would be illegal."

"What's it doing here?"

"It was here when I drove up." Feigning a flippancy he didn't quite feel, Dex reached into the car seat and pulled aside the blanket to reveal the tiny head of a sleeping infant. The baby's skin seemed impossibly pale in the moonlight, its delicate rosebud of a mouth the only color in its face.

The infant was so still, he couldn't even tell if it was breathing. Feeling a burst of panic, he pulled loose the pink blanket and pressed his palm to the tiny cotton-covered chest.

The infant drew in one shuddering breath, then exhaled slowly. As he felt the warm breath drift across his hand, he felt something tighten inside of him, even as relief rocked him back on his heels.

"It's alive?" Derek asked.

"Thank God."

"What's that?" Derek asked.

Dex looked to where Derek was pointing. When he'd untucked the blanket, he'd dislodged a note. He picked it up and stood.

Derek took it from him and stepped out of the shadow of the doorway so that the landscape lighting from the yard shone on the note.

> D—
> Her name is Isabella. She's yours. You'll have to take her for a while.

The note wasn't signed.

For a long moment, Derek and Dex merely stared at each other. Then they both turned to stare at the baby.

"This is quite the mess you've gotten into this time." There was a note of grim censure in Derek's voice.

"*I've* gotten into?" Why it surprised him that Derek assumed this was his mess, he didn't know. "Who says it's mine?"

Derek propped his hands on his hips. "It's not my baby. I'm scrupulously careful about that kind of thing."

"Trust me. About that kind of thing, so am I."

"You found her," Derek pointed out.

"Yes. At *your* house."

"Where we both live."

They stared each other down, neither relenting.

Even as he looked into his brother's steely-blue eyes, Dex knew how ridiculous the conversation was. Yet conceding that they had no way of knowing who'd fathered the baby was like admitting that it could be his.

A little mewing sound came from the car seat and they both turned to the baby. She moved her head, her mouth opening and closing as if searching for something. He'd been on enough flights with crying babies to know that this could go very bad if they didn't do the right thing.

He dropped to his knees, ran his hand along the edge of the car seat and found a pacifier attached by a cord. With the precision of a movie hero disarming a nuclear weapon, he eased the pacifier into her mouth.

Holding his breath, he watched her suck contentedly, bringing a hand to rub against her cheek and then fall back asleep.

From behind him, Derek let out an audible sigh. "This is ridiculous."

Pulling his phone out of his pants pocket he spoke into the phone. "Call Lorraina."

"You're calling Raina?" Dex asked in a whisper as he pulled Derek farther away from the baby. "It's after midnight on a Sunday night."

"So?"

"It's a little late to be calling your assistant. Besides, someone abandoned a baby on your doorstep. We should call the police."

Derek's gaze narrowed. "Absolutely not. That would be a public relations nightmare."

"And naturally the public image of Messina Diamonds is more important than the welfare of this baby."

He didn't know if Derek heard him or not because by then Raina had picked up and Derek was talking to her. A few minutes later, he flipped his phone closed. He stood, hands clasped behind his back, glaring at the tiny infant.

"She said she can't come."

"I can't blame her."

"She did give me some…advice." Derek sounded disgusted. "She said if the baby wakes up, we should feed her."

"Then I guess we're on our own."

Dex stared at the car seat before mustering the courage to approach again. Derek, he noticed, didn't seem any more eager than he was to move the child off their front door step and into the house.

Finally, Dex pushed himself forward, plucked the car seat up by the handle and headed inside. Derek stopped him before he reached the door.

"Do you think that's wise?"

"She's a baby. Not a vampire. We've got to bring her into the house at some point."

Derek nodded reluctantly and followed them into the front room. Dex set the car seat down in the shadow of the sofa, where the lights wouldn't shine on her face, then sat down in the chair beside her to wait.

Derek handed him a brandy before lowering himself to the armchair opposite. "You'll have to stay with her tomorrow."

Dex nearly choked on the brandy. "Why me?"

"I leave for London at noon."

"Why can't Raina watch her?"

"Raina's coming with me. She'll be back by the end of the week, but she's going to be busy planning the reception for next week. You'll have to find someone to watch the child soon. Someone you can trust. I need you in the office by Tuesday for the board meeting."

Dex took another sip of his brandy. "Good thing you're not leaving until noon."

Derek looked up. "Why's that?"

"Because first thing in the morning, we're going to go get paternity tests."

Lucy Alwin—as a rule—didn't lie. She didn't like doing it and she wasn't any good at it.

But today, she was going to have to lie her butt off. And she'd better damn well be convincing at it. Isabella's future was at stake.

She double-checked the address one last time and turned her Toyota Prius onto Briarwood Lane. The sight of one mansion after another did little to quell her nerves and only reinforced what she already knew. The Messinas were filthy rich. And very powerful.

She eased her car to a stop across the street from number 122, mentally cursing her twin sister yet again. She'd warned Jewel a year ago, "You have to tell Dex Messina you're pregnant now. He needs to know he's going to be a father. Because if he finds out later that you've deceived him, he may do everything in his power to take your baby away from you."

But had Jewel followed her advice? No. Instead, she'd been determined to do this her own way. And on her own. Of course, Jewel's definition of "on her own" involved relying heavily on Lucy. From the moment she'd first held her darling niece in her arms Lucy hadn't minded one bit.

But over the past month, Jewel had slowly been withdrawing from both Lucy and Isabella. Then, late last night— long after Lucy was asleep—she'd dropped sweet baby Isabella on Dex's doorstep, then hightailed it out of town.

It was morning before Lucy had even realized they were

gone. Jewel, apparently in an attempt to reassure Lucy, had left a note saying she was going out of town for a couple of weeks, but that Lucy shouldn't worry, she'd left Isabella someplace safe.

For the first time in her life, Lucy was thankful for her sister's laziness. Jewel hadn't bothered to move Isabella's car seat from Lucy's car to her own. Instead she'd borrowed Lucy's Prius only to exchange it later on her way out of town for her own car. Thank God she had. Jewel had used the car's GPS system to look up Dex's address. That was the only way Lucy had known where Jewel had left Isabella.

It had taken Lucy another three hours to design and execute a plan to get Isabella back. A plan that involved raiding her sister's closet and having her hair cut and dyed to match Jewel's vibrant red.

In short, Lucy had to convince Dex that she was Isabella's mom and that she'd made a terrible mistake abandoning her baby. To do that she'd have to first convince him she was the woman he'd had a one-night stand with fourteen months ago.

How exactly she was going to do that was the question that had plagued Lucy since she'd developed this harebrained plan. She and Jewel didn't just dress differently.

Lucy was sensible, no-nonsense practicality while Jewel was exotic, seductive sexuality. In short, Jewel had a way of manipulating and controlling men that Lucy had never comprehended, let alone replicated.

If Dex remembered Jewel at all—and men never forgot a woman like Jewel—then Lucy was going to have a hell of a time convincing him that she was her twin sister. Her best hope was to get in and out of there as quickly as possible and pray that he wouldn't look too closely at her.

She didn't know if she could pull this off. She only knew she had to try. For Isabella's sake.

The Messinas, for all their wealth and privilege, were known for their ruthlessness. For their cold-hearted pursuit of the all-mighty dollar. No way Lucy was going to let one of those men care for her niece.

No, Isabella needed someone in her life who would always do the right thing for her. Since that person obviously wasn't going to be Jewel, Lucy was more than happy to step up to the plate.

With that thought spurring her on, Lucy stalked up the winding front path and rang the doorbell. She heard Isabella's cries from the behind the door and distress clutched her throat. Any lie she told today was well worth it.

She had to remind herself of that when the massive front door swung open to reveal Dex Messina, looking just as attractive as he had the first time she'd seen him, but considerably more rumpled and annoyed.

"Are you the nanny?" he asked.

"No. I'm the mother."

Two

Dex hadn't realized a baby could scream so loudly. Or for so long.

The baby had started crying the minute he'd been left alone with her and hadn't stopped nearly ninety minutes later.

Convinced her piercing cries had destroyed his hearing, he thought he'd misheard the woman at the door. "You're the what?"

"The mother," she repeated. "I'm Isabella's mother."

Isabella chose that instant to stop crying, so this time, Dex had no trouble hearing the woman. Instinctually, he brought up his arm to block the door as he studied her. But maybe Isabella was just catching her breath because, after a moment, she let out another bloodcurdling scream.

The woman rose onto her toes—for all the good it did her—trying to see Isabella over his shoulder. She bobbed first to one side, and then the other. Then, with unexpected speed and grace, she darted under his arm and into the house.

She dashed through the foyer to the living room with what he could only assume were a mother's instincts, straight to the car seat where he'd deposited the crying Isabella when the doorbell rang.

She scooped up the baby, held her at arm's length for a moment as if assessing the damage, and then cradled her close. The woman crooned softly to the child, swaying back and forth. Instantly the cries stopped.

In the blessed silence that followed, Dex's ears continued to ring. Hours of listening to Isabella cry had left his head throbbing and his thoughts muddled. And despite all that, the woman looked familiar.

She was dressed in a denim miniskirt and a pink tank top that barely covered her generous curves. Her pale, heart-shaped face was dusted with freckles. Her garishly red hair cut into a wedged bob.

It was the hair he remembered first. That and her hips. There was something sensuous in the way they shifted from side to side as she swayed. Something deeply erotic that pulled at him on an instinctual level.

Pick up the beat a little and add in the heavy throbbing bass from the bar and he'd think he was having a flashback to…when was that? A year ago? Longer?

His father had just died. There'd been the funeral followed by endless meetings and conferences divvying up the estate and business. Within a week, he'd been sick to death of death. Ready to lose himself in a bottle of Scotch and a warm, willing body.

He vaguely remembered that night. Had she been that body he'd lost himself in?

It was exactly the kind of relationship at which he excelled. No emotion. No future. No commitment.

But apparently something had gone terribly wrong.

* * *

Lucy kept waiting for Dex to say something. Anything.

Instead, he just watched her. His face inscrutable, but the tension evident in every line of his body.

With every minute that passed, her own apprehension grew. Finally, in a burst of defiant anxiety, she blurted out, "I made a mistake."

He lifted one eyebrow in silent, sardonic question.

"Okay, a big mistake. Huge really."

"You abandoned your baby on my doorstep. That's more than a mistake."

"But—" she held up her index finger to emphasize her point "—I realized it was a mistake, and I came back for her." Her heart was pounding and her nerves loosened her tongue. "So no harm done, right? And since you obviously don't want her, I'll just pack her up and we'll be on our way. You'll never hear from us again."

Holding her breath, she clutched Isabella tightly in one arm, swooped up the car seat in the other, and dashed for the door. For an instant, she even hoped it would be that simple.

But of course, it wasn't.

He grabbed her arm as she strode past, pulling her to a stop. His grip on her arm was almost painfully firm.

"Is she mine?"

Damn it. Why couldn't she be the kind of woman who would lie about this sort of thing? But, for better or worse, she wasn't.

When she hesitated, he continued. "In two weeks I'll have the results from the paternity test. I'll know for sure then."

"Two weeks?" she asked, her heart constricting at the thought of what might happen at the end of those weeks.

"Yes. Two weeks. That's how long the results will take since Derek and I both sent in samples to be considered. Apparently it takes that long when the possible fathers are brothers."

"I wasn't surprised at how long it would take. I was surprised you'd already done the test. Didn't take you long. Eager to dodge the bullet of fatherhood, aren't you?"

"Is she mine or isn't she?"

"She's yours."

"Then why did you hesitate?"

"I thought if you didn't know she was yours, you might just let us go."

"Even if she wasn't mine, you abandoned her."

Lucy hadn't counted on this.

In fact, she'd been so sure Dex would be so eager to get rid of Isabella, that he wouldn't think twice about handing her over.

Anger and frustration welled up inside her as she clutched Isabella even tighter. She blinked back tears, held Isabella even more tightly and made the only argument that had even a chance of winning him over.

"You can't possibly want to keep her yourself. Even if she is yours."

"Whether or not I want her is irrelevant. There's a reason abandoning a child is illegal. You're obviously not a fit parent."

And yet he hadn't called the police. That was something, wasn't it?

Knowing she couldn't possibly win an argument about whether or not she was a fit parent, she turned the tables on him. "No offense, but by the sound of things when I got here, it didn't seem like you were doing much better."

His eyes narrowed. "You're right, I don't want a baby. But if she really is mine, then I don't have a choice. To be honest, I don't have the faintest idea what to do with her. But you obviously do."

"I'm her mother," she insisted. "Of course I know what to do." And for a moment, she imagined she still might get out of this. But first she'd have to convince him he really could trust her with Isabella. But how could she do that when every cell of her body abhorred what Jewel had done?

As inconceivable as Jewel's actions were, Lucy tried to imagine what could possibly have been going through her sister's mind last night. Still swaying with Isabella in her arms, she gazed up at him, letting all her love for Isabella show in her eyes.

"The truth is, being a single mother is harder than I thought. But I've been doing this for five months now. After all that time, I had one night—just one night— when I got freaked out and felt like I couldn't do it anymore. Leaving her on your doorstep was stupid, but surely every parent is allowed one mistake. Even if it's a big one."

She held her breath, waiting for his response. If he didn't let her leave with Isabella now, she didn't know what she would do.

Finally, he responded. "You're right. I'm clearly not equipped to take care of an infant. But there's no way I'm handing her over to you, either. However, since the nanny service I called this morning appears incapable of sending someone over in a timely manner, you can stay here with the baby until I find someone suitable to watch her."

Before she could even feel relief, he pinned her with another of his cold stares.

"Just remember this is temporary. And I'm not letting you out of my sight."

* * *

Thirty minutes later, Lucy steered her car onto the Dallas tollway toward her condo. Normally she was a fairly calm driver—if perhaps overly cautious. But who wouldn't be in her profession? After all, she spent her days crunching numbers, calculating the odds of a person dying in a fiery car crash. In general, actuaries were very safe drivers. Today, however, she was a nervous wreck.

No doubt it had something to do with the fact that Dex was seated beside her. Since she and Isabella were going to be living in his house for at least the next few days, they needed clothes, formula, diapers…the gazillion things an infant needed. When she'd pointed this out to Dex, his first reaction had been to call the local baby superstore and have one of everything delivered. She'd quickly vetoed that idea.

No, if they were going through with this ridiculous plan, then Lucy wanted to retain what little control she had. And the very last thing she wanted was to make any of this easier on Dex. She certainly wasn't going to help him outfit a nursery for Isabella at his house. At the end of the two weeks—if not before—she intended to walk out of his life, taking Isabella and all of her stuff with her.

As she navigated the busy Dallas traffic, she kept up a constant mental litany of reasons why he should trust her with Isabella.

The second he'd gotten into the car, he'd shoved the seat back as far as it could go, stretched his denim-covered legs out in front of him, tipped his head back and closed his eyes. Unless she was mistaken, he'd fallen asleep. Probably taking advantage of the few blessed minutes of silence.

She remembered all too well the few nights she'd been up all night long with Isabella. They were as frustrating as they were exhausting.

Perhaps fatigue explained his behavior so far, which had ranged from rude to suspicious to downright insulting. Or perhaps he just thought she had it coming, after abandoning Isabella on his doorstep. But she couldn't feel sorry for Dex, despite what Jewel had put him through in the past twenty-four hours. Her first concern had to be Isabella's welfare.

Before showing up at his house, only two possible scenarios had occurred to her. Either he would have immediately contacted child protective services or he would have been so eager to get rid of Isabella, he wouldn't have questioned Lucy when she came to take her off his hands.

She'd never considered the possibility that he wouldn't want to give up the baby.

After all, from what she knew about Dex Messina, he was the jet set, playboy, black sheep of the Messina family.

As soon as she'd found out Jewel was pregnant with his child, Lucy had given in to her curiosity and run a Google search him. As wealthy and powerful as the Messina family was, it wasn't hard to find information about him.

What she'd learned had only been confirmed this morning when she'd met him in person. He was surly, un-approachable and…just difficult. More importantly, he didn't want to be a father. His rush to take the paternity test proved that, didn't it? And how could she help but resent being accused of being irresponsible by a man with Dex's reputation?

By the time she pulled her car into the spot outside her condo, she was practically fuming.

No one loved Isabella like she did. She was the best person to care for her. She knew it in her heart. Now, she just had to convince Dex.

Three

"Is all this really necessary?" Dex eyed the growing pile of baby accoutrements, which had begun to collect by the door.

"Babies need a lot of things," she called from the upstairs bedroom. "This is why I didn't want you to buy all new things."

Isabella—no doubt exhausted from her earlier rampage—lay asleep in her car seat on the living room floor.

The woman—and, damn it, why couldn't he remember her name?—emerged from the stairs carrying a suitcase. She dropped it by the door and immediately moved on to the kitchen. She'd changed from the miniskirt and heels into jeans and white Keds, a combination that took her skimpy pink tank top from tawdry to tomboy. The effect was oddly appealing in its wholesomeness. He half expected her to pull a baseball glove out of her back pocket and suggest they toss a few around in the backyard, or maybe offer him a slice of apple pie and a glass of lemonade.

Dex followed her into the kitchen, propped his shoulder against the doorway and watched as she moved about the tiny room.

She wasn't the sort of woman whose company he normally sought out. Despite the bright hair, there was nothing exotic about her. Nothing overtly sexual and enticing. Nothing flamboyant. Nothing that screamed, "For a good time, call…"

Instead, there was an efficiency about her, a sort of no-frills, no-nonsense simplicity that made her a pleasure to watch.

It wasn't that he was only attracted to party-girl bimbos. But he wasn't a long-term relationship kind of guy. He traveled a lot and didn't have the time or energy to devote to relationships. When he was in the country, his business commitments kept him busy enough without adding a needy girlfriend into the mix.

So how had he ended up sleeping with… "Damn it, what is your name?"

She looked up, her eyes wide and startled. "Lucy." Then she looked back down to frantically dig through the cupboard. "I mean, my legal name is Jewel. But I go by Lucy. Lucy Alwin."

She dropped a handful of plastic baby bottles into a paper grocery sack and rubbed her palms on her jeans.

"I make you nervous."

She started to lick her lips, but seemed to realize that only proved his point and pressed them firmly together. "Yes, you do."

"Why?"

She giggled. "You have to ask? You hold the fate of my child in your hands."

"Our child," he corrected. As he said the words, he felt something shift deep inside him.

That infant in the other room—the one who had frustrated and annoyed him so, who had thrown his life into upheaval—had been created when he'd had sex with this woman. When he'd stripped off her clothes, caressed her skin and plunged his seed deep into her body.

Almost as if she could read his thoughts, Lucy's eyes grew wider and she took a step backward. Her chest was rising and falling rapidly and the movement drew his gaze to the soft curve of her breasts.

He willed himself to remember what her breasts looked like, how they'd felt in his palms, but the memory didn't surface.

It had been so long ago. His memories of her were just snatches. Her enticing smile, the sway of her hips, the taste of tequila on her breath.

None of those images jived with the woman standing before him.

Maybe it was the way her simple jeans and tank top minimized the luscious curves of her body without hiding them. Or maybe it was the way she'd rocked Isabella in her arms, the very icon of maternity. Or the way she smelled faintly of baby powder.

Combined, they made her seem so wholesome. Almost innocent.

He might even buy it, if he hadn't picked her up in a bar and slept with her.

But because he had, he couldn't help wondering what it would be like to do so again. Without the liquor this time. With his senses fully intact. And he couldn't think of a damn reason not to.

Other than the fact that she'd already deceived him. She may not have lied outright, but wasn't having his child without telling him the worst lie of omission? But of course, sleeping with her and trusting her weren't the same thing at all.

He smiled wickedly at her. "I do hold your fate in my hands. You should remember that."

Part of him expected her to balk or shy away from him. Instead, she bumped her chin up and met his gaze straight on.

"Yes, you do. But that doesn't mean I'm going to let you bully me."

"Bully you?"

"Don't pretend you don't know what I'm talking about." She faced him with her hands on her hips. There was the faintest tremble in her voice, but he could tell she struggled to control it. "There you are, looming in my kitchen doorway, leering at me like the big bad wolf, ready to gobble me up if I make one wrong move."

He closed the distance between them. "If I'm the big bad wolf, what does that make you?" He tweaked a lock of bright red hair. "Little red riding hood?"

She swatted his hand away and narrowed her gaze at him. "Just remember how that story ended. Little Red Riding Hood learned her lesson and the wolf came to a bad end."

"Don't worry, red. I have no doubt you know how to take care of yourself. You've done a bang-up job so far."

"What's that supposed to mean?"

"The elaborate show of maternal care. The wide-eyed innocence. The sorrowful regret for your mistakes. It's all very touching. But don't think for a minute I've fallen for it."

"All very touching?" The pitch of her voice rose sharply and her chin bumped up another notch.

She stepped closer to him, hands still propped on her hips defiantly as she got right in his face. Or as close to his face as she could get, considering she had to be close to a foot shorter than him.

"You think I'm somehow faking my emotions? That my concern for Isabella, that my regret, is somehow planned? Is part of some scheme? Why would I do that? What could I possibly hope to achieve?"

"I don't know. You tell me."

For a moment, her mouth opened and closed rapidly, like a fish gaping in the air. Then she snapped it closed and shook her head. "What kind of person do you think I am?"

He stared down into her green eyes and felt bitter anger coil through his gut.

"I think you're the kind of woman to have a baby without letting the father know it's his."

Her face went white, then she threw up her hands in frustration as she turned away from him. "Well, that's hardly my fault."

He grabbed her arm and spun her back around to face him, surprised by his sudden burst of anger and looking for a way to vent it. "Then whose fault is it?"

She pressed her hands into his chest, trying to wedge some room between them, but he didn't release his hold on her. "This is the twenty-first century. It's gauche to blame a woman for getting pregnant. Not to mention ignorant. We're both responsible for what happened that night."

"I'm not talking about what happened that night. I'm talking about your decision afterward not to tell me you were pregnant."

"Funny, I don't recall us exchanging phone numbers before we parted ways. Maybe you should make a note of that for the next time you decide to pick up a woman in a bar."

The words "pick up a woman in a bar" were said with more than a hint of scorn. As well as a healthy dose of indignation. As if she were an innocent bystander to this train wreck.

"Don't make me into the villain here."

"Then don't me make into the villainess." She tugged again at her arm and this time he let her pull herself free. "I made a decision. I thought it was the right one at the time. You're not exactly a model of upstanding responsibility. It never occurred to me that you'd *want* to know you were going to be a father."

And until this moment, it hadn't occurred to him, either. Hell, he still wasn't sure he *wanted* to be a father. That was an issue that was going to take a lot more than just one day to get used to.

But he did know this: given the choice of having a five-month-old baby sprung on him versus having eight or so months to get used to the idea, he definitely would have preferred the latter.

This whole damn situation made his head pound and his gut twist into knots. And the woman before him—innocent appearance aside—was the one responsible. If that wasn't bad enough, she honestly thought she had his whole personality—his whole life—summed up in one word: *irresponsible*.

"Look, you don't know anything about me. You knew me for less than one night. If you want to judge whether or not I have what it takes to be a father, you're going to have to stick around a lot longer than that."

"Don't worry. I plan to. But for the record, I didn't base my decision not to tell you on just one night."

"Okay, I know that's the only time we met. Unless there's something else you're not telling me."

She blanched but recovered quickly. "That's not what I meant. You don't exactly live a low-profile life. You're in the gossip columns every time you're in the country. And Messina Diamonds is in the business section when you're not."

He rocked back on his heels. "Ah, so that's what this is about."

"What?"

"Your sudden appearance on my doorstep. You were flipping through the paper one day, happened across a mention of me and put two and two together. I'm only surprised it took you this long to figure out what I was worth."

"You think this is about money?"

"What else would it be about it?"

"Not that. I can tell you that much. Financially, I'm doing just fine."

He looked around the generic two-bedroom condo. "Yeah, you're really rolling in it."

Indignation shot through her, stiffening her spine. She must have grown a full inch. "I'll have you know I make very good money. For a normal person. If I appear to live modestly, it's because I put plenty of money into my retirement fund and because I live within my means. But I do live very comfortably, thank you very much."

Her indignation was so complete he might have been convinced. If his gut wasn't screaming at him that she was hiding something.

"If it's not money you want, then what is it?"

"I just want Isabella. That's all. Is that so hard to believe?"

"Yes it is. Considering that less than twenty-four hours ago you abandoned her."

Four

"I assume this room will be sufficient."

Lucy looked around the elegantly appointed guest room. A room large enough that even the king-sized mahogany bed didn't seem out of place. The classical lines of the furniture blended beautifully with the beige raw silk duvet cover and the ecru mohair throw draped artfully across the corner of the bed. The attached guest bath, outfitted with travertine tile and buff marble, was as large as her bedroom and twice as luxurious. It was all very…cream.

The room was lovely in a blandly elegant kind of way. The rest of the house—that she'd seen so far—was the same: ridiculously spacious and decorated with refined sophistication. In short, the house looked unlived in. It wasn't a home, it was a museum. And clearly one in which a baby had never spit up her iron-fortified formula. Isabella was sure to change that.

From the corner of her eye, she shot Dex a dirty look. "Yeah. It'll do."

It would constantly remind her that she didn't belong here. That despite her protestations that she lived comfortably, the Messina definition of *comfortable* varied greatly from hers.

A reminder she didn't need and appreciated even less.

"Shall I set up this…thing?"

He held the twenty-five-pound portacrib in one hand as if it weighed no more than a briefcase.

"No. I'll do it. They can be tricky."

In truth, it wasn't that difficult. But she didn't want him feeling comfortable with any of Isabella's things. Besides, after the visit to her condo, she needed a break from him.

He looked from her to the ExerSaucer, where Isabella sat gurgling happily while she spun one of the chair's many doodads. Lucy took little comfort in how nervous he looked. But, she supposed, a little comfort was better than none.

"Well, then. I'll let you get settled. Dinner will be served at seven."

"Dinner will be served?"

"While you were packing, I called Mavis, our house-keeper, and arranged for her to make a full meal. Normally, she just leaves something in the fridge for Derek or me to heat up. But with Isabella here I figured she'd need something more."

She stared at him in confusion for a moment, trying to make sense of his words. "Isabella is five months old. She doesn't even eat baby food yet."

"Oh."

"You didn't try to feed her real food when you were alone with her, did you?"

"No. There were two cans of formula in the bag you left. I fed her those."

"Thank God."

But the way his lips tightened made her wonder if he tried the formula before or after trying to feed her a hamburger or something absurd.

"Dinner will be served at seven," he repeated. "Even if she won't eat it, presumably you will."

"Of course." He was already out the door when she muttered, "But I could have just cooked my own food like a normal human being."

He stuck his head back through the doorway. "What was that?"

"Sounds great." She smiled brightly in the face of his suspicious glare. "I'm looking forward to it."

"Yeah. That's what I thought you said." Though his expression made it clear he didn't believe anything of the sort.

This time, she followed him to the door, closed it behind him and then collapsed against it with a sigh. Across the room, Isabella sat in her ExerSaucer.

"Look at the mess your momma has gotten us into this time."

Isabella's head tilted to the side, a slightly puzzled expression on her face.

"Don't you worry, though," Lucy said, crossing to the bed where her purse lay. "I'll fix this. I promise."

Lucy dug through her purse and pulled out her cell phone. When her call was shuffled over to Jewel's voice mail, she spoke low into the phone.

"Damn it, Jewel, I need to talk to you. Still. I've got Isabella. She's fine. But I'm staying at Dex Messina's house, so don't bother trying me at home." She almost hung up, but then at the last moment added, "And by the way, I've got over a dozen books on how to take care of babies. You couldn't have stuck one of those in the diaper bag for Dex?"

As she dropped the phone back in her bag, she noticed the thin sheaf of papers she'd gotten from her lawyer just last week. Papers that would give her full custody of Isabella. Papers she hadn't yet gotten Jewel to sign.

Pulling her suitcase behind her she crossed to the dresser. She quickly unpacked her clothes into the top two drawers, carefully burying the bundle of papers beneath her stash of bras and panties.

How in the world had she found herself in this mess? And here, she'd always tried so hard to do the right thing. To be the good sister.

Sure, she'd been cleaning up her sister's messes all her life. She usually did it in her own way—logically, without lies or deception. But this? This desperate scheme to get Isabella back seemed almost like something Jewel would do. Living in Dex's house for two weeks while she pretended to be Isabella's mother? The plan was farcical. No, scratch that. It wasn't a *plan* at all. It was a series of irrational decisions held together with nothing more than hope and luck. It would never work. Except it *had* to work.

She rubbed her fingers over her forehead, wishing she could rub away the tension gathering there. Unfortunately, that was as futile as trying to coax some warmth out of Dex.

"I'm not going to let that awful man raise you."

Isabella looked toward the door and cooed. Almost as if she knew exactly which awful man Lucy was talking about. Lucy frowned. Isabella's coo hadn't sounded nearly as traumatized as Lucy would have expected, given all the poor girl had been through.

"Okay, honey, you're just going to have to take my word on this. That is not the kind of man you want raising you. He's cold and emotionally unavailable."

Not unlike her own father. After their mother had up and

walked out on them, he had left them to be raised largely by nannies and sitters. They had both suffered from his neglect in their own way.

Lucy had often thought things had been worse for Julie—this was back when she was Julie, before she'd legally changed her name to the more sophisticated Jewel.

Jewel had been their mother's darling, whereas Lucy had been largely ignored. Jewel had been spoiled and coddled, treated like a pampered lapdog. Until the day their mother had just left without warning or apology.

For Lucy, who was used to being ignored by both parents, things had gone on pretty much as they always had. Jewel, who was used to their mother's elaborate shows of affection, had pulled one outrageous stunt after another trying to get their father's attention. And when that hadn't worked, the attention of any man.

And now Jewel had done the unthinkable. She'd abandoned her own baby. But Isabella would never suffer from it. Not if Lucy had anything to say about it.

She dropped down on her knees before Isabella. "I'm not going to let that happen to you. No psychological freezer burn for you."

And Dex was certainly the kind of man to freeze out his child. She'd seen the way he'd treated Isabella so far. He hadn't held her. Had barely even looked at her.

"Here's the thing about Dex Messina. He fools a lot of people, but you can't let him fool you. He pretends to be the laid back, easygoing younger brother. The one you don't have to worry about. But you've got to keep your eye on him. Don't let him too close."

Lucy saw past that facade of his.

She'd done her research—long before she'd ever even met him. She'd read everything she could find about him.

Derek may have the reputation as the heartless businessman, but Dex wasn't to be trifled with, either. He was the
brother who negotiated deals and wooed investors. The
more she thought about it, the more she realized he wasn't
really the black sheep of the family. No, he was the wolf
in black sheep's clothing.

Definitely not the warm and responsive dad she'd
choose for Isabella.

Emotionally unavailable, certainly. But cold? Maybe that
wasn't quite the right word. Heat had simmered in his gaze
every time he'd looked at her. His touch had nearly scalded
her. Passion seemed to lurk just beneath his surface, surging
forward at every reminder of the night they'd spent together.

Except *they* hadn't spent a night together.

They had never met before twenty-four hours ago.

He might remember a night of passionate sex with a
tempting vixen, but it wasn't *her* he remembered. No,
whatever emotion or passion he remembered was for
another woman entirely.

She sighed and rocked back on her heels, resisting the
urge to bury her head in her hands and just cry. Because
whether or not Dex wanted her or not was completely
beside the point. Because if he ever found out that she
wasn't the woman he'd slept with—that she wasn't
Isabella's mother—he'd guarantee she never got custody
of Isabella. He'd destroy all her hopes for the future.

And she wasn't going to let that happen.

Jet lag followed by a near sleepless night up with
Isabella should have been enough to knock him out completely. And it did. But for only a few hours. By three in
the morning he was awake again and pacing the length of
the guesthouse's living room.

Not for the first time, he crossed to the bay of windows looking out over the pool. He pressed his forearm to the window and leaned his forehead to his arm. He couldn't take his eyes off the window of the room where he'd put Lucy and Isabella.

Dinner had been a chilly affair. Even little Isabella seemed to feel the tension. If he didn't know better, he'd say they'd had some kind of powwow and had mutually decided to give him the cold shoulder.

Or maybe they just both sensed how nervous he was. What did he know about babies?

Absolutely nothing.

Until last night, it had never even occurred to him that he might have one in his life.

The concept of settling down, getting married, having kids…those were just things Derek hassled him about. Which Dex had always considered ironic since Derek wasn't exactly Mr. Commitment himself.

No, Derek was one hundred percent married to his job, with only the occasional extramarital affair with things like dinner and sleep. Women ranked a distant fourth. *Marriage* might as well have been a word from another language. Dex's list might look different, but kids were just as far down it.

Except now he had one. And he didn't know what the hell to do with it.

All he knew was that he was damn sure going to do a better job than his own father had done.

Which was probably why, when he saw the light go on in Lucy's room, he immediately headed for his closet and pulled out a pair of jeans.

By the time he'd pulled them on, a procession of lights blazed from the second story east wing down to the kitchen. He slipped down the stairs and crossed the slate patio to the French doors of the kitchen, where he let himself in with his key.

Lucy looked up when he entered. She was dressed in a white cotton tank top and a pair of denim shorts that left the length of her legs exposed. Her legs were lightly tanned without being the baked brown of a woman who frequented the tanning salon. Her feet were bare, her toes painted a delicate pink.

The picture she presented would have been nearly irresistible if it hadn't been for the crying infant she held in her arms.

"She did that last night when I was taking care of her, too," he said as he typed in the code to disarm the alarm.

"Did what?"

"That crying thing. I couldn't get her to stop."

"Did you feed her?"

"No. Raina—Derek's assistant—said to give her a bottle when she woke up at one. But this was at four or five."

The look Lucy shot him said it all.

She crossed to a cabinet and pulled out a bowl, which she filled with water and then stuck in the microwave to heat. The hum from the microwave must have soothed Isabella because her crying slowed to the occasional whimper.

Lucy's silence confirmed it. She thought he was an idiot.

"Hey," he said in his defense. "She couldn't have been hungry, she'd just eaten a couple of hours earlier."

This time he could have sworn even Isabella shot him a dirty look before nuzzling her face into Lucy's neck. The scene they made, snuggling together in the dimly lit kitchen was charmingly intimate. Not to mention exclusionary.

They were a pair, those two. A family complete without him.

Resentment rushed through him. That was *his* daughter.

His daughter who cringed away from him. His daughter who cried when he held her. Whom he didn't know how to care for or feed.

All because Lucy had kept her from him. Because she'd denied him his rights.

Part of him wanted to lash out at her. Yet something held him back. Maybe it was the darkened intimacy of the kitchen. The late-night feeding. The simple domesticity of it.

He didn't want to be angry with her. He just wanted to be a part of it. To have his daughter not flinch from his touch.

The microwave beeped just as Lucy returned from the pantry with a canister of formula. She blinked as if surprised he was still there.

"You don't have to stay. I don't need your help."

"Obviously." Derek accused him of always taking the easy way out. Well, not this time. "But I'm up. And I have to learn how to do it sometime. It might as well be now."

She eyed him suspiciously for a moment, then stepped away from the can of formula. "Okay. First you wash your hands."

She guided him step by step. She stood stiffly beside him, with Isabella turned carefully away from him, almost as if Lucy didn't want her to see him preparing the bottle.

A few minutes later the bottle was warmed and he held out his arm for Isabella. Lucy frowned but handed her over. Her expression made him feel like he was ripping the infant from her arms. Isabella's instant cries of protest didn't help matters.

He lowered himself to one of the bar stools along the counter and mimicked the posture he'd seen Lucy use when she'd fed Isabella after dinner. He held Isabella out in front of him, cradled along one arm, her head in his hand, so she faced him. Her face scrunched up in apparent agony as she waved her little fists around, howling all the while.

Lucy hovered nervously behind him, ratcheting up his tension level.

"Do you want me to take her?"

"No, I can do it."

"Oh, I'm sure you can do it. But maybe you could try some other time. When she's not hungry."

He'd done some pretty crazy stuff, back before he'd settled into his current respectable position in the company. He'd crossed the Alaskan tundra in a dog sled. He'd spent a season living with a Bedouin tribe in the Sahara. He'd climbed Mount Kilimanjaro, for Christ's sake. He could do this.

He could feed one tiny infant.

Lucy must have sensed his determination because she leaned over his shoulder and wrapped her hand around his hand holding the bottle.

"You don't just shove it in her face. You have to let her know it's here if she wants it. Just rub it across her lips like this."

She moved his hands to run the bottle's nipple along Isabella's bottom lip. Slowly, Isabella's cries faded and she sucked the bottle into her mouth. She continued to gaze at him with rebellion in her eyes, but she drank greedily. Triumph surged through him.

After a moment, he became aware of Lucy's hand on his shoulder, of the warmth of her pressed against his back and along his arm. The smell of her seemed to envelope him. Something feminine and sleepy and sweet. If he turned his face, his lips would brush her cheek.

For an instant, he felt like he was part of the family. Part of the bond they shared.

Instantly, panic blossomed in his chest. *Run!* it screamed. *Get out now. Write the woman a generous check and show her the door!*

But he shoved the feeling aside, forced his heartbeat to slow and bellied up to the bar of responsibility. He wasn't that guy anymore—that guy who dodged his obligations in favor of a good time. He didn't want to be that guy. Okay, he *mostly* didn't want to be that guy.

With no appreciation for his internal struggle at all, Lucy jerked her hand away. She quickly put space between them, rounding to the other side of the counter where she bustled around the kitchen putting up the formula and rinsing out the bowl she'd heated the water in.

Isabella's eyes had drifted closed. She had one hand on the bottle, as if she was trying to hold it herself. With the other hand, she reached up and grabbed one of his fingers where it held the bottle. The tiny palm was warm against his skin. Something clenched deep within his chest.

"You do this every night?"

"Feed Isabella? Sure. It's usually only once or twice."

And she'd been doing this every night since Isabella was born. "You must be exhausted."

"Oh, it's not so bad. This time, in the middle of the night, it's kind of our time. I don't get to see her during the day when I'm at work."

"You work?" He asked the question without thinking and immediately wished he could take it back.

She stiffened, her head jerking up. "Of course I work. How did you think I supported myself?"

"What was I supposed to think? You said you could take care of Isabella during the day for the next couple of weeks."

She stilled, ducking her head. "I have to take time off work. It's not a big deal. I've got some vacation coming."

He didn't press her on this vacation time she'd be taking. It was obviously not something she wanted to talk about.

Besides which, after a few more minutes, Isabella began

to drift off to sleep, her body growing more and more relaxed, her eyes drifting closed, her rhythmic sucking slowing to just the occasional twitch.

When her mouth fell open and he pulled the bottle from her lips, his sense of accomplishment was astonishing. Mount Kilimanjaro? Bah. That was nothing.

Lucy took the bottle from him and brought it the sink to rinse out. When she returned, she held out her arms to take Isabella.

How crazy was it that he didn't want to let her go? Twenty-four hours ago, before he'd known she was his, when she was crying her head off, he would have been happy to hand her off to the first stranger who walked through the door.

But now? Now that he'd fed her and felt her fall asleep in his arms. Now that he seemed on the verge of…

Of what? He didn't know, but he just didn't want to let her go.

"I'll take her now."

He looked up at Lucy and felt the familiar stab of resentment. He had to force himself to hand Isabella back to Lucy, but he did it. After all, he wasn't the expert here, she was.

What did he really know about taking care of a baby other than it was a hell of lot harder than the sitcoms made it look.

The tender way Lucy took Isabella from his arms, the way she shushed her when she stirred and rocked gently from side to side, the almost greedy way she clutched her to her chest as she silently walked from the room—it left him wondering.

Lucy clearly adored Isabella. She would do anything for her. Hell, she'd taken two weeks of vacation so she could move into a stranger's house and care for her.

So how had this woman abandoned her baby on that same stranger's doorstep?

Once again, his gut was telling him something wasn't right with Lucy. It was time to find out what.

Five

The following afternoon, Lucy sat in her idling car, her frustrations mounting. She and Isabella had escaped the oppressive atmosphere of the house for the morning. If she had hopes of sneaking back in unnoticed, they were dashed before she even made it inside. Dex's SUV was hogging the driveway. Big, arrogant, presumptuous.

She'd never liked SUVs. They took up too much of the road. They were pushy. Insensitive to the needs of others. And this one practically gloated that it would be a better mode of transportation for Isabella.

Stifling the sudden urge to gun her car and ram the thing, she shifted into Park and set the brake.

Okay. So she was irrationally transferring her resentment to an innocent SUV. The truth was, she was scared.

Not just a little nervous, but honest to God, quaking-in-her-boots terrified that she was going to lose Isabella and that nothing short of absconding to Mexico could prevent it.

She'd been to visit her lawyer that morning. The news wasn't good. In addition to giving her a talking down the likes of which she hadn't had since grade school, he'd told her what she already knew. By bringing Dex into the equation, Jewel had really mucked up Lucy's chances of getting full custody of Isabella. Lying to him about her identity had only made things worse. Much worse.

Her lawyer had thrown around terms like "fraud" and "culpability." He was almost as bad as her own conscience.

"Damn it, damn it, damn it." She banged her head against the steering wheel with each "damn it." Unfortunately, it didn't make her feel any better. And it didn't stop her mind from racing.

So far, lying to Dex had only pushed her further away from what she wanted. When she'd decided to pretend to be Isabella's mother, it had seemed so simple.

But now she was caught in her lies. If she told him the truth, he'd never let her see Isabella again. But could she really continue to lie to him? She didn't have a choice.

A sharp rap sounded on the door frame. She jumped guiltily and whipped to face the noise.

Dex. Of course.

She pressed a palm to her chest to calm her thundering heart, then leveraged the door open and climbed out.

He eyed her suspiciously. "What's wrong?"

She couldn't meet his gaze. "You startled me. That's all." She glanced down at her watch. "It's only four. What are you even doing home?"

"I came home early to check on you. I got worried when you didn't answer the phone."

He was standing entirely too close, with one hand pressed to the roof of the car. His mere presence made her feel all jittery.

It's only because he has so much power over you.

But no matter how many times she told herself that, she wasn't sure she believed it.

"Let me guess," she quipped as she ducked under his arm to reach Isabella's door. She swung open the door so she'd at least have that barrier between them. "You thought that in an act of rebellion, Isabella had knocked me unconscious and gone out for a joy ride."

"No. I thought you'd panicked again, taken Isabella and left."

There seemed to be a note of genuine concern in his voice. She paused and looked up at him. The sun was in his eyes and he squinted as he looked down at her, making his expression unreadable.

"I would never do that."

And yet, just a few minutes ago, she'd been contemplating just that. Not seriously, true. But the thought had crossed her mind.

"I mean it," she said, and found to her surprise, she really did. "I won't just leave. I promise. I'll do everything in my power to convince you to let me keep Isabella. But I won't skip out on you."

Was it her imagination, or did he relax a little at her words?

Guilt stabbed at her conscience. Was she judging Dex unfairly? Was she assuming he was a coldhearted monster merely because that was how she wanted to see him? The thought disturbed her more than she wanted to admit.

To keep him from asking where she'd been, she lied preemptively. "I just had to stop by the office to pick up a couple of files." She held up her briefcase as evidence, thankful she'd tossed it in the back of her car last Friday before any of this had happened. "I can usually get a little work done while Isabella is sleeping."

When she stood up holding the clunky car seat, he took it from her. Together—he carrying the baby, she carrying her briefcase and the diaper bag—they walked up the driveway to the house. For a moment, they felt eerily like any normal couple meeting in the driveway after work.

"What exactly is it you do?"

"I'm an actuary."

"An actuary?"

"I crunch numbers for an insurance company. Calculate risks, that kind of thing."

"I know what an actuary does, I'm just surprised. I've never met an actuary before. I didn't expect something so—"

"Geeky," she supplied.

"That's not what I was going to say."

"No, but you were searching for a more diplomatic word for it, weren't you?"

They'd reached the door, and as he opened it, he turned to face her fully, blocking her way in with his body. "Actually I was thinking I expected something more feminine."

The appreciative gleam in his eyes sent heat spiraling through her body. Once again she was aware of how tall he was. How much bigger than her. There was something predatory in his gaze that simultaneously made her want to surrender and flee. Or just tilt her head up to his, let her eyes drift closed and wait to be kissed.

Instead, she scoffed. "Trust me. Being an actuary is the perfect job for me."

It may be geeky—which was how Jewel always described it—but it was challenging and logical. It was a no-nonsense, fuss-free kind of job. Perfect for her.

Of course, she couldn't explain any of that to Dex because he didn't know what kind of person she really was. He thought of her as the exotic, charismatic woman he'd met in a bar one night. The kind of woman who enticed men and let them pick her up for one-night stands.

No wonder he thought the job wasn't feminine enough for her.

Just one more reminder of the deception she was perpetrating. If he found out who she really was, he wouldn't be looking at her with something akin to desire in his eyes. And of course her train of thought was ridiculous, anyway. If he knew the truth, whether or not he wanted her would be the least of her concerns. Whether or not he was going to kill her with his bare hands would be a tad bit higher on the list.

Equally unsettling was the easy way they'd been talking just now. At what point had they developed this easy rapport? She didn't remember it happening. Hadn't planned on being friendly with him.

He's the monster, remember? she told herself. *He's the man who's going to take Isabella away from you. He's not friendly. He's not charming. He's ruining your life.*

He walked ahead of her, still carrying Isabella, asleep in her car seat. Lucy stood by the back door, watching him as he headed into the living room. As he settled Isabella's car seat into a darkened spot, he reached down and brushed a fingertip across her cheek.

The tender gesture made Lucy's throat close and her heart tighten. She sank against the kitchen door as her strength of will drained out of her.

He might not be a monster, but he *was* going to take Isabella away from her. Watching him in this unguarded moment brought that home in a way nothing else yet had.

Until now, despite everything, she'd had hopes that… that what? Dex would just hand Isabella over to her?

No. That wasn't going to happen. As long as he believed he was her father, he would fight for custody.

But what if…

Lucy straightened and stared blankly ahead in shock.

"What if she's not his?" Almost without meaning to, she muttered the words under her breath.

"What do you mean she might not be mine?"

She jerked her head around to find him standing not four feet away. For a long moment, Lucy simply gaped at him, panic clutching her heart.

"Well," she began nervously. "It's not like we've done a paternity test yet, right? Until then, we won't really know for sure, now will we?"

"Is there someone else who could be the father?"

Ah, there's the rub.

She didn't think so. She had been at the bar the night Jewel had hooked up with Dex. She'd watched the whole thing from a distance, shocked her sister would even flirt with one of the men who ran the company where she worked. Only later had Lucy learned that Jewel had been fired from Messina Diamonds mere days before.

As far as Lucy knew, Dex was the only man Jewel had slept with that month. And Jewel had always been one to kiss and tell. Usually in way more detail than Lucy wanted. But what if Lucy was wrong? What if she didn't know her sister as well as she thought she did?

"I don't know," she answered honestly.

He eyed her for a long, slow minute, his gaze raking across her face, no doubt looking for signs of deceit. She prayed he wouldn't find them.

Finally, he said, "It's a simple question. The month you

got pregnant, how many men did you sleep with? Just me? Or did you sleep with some other guy, too, but you left Isabella on my doorstep because I was worth more?"

For an instant, the question actually confused her. *She* hadn't slept with any men the month Isabella was conceived. But of course that wasn't what he was really asking.

And as insulting as his insinuations were, she had no one to blame but herself. After all, it was her big mouth that had gotten her into this conversation.

As annoyed with herself as she was with him, she snapped, "What makes you think it's between just you and one other guy? Maybe there were dozens."

There. That ought to shut him up.

Instead of looking shocked or even offended, he laughed. Out loud, dang it.

"Nice try." He studied her for a minute more while his laughter subsided. Shaking his head ruefully, he said, "No, I don't buy it. I don't believe for a minute there was even one other guy, let alone dozens."

"There could be," she insisted defiantly.

"No. There couldn't be. You just aren't the type. You know what I think? I think our one night together was out of character for you."

He stepped closer to her, and she found herself backing up against the door.

"You don't know me well enough to know anything about my character," she protested. She was surprised how breathless her voice sounded, how weak her protest was. How the pounding of her own heart seemed to close in on her.

"Ah," he murmured, reaching up to tuck a lock of her hair behind an ear. "But I'm an excellent judge of character. And you don't strike me as the kind of woman who's been with a lot of men. You're too innocent for that."

She felt a blush moving into her cheeks and cursed herself. Jewel wouldn't blush at this. Jewel never blushed.

"Look at you," he continued, brushing the backs of his knuckles against her hot cheeks. "You're blushing. Women who've slept with a dozen men in a month don't blush."

Trying for far more bravado than she felt, she knocked his hand away and said, "Oh, and I suppose you know women like that."

But he chuckled and ignored her. "Besides you're an actuary."

"So?"

"Actuaries don't take risks. They think things through. They plan. They organize."

She couldn't deny it. And why would she want to. She'd always taken such pride in her logical approach to life.

Yet standing here, with Dex so close she could feel the heat of his body… So close she could smell him, musky and masculine. And dangerous. She wanted to be the kind of woman who did take risks. Who threw caution to the wind.

"No," he continued, stroking her jawline with a light, tremor-inducing touch. "I bet our night together was a once-in-a-lifetime thing. I bet it really threw you for a loop. I bet you've been wondering how you could ever have done such a thing."

Of course, he was right. How many times had she wondered just that? How could Jewel sleep with men she barely knew? How could she engage in such reckless, selfish behavior?

And yet, in that instant, Lucy knew exactly how Jewel must feel. She wanted a little recklessness herself. She craved that wild restless heat.

"And I bet you haven't stopped thinking about it for a

minute. I bet you're even wondering what it would be like if it happened again."

She was. Which was why, when he leaned down to kiss her, she rose on her toes meet him.

Six

Kissing Lucy was pure heaven.

Her lips were soft and silky. Her mouth, warm and sensual. The heat of response shocked him. She didn't just kiss him back, she plastered herself against him, pouring herself into the kiss.

Her lips parted almost instantly, her body pressing up to his, her tongue stroking against his with an eagerness that inflamed his blood.

Even as he felt his body hardening in response, he knew he'd been right about her innocence. There was no expertise in her. No pretense or artifice.

Just passion.

And he couldn't wait to explore that passion.

His hands sought her hips, pulling her even closer, his fingers slipping up under her shirt to the silky skin of her midriff.

A moment later, he filled his palm with her breast. She moaned low in her throat as he rubbed his thumb across her nipple.

He couldn't get enough of her.

He wanted more. More than this teenage groping. He wanted her naked and arching against him.

But before he could maneuver her toward a horizontal surface, she pressed her palms against his chest and shoved.

He pulled back from her, satisfied that at least she was breathing even harder than he was.

"That was a mistake," she said almost immediately.

"I disagree." He'd stopped kissing her, but he wasn't about to stop touching her altogether. His hand lingered at her hip, relishing her voluptuousness, the lush generosity of her body. "In fact, I can't imagine why we haven't done this before."

"Stop that," she ordered, swatting at his hand and moving out of his reach. "We haven't done this before because it's a bad idea. We can't get involved."

He raised his eyebrows. "We have a child together. We're already involved."

She glared at him, her eyebrows knitting into a fierce frown. "I meant, involved beyond that."

Damn, but she was cute when she was trying to look fierce.

"I know what you meant. But we've already slept together once. There's nothing keeping us from doing it again."

"That's male logic for you," she quipped.

"No, that's just logic. But if that doesn't work, how about this. We're adults. We want each other, that should be enough."

"But it isn't. Regardless of whether we want—" she stumbled over the word *want* and another blush crept into her cheeks "—each other, there are other things to consider.

You said it yourself, we're adults. To me at least, that means we act responsibly. We don't just do whatever we want the instant we want to do it."

The way she emphasized the word *responsibly* set his teeth on edge. "Don't you think it's a little late to be lecturing me about responsible behavior?"

She seemed to be biting back a response. Or maybe just searching for an answer that would turn the conversation to her liking.

"Whatever else I may have done in the past, you've got to believe that now my biggest concern is doing what's right for Isabella." Her voice was hot with emotion, dense with yearning to make him understand. "I know I've made mistakes, but from here on out, I swear I'm always going to put her first. And she deserves more than two parents who would make a bad situation worse because of a momentary flash of desire."

With that, she scooped Isabella's car seat off the floor and escaped toward her room with the still-sleeping child.

He let her go, smart enough to realize she was right about one thing. This wasn't the time.

For one thing, he still had too many questions about her. If he was right—and he'd bet half his fortune he was—and she really was that inexperienced, then what had she been doing in that bar fourteen months ago?

Why after years of cautious, responsible behavior had she picked him for her one-night stand?

If they'd met under other circumstances, he might have believed her uncharacteristic behavior that night was due entirely to the chemistry between them.

But she had approached him. And when she'd done so, she hadn't been timid or shy. She'd been bold and flirtatious in a way he hadn't seen since. She'd set out to seduce him. Which again brought him back to the question: why *him?*

Only one answer came to mind. She must have known about his money.

And if she'd known about his money, he wondered if she'd gotten pregnant on purpose. Had this seemingly sweet and innocent woman targeted him for a pregnancy scam for money?

Every bone in his body said she wasn't capable of doing that. Yet he knew she was lying about something.

Just that afternoon, he'd visited Quinton McCain. Quinn ran McCain Security, the firm that handled all the security for Messina Diamonds. He also happened to be one of Dex's best friends.

As head of his own very successful company, digging up dirt wasn't exactly the kind of thing Quinn normally did, but when Dex had explained the situation, Quinn hadn't blinked an eye. He'd merely whipped out his BlackBerry, jotted down what little Dex knew about Lucy and promised to find whatever dirt there was. Dex had the nagging suspicion Quinn wouldn't find much.

If conning money out of Dex had been her plan all along, why had Lucy waited so long to execute it? Why not come to him when she was pregnant? Why struggle through raising an infant alone for five months? And why had she left Isabella on his doorstep at all?

He kept coming back to that question. He simply couldn't reconcile the woman he knew with that one action. The longer he knew her, the more absurd it seemed that she'd done it at all.

Shaking his head, he crossed to the fridge, pulled out a cold Shiner and twisted off the cap. He sipped it as he crossed the patio to the guesthouse.

He needed something to clear his head, so he changed into his swim trunks and headed for the pool to swim laps.

As he stood poised on the diving board, he couldn't help wondering if Lucy was right. Maybe Isabella did deserve more.

But she was wrong about at least one thing. This wasn't some fleeting flash of desire. She may not have enough experience to know better, but he did. The chemistry between them was off the charts. Merely avoiding each other for the next two weeks wouldn't make it go away. At some point, they were going to have to deal with it.

Laps in a cold pool wouldn't work forever.

From the window of her room, Lucy watched Dex dive into the pool. As his lean, muscled body cut effortlessly through the water, she tried to tell herself she'd made the right choice. She'd made the *only* choice.

Her first concern had to be Isabella's welfare. Her own wants and needs were irrelevant.

Oh, but she had *wanted*. His kiss had sparked a fire in her she hadn't imagined she could feel. His touch had made her tremble. Even now, her breasts felt overly sensitive. Her blood seemed to pound, throbbing between her legs.

Frustrated, she spun away from the window and crossed to sit in the armchair beside Isabella's car seat. She crossed her legs, pressed them together, but that did little to ease the ache.

Damn him.

Damn him for making her want what she couldn't have. For making her miss what she'd resisted for so long.

He was right of course. It had been years—forever, it seemed—since she'd been with a man. So many of her previous relationships had been mediocre at best. And she wasn't Jewel, jumping carelessly from one man to the next, mindless of the risks such behavior incurred. She could never be so cavalier with her body or her emotions.

And now, apparently, she was paying the price in sexual frustration. Maybe if she had a fling every couple of months, she wouldn't now be in the position of desiring the one man she shouldn't want.

Lucy was avoiding him.

He'd come home earlier and earlier each night, yet every time Mavis had handed him his warmed-over food and told him Lucy had already eaten and was up in her room, "Trying to put Isabella down."

By day four, the phrase set his teeth on edge, probably because it evoked images of lame racehorses being shot out behind the stables.

Why Lucy's obvious avoidance of him bothered him so, he couldn't say. But he hadn't felt this ignored since child-hood, and that sure as hell wasn't an experience he wanted to revisit.

He told himself he should just be glad she was making this fatherhood thing so easy on him. So far, other than that first day he'd had Isabella all by himself, he'd done almost nothing to take care of her. He should be rejoicing. Instead, he was just plain irritated.

Which was why he left work at two on Friday, to force his way through the already chocked downtown traffic, to make it home by three in the afternoon. Unless Lucy was going to have Mavis smuggle her food up to her room, then damn it, she was going to eat her meal with him.

He bypassed the guesthouse altogether and headed straight for the main house, determined to catch Lucy in person. He stopped a few feet into the living room to stare at the scene before him.

The living room furniture had been shoved aside. Lucy had covered the floor with several fluffy cream-colored blankets, all of which bore suspicious brown splotchy stains. Mavis—who before today Dex had never once seen crack a smile—sat cross-legged on the floor, jostling a giggling Isabella on her knee while dangling a chain of plastic links before her grasping hands. Lucy lay on the floor beside them, her head propped up on one of the sofa's pillows, her bare feet resting on the edge of one of his brother's priceless Eames leather chairs. Mozart's "Eine Kleine Nachtmusik" played softly in the background. Over the music, Lucy was reading aloud from a paperback, the cover of which she'd folded back, so that she held it in one hand.

"'This little explanation with Mr. Knightly gave Emma considerable pleasure.'" A bowl of red grapes sat by her other hand, and she paused to pop a handful in her mouth before continuing. "'It was one of the agreeable recollections of the ball.'"

At that moment, Mavis looked up. For a second, she stared at him incomprehensibly, as if she didn't recognize him or couldn't imagine why he'd shown up to disrupt their idyllic afternoon.

"Miss Lucy." Mavis cleared her throat and sent a pointed look in his direction.

"'She was extremely glad…'" Lucy trailed off as she turned her head to glance in his direction. "Oh." She swung her feet off the chair and sprang up from her reclined position, knocking over the bowl of grapes in the progress. "Oh. Dex. What are you doing here?"

"I live here."

"But it's a Friday." She didn't meet his gaze, but hustled to pluck up the grapes, which were rolling haphazardly around the hills and wrinkles of the blanket. "In the middle of the afternoon. Shouldn't you be at work?"

"One of the benefits of being a VP," he said tersely.

Why did it bother him, how relaxed and calm she'd been just a moment ago and how nervous and tense she now seemed?

"Oh." She dropped a few more of the meandering grapes back into the bowl. "Yes. I suppose."

She stood and as she did so, he heard a faint pop and at the same time an expression of surprise crossed her face. "Oh." This time she muttered it with a cringe. She lifted her foot to reveal a squashed grape on the ball of her foot and a bright, oblong stain on the blanket. She sighed. "Well, I suppose we wouldn't have been able to get the formula stains out, anyway."

Mavis stood as well, clucking sympathetically. "Never you worry. It's just a comforter." She waved a hand dismissively. "I'll have it replaced and Mr. Derek will never know the difference."

Mavis shot him an angry glare as if daring him to whip out his cell phone and tattle on them that very instant. Then she handed Isabella over to Lucy and dusted her hands off on the dish towel she had hanging from the waistband of her khaki pants. Then she pulled the dish towel out and handed it to Lucy as well, who used it to wipe off her foot.

"Well, dinner won't be cooking itself, now will it?" she muttered as she huffed off in the direction of the kitchen, shooting him one last rebellious look.

"So." He shoved his hands into his pockets. "This is how you've been spending your days."

Lucy shifted Isabella into her other arm, without meeting his gaze. "Yes. I suppose it is." She passed the dish towel from one hand to the other as if unsure where to put it.

"Seems fun."

She bristled visibly and her eyes shot up to his. "This isn't just a vacation for me, if that's what you're implying."

"It wasn't."

"I rarely get to spend whole days with Isabella like this, but when I do, I make the most of our time."

"I didn't—"

"Listening to music, particularly classical music, has been shown in countless studies to increase a child's cognitive math and reasoning skills. And reading aloud to children, even babies, helps them develop a love of literature."

"I'm sure she's really enjoying—" he glanced down at the paperback Lucy had discarded when he'd entered "—Emma, is it?"

Lucy's already stiff spine straightened even more. "You think this is just a big joke?"

"Not at all."

She stomped off the blanket and bent down to pick it up. "I'll have you know, I take this very seriously."

Mozart continued to lilt in the background, a discordant backdrop to her harsh tone.

"Obviously."

Still holding Isabella, she struggled to bunch up the king-sized comforter. "Well, I'm sure you have more important things to do than belittle my work with Isabella. So we'll just get out of your way so you can have the living room all to yourself."

With that, she spun on her heel—as much as she could—and stalked—or rather tried to—from the room, the blanket trailing behind her like a train.

"Lucy, wait." The words left his mouth before he could stop himself.

She stopped but didn't turn around.

What was he doing? Why wasn't he just letting her go?

This was exactly the kind of emotional entanglement he'd spent his whole life avoiding. He'd never wanted a kid. Certainly not with a woman like Lucy. Not with someone he couldn't trust. So why didn't he just let her walk away? Why *couldn't* he let her walk away?

He didn't know. But he did know this—he'd come home early because he wanted—no, needed—to spend time with Isabella. Not just Isabella.

"I didn't come home early to belittle you."

Slowly she turned to face him, her expression guarded, her arms overflowing with both baby and comforter.

"I haven't seen you or Isabella in four solid days. There's no point in you living here with her if I never get to see her."

Lucy narrowed her gaze in a calculated manner, then gave a slight huff of indignation. "I couldn't agree more. I'll pack up our things and be out of here within the hour."

"That's not what I meant."

A sigh deflated her chest. "I was afraid of that."

"If this—" he gestured to spot in the living room where they'd been lounging "—is what you do with her during the day, then I'd like to—" he hesitated, looking for the right word "—participate."

"How?"

He crossed to her, mincing around the comforter and taking it from her arms. "Let's start by putting this back. And you can show me what you normally do with her."

She frowned as he spread the blanket out over the floor. "It's not complicated," she hedged.

And he could see from the glint in her eyes, she was looking for an excuse to bail on him.

"But as you said, it's important. Why don't you talk me through it?"

He kicked off his shoes and settled down on the comforter with his back against the sofa.

"Well," she began hesitantly. "She can't roll over yet, but she's close."

"Okay."

"So she needs a lot of belly time." When he looked at her blankly, Lucy added, "To strengthen her neck and arm muscles." She sat down a few feet away from him. "Here, like this."

She placed Isabella on her belly on the blanket and then lay down beside her, so their faces were at eye level. Isabella automatically wedged her arms under her shoulders and levered herself up to get a better look at Lucy.

"That's great, Isabella."

Isabella grinned in delight at her success.

Once again feeling excluded, Dex lowered himself to Isabella's other side. When he was at her level, she twisted to get a look at him, flashing him one of her adorable toothless grins. A band of emotion tightened around his heart.

He gazed past Isabella to Lucy, wanting to share the moment with her. For a moment, she just stared back, her eyes wide. Then she sucked in an audible breath and jerked to a sitting position.

"Well, looks like you've got that down pat." She scrambled back toward the chair. "If you want I can just leave you two alone."

"Aren't you going to read?"

"Read?"

"Yeah. You were reading to her when I came in. Didn't you say it would improve her cognitive abilities or something?"

"Um…yes. Something like that." Lucy fumbled to pick up the worn copy of *Emma* before raising herself to the chair and tucking her feet under her self-consciously.

As she flipped through the book to the spot she'd left off at in chapter thirty-nine, she was all too aware of her heart pounding in her chest. She didn't want to consider why it was beating so fast, though it seemed all too likely that Dex was the cause. The intolerable man was as sexy as he was annoying.

And what did he mean, coming home in the middle of a workday just so he could bond with Isabella? What was he doing, trying to be a real father? Ha! Likely story.

His appearance here just reminded her that she was living on borrowed time. What she needed was a plan of action. A surefire way to convince Dex that he should hand Isabella over to her. And maybe—just maybe—she knew just what needed to be done.

Seven

"I'm sorry," she lied. "There's nothing I can do about it."

Dex's expression was grim, but he nodded. "No problem."

"Are you sure? You'll be all alone with her for four, maybe five hours."

His mouth tightened, but when he spoke he sounded more resolute than scared. "I'll handle it. If you can't get out of this business dinner, then I'll watch her while you're gone."

It had been several days since he'd kissed her. In that time he'd made no further attempts.

She, however, had been very busy. She'd spent her time hatching a plan guaranteed to make him lose confidence in himself as a father.

It was ruthless. It was cruel. But it was for Isabella's own good.

Massive twinges of guilt aside, it was a good plan. She was going to leave Isabella alone with Dex for the evening.

Sure, it seemed simple enough, but Lucy had spent enough evenings alone with Isabella to know they could be brutal. The hours from six to ten were often fraught with crying, colic, sleeplessness and general fussiness. Plus, Isabella hadn't napped well today, so tonight was likely to go particularly badly.

As if to prove Lucy's point, Isabella picked that moment to scrunch up her face and let out a wail.

Dex shot a look of grim determination toward Isabella, who had been lounging innocently in her bouncy chair on the living room floor.

"Is there a number where you can be reached?"

Lucy sighed, as if it were a huge imposition, before rattling off her cell-phone number. "But this is a very important meeting for me. Call only if it's a true emergency."

He nodded as he typed the number into his own cell phone. "Got it. Only in an emergency."

And she felt only a teeny tiny bit guilty about leaving him alone with Isabella. He wanted to be a father? Well, here was his chance. This was what being a parent was all about. Making it through the rough times. Learning how to do it on your own.

She'd had plenty of nights when Isabella hadn't stopped crying no matter what she'd tried. Plenty of nights she'd wanted to pull out her hair. Or had wanted to just shoot Jewel for blithely going about her own life while she left Lucy to care for her daughter.

The simple truth was, this parenting gig wasn't for pansies.

And if she didn't leave now, she might not have the strength to put him through this ordeal, even though it was her last chance to convince him to give her Isabella.

She grabbed her purse and headed out. She turned one last time at the door. Dex stood under the imposing arch doorway leading from the foyer to the living room. His hands were on his hips as he stared down at the tiny crying Isabella.

"You going to be okay?" But she wasn't one-hundred-percent sure if it was a question or meant to be reassurance.

He looked up at her, his gaze steely and focused. "We'll be fine."

She nodded, but as she closed the door behind her and headed for her car, she knew they wouldn't.

Dex stared at Isabella for a long minute before letting panic settle over him. What kind of diabolical scheme was Lucy up to now?

He could hardly protest when she'd asked him to watch Isabella for a couple of hours tonight. After all, she'd been caring for her nonstop for a full week. Well, who was he kidding, for the past five months. Who was he to complain about just one night?

After all, he could do this. He'd been alone with her before and nothing bad had happened. Sure, she'd cried a lot and he'd ended up with a headache, but he could do this.

He could, he repeated to himself as he bent down, unlatched the straps from the seat and picked her up.

If possible, her cries grew even louder. She swung her fists toward his face like a tiny boxer, her lovely face turning red from exertion.

He held her at eye level to scope out the situation. Assess the damage. This was just a problem like any other. He could solve it. He just needed the right approach.

But man, was it good for her to be crying like this?

Great sobs shook her body and finally she had to pause to suck in a shuddering breath, before letting out another howl of outrage.

"Okay, there are only a few things that could be wrong with you to make you cry like this."

At the sound of his voice, Isabella's crying slowed. She opened her eyes to glare at him. She snuffled as if waiting to hear his opening offer.

"You could have a dirty diaper." He shifted her in his arms to peek through the leg of the tiny pink jumper she wore. "Nope. Not it. You could be hungry."

Except he'd seen Lucy feed her a bottle just before leaving.

"You could be tired. In which case you'll fall asleep before long."

Except he knew there were plenty of times he'd been traveling all day when he was just too tired to fall asleep. Hopefully that wouldn't be the case here.

Dex rattled off the next few options quickly, feeling less and less optimistic about them.

"You could miss Lucy. You could know that you're in the hands of an amateur. You could be panicking because you know I don't know what the hell I'm doing.

"And if that's the case, then we're both screwed."

Unfortunately, he'd been right.

Two hours later, after countless diaper changes, several warmed and then tossed bottles of formula, and what he was sure were ruptured eardrums, Dex could finally imagine why Lucy had left Isabella on his doorstep. Five months of this, and he might be willing to do the same.

In the end, he'd resorted to doing what he'd seen Lucy do to soothe her. He'd held her close to his chest, hummed in her ear and waltzed around the living room. By the time she started to calm down, his own pulse was returning to normal. After a solid forty-five minutes of waltzing, he was ready for a break. Since she seemed nearly asleep, he danced toward the sofa and sank to the edge.

Her eyes immediately opened and she let out a mewling protest.

"Come on, Izzie. Don't look at me like that. You just quieted down."

Remarkably, instead of howling her outrage, she cocked her head to the side, blinked her impossibly wide blue eyes at him and seemed to listen.

As soon as he settled back on the sofa to relax, she screwed up her face again and looked ready to scream, so he kept talking.

"I had no idea babies were this much work. Sure, you see little kids wreaking havoc at restaurants and stores, but those are the older ones. By then, they're mobile. They can get into trouble. Play with matches, that kind of thing."

The truth was, the sum total of his experience with infants was what had happened in the past week. For him, Izzie was it.

"I suppose I had it coming, though. I was the trouble-maker in the family. Derek—your uncle—he was so serious, even as a kid. Never a step out of line for that guy. Me, I was the one climbing out the second-story window to jump from the roof into the big pile of leaves in the lawn."

Thank God, he'd broken only one leg with that stunt. He'd nearly given his mother a heart attack.

He chuckled as he remembered how she'd yelled at him, shaking her fists, her face all red with anger. She could sure throw a fit, his mother could, back before the cancer had sapped all her strength and left her too weak to fight back.

To Izzie he said, "Your grandmother would have loved to have seen you."

Instead, she hadn't lived to see either of her own children even make it out of high school.

And because she seemed to be listening, he told Izzie about his mom and all the things she'd missed in his life.

About how she'd died when he was only ten. How she'd married a poor, ornery geologist who'd believed there were diamonds to be mined in the Northwest Territories of Canada when everyone else thought he was crazy. How she'd died without ever losing faith in her husband, even though he wasn't proved right until years later.

"That very first diamond Dad found, he had set in a ring for her, even though she'd never wear it. He always said she was the love of his life and there'd never be anyone to replace her."

And there hadn't been. Not in the nineteen long years from her death until his.

Dex leaned back, propped his feet against the coffee table and rested Izzie against his legs, where he could look at her. During one of the many diaper changes, he'd given up the pink jumper. Now she was dressed only in her diaper, leaving her cubby little belly exposed.

With a resolute nod, he reached into his pocket and pulled out the box from the jeweler he'd visited over lunch.

Holding Izzie with one hand, he flipped up the top of the box to reveal the thin platinum chain and the simple diamond solitaire ring dangling from it.

Just before his father's death, he'd given the ring to Dex, extracting the promise that someday he'd give it to the love of *his* life. Today, Dex had had a jeweler attach the ring to a necklace for Isabella.

"You're a little young for it, Izzie, but I figure…" He hesitated, choked back a surge of emotion and finished with, "Hell, it's a family heirloom if nothing else."

He held the box out to her and she reached one tiny finger toward the ring. He pulled the chain from the box and let it dangle from his hand. The ring spun back and forth, the diamond catching in the light. Izzie reached for it, smiling with delight when he pulled it from her grasp.

Something bloomed deep inside of him as he gazed at her toothless grin.

Once again he was struck with amazement. This child was his. This perfect little human being had come from him.

He'd spent all his adult life avoiding emotional commitments. Keeping everyone at arm's length. It's the way he'd wanted it.

But now? Now that Izzie was here, he wasn't so sure anymore. Yeah, he could push her away like he had everyone else in his life, but would that be fair to her? Maybe it would be. After all, what did he know about being a father? Maybe Izzie's childhood would be happier if he just bowed out now. Quietly walked away and let Lucy raise her.

Yet every cell in his body rebelled at the idea of never seeing her again.

Besides, wasn't pawning her off on Lucy just taking the easy way out? He thought briefly of his own miserable childhood. How many times had he berated his parents for putting their own wants and needs before his. If he bailed on Izzie now, wouldn't he be doing the same?

And that's when it hit him. She wasn't crying. He wasn't stressed. They'd been alone for nearly three hours. He really *could* do this. He could be a father to Isabella.

Whatever else he needed to know, he could learn on the way.

As he swung the ring back and forth in front of Isabella, he felt a deep contentment settle over him.

His cell phone rang just as she grabbed the chain in her tiny fist. He let go of his end to reach into his pants pocket and dig the phone out.

He frowned when he spied the listing. Lucy.

"How's it going?"

"Great," he answered honestly, relieved she hadn't called an hour ago when Izzie was screaming her head off.

"Really?"

"Yes, really."

"She isn't crying."

He couldn't tell if it was a question or if she was commenting on the lack of squalling in the background.

"No. She quieted down about an hour ago. We're doing great."

And that's when he looked back at Izzie and didn't see the chain in her hand.

"That's…fantastic," Lucy said unenthusiastically.

But her comment barely registered.

"Great. See ya soon," he muttered and hung up without waiting for a reply.

Where was the necklace?

What in the world could she have done with it?

She gurgled contentedly, one tiny fist shoved entirely into her mouth. He stared at her for a long minute as dread built in his stomach.

"Oh…you didn't. Tell me you didn't put it in your mouth."

She actually giggled in response. The little imp.

After gently prying her fist out, he ran his forefinger along the inside of her mouth. Nothing.

He held Isabella up in both hands, hoping the necklace would fall to the floor. It didn't. He had to resist the urge to shake her lightly to see if it would drop out.

He dusted himself off. He dusted her off. He ran his hand

across the cushions of the sofa. He even got down on his knees and ran his hand along the floor and under the sofa.

Then he rocked back on his knees, clutched her to his chest, and fought the urge to panic.

Damn it.

How could he have made such a rookie mistake?

And why did Isabella have to pay for his stupidity?

Standing, he grabbed his cell phone from the sofa and quickly scrolled through the numbers to the home number of Derek's secretary. Thank God she'd just gotten back from Antwerp.

"Raina, this is Dex," he said when she answered after six rings.

"Dex?" There was a sleepy note in her voice that vanished almost instantly. "What's wrong? Has Derek been in an accident?"

"Derek? No. I'm here with the baby. I think she may have swallowed something. What do I do?"

"Okay." There was a beleaguered sigh from the other end of the phone. "Well, first off, she's not choking on it, is she?"

"I don't think so. How would I know?"

"Is she turning blue? Not breathing? Any of those things?"

"No. She's still breathing."

"That's good. But for the record, if she ever is choking, you don't call me, you call 9-1-1, got it?"

"Got it. And Raina, I'm sorry about this." And he truly was. Derek pulled this kind of crap with Raina all the time—using her like his personal slave, calling her in the middle of the night. "I didn't know who else to call."

Of course he could have called Lucy, but she'd been waiting for him to fail.

"No problem. Okay, as long as she's not choking, don't

panic. But you should take her to the doctor. They'll know what to do." He heard the rap-tap-tap of computer keys in the background. "There's a children's hospital just down the tollway from your house. I'll get you the address."

He squeezed his eyes shut as he paced back and forth, holding Isabella in one hand and the phone in the other.

"But, Dex, you should know. They may make this difficult for you. If she has to be admitted to the hospital, they'll need to see her birth certificate. When you can't provide it, they'll have to call CPS."

He thanked Raina, hung up and began putting Isabella in her car seat. He would have to call Lucy after all. She could meet them at the hospital. She'd have the birth certificate if it came to that. But even if they did have to call CPS, that was okay, too. Nothing mattered but making sure Isabella was safe.

Eight

The doctor was one of those gratingly jovial types destined to drive parents crazy in a time of crisis. However, the nurse more than made up for his attitude with her disapproving, scornful frowns.

"Well, well, well." The doctor flashed them a broad grin and chucked Isabella under the chin. "Swallowed a necklace, did you?"

The nurse looked at her clipboard, then glared at Lucy. "And a diamond ring, according to the chart. Who was watching the child when this happened?"

Lucy sensed Dex about to answer, but she didn't let him. "What does it matter? Accidents like this happen." She turned her attention to the doctor. "What can you do?"

"Well, first, we'll have to take an X-ray. See how far down the intestinal tract the necklace has made it. Of course, our main concern will be the chain catching in her stomach or intestines. If the X-ray shows the necklace hasn't progressed very far, we may just fish it out."

Beside her, Dex paled, but nodded resolutely. Lucy squeezed his hand.

The doctor took Isabella from Dex's arms. "Little lady, you sure are making your parents worry tonight." The doctor wrinkled his nose. "And unless I'm mistaken, the first procedure you're going to need is a diaper change."

If possible, the nurse's expression soured even more, as if this was the final insult. The ultimate proof they were unworthy parents.

Lucy felt her cheeks heat. In the anxiety of the moment, she hadn't even thought to check Isabella's diaper. She took the baby from the doctor. "I'll do that."

"I didn't bring the diaper bag." Dex's expression was crestfallen. Apparently, he wasn't invulnerable to the nurse's disapproval, either.

She laid her hand on his arm. "Don't worry. I carry a spare diaper and some wipes in my purse."

The doctor and nurse left them alone in the exam room so they could change the diaper. As she went through the familiar motions, her mind raced.

Logically, she knew kids swallowed things all the time. Usually, they just passed right through. But that didn't keep her from worrying.

What if she needed surgery? Oh, God. An anesthetic. She was so young for surgery. What if…

Then she looked down. Actually looked at what she was doing.

"Dex, you thought she swallowed a ring, right?"

"Yes."

"A solitaire. Not too big. Half carat maybe?"

"Yeah."

Lucy chuckled as relief flooded over her. She stepped back so Dex could look at the open diaper. There, right on top, was the ring. Dirty and definitely in need of cleaning, but intact.

"She didn't swallow it, Dex. She stuck it down her diaper."

It was the obvious conclusion since there was no way it could have passed so quickly.

Dex scowled as he stared at the incontrovertible evidence before him. "She had to have swallowed it. I looked everywhere."

"I guess—" Giggles welled up inside of her and she paused, sagging against the exam table, feeling weak and giddy. "I guess you didn't think to look there."

Dex seemed more irritated than relieved. Somehow his annoyance only made her giggle more.

He didn't see the humor in the situation. "Why would she do that?"

"She's a baby. They stick things down their diapers. It happens." Suppressing the last of her giggles, she continued. "Besides, in her defense, that diaper was on very loose."

This earned her a glare. "You finish changing the diaper. I'll go tell the doctor."

Dex all but stomped from the room, his frustration palpable.

Which somehow just made the whole situation funnier to Lucy.

She chuckled as she used a wipe to fish out the ring. A few more wipes and Isabella was clean and tucked into a fresh diaper.

For a long moment, she stared at the ring dangling on its delicate platinum chain. When he'd mentioned losing a ring, she'd wondered—absently and beneath her fear— what he'd been doing carrying around a diamond solitaire. After all, diamond rings were the classic engagement ring.

The thought had flashed through her mind—however briefly—that he might be thinking of asking her to marry him. After all, that would be the ultimate easy way out. Why hire a nanny when you can marry one instead?

Thank goodness he hadn't done that. She saw now that had never been his intention. The ring had been attached to the necklace by a single link of chain, and the necklace itself was exactly the length for a girl. This wasn't a ring meant to be worn by an adult, but around a child's neck.

Funny how relieved she was that he hadn't planned the blundering mistake of asking her to marry him purely for his own convenience. She didn't think she could have borne it if he had.

After folding the rather dirty ring into the baby wipe, she tucked it carefully into the inner pocket of her purse and returned her attention to Isabella.

"Don't you worry about Mr. Grumpy there," she cooed as she leaned over Isabella to fasten on the new diaper. Lucy couldn't resist blowing a raspberry on the sweet, chubby belly. Isabella giggled in delight. "You just gave him a scare, you little bugger. That's the only reason he's so grumpy."

Slowly, Lucy straightened. Staring straight ahead, she mused aloud, "You really did give him a scare."

Dex had been terrified. Really, truly freaked out.

In fact, he'd been more upset than she had. Now, true, he didn't have as much experience with kids. He hadn't yet lived through the dozens of little traumas babies put their parents through. The scares and anxieties.

Not that she was actually Isabella's mother. She was just the aunt. Nevertheless, she felt all of the worries as deeply as any mother could.

She just hadn't expected him to feel them, too.

Earlier that day, if someone had asked her how Dex would respond in this situation, she never would have imagined his palpable fear and genuine distress.

Mindlessly, she put the wipes back into her purse. She picked up Isabella before crossing to the sink and washing her hands. But her mind was racing.

She'd been so sure that Dex wouldn't be a good father. So sure, he was cold and unemotional. Exactly the kind of father she didn't want for Isabella.

Everything she'd done had been predicated on that assumption. All the lies she'd told. All the deception. All because she'd been so sure—so sure!—Dex didn't really care about Isabella.

But what if she'd been wrong?

Dex drove back to the house alone, having put Isabella and her car seat back into Lucy's car and into Lucy's care. Where she belonged.

His hands clenched the steering wheel with a grip almost as firm as the one tension had over his body. Recrimination after recrimination pounded through his head.

Of all the stupid mistakes. What kind of an idiot gives a baby a ring to play with? What kind of an idiot doesn't think to check the diaper once he'd lost it?

If he had checked Isabella's diaper, then at least he wouldn't have had to call Lucy. At least she wouldn't have known about his stupidity. But he probably would have told her anyway. No, she needed to know about his incompetence.

Of course, his mistake, minor as it was, was nothing in comparison to the many, much bigger mistakes he'd made tonight. The truth was, they were lucky. They'd gotten off easy. No help from him.

It all came down to this. He didn't know jack about being a father. And knew even less about caring for an infant.

He pulled into the driveway to find Lucy had arrived before he had. She was bent over, removing an already sleeping Isabella from her car seat.

Izzie opened her eyes blearily, then fisted a hand around Lucy's shirt, nuzzled her neck and drifted peacefully back to sleep. A few minutes later, when Lucy laid her down in the crib that had been set up in her room, Izzie didn't even stir.

Watching Lucy bend over Izzie's crib, he felt his chest compress with relief and mingled fear. Tonight, he'd come so close to losing her. To losing them both.

He sure as hell didn't blame Lucy for the distant, cold look in her eyes when she straightened and found him standing in the doorway.

As she shut her bedroom door behind her, she whispered, "I suppose we need to talk about this." She shoved her hands into her back pockets as she headed down the stairs. "And you're certainly not the type to put things off, are you?"

"And here I thought you'd be eager to rake me over the coals. After all, you've been proven right."

She didn't answer until they'd reached the living room and he got the impression that she'd been searching for the right words.

"Yes. I suppose you would think that." She sank down to the sofa, propped her elbows on her knees and looked up at him, regret lining her every feature. "I expected you to fail tonight. I was *counting* on it."

"And I never doubted I wouldn't," he admitted, not bothering to hide his chagrin. Since his fear was still palpable, he crossed to the bar, poured himself a brandy. After glancing at her, he poured a second. If her nerves were half as rattled as his, she needed it. "I'm not used to failure."

She took a tiny sip of her brandy and swallowed her grimace. "No. I don't suppose you are. But what happened tonight wasn't your failure. It wasn't your mistake. It was mine."

"Lucy—"

"No, let me finish." She stood, setting the brandy snifter on the coffee table. "I didn't have a business meeting. That was just an excuse to leave you alone with Isabella." Guilt echoed in her voice. "I knew you couldn't handle it. I knew you weren't prepared. This is all my fault."

She sounded so dejected, he wanted to pull her into his arms. Instead, he smiled ruefully. "You wanted me to see how difficult it was. You thought I'd realize how hard it was and I'd give up. That I'd let you take Isabella."

She looked at him in surprise. "You knew what I was up to?"

"You didn't really think you could out-strategize me, did you?"

"Yes, I suppose I did." She laughed ruefully. "And here I thought I was being so clever."

"Don't be so hard on yourself. You were right. I don't have what it takes."

Once again, surprise flickered across her face. "But you do."

Now it was his turn to laugh bitterly. "Right. I nearly killed her."

"No, you didn't. She was never in any danger. And even if she had swallowed the necklace and ring, much worse things could have happened. She could have swallowed bathroom cleaner, someone's medication, drugs. Anything. Kids put stuff in their mouths. It's why you have to be so cautious."

With each item she ticked off on her fingers, he felt his stomach roil. He didn't even know where Mavis kept the bathroom cleaner. But surely they had some. As for medications or drugs, he knew neither he nor Derek took illegal drugs or even prescription drugs regularly. But who knew what over-the-counter medicines they had lying around.

He vaguely remembered Tim from marketing talking about hiring a professional to baby-proof his house. At the time Dex had laughed his ass off. First thing in the morning, Dex was getting this guy's name from Tim. He needed professional help.

Lucy, however, didn't seem nearly as worried as she should be. She just continued chatting away.

"The important thing is, when you thought she'd swallowed the ring, you didn't panic."

He tossed back the rest of his drink. "Excuse me, but I'm afraid I did."

She crossed to stand beside him. "You were scared. Terrified maybe." She ran her hand up and down his bicep in a way that was surprisingly soothing. "Any parent would be scared under those circumstances. I know I was. But still you did the right thing. You took her straight to the hospital."

At her touch, he felt the anxiety begin to ease from his body, only to be replaced by a different kind of tension. Staring down into her wide green eyes, which were so full of reassurances, so full of trust, he wanted to believe he could be the kind of father she thought he was capable of being.

But that certainly wasn't all that he wanted.

There was a hell of a lot he didn't know about caring for a child. But there were things he did know. He knew sex was the best release after an intense experience. He knew how to make a woman groan with pleasure. He knew how to make her ache. And he certainly knew how to bury all of his self-doubts and recriminations in the pleasure he could find in a woman's body.

He raised his hand to brush a lock of bright-red hair from her cheek. "This must have been very hard on you, too."

She licked her lips nervously as her hand slowed, then stilled on his arm. "I'll be okay." As if she just realized she was touching him, she jerked her hand away. "But I'm tired and should—"

But he didn't let her retreat. Instead, he snatched her hand from midair and used it to pull her into his arms. "Don't. We both need this."

He pulled her to his chest, more roughly than he intended to. But she didn't protest when he lowered his mouth to hers and kissed her.

Nine

Her body melted against his, all soft curves and pliant woman. He tasted her need. Her passion. But also her fear and desperation. Her need for reassurances.

What surprised him was his own echoing emotions. She may have needed this, but so did he.

He lost himself in her touch. In the way her mouth opened under his lips and her tongue arched up to meet his. The way her hands clutched at him, burrowing into his hair. The way her breasts pressed into his chest, full and soft in contrast to her hardening nipples.

He stepped his feet between hers, forcing her legs wider apart. Her thighs parted, one calf creeping up the outside of his leg, her pelvis bumping against his erection.

Groaning as his desire spiraled, he pulled her even closer, plastering her body against him, sinking his fingers into the flesh of her buttocks. Her body felt so warm, so solid beneath his hands. So reassuringly feminine.

He pulled his mouth from hers to bury his face in her neck. She moaned, low in her throat as her head dropped back to give him access. Her skin was hot, replete with the scent of her, musky and filled with desire. Her desperate need called out to him, resonating with a pounding urgency. He backed her up, one step and then another, until they fell back together into the plush depths of the sofa.

In the moment their bodies were apart, her hands reached between them, tugging at the buttons of his shirt for one frustrating minute before abandoning them for the button and zipper of her jeans.

Still kissing her, he felt more than saw her tugging her own jeans down her hips and kicking her legs free. That was all the invitation he needed. A moment later, he buried his fingers deep into her heat. Her folds were moist and plump against his hand, pulsing with desire.

The feel of her, the heat of her, made his erection tighten and strain against his jeans, bucking to get free.

She arched and moaned against him. "Please, tell me you have a condom."

It took a moment for her words to register. When they finally did, he nearly cursed. A condom was the last thing on his mind. Still, he groped for his jeans, found the foil packet he knew was in his wallet and a moment later he was back in her arms.

The sight of her there on the sofa, shirt unbuttoned to reveal her perfect breasts still encased in her pale pink bra, her creamy thighs parted, nearly sent him over the edge.

She opened her arms to him, urgency writ clearly on her face, but he forced himself to slow down. "No. Not yet."

With excruciating slowness, he unclasped her bra then peeled away the silken fabric to reveal breasts that were firm and lush, nipples peaked and darkened with desire.

He'd never seen more perfect breasts. But as tempting as they were, her faint gasp of anticipation was even more erotic. The fervency of her passion turned him on in a way no other woman ever had.

With hands that nearly trembled, he stripped off her remaining clothes, relishing every inch of her body as it was revealed.

A moment later, he buried himself in her. He lost himself in the heat and energy of her body. In the thrusting of her hips and desperate clutching of her hands. In the soft moans of pleasure resonating in her chest.

She wrapped her legs around his waist and arched further into him. Her eagerness only turned him on more. God, she was amazing.

This wasn't the practiced seduction he'd imagined. On his part, there was no skill. No pretense. No art.

Just lust and exquisite passion.

And Lucy.

She was everywhere. She was pounding through his mind, thundering through his blood.

With every stroke of his body, his pleasure built until he could feel nothing but the heat of her body, the clenching of her muscles around him, the spasm of her climax. Until it seemed as if her very soul was imprinted on him.

As his own climax rocketed through him, he knew he'd never forget that moment. Never forget her.

How had he ever forgotten her?

Waves of pleasure still undulated through her body. Dex, heavy and warm, lay on top of her, their bodies still intimately joined. And already she was having doubts.

Okay, not doubts, exactly. More like a full-fledged onslaught of panic.

One part of her—the logical, intelligent part that had guided every decision she'd made since she was eleven—had launched into reprimand mode.

What were you thinking?

You don't sleep with men you barely know. And this wasn't just any virtual stranger, either. This was Dex. Isabella's father. You shouldn't even be alone with him. You've lied to him. Deceived him. This is a man who could crush you like a bug if he finds out.

And by sleeping with him, she'd greatly increased the risk that he *would* find out. After all, he'd slept with Jewel. Sensual, exotic Jewel, who knew how to tempt and entice a man beyond endurance.

Lucy had none of Jewel's skills in bed and only a tiny fraction of her experience. Was there any chance at all that Dex wouldn't notice the woman he'd had sex with just now was nothing like the woman he'd slept with fourteen months ago?

She held her breath, waiting for him to comment on the differences, praying that he'd chalk it up to the high emotions of the evening. And all the while, her mental debate continued.

This man isn't just some heartless automaton, the emotional side of her argued. *He was just as worried as I was this evening. Surely it was natural to take comfort in each other.*

Natural? It was convenient, that's what it was. And what now? How many more times in the next few weeks will it be natural to seek comfort in sex again? How many more times will you make that mistake? And how much harder will it be now to take Isabella and leave when the time comes?

Ah, it always came back to that, didn't it? Back to her pledge to do whatever it took to get Isabella back.

But what if she wasn't right? Who was to say taking Isabella away from Dex was the right thing to do?

Sure, when she'd thought he *was* nothing more than a heartless automaton, doing everything in her power to get custody of Isabella had made sense. It had been justified. But she no longer believed that. As of tonight, she knew he cared about Isabella.

Lucy thought briefly of the diamond ring necklace still tucked safely in her purse. Obviously, giving his daughter a diamond ring wasn't a romantic gesture, but it was a gesture of some kind. It showed how much Isabella meant to him, almost as much as his panic had when he'd thought she was in danger. Just more proof that he'd grown to care for Isabella.

Maybe as much as she did.

So what gave her the right to decide what was best for any of them?

She was so lost in her mental debate that she barely noticed when he rolled off her and left for the bathroom. He returned a few minutes later with a glass of water for her. She took it from him without meeting his eyes.

"Where did you go?" he asked.

She looked up at him in surprise at his question. "What?"

"One minute there was a passionate woman in my arms." He pulled on his jeans as he spoke. "The next it's like you're not even here."

She turned her back on him, suddenly embarrassed by the intimacy of the situation. She placed her glass on the table, then pulled on her own jeans before turning back to face him. But instead of answering his question, she posed one of her own.

"You're not going to give me custody of Isabella, are you?"

"Sole custody?"

"Yes." Her breath caught in her chest as she waited for

his answer, even though she already knew what it would be. It all came down to this. Sex aside, emotions aside, this was the issue that stood between them.

"No. Not sole custody."

"No matter what I do? No matter how good a mother I prove myself to be? You won't even consider it, will you?"

She gazed into his eyes as she spoke, willing him to see her desperation. Her need.

Forcing herself to really see him as well. Not as just the man who could take Isabella away from her. Not as just some rich man with more money than heart.

As a father. As a man who had sought and given comfort. Not to mention tremendous pleasure.

Oh, it might be all too easy to demonize him. To pretend he didn't have any needs or rights for her to consider.

But wasn't it bad enough that she'd been lying to him? Did she really need to continue lying to herself as well?

Grief welled in her chest, forcing her to turn away from him.

He must have seen the desperation in her gaze, because he quickly closed the distance between them. Tenderly, he cupped her cheek, tilting her head up to his.

"This isn't about how good a mother you are," Dex said. "This is about what's best for Izzie. I don't doubt you're the best mother for her. But she needs a father, too."

Somehow his use of the nickname, Izzie, was like a stab in her heart. Like suddenly he had a piece of Isabella that she didn't. A piece that she'd never get back. She protested automatically. "But—"

"There are lots of single mothers out there who would disagree with me, I'm sure. But you don't have to do this alone. Besides, I have financial resources you couldn't hope to match."

"Money?" she asked incredulously, jerking away from his touch. Why had she brought this up now? Why couldn't she have just enjoyed lying in his arms? Instead, she'd brought up the one subject guaranteed to drive a wedge between them. "You're making this about money?"

"I'm just being honest."

"By pointing out that if it came down to a court battle, you would win by the sheer size of your wallet?"

"That's not what I meant. You know as well as I do that raising a child is expensive."

"Ah." She held up her palm to silence him. He didn't need to go on, she could do that for him. "I suppose you're going to point out that if you raise Isabella, she'll have the best of everything. The best schools, the best clothes, the best education."

"And you're…" he interrupted her, "…undoubtedly going to point out that there's more to life than material wealth."

Of course, that was what she was going to say. But in truth she couldn't deny that money made things easier. Instead, she sank to the edge of the sofa and rested her elbows on her knees, as resignation settled over her.

Growing up, her own family had been lower-middle class, not poor by any means, but well out of the league of most of the families in their upper-middle-class school district.

Her father had done what he could to provide for them—he'd made sure they got an excellent education—but she remembered all too well the yearning for nicer things, for the clothes and baubles other girls wore. Clothes were the least of it, of course. She would have been thrilled with the occasional warm word of encouragement from her father. But in lieu of that, there had been material things that would have made her feel less like an outsider. Less pitiable, perhaps.

"You're right, of course. Money isn't everything, but it does help."

Since she'd had the love of neither a mother nor a father, she'd simply held her head high, worn her shabby clothes with all the dignity she could muster and made sure that no one had had the chance to feel sorry for her. Not for anything she had control over, at least. She hadn't asked for handouts. She hadn't complained. And she had never, ever let anyone know that *she* knew she was second-class.

She wanted better than that for Isabella. How could she not?

Standing, she wrapped her arms around her waist and crossed to the massive fireplace at the far end of the room. On this warm spring night, it was empty, of course, except for an artfully arranged triad of pillar candles. "I was accepted to Brown and Princeton, but my dad didn't have the money to send me to either."

"Financial aid," he pointed out, ignoring the apparent non sequitur.

"Naturally I qualified, but I still would have been left with a mountain of debt." She chuckled, making light of the decision that had broken her heart at eighteen. "And I was far too practical to take that on. Not when I had a perfectly good scholarship from the University of Texas." She turned back to him. "So you see I know all too well that money *does* matter. I'm not saying it doesn't. Just that it's not everything."

"I couldn't agree more. And I would never dream of trying to raise Izzie all on my own. You're her mother. She needs you. She's going to continue to need you her whole life. I won't give you sole custody, but I'd never dream of taking her away from you altogether."

Oh, but he would.

Just as soon as he found out she wasn't really Isabella's mother, he'd do everything in his power to make sure she never saw Isabella again.

And now, she was beginning to realize, that wasn't the only heartbreak in her future. Never seeing Isabella again would be bad enough. But of course she'd lose Dex as well. Even if she could survive the one, could she survive the other?

Ten

Dex spent the following day hounding Quinn about Lucy. Unfortunately, Quinn had found out nothing Dex didn't already know. By all appearances, Lucy Alwin was a model citizen. She paid her taxes, earned a comfortable income and returned her library books on time. She'd never gotten so much as a speeding ticket. Nothing in her past or present raised a single red flag.

It was beginning to look as if she'd made only two mistakes in her whole life. Sleeping with him and abandoning Isabella on his doorstep. He'd been complicit in the first, so he could hardly blame her for that. As for why she'd abandoned Isabella, that was still a mystery.

But one thing was obvious. Since he and Derek had never reported that incident to the authorities, and since Lucy's record was otherwise squeaky-clean, he would have a hell of a time convincing a judge Lucy was an unfit mother.

If he wanted to go that route, that was.

But dragging Lucy and Isabella through a nasty court battle was no longer something he could imagine doing. Which left him with only one option. If he wanted custody of Isabella, he was going to have to marry Lucy.

Dex's neighborhood was not the kind of place where salesman traveled door to door hawking their goods. So the chime of the doorbell ringing at two o'clock in the afternoon, mere moments after she'd put Isabella down for her nap, definitely took Lucy by surprise.

As she walked to the front door she made a mental list of who could possibly be on the other side. Girl Scouts selling Thin Mints? Ed McMahon with a giant check? That skinny chick from *What Not to Wear,* there to overhaul Lucy's wardrobe?

She swung open the heavy mahogany door to reveal a tall woman, not quite as thin as the *What Not to Wear* woman, but darn close. The similarity was accented by the bulky, black garment bag she held in her hand. The woman's dish-water-blond hair was pulled back in a tight cinch, which either caused or exaggerated her pinched expression, Lucy wasn't sure which. Either way, Lucy got the distinct impression that this woman did not want to be there.

"May I help you?" Lucy hesitated to ask the question, in case it pissed off the ice queen even more.

"Raina Huffman." She held out her hand, but the handshake was anything but warm. Then she breezed through the door without waiting to be invited in. "I'm Mr. Messina's assistant. Mr. Derek Messina's assistant, that is. Dex sent me to bring you these."

Raina held out the garment bag, at which Lucy stared blankly.

"His dry cleaning?" she asked flatly.

"No." There was an exasperated eye roll in Raina's tone that she somehow managed to convey while keeping her expression carefully blank. "This is a collection of outfits Dex thought might be appropriate for you to wear to tonight's gala event."

"Oh…"

When Lucy didn't rush to take the bag from Raina, she draped it over the back of the sofa. "I've included—"

"What gala event?"

"Tonight Messina Diamonds Dallas is hosting a black-tie reception to celebrate the opening of their Antwerp office. Dex thought you should attend. He told me to make sure you had an appropriate gown and suggested you might like to have your hair and makeup done for the event."

"Ah. That gala event," she snapped peevishly. Dex had mentioned a couple of days ago that he had a business function to attend that night. And now he was ordering her to attend, too. Typical Messina autocracy. "Well, you can just tell him that you tried, but that I can't attend any event, gala or otherwise, appropriate clothes or no appropriate clothes. I have Isabella to look after. I can't leave her here alone."

"That has been arranged as well. I've hired a very reputable babysitting service. They'll be sending someone over shortly." Raina glanced at her watch. "A driver will be here to take you to your hair appointment in an hour. Also, I would suggest a slightly more—" her gaze lingered unpleasantly on Lucy's Jewel-inspired bright red hair "—conservative hairstyle."

Irritation spiked through Lucy, despite the fact that she didn't like the garish red of her hair any more than Raina appeared to. She didn't know who she was more annoyed

with: Raina for judging her with such disdain after an ac-
quaintance of less than ten minutes, or Dex for siccing this
woman on her.

Okay, Lucy told herself. *Don't take this out on her.
Maybe she's just doing her job. Or has an enormous stick
shoved up her butt.*

All but biting her tongue, she ignored Raina's "suggestion" and crossed the room to the garment bag, curious
what the ice princess would deem appropriate cocktail
wear. A starchy Victorian gown, perhaps?

The corner of the bag bore the embossed logo of an exclusive retail shop. The kind of place Lucy could barely
afford to drive past, let alone shop at. Just her luck. The
only time in her life she'd ever even touch a dress from that
shop and it had been picked out by Ms. Congeniality.

However, when she unzipped the bag, a soft gasp of
surprise slipped out unbidden. The first dress inside was a
deep teal silk with a ruched bodice and a long, flowing skirt.

"You don't like it."

"No, I—" She reached out a tentative hand to touch the
dress, only to pull back, all too aware of the baby drool
that likely lingered on her fingers. "It's gorgeous. You
picked it out?"

She couldn't keep the surprise from her voice and Raina
frowned in response to it.

"There are three dresses. One of the other ones may be
more to your liking."

"No. This is beautiful. But is the reception really this
formal?"

Raina stiffened. "This isn't my first reception at
Messina Diamonds. I picked out what I thought would be
appropriate and—"

Great. She'd offended her again. Lucy held up a hand

to halt Raina's sputtering. "Oh, I trust you. It's just the last time I wore a dress this fancy, Jake, my prom date, drank too much and puked all over it at three in the morning."

"I'm sure he did."

"It's a beautiful dress," Lucy said sincerely, since humor didn't seem to be working at softening Raina up. "You have excellent taste." Lucy looked up to find Raina scowling, clearly annoyed by the compliment. "Why do I get the feeling you don't like me very much?"

Raina blinked in surprise, then pressed her lips together. "I don't know what you mean."

"Sure you do. You're going to get a crick in your neck if you look any farther down your nose at me. Now, don't get me wrong, I can understand your being annoyed that Dex sent you to be my personal shopper—that would annoy anyone." She cocked her head to the side, studying the other woman, trying to see beyond the cool haughtiness. "But this is more than that. You really don't like me."

"Well, if you must know, Jewel…" Raina put a little sneer into the word *Jewel* "…Dex may not remember your stint working at Messina Diamonds, but I do."

"Oh." Lucy bit down on her lip, trying to hide her distress. She'd been so focused on convincing Dex she was the woman he'd slept with, she'd completely forgotten that Jewel worked for Messina Diamonds at one point. It had never occurred to her she might have to convince anyone else she was Jewel. Having a fellow employee pop up who remembered Jewel from her days there was completely unexpected.

Lucy fought the urge to defend her sister. What could she possibly say, when she had no idea what history this woman shared with Jewel?

Since Raina obviously expected some kind of response,

Lucy shrugged and went for something vague. "I guess I wasn't an ideal employee."

"You guess? Dressing inappropriately, flirting outrageously. Constantly throwing yourself at—"

But Raina stopped herself. Again her cheeks flushed and her gaze darted away from Lucy's. Apparently, she'd said far more than she'd intended.

Suddenly, Raina's attitude began to make sense. Her voice had been laced with scorn, but Lucy could tell it hid a deeper, darker emotion. Jealousy.

And this, she realized, was what it was actually like to be Jewel. Jewel's sexuality had always been her greatest strength and her greatest weakness. She used it to lure men in and keep women at arm's length.

"Ah. So you don't like me because I was always throwing myself at Dex?"

"Not Dex. Derek." Raina frowned at Lucy's slipup, but then continued fiercely, "But Derek would never sleep with an employee."

Derek? Jewel had been throwing herself at Derek?

Lucy recovered quickly. "Which is why I threw myself at Dex. That's what I meant."

The twisted machinations of Jewel's love life were becoming more and more…well, twisted. And yet, somehow, it all made sense. Jewel had a long history of developing crushes on unattainable men. After all, a skilled hunter isn't satisfied hunting deer. Sooner or later, she'll give in to the lure of big game.

Derek must have posed quite the challenge. Undoubtedly, the more he'd resisted, the more determined Jewel had become. She'd probably thrown herself at him the whole time she'd worked at Messina Diamonds. When he hadn't nibbled, she'd set her cap on Dex instead.

And all the while, there was poor Raina, who obviously cared about Derek, though she was doing an admirable job of hiding it. But Lucy knew the signs well. The jealousy, the fierce protectiveness, the way her voice thickened when she said his name.

Well, if Jewel had a long history of manipulating men, Lucy had an equally long history of smoothing over her sister's mistakes.

"Raina, I'm sorry." Since the other woman was standing only a short distance away, Lucy reached for Raina's arm. "I didn't know you were in love with him."

Raina jerked away. "I'm not in love with him."

But the vehemence of her response and the heightened color in her cheeks proved her a liar.

And Lucy knew all too well what it felt like to have someone she was interested in lured away by her sister's innate sensual appeal.

"If it makes you feel any better," Lucy pointed out, "he didn't sleep with me, either. Derek really wouldn't sleep with an employee."

"Really?" A glimmer of something like hope flashed in Raina's eyes, but there was caution there as well.

Lucy certainly couldn't blame Raina for not trusting a gesture of friendship from someone like Jewel. However, she felt too much kinship with Raina to not try. After all, how many times in her own life had men overlooked her because she lacked Jewel's overt sensuality? How many broken hearts had she nursed while watching her sister ride off in the front seat with some guy Lucy had secretly had a crush on?

Too many. She knew all too well that it was no fun.

And in some weird way, wasn't that what was happening all over again? Here she was, well on the way to losing her heart to Dex and the only reason he even knew she existed was because he thought she was Jewel.

She was as much a victim of Jewel's power over men as Raina was. Besides, she could certainly use a friend tonight at this gala event she'd been ordered to attend. That alone was reason enough to extend the olive branch again.

"Can I assume you're going to this reception, too?" she asked Raina, who nodded. "Well, it certainly wasn't very nice of him to send you here to do his dirty work when you probably need to be getting ready, also."

Raina shrugged in a gesture of beleaguered resignation. "I'm Derek's go-to girl. And sometimes Dex's by proximity. I do what they need me to do."

"Gawd, I hope they pay you bundles to do it."

Finally, a smile cracked through Raina's icy facade. "Well, at least there's that."

Lucy laughed as inspiration struck. "Look, if Dex is footing the bill for this spa afternoon thing, why don't you come with me? I'd be thrilled to have someone tackle this mess I've made of my hair…" The garish red favored by Jewel gave her a fright every time she looked in the mirror. "But I certainly don't need a manicure or a pedicure. It'll be a girl's afternoon out."

In the end, they both got their nails done. The few occasions when Lucy had had a manicure and pedicure, she'd just gone to the Walk-Ins Welcome nail salon in the strip mall near her condo. She'd never been to a full-service day spa before. Between the soft classical music, the dimmed lights, the massage chair and the fragrant herbal tea, it was all Lucy could do not to fall asleep while getting her hair dyed.

Four hours later, she emerged from the cocoon of the salon like a pampered and rested butterfly. Two hours after that, she found herself swathed in shimmering teal silk, seated next to Raina in the back of the limo Dex had sent to pick her up, grateful she wasn't having to navigate the downtown Dallas traffic.

Raina, who'd been thawing all afternoon, looked at her appraisingly. "You look good with that hair color."

"I do?" Remarkably, the hairdresser had picked a shade very close to her own natural brown. He'd added a few auburn highlights and trimmed up the shaggy bob, which had left Lucy feeling less like a pale imitation of Jewel and rather like a slightly more glamorous version of herself. She smiled. "Maybe I'll keep it like this."

"You should." And then Raina hesitated, biting her lip before adding, "You're not at all like I thought you were."

"Yeah. I'm getting that a lot lately," she muttered wryly. When Raina raised her eyebrows in question, Lucy added, "I guess becoming a mom has really changed me."

"I can see that. I'm the oldest of five. Dealing with the little ones either makes you crazy or makes you a better person. Usually both."

Lucy chuckled, but it felt forced. She really liked Raina and, in the end, she was yet another person Lucy was lying to. Imagining how Raina would respond when she found out the truth—as she inevitably would—made Lucy squirm. More lies. More deception. And it was getting harder and harder to tell herself her motives were pure.

Luckily, she was saved from having to come up with an answer as the limo pulled to a halt in front of the towering building that housed Messina Diamonds. Even though she'd lived in Dallas for most of her life, she'd never really been downtown at night. Downtown Dallas wasn't alive at night like Chicago or Manhattan. The streets were well lit, but empty of pedestrians. There was road traffic, but no crowds spilling out from restaurants or bars. However, this swath of downtown was aglow. Cars lined up before the building, elegantly dressed men and women stepping from limos like glitterati.

Lucy double-checked to make sure she had her evening clutch before climbing out of the limo. That morning, she'd dropped by the jewelry store to have Dex's ring cleaned. She hadn't felt comfortable leaving the ring at the house, so she'd been carrying it around in its velvet jewelry box until she could give it back to Dex.

By the time they made it up to the Messina Diamonds offices on the fifteenth floor, Lucy was feeling decidedly outclassed, even in her stunning teal gown. She'd never even ridden in a limo before tonight, let alone attended a gala event. For her, a big night out was getting popcorn at the movies. She didn't belong in this elevator full of sparkling, laughing people. What could she possibly have in common with any of them? As the elevator doors opened, Raina placed a hand on Lucy's arm.

"Take a deep breath," Raina murmured. "It'll help you calm down."

"That obvious, huh?"

"You look ready to pass out."

"Ah, but the question is—" Lucy smoothed her hands down over her hips as she spoke "—does peaked go with formal wear?"

Raina chuckled under her breath. "Just remember, no one here is any better than you, no matter how they may act. Besides, you're the only woman here tonight personally invited by Dex."

"Invited? Ordered was more like it," Lucy grumbled.

"Just try to have fun."

As Raina spoke, the crowd parted and Lucy got her first

glimpse of Dex's office. The Messina Diamonds offices were both more and less impressive than she'd expected.

Less, because she somehow thought they'd be bigger. The office took up a modest six floors of a downtown skyscraper. Only six. Which seemed tiny for a multi-billion-dollar business. Of course, they also had offices in Toronto, New York and Antwerp.

At least the logo etched in the massive wall of glass that faced Lucy when she exited the elevator on the fifteenth floor said so. The words *Messina Diamonds* arched across the glass, and underneath was the image of a diamond ring laying on its side, the diamond cut in a distinctive elongated oval. In smaller letters underneath that the four cities were listed.

She stared at the image of the ring for a long moment. "I know that ring."

"The legendary Messina family diamond." Raina nodded.

"Legendary?"

"Of course." Raina pushed open the heavy glass door and led the way into the lobby. "That's the first diamond discovered by Derek and Dex's father. The elder Mr. Messina, I mean. By the time the diamond mine was operational, their mother had already passed away. But Mr. Messina had the diamond set in a ring for her anyway because she's the only woman he ever loved." A hint of wistfulness had crept into Raina's voice, revealing the romanticism she tried so hard to hide. "He carried it with him until the day he died."

"And then he gave it to Dex," Lucy murmured as her heart sank under the weight of the story.

So it wasn't just any ring Dex had given to Isabella. Not just a trinket a diamond magnate would thoughtlessly bestow on his child. This was a ring of great importance to Dex.

Raina's head whipped around and stared at Lucy. "How did you know that?"

"Not because he gave it to me, if that's what you're worried about." She had to work to keep her own hint of wistfulness from her voice. Her disappointment was too illogical to share with someone else.

Raina flushed. "I wasn't worried, I just…"

"Ah. You thought I might abscond with the family heirloom?"

"It's not that. I was just surprised. Mr. Messina gave it to Dex on his deathbed. He wanted him to give it to the love of *his* life."

"Which explains why he gave it to Isabella."

Raina's expression softened. "To Isabella? That's charming."

"Yes. It is."

Dex really loved Isabella. And the fact that he'd given the ring to her was a sign he'd really welcomed her into his heart.

She should be thrilled. So why did the smile plastered on her face feel like it was cracking around the edges?

Surely not because she was jealous? That was absurd. It wasn't as if she wanted Dex to love her. Was it?

Eleven

"Champagne?"

"Hmm?" For a second, Lucy stared blankly at Raina, who had snagged a waiter wandering by with a tray of champagne flutes.

"Or there's an open bar if you'd prefer wine."

"No. Champagne's great." And maybe if she sounded excited enough about it, Raina would even believe her.

The reception was being held in the lobby of Messina Diamonds offices, with the open bar set up in one corner and tables of appetizers along the walls. However, the crowd of tuxedoed men and elegant women had spilled out to the elevator bay and beyond the lobby to the conference rooms.

Though she wouldn't have thought the lobby of a business was the perfect place to hold such a glamorous event, somehow it seemed appropriate. Everything about the lobby spoke of austere elegance—frosted glass, brushed metal and creamy, golden marble. The room was crescent-shaped, with the glass wall facing the elevator forming the shorter side, and the opposite wall arcing from corner to corner in a broad arch.

The center of that wall also bore the Messina Diamonds logo. On either side of it, in two wide columns of foot-high letters, was printed "The Story of Randolph Messina."

"I can give you the nickel tour if you'd like?" Raina asked.

"Maybe later. You don't have to babysit me all evening." Even in the short time they'd been there, several people had nodded at Raina in greeting. "I'll be fine here. I'm just going to…" Lucy let her words trail off as she pointed to the paragraphs printed on the wall.

After a few minutes of convincing, Raina wandered off to work the room, leaving Lucy to read about Messina Diamonds. She felt slightly voyeuristic, but excused the feeling by telling herself that—if Dex had anything to do with it—Isabella would someday be heir to this company. Besides, it wasn't as if Dex had been exactly forthcoming about his family history.

Of course, her curiosity was ridiculous. She knew that. Despite the single night of breathtaking passion they'd shared, nothing had changed. He still wanted Isabella. She was still lying to him. They still had no future. So why did her heart ache a little at the idea of losing him? Surely she hadn't gone and done something really stupid, like fall in… No. Even she wasn't that dumb. No, if anything, she was merely vulnerable to his charisma. Whatever she was feeling was a temporary glitch in her emotions. Nothing more.

Forcing her attention away from her troublesome feelings and back to the real world, she scanned the text before turning her attention to the picture inset into the left column of text. The black-and-white photo of a stocky, rough-looking man in a cowboy hat with his arm around a willowy woman with flowing long hair. He indeed looked like he'd stepped out of a gold mine from 1849. She, however, looked like she'd stepped off a runway in Paris.

Dex had obviously gotten his height from his mother's side, but she could see his father in the curve of his lips and the shape of his eyes. And unless she was mistaken, Randolph's eyes would be the same piercing blue-gray as Isabella's.

"There's a better picture of them upstairs."

Lucy spun around to see Dex with his elbow propped on the receptionist's desk. Like all the men she'd seen tonight, he was dressed in a tux. Somehow on him, it looked even more impressive. It might have been the breadth of his shoulders or the clean lines of the tux, which was obviously custom-made. Or perhaps just the casual confidence with which he stood there. Dex may pretend he was just an ordinary guy, and until tonight she'd been fooled, but he was obviously as much in his element here as he was back at the house playing on the floor with Isabella or sitting by the pool drinking a Shiner.

"You look lovely."

The appreciative gleam in his gaze warmed her to the core, reminding her of the intimacy they'd shared. She blushed, remembering, and had to force herself to respond. She ran a hand down the front of her gown. "Raina has excellent taste."

"I wasn't talking about the dress."

Her blush deepened at his compliment and she found herself at a loss for words. *You look better in a tux than James Bond* were the words that popped into her head.

After a moment, he took pity on her and asked, "Would you like to come up and see the rest of the offices?"

"Actually, I've been enjoying the story."

Dex grimaced. "That was the PR department's idea."

"It sounds like your dad was a bit of a character."

"He was the last of a dying breed."

Lucy looked sharply at Dex. "And there's no pride in your voice when you say that."

He looked a little surprised at her observation. "No. I suppose not."

"And yet," she pointed out, "it says here he was devoted to your mother and to his family. That he was a brilliant geologist."

"That's the work of the PR people again. 'Devoted to his family' merely means he dragged us all over South America when we were kids. 'Brilliant geologist' really means headstrong and foolhardy. He believed he'd find diamonds in Canada and no one else could convince him otherwise."

"But he was right."

"In the end, yes he was."

Dex didn't continue and she guessed there was a lot he wasn't telling her. Resentment, perhaps, at being "dragged all over South America" as a kid? Or perhaps just a troubled relationship with his headstrong and foolhardy father?

"You don't talk much about your family."

"You haven't said much about yours, either."

"True enough." She shrugged and then rattled off the highlights. "Raised by a single dad. Mom left when we were young. I have one sister." Better to be as vague about that as possible. "Dad was a CPA," she added quickly.

"You must have gotten your love of numbers from him."

"My love of—" Then she broke off with a chuckle. "Oh, I see. Because I'm an actuary. Um. No. Sorry, not from him." If her father had loved his job, he certainly hadn't let her see it. He hadn't passed a love of anything on to his children. Doing so would have required showing too much emotion.

Feeling suddenly self-conscious—as if she'd given away far more than she'd intended—she rushed on. "No. The whole actuary gig was just more of me being practical. I was always good in math. And there are lots of scholarships and job opportunities in that field. Especially if you're a woman."

"You remind me of my mother."

When she looked up at him in surprise, an odd expression crossed his face, giving her the impression he hadn't meant to say that aloud.

"That sounds like something that could have been a compliment, but wasn't," she observed.

"Always so practical. Always doing the right thing. Making sacrifices for other people."

"Those aren't bad qualities."

"They are if they keep you from doing what you really want with your life."

Lucy returned her attention to the photo on the wall, to the smiling faces of the couple. Randolph was smiling into the camera, but the woman, Sara, had her head cocked just slightly toward her husband. The expression on her face, the tilt of her lips, suggested she was seconds away from a full-blown chuckle, as if her husband had said something outrageously funny mere seconds before the picture had been taken.

Nothing in her expression bespoke a woman unhappy with her choices.

"Who's to say she wasn't doing exactly what she wanted to do?"

"Trust me, prospecting for gold and diamonds isn't the

glamorous work you might imagine it to be." A note of bitterness crept into his voice. "Prospectors travel to crappy little towns in the middle of nowhere. That's if there is a town. Typically, there are no hotels. No shops. More often than not, there isn't even any running water. Diamond mines aren't found in New York City half a block away from the Ritz-Carlton."

"I never said they were."

"It's hard work. Under brutal conditions. No one deserves to live like that."

"Are you talking about why you think your mother was unhappy or why you were unhappy?"

The expression that flickered across his face was positively chilly. But it was gone in an instant, replaced by cool disinterest.

"Oh, I get it now."

"Get what?"

"All those years of rebellious behavior that you pretend to be so proud of."

He appeared to be gritting his teeth, "I'm not proud of—"

"Well, of course not. Because you're not really a rebel. The media portrays you like the renegade of the Messina family. But that's not it at all. You didn't travel around the world, refusing to accept a position at Messina Diamonds because you're some kind of renegade. You know why you did it?"

"I'm sure you're going to tell me."

She ignored his obvious annoyance. "You did it to get back at your father and brother. On the one hand, for the first time in your life you had control over where you lived and what you did. After years of being dragged all over the world—your words, not mine—you probably wanted to settle down in one place. Put down some roots. But by then,

Messina Diamonds was taking off. Your father needed you to settle into the family business. So you were torn between the desire to do what you wanted and the compulsion to disappoint your father. After all, he'd disappointed you for so many years. So you made yourself into the rebel loner. Traveling all over the world, keeping everyone at arm's length. All to protect yourself."

She felt a surge of triumph at her explanation. For an instant it even seemed like maybe she understood him. He, however, didn't give even a flicker of a response. In fact, he spoke as if she hadn't said a word.

"Why don't I show you the rest of the office." He placed a hand at the small of her back and guided her to the doors behind the receptionist desk.

Wow. Wasn't that interesting?

Apparently, he had a nice big tender spot where his childhood was concerned and she'd just trampled all over it.

As soon as they were out of earshot of the other party-goers, she pulled away from him. "Look, Dex, I didn't mean to offend you."

He raked her face with a dispassionate gaze. "I'm not offended." With one hand shoved firmly in his pocket, he gestured broadly with the other one. "These offices—"

"Excuse me, but you obviously are offended." When he turned back to face her, she saw that his jaw was clenched, his eyes shuttered. "You've clearly got this enormous Do Not Disturb sign right where your childhood memories should be and—"

"Don't analyze me."

She held up her hands in acquiescence. "Trust me, I'm not *trying* to. It doesn't take much effort to see that you still resent your parents for mistakes they—"

"The word *mistake* implies 'accident.' When you take

your kids out of school and drag them halfway across the continent every time you want to dig in the dirt, that's not a mistake. That's a decision."

"Okay, so maybe your parents made some poor decisions." She gentled her tone. "You will, too, someday. All parents do."

"No," he said quietly but with firm finality. "Parents should do what's right for their child. Not just what they want, but what their child needs." With that, he turned his back on her and gestured toward a wall of cubicles to his left. "These offices belong to the junior researchers…"

Just like that, he continued with his tour of the office like she'd never even brought up the subject. And here she thought she had issues with her own childhood.

Of course, she did have issues—maybe everyone did. But she worked to overcome them. To find success and happiness in life despite the rough patches of youth.

In recent years, she and her father had come to a kind of peace in their relationship. And until this recent debacle, she'd have said she and Jewel were closer than they'd ever been. And she had Isabella. Her last, best hope to have the kind of family she'd always dreamed of.

But Dex?

He seemed closed off from everyone in his family. If he had any fond memories of his childhood, he sure wasn't sharing them with her.

Which, she supposed, wasn't surprising.

After all, what connection did they really share? They'd lived in the same house for a while and had had sex once. Well, twice, if you looked at it from his point of view.

Yes, they had Isabella in common, but that was it.

It was time she faced facts. He may be ready to let Isabella into his heart, but he was keeping that door firmly closed to her.

Twelve

Lucy barely paid attention to the tour she received of Messina Diamonds' six floors of offices. It was much as she expected: cubicles, offices, hundreds—if not thousands—of geological maps rolled up and stored, taped down to tables, tacked to walls. Most of the research and development was out of this office, Dex had explained.

He talked to her about the process of looking for diamonds, where they thought the next big find would come from, how long they estimated the mines would stay in production. And he did it all with a cool efficiency that bordered on impatience. Blah de blah, blah, blah. He told her nothing she *wanted* to know.

All of that information he kept firmly under wraps.

From what she'd read, she gathered his one true childhood home had been in Dallas. Was that why Messina Diamonds still had an office here? And if he had no fond memories of his childhood, why did he still live here? Why not in Toronto, New York or Antwerp?

But Dex didn't answer any of those questions. Geesh, he didn't even give her time to ask them. Her tour of Messina Diamonds was like a military strike. Fast, precise and a little chilling.

And just when her patience was about up, he ushered her into a spacious corner office with breathtaking views of the city. Unlike the other rooms she'd toured, this one was warm and inviting. The two walls not made up of windows were wood paneled. Centered in each of the shadow-box panels was a framed photo of his family. An oversized mahogany desk dominated the room, flanked on either side by dark leather chairs. Stacks of papers and folders littered one wing of the desk.

The overall effect was elegancy tempered by a sort of cozy clutter. It was a pleasantly intimate glimpse of his everyday life.

"So, this is your office," she murmured.

To her surprise, Dex turned around. "No. Actually, this is Derek's office."

"Oh." And if that wasn't enough to deflate what little enthusiasm she'd had for the tour, she didn't know what was.

"Have a seat."

Why had she even come here? she wondered as she lowered herself to the cushy leather wingback.

She'd never felt more out of place and she couldn't help wondering if this tour had been designed to impress or intimidate.

"If it's not your office, why are we even here?"

"Because of this." Dex turned to one of the larger framed photos of his family.

But before she could even glimpse the picture, he swung the frame away from the wall to reveal a wall safe.

"Oh." She sank back into her chair. "How exciting."

Why wouldn't he tell her something? Anything about his past? And why was she so desperate to know? But she knew the answer before her mind had even finished forming the question. Once he trusted her, once he opened up and told her a truth about himself, somehow it would be easier to tell him her truth. Tell him all about her charade and hope that it wasn't too late to ask for some forgiveness.

If Dex noticed her sarcasm, he didn't comment on it. He spun the dial on the wall safe a few times and then that door swung open, too.

From it, he pulled out a roll of black velvet. Not unlike the fabric used by the jeweler she'd visited earlier that day. She couldn't say why, but dread began to swirl in her stomach.

"For years now, Derek has been working toward vertical integration."

"I see," she murmured, even though she had no idea what that had to do with anything.

"Owning the diamond mines is certainly profitable. But he's been working to open a subsidiary of Messina Diamonds in Antwerp to handle the cutting, polishing and wholesale selling of our stones, as well."

This cold and formal discussion of business expansion actually relaxed her. He wasn't going to do something stupid. To him, diamonds weren't jewelry, they were business.

He crossed the desk in front of her, cleared a spot and unrolled the velvet. The rectangle of fabric was only slightly larger than a legal sheet of paper. A dozen diamonds glittered against the inky velvet.

Still, she couldn't quite stifle her gasp at the sight of all those rocks twinkling up at her. No woman in the world was immune to such beauty.

Unsure what he expected her to say, she said, "And these are from your mine?"

"They're the first batch to come out of the newly formed Messina Cutting House. I inspected them and brought them back during my recent trip to Belgium."

"I see." Though of course she didn't. His world was miles apart from her own. Diamonds, cutting houses, trips to Europe—it was all so foreign to her. She'd once been sent to corporate headquarters in Des Moines, but that was hardly the same thing.

"I personally inspected each of these stones. You won't find a finer diamond anywhere in the world. One of them could be yours."

A bark of panicky laughter escaped. "Not unless I wanted to clean out my savings and my retirement fund. Even then I'd be pushing it."

"That's not what I meant."

"That's what I was afraid of."

"I'm asking you—"

"Look, Dex—"

"—to be my wife. All you have to do is pick out the diamond for your ring."

That feeling of dread in her belly solidified into something hard and ugly. Something that felt a little like anger and a little like envy. But who was it she envied?

Dex had proposed to *her*. So why did it feel like it wasn't her he really wanted?

The anger was easier to put her finger on. All her life she'd waited for—dreamed of—this moment. The moment a man she genuinely cared about asked her to marry him. And here he had to go and ruin it by sucking out all the romance, all the warmth. He could have been asking to borrow a pencil for all the emotion he showed.

She stood up. "No, Dex. This is all wrong."

"Think about it, Lucy. I can give you everything you want."

"What do you know about what I want?" Her voice rose sharply in accusation.

In contrast, his voice came out smooth as butter. Soft and low, like the purring of a cat. "I know you. I know what you want."

"I'm sure you think you do." She cast a scornful glare at the diamonds on the desk between them.

"You want Izzie. You want a family. More important, you want to do the right thing for Izzie."

Her chest tightened as if he'd punched her in the solar plexus. She had to consciously suck in one breath after another before she could speak.

It was crazy, of course, how for an instant she was tempted.

She couldn't marry him. Every practical bone in her body knew the real reason she couldn't say yes. He didn't even know who she was. The lies she'd told stood between them like some huge, insurmountable obstacle.

And yet it was the impractical, romantic heart inside her that protested the loudest. Somehow, the biggest obstacle between them wasn't really the lies she'd told, but the fact that he didn't love her. Not even a little.

All her life, she'd been the practical one. It was a quality she nurtured in herself and admired in others. Yet here he was, being oh so practical. So *reasonable*. And every cell in her body recoiled at the thought.

"You're right. I do want a family. Of course I want a family. I want to be a mother to Isabella and to whatever brothers or sisters she has. But what you're describing isn't a family. It isn't a marriage. You're talking about a convenience."

"I'm talking about doing what's right for Izzie." He rounded the desk to stand before her, crowding her space, making her fight the urge to step back, to retreat. "Think about it. Izzie needs both her parents. How much easier will her life be if they live in the same house?"

"Easier? Because you could tell yourself you'd done the right thing by Isabella, but I'd be the one doing all the work. Yes, it would be easier for you, wouldn't it?"

"Easier for both of us. You could quit your job if you wanted to. You'd get to be with Izzie all the time. Both of us would." He raised his hand to her face and brushed her hair back in a sensual, seductive gesture. "And we know we're compatible."

For the briefest instant, she felt a burst of hope—that maybe, after all they'd been through, after the emotional turmoil of the past week-and-a-half, after they'd made love, that maybe he was starting to develop some tender feelings for her.

Maybe.

But then she saw the glint of sexual desire lighting his gaze.

Resignation threatened to smother her. He didn't mean they were emotionally compatible. He meant in bed, of course. And they were.

The sex had been incredible. But a marriage—a real marriage, the kind of marriage she wanted—wasn't based on sex and lies.

As if he sensed her wavering, he took her hands in his and added, "I know what you want most is Izzie. But surely there are other things you want. I'm a wealthy man, Lucy. I can give you whatever you want. Travel, cars, clothes, jewelry. Name it and it's yours."

"Ah." She stepped back, pulling her hands from his. "So that's what this is all about. You planned this all out, didn't you? From the moment Raina showed up on the doorstep. The dress. The trip to the day spa. Arriving via limousine at this glamorous affair. You created this perfect Cinderella evening, all so you could propose."

What a stupid, stupid man.

He said nothing, but the very corner of his mouth twitched upward, as if he was pleased with himself.

She laughed, for a moment genuinely amused by the absurdity of the situation. But when she spoke, her voice sounded brittle and hollow. "You know the thing men don't get about that story? Women don't love Cinderella only because Cinderella gets to dress up in fancy clothes and go to the ball. They love Cinderella because when the prince finds out that she's just a poor servant girl, he still loves her."

The beginnings of a frown settled on Dex's handsome face. As if he didn't quite get where she was going with the metaphor. So she made it easy for him.

"You want me to believe I can have anything I want. All I have to do is pick out a diamond. Any diamond in this room, right?"

Success glinted in his eyes. "Right."

"Any diamond—" she reached into her bag and pulled out the box from the jeweler "—except this one."

When she flipped open the box with her thumb, his gaze hardened. His lips compressed into a thin line, but he said nothing.

Bitterness laced her tone when she spoke. "Because this is the one diamond that means something to you, isn't it?"

Again, he said nothing and again she pressed on. "I'm not an idiot, Dex. I put two and two together. This is the ring from the logo. And Raina told me its history. It's the first diamond your father found. The ring your father had made for your mother, long after she'd passed away."

He didn't deny it, not that she expected him to.

He didn't meet her gaze, either, but turned away from her to face the bank of windows overlooking downtown. He shoved his hands into the pockets of his tuxedo pants. His back was a broad, impenetrable barrier.

Despite that, she kept talking, because her point was too important to let drop. Not for her, but for Isabella. And for Dex.

"You've worked so hard to push your family away, but this ring means something to you, Dex. That's why you gave it to Isabella the other night. You did it because you're starting to open up to her."

She waited for him to say something. Anything.

But his silence, his stubborn refusal to even turn and face her, hung between them, as insurmountable as her deception had ever been.

True, she couldn't marry him because of her lies. But it was funny, really, how *that* had become the least of the problems between them. It seemed a small thing compared to the fact that he didn't love her. That over and over again, he'd shut her out of his heart. That he was asking her only because she'd make the perfect long-term babysitter.

"Do you know what would happen if I did say yes?" she murmured. "Things would pretty much go back to how they were the first week Isabella and I lived with you. I would take care of her. I would love her heart and soul. And you would stop by to visit once every week or so. Yes, you'd be her father in the biological sense, and certainly in a financial sense, but in no other way.

"That's why I can't marry you. Well, actually—" a nervous little chuckle escaped "—there are a lot of reasons

I can't marry you. But the real reason is because you're asking for all the wrong reasons.

"If you married me, I'd take care of Isabella. Not just her physical needs, but her emotional ones, too. You'd have the perfect excuse to hold her at arm's length forever. All you'd have to do is pay for everything. You could have a daughter and a family, but you wouldn't have to care about either. Marrying me would let you push Isabella away, just like you've pushed away everyone else in your life."

She paused, holding her breath, praying he'd deny it.

When he didn't, she added, "But I can't let you do that to her. I can't let you do that to you."

Thirteen

Dex didn't turn around to watch Lucy leave. What would have been the point?

She was going. She would take Izzie with her. And he couldn't say that he blamed her.

As soon as she'd started babbling on about Cinderella, he'd known he'd lost. He'd made one fatal mistake. He'd appealed to her practical side.

What he hadn't realized until too late was that under all that practicality beat the heart of a romantic. Deep down, Lucy was the kind of woman who wanted it all. The whole sappy, romantic package.

Raina—a bit of a closet romantic herself—had told Lucy all about the damn ring at the reception and Lucy had fallen head over heels for the story.

He, on the other hand, had done everything in his power to avoid so much as walking past the damn PR display.

He'd read it exactly once, his stomach knotting with disgust. It was nothing more than a bit of revisionist history cooked up by the PR department in conjunction with an overpriced decorator.

What made for a charming press release did not make for an enjoyable childhood. The fact that his father eventually did strike gold—or, rather, diamonds—didn't make up for the fact that he'd dragged them across three continents, that they'd barely lived in the only home they'd ever known or that he'd squandered the last few years of their mother's tragically short life obsessively prospecting in Canada's kimberlite pipes for diamonds.

Sure, having the first diamond he'd found cut and set into a ring for her years after her death had certainly been a romantic gesture. But that hardly made up for the fact that he hadn't loved her enough to settle in one place when she'd been alive.

The one time he'd read the history of Messina Diamonds, all he'd seen were the stretched truths romanticizing a childhood that had barely been bearable for him.

But that wasn't what she'd seen. She'd seen exactly what the PR department had wanted her to see. Love, devotion and tragedy. A recipe for timeless romance.

And she'd fallen for it.

The ultimate proof that she wasn't nearly as practical as she wanted him to believe.

Though her ridiculous theories about his behavior certainly should have given him a clue what to expect. Apparently, she wanted to see him as some kind of wounded soul, tortured by his past. Her theory was damn near laughable.

But if he could use her sentimentality to get a yes out of her, then he would. If she was a closet romantic, he could give her romance. He could woo and seduce with the best of them. He certainly wasn't going to make the same mistake twice.

He felt only the briefest pang of concern for his motives, but he quickly buried it.

Isabella needed her mother. And since he wasn't willing to give up Isabella, marrying Lucy was the logical choice. After all the years he'd spent resenting his parents for the way they'd raised him, he took a certain amount of gratification in knowing that he would not make the same mistakes they had. He would put Isabella's needs and wants before his own. His proposal certainly was not the manifestation of some deeper desire to make Lucy his own. It was simply a matter of logic.

And next time, he wouldn't ask until he was sure of her answer. But eventually he would get a yes out of her. Because no wasn't an option.

Besides, if there was one lesson she should have learned by reading that garbage downstairs, it was that Messina men always got what they wanted.

"Don't look at me like that."

Lucy couldn't even meet Isabella's eyes as she ducked to pull her suitcase out from under the bed where she'd stashed it when she'd first arrived.

Isabella was currently having a little bit of "belly time" on her blanket in the middle of the king-sized bed. Her chubby little arms wobbled as she struggled to raise herself up enough to shoot Lucy what could only be described as an accusing glare.

"I'm not running away," Lucy continued in her own defense. "This is a strategic retreat, that's all." And really, she thought she'd shown quite a bit of fortitude in not retreating earlier. She'd allowed a whole nineteen hours to pass between Dex's proposal and her retreat. She hoisted the suitcase onto the foot of the bed and unzipped it. "I'm only leaving you with him temporarily."

But even as she said the words, she knew they were a lie. This wasn't temporary because chances were good she'd never get custody of Isabella. But if she was very lucky, and Dex was very forgiving, she'd at least get visitation rights.

She pulled a stack of clothes from the dresser drawer and tossed them into the suitcase. It seemed impossible that less than two weeks had passed since she'd first arrived at Dex's house. How had so much changed in so little time? How had she gone from mistrusting him to caring about him?

Moving about the room, she caught a glimpse of herself in the mirror over the dresser and stilled. Her eyes looked wide and haunted. Her cheeks sunken. Her skin pale. A sleepless night will do that, she told herself. Or maybe she'd had too much to drink last night.

But who was she kidding? Really?

She'd been lying to so many people lately, did she really need to start lying to herself as well?

This wasn't sleeplessness. This wasn't too much alcohol. She'd only had a single glass of champagne, for goodness' sake. This was good ol' fashioned misery. This was a broken heart.

Because she really had gone and done something stupid and fallen in love with Dex Messina.

What an idiot.

She'd fallen hard and fast for him. And she very much feared that her heart would be his forever. But that wasn't the reason—at least not the *only* reason—she was leaving now.

"Here's the plan, Isabella." She knelt down so she was eye to eye with the other person who owned a nice big chunk of her heart. "I'm going to tell him the truth."

Isabella parted her little rosebud lips.

"No, no." Lucy held up a hand as if staving off a protest. "Hear me out. He deserves to know. He deserves a chance to be a real father to you." She sucked in a deep breath. "And I'm going to track down your mother and sort this whole mess out. And in the meantime, I'm going to contact my lawyer and see if he can't arrange visitation rights."

Even though she should be packing, she couldn't resist picking up Isabella. She sat cross-legged on the bed and balanced Isabella on one knee.

"Don't you worry. He'll cave on visitation rights. I know he will. He's a stubborn man, but he's fair. He might be tempted to keep us apart just to punish me, but he'll do what's right for you."

Isabella frowned, giving Lucy the impression—not for the first time—that she really was listening. And while the practical side of Lucy knew she was mostly talking aloud for her own benefit, there was another side of her that truly believed Isabella understood—if not the words—at the least the emotions behind them.

"Here's the thing about dealing with your Dad. I know I warned you about letting him too close earlier. But I was wrong. Getting close to him is exactly what both of you need. Now, you may have to really work at this, because he's going to resist you every step of the way. But—" she met Isabella's gaze with a smile "—you have the advantage. You're cute and defenseless. You'll get him to open up. I've already seen you starting to work your magic on him. Besides, you worked your magic on me, didn't you?"

An instant later, her smile wavered.

Yes, Isabella had worked some pretty amazing magic on her.

Lucy hadn't needed anyone. And then Isabella had come

along, with her wide blue-gray eyes, her pink little mouth and soft fuzzy hair. One coo, one wobbly little smile and every defense Lucy'd had, had shattered.

Isabella had left Lucy's heart open and vulnerable.

And then Lucy had watched Isabella do the same thing all over again with Dex.

Lucy hadn't stood a chance. Dex didn't, either.

But now that she had to give Isabella up, Lucy didn't know how she was going to bear it. How could she possibly walk away from this sweet little girl?

Only one thing made it bearable. Knowing that Dex would be there to pick up where she'd left off.

"You're going to be just fine with him. You really are. He may not know it yet. But he loves you. And he's going to be a great father to you."

Lucy clutched Isabella to her chest. She squeezed her eyes closed, but couldn't keep the tears from seeping out of the corners of her eyes.

No, Isabella and Dex would both be fine. Lucy, on the other hand, felt like her very soul would be crushed by her sorrow.

By the time he found what he was looking for and made it back to the house, her bags were already packed and waiting by the front door.

Lucy stood in the entry hall, holding a sleeping Isabella in her arms, rocking slowly back and forth. Apparently waiting only to say goodbye to him before leaving.

"I won't let you take her."

Lucy looked up, frowning. "If I'd been planning on just taking her, I wouldn't still be here."

"Then what are you planning?"

"We need to talk." She gestured behind her and for the

first time he noticed the woman standing in the house, just beyond the foyer. "This is Mrs. Hill. She's a babysitter I've hired before. She's very reliable and Isabella knows her, so they'll be fine together."

"How long were you planning on talking?"

"I know I'm leaving you in a lurch, so tonight she's agreed to stay overnight with Isabella. She doesn't work weekends, but she's an experienced nanny. As long as you're home by seven most evenings, she can be here during the day while you're at work. I'm sure eventually you'll want to hire your own nanny, but until then—"

Tension knotted his belly as her words sank in. She was leaving.

Which, of course, the packed bags by the door indicated as well, but this was different. If she left and took Izzie with her, he had a built-in excuse for chasing her down. But if she left Isabella with him, that was something else entirely.

"I'm not going to hire a nanny. I want you to stay."

Exasperation crossed her face. "I can't stay indefinitely, Dex. You know that. You're going to have to hire a nanny eventually."

"I—"

But she raised a hand to cut him off. "We really do need to talk."

Wasn't this exactly the opportunity he'd been looking for? She wanted grand romance. Well, he was prepared to give it to her.

"In that case, we should go to the guesthouse where we can be alone."

With reluctance that was obvious even to him, she handed Isabella over to Mrs. Hill and followed him through the living room and kitchen out the back door and across the patio to the guesthouse.

The guesthouse was far more comfortable than the main house. Before moving into it six months ago, he'd had his own furniture moved in, so it reflected his more modern sensibilities.

When Lucy followed him in, her eyes scanned the room hungrily, taking in every detail.

"I wondered when I'd see it," she murmured.

"What?"

"Some scrap of your real personality."

A little fissure of irritation cracked through his grand plan to seduce her with romance. "It's just a room, don't make too much out of it."

He looked again. The leather sofa and armchair had clean, modern lines. The space was decorated in deep chocolate browns, smooth creams and cool, pale blues. It felt as much like home as anywhere he'd lived in the past decade. Which was to say, it was pleasant, but he was no more attached to it than to the hotel room he regularly stayed in at the Windsor Arms in Toronto.

"No, it's more than just a room. This is where you live." She swept the room with a gesture. "It suits you. It's restrained. Comfortable, but not fussy. I knew the big house—" she nodded in that direction "—wasn't you at all. It's too…"

When her words trailed off, he offered, "Garish."

Her lips twitched slightly. "I was going to say it's too comfortable with its wealth. You never seem at ease there."

He wasn't. But it annoyed him that she saw through him so completely.

"You're stalling," he pointed out. "There was something you wanted to talk about."

Instantly tension sprang into her body and he regretted changing the subject.

"I did." She turned away from him and paced to the far side of the room.

He watched as she put her purse down on the sofa and then picked it up again. Then put it down again. When she turned to face him again, her palm was pressed to her belly as if to quell her nerves.

"The thing is—" she broke off, sucked in a deep breath and started again. "Here's the thing. I'm not exactly who you think I am."

"I know."

Fourteen

"You do?" Her gaze darted to his.

He crossed to her side and took her shaking hands in his. "You haven't hid it very well." Confusion lit her face. "Oh, you had me fooled at first. You seemed so practical. So down to earth. But that's not who you are. Not deep down inside."

Her frown deepened. "I don't know what you mean."

He brought his hand up to cup her face. The skin of her cheek was impossibly soft. Her lips were parted and dampened from her nervous licking. Her gaze softened. For a moment, the role he was playing faded into the background. The practiced seduction slid aside and in its place was some emotion he could barely name, let alone understand.

"You pretend to be so tough, but that's not who you are deep inside. You're a romantic. I didn't see that at first. But I do now."

She ripped her hands away from his, turning her face aside. "This isn't about me being a romantic."

"Of course it is. Last night when I proposed I did it all wrong. I didn't know you wanted a grand gesture."

She rolled her eyes. "Trust me. Unrolling about a million dollars worth of diamonds was grand enough. If I could have said yes, I'm sure I would have."

"Okay. The diamonds were grand, but they were impersonal. You wanted more." The role she needed him to play was coming more easily now.

When he handed her the wrapped package he'd taken out of storage earlier that afternoon, it almost felt natural.

"What is this?" she stared blankly at the gift-wrapped present.

"You wanted me to give you something personal. Unwrap it."

"Dex, I—"

But he cut off her protest. "This isn't easy for me. Just unwrap it, okay?"

Frowning, Lucy slipped her fingers under the edge of the wrapping paper and pealed it back to reveal a tattered, used copy of Mark Twain's *The Adventures of Tom Sawyer.*

This was no first edition family heirloom. No elegantly leather-bound copy. This was a cheap paperback. The cover creased, the pages yellowed and dog-eared and on the title page, stamped in faded blue print were the words, "Property of Spence Middle School."

She looked up at him as confusion replaced her distress. "I don't understand."

"I was in the seventh grade the year my mom was diagnosed with cancer. It was the only year we were in school the whole year. My English teacher read this book aloud." His voice was oddly flat and emotionless as he spoke.

But as he had said, this wasn't easy on him. And she didn't need tears or outbursts of emotion to guess what this book had meant to him.

She could picture it all too well. The skinny, defensive adolescent boy, sitting in his English classroom, feeling so angry at the world—at his mother for being sick, at his father for not doing more—and slowly finding himself won over by the story of Tom Sawyer. The pranks, pratfalls and adventures would win the heart of any boy.

And then there was the fact that Tom was an orphan, drifting through life without need of parents or adults. How that must have appealed to Dex at a time when he'd felt his own parents had abandoned him.

Looking at the tattered old cover of Tom Sawyer, her heart seemed to swell and unfurl. Whatever few remaining defenses she had against this man crumbled and fell, leaving her completely vulnerable to him.

As she looked from the book to Dex she felt tears well in her eyes. "I…I don't know what to say."

"Say you'll marry me."

"I—"

"You wanted a romantic gesture." His mouth curved into a wry smile. "Personally, I thought the diamonds were much more romantic, but…"

He let his words trail off. He was waiting for her "yes."

She could feel it hanging there in the air between them. The expectation of acceptance.

He'd gone to all this trouble, searched his life—his whole history—for something personal enough to give her. Something "romantic" enough for her.

And she still couldn't say yes. He didn't know who she was. He would hate her when he did know.

Yet she found she couldn't say no, either. The word

seemed to have vanished from her vocabulary. Since she couldn't say yes and she didn't have the heart to tell him no, she did neither. Instead, she kissed him.

Sure, there were a thousand reasons why kissing him was just as stupid as saying yes. It was a momentary reprieve and nothing more. Yet she could think of nothing she wanted more at that moment than to press her body to his and pour into her kiss all the things she couldn't say. All the doubts and regrets. All the longing.

And she'd never get another chance. She'd have to come clean very soon, and the moment she did, he'd despise her. In all likelihood, this would be the last time he ever kissed her.

She had every intention of making the most of it.

His body was hard and solid beneath her hands. His muscles firm without being sculpted. His mouth was warm and bold against hers.

He accepted her kiss completely, without question. Maybe he thought it alone was the answer he sought. Whatever pang of conscious she felt at that, she quickly buried it. Maybe her acquiescence wasn't the answer he thought it was, but it was the answer of her heart.

When his hands sought the edge of her T-shirt and eased under the fabric to her bare skin, she didn't stop him. Instead, she relished the sensation of his roughened fingertips against the flesh of her stomach. His touch sent tendrils of desire pulsing through her.

Blood seemed to pound through her body, tightening her nipples, making the flesh between her legs throb. Her desire built all the more quickly because she knew what was coming. She knew what a powerful lover he was. How his touch would master her body. Make her tremble. How he would feel plunging into her, strong and hard.

She gasped aloud when his hand—finally—reached her breast. His touch was a little rough. Not painful, but firm. In control. Exactly what she wanted.

She didn't think twice before allowing him to nudge her legs apart with his knee. She welcomed the pressure against the apex of her legs and found herself bucking against him, aching for him to touch her there. To strip her jeans from her body, pull her panties down her legs and find the moistened folds of her flesh. To probe her body with his fingers, his mouth, and of course that glorious erection of his pressing against her hip.

She pulled her mouth from his, panting. "I want…"

But she trailed off, unsure how to put into words all she desired.

He looked down at her, his gaze clouded by desire, but a hint of amusement lingering on his lips as he toyed with her hardened nipple. "You want?"

"More," she gasped out. "I want you. All of you."

She'd never said truer words. It wasn't just his body she wanted thrusting against and into hers. She wanted his heart. She wanted him to give himself completely to her. Without reservations or doubts. She wanted to feel as if they were completely joined. Because when morning came and she had to tell him the truth, they would never be together again.

But she wouldn't let herself think of that for now. Now was just about them. About pleasure. About pouring her heart into every touch in hopes that someday he'd understand that she loved him despite the lies she'd told.

When he began backing her toward the bedroom, she let him. But she never released her hold on him. She clung to him as they moved through the living room, like a couple slow dancing to the rhythm of some sultry ballad. A kiss for every step. A tie loosened. A shirt pulled off. A snap undone. One shoe, then another kicked off.

By the time she felt his mattress bump against the back of her legs, she was down to just her jeans, unsnapped, unzipped, shoes off. His tie was gone, his white dress shirt unbuttoned. Still, she felt delightfully exposed by comparison. Wickedly naked.

He looked unbearably sexy, half-dressed as he was, the smooth muscles of his chest visible between the two halves of his shirt. The sprinkling of chest hair, the occasional glimpse of his nipples was enough to tempt her beyond endurance.

Pressing her hands against his shoulders, she spun him around so his back was to the bed. Then she shoved the shirt off his shoulders. It caught on his wrists, trapping his hands just long enough for her to give him one more light shove. He allowed himself to be toppled over, arms trapped at his sides, legs hanging over the sides of the bed.

She smiled in delight at the image he presented. He was completely at her mercy. And she intended to have none.

But first, she nudged her jeans down over her hips and let them fall to the floor. Any self-consciousness she might have felt standing nearly naked before him vanished at the sight of his appreciative smile curling his lips.

She supposed he could have been comparing her to the legions of women he'd no doubt been with before her, but the look in his eyes said he wasn't thinking of anyone else. Right now, at this moment, neither of their pasts existed. His other lovers didn't matter anymore than her lack of experience did.

All that mattered was tonight. This moment. This instant, as she was climbing on top of him, straddling his waist, staring down into the laughing eyes of the man whose body seemed to have been handcrafted for her pleasure.

She ran her hands over his chest, using his temporary confinement to explore his body and drive him crazy all at the same time. His skin was hot beneath her touch. His nipples were as hard as hers were and she took great pleasure in sucking each of them into her mouth, in the low moan of pleasure he gave as she raked them with her teeth.

"I think you're enjoying this," he ground out.

Leaning over his chest, up on her knees, she looked up at him. "I'd rather hoped you were, too."

He chuckled. "Oh, I am." Then his wicked smile vanished and his look intensified. "Don't forget. I'm not entirely without resources here."

His arms may have been trapped by his side, but his hands were still free and he was able to just reach the back of her knees. He grabbed her and with a swift tug, pulled her body up so that her mouth was even with his. He gave her a fast, fierce kiss.

"Unbutton my arms," he ordered.

"No."

Then, with another tug, he pulled her breasts within reach of his mouth. He laved first one breast and then the other with exquisite attention. His hands were at the back of her thighs now. She didn't know what was worse, the persistent sucking on her nipples or the aching anticipation of wondering how much range of motion he had in his arms.

Could his fingers reach her panties? Could they slip underneath?

His hands tightened on her thighs, branding her with his touch.

"Unbutton my arms."

"Make me." But the words came out as a pant. More begging than ordering.

Then with excruciating slowness, his hands moved from the backs of her thighs to the front. First one thumb and then the other slipped under the elastic edging of her panties. His thumbs moved to her entrance, where moisture clung. Moving in slowly expanding ovals, his thumbs circled from her entrance and then up, almost to her bud, and then back down.

With every movement, the tension seizing her body racketed up another notch. Almost there. Almost.

When his thumb finally brushed her center, her whole body clenched in a spasm, her back arching.

His hands tightened on her legs once more. This time, when he pulled her forward, she found herself poised directly over his mouth. His fingers tugged aside the only barrier separating them. He pulled her hips down and sucked her into his mouth. His tongue swirled around, his fingers slipped into her from behind and whatever remaining inhibitions she clung to vanished.

Suddenly, she was uncontrollable, bouncing on his fingers, moaning in pleasure, begging for more. Every muscle in her body tightened, poised for release. And then it came, as shock wave after shock wave of pleasure washed over her.

She was still trembling when he flipped her over onto her back. The last of their clothes vanished in the hazy aftermath of her climax. A second later his erection prodded her tender, sensitized fleshed, stirring her desire once more. He pounded into her, hard and fast. Touching the deepest part of her, pushing her to new heights of pleasure.

For an instant, her eyes drifted open, just long enough to see his expression, taut with desire, mindless with passion. And then she lost herself again as another climax shook her body and soul.

Fifteen

He still couldn't imagine how he'd possibly forgotten a sexual encounter with this woman. When he woke up the following morning to find her warm, naked body draped over his, he felt as if every instant of the previous evening had been branded into his mind.

The feel of her silken skin. The sight of her poised above him, head thrown back. The honeyed taste of her on his lips. The shuddering of her climax as her body had clenched around his.

She was, quite simply, unforgettable.

Every other woman he'd slept with faded into the recesses of his memory. All these years, he'd drifted from woman to woman, having one meaningless sexual encounter after another. He'd never before appreciated that knowing a woman would add so much to sex.

A glance at the clock told him it was far too early to wake

her. As appealing as early morning sex sounded, after the night they'd had, he wanted her to catch up on her sleep.

He slid out from under her, lingering only for a moment to brush the hair off her cheek. He didn't let himself stay longer. She was far too tempting as it was and he'd indulged his passions enough.

Last night's touching presentation of his old copy of *The Adventures of Tom Sawyer* had achieved his goal. She was going to marry him. She had, perhaps, not said the words, but her response hadn't left any room for doubt. Since he'd gotten what he'd wanted, he certainly didn't need to overplay his hand.

There'd been moments last night when he'd even felt himself swept up in his performance. Which, in the harsh light of morning, only reminded him that when they were married, he'd have to go the extra mile to make sure she didn't get too close.

He was his own man, in charge of his own destiny. He didn't need anyone. Not a seductive temptress like Lucy and certainly not a little imp of a baby girl. Trusting people, letting them close, meant heart-wrenching vulnerability. He'd learned that lesson long ago and it wasn't an experience he intended to repeat.

All the more reason—he thought as he pulled on a pair of jeans—not to linger in bed with her. Sex was one thing in a marriage. Explosive, amazing, best-sex-of-his-life sex—well, that was just a bonus. But he wasn't about to let himself be trapped by deeper emotions. He'd seen first-hand that love brought nothing to a marriage but heartache.

And he respected Lucy too much to break her heart.

He slipped into a pair of loafers and silently shut the bedroom door behind him before heading over to the main house.

It was only a little past six. The night before, Lucy had explained that she'd paid Mrs. Hill to stay the whole night. Originally, Lucy hadn't planned on being at the house much past their big "discussion." So Mrs. Hill had spent the night in the guest bedroom Lucy had stayed in previously, watching Izzie all through the night.

However, he knew Izzie sometimes woke up early. And since she'd been all night long without either parent, he'd like to be nearby when Mrs. Hill brought her down for her morning bottle.

Unfortunately, when he crept in through the back door, the house was silent and still. He quickly disarmed the alarm, then made his way over to the coffeemaker. While he waited for the machine to work its magic, he flipped absently through the pile of mail Derek's housekeeper had left at the kitchen desk the day before.

He shook his head in exasperation at the sight of a Pottery Barn Kids' catalog. How in the world had Pottery Barn found out he had a kid less than two weeks after he'd found out?

He tossed it aside along with the Hammacher Schlemmer catalog, quickly shuffled through a stack of bills and hesitated with the eleven-by-thirteen-inch envelope marked Confidential. The return address was Geneletic Labs. He stared at the envelope a moment before recognition sank in.

Geneletic Labs was the company he and Derek had sent their paternity test to the morning after Izzie had arrived on their doorstep.

Funny, when he'd taken the test just under two weeks ago, he'd been desperate to get the results. Desperate to know whether or not he could foist the responsibility for Izzie off on Derek.

He hadn't wanted her. Hadn't wanted to be tied down

by a child. Now, he knew there was nothing he wouldn't do for her. He'd even gladly made the sacrifice he'd once sworn he'd never make. He'd asked a woman to marry him. Hell, he'd damn near begged her.

Dex nearly tossed the unopened envelope into the pile of junk mail and catalogs. After all, he already knew he was Izzie's father.

But for some reason, he hesitated. With a why-the-hell-not shrug, he slipped his forefinger under the flap of the envelope and pried it open.

A moment later, he stared at the paper inside as shock rocketed through his body.

Isabella wasn't his.

So this, Lucy thought groggily, *was the meaning of the phrase "rude awakening."*

"Lucy, wake up," the stern voice repeated.

She rolled over onto her back, rubbing at her eyes and the words and the voice sank in.

That was Dex's voice. Dex, with whom she'd made beautiful, amazing love the night before.

Just as something warm and delicious began to unfurl within her, she was hit by another thought.

Dex, whose voice did not sound at all sleepy and sex-sated. Dex, to whom she still had not told the truth.

Dread quickly squashed any of her warmer emotions. Regardless of what had made him so grumpy this morning, the day couldn't end well. Not when she had such bad news to break to him.

Well, nothing like a cold dose of reality to wake one up, was there?

She sat up, pulling the sheet up to her shoulders as she did so. "What do you want?"

She tried not to sound defensive, but she wasn't at all sure she'd pulled it off. It would have been tricky, given his chilling scowl.

He stood at the foot of the bed dressed in jeans. Last night's dress shirt hung unbuttoned over his bare chest. His arms were crossed, his expression thunderous.

It was all she could do not to shrink into the bed and hide under the covers.

"Is Isabella okay?"

"Isabella is fine. At least, I assume she is." His scowl deepened. "She is not, however, mine."

Somehow his words just didn't register. "What are you talking about?"

"Isabella." He bit out the words. "She isn't mine."

"That's impossible." But even as she said the words, dread began to build in her stomach.

She looked up at him, but his expression—which was normally so cold—was thunderous.

"I don't understand."

He held up a sheaf of papers. "These are the test results from Isabella's paternity test. I'm not her father."

"But…I was so certain. I was so sure."

Her protests did little to soften his expression. He reached down, snatched up her shirt from the floor and tossed it on the bed. "Get dressed and get out of my bed."

Before she could respond, he stormed out, slamming the door to his bedroom. For a long minute, she just sat there in bed, staring at the yellow cotton T-shirt crumpled on the bed, her mind reeling and her stomach roiling.

How in the world had she made such a mess of things?

And could Dex really be right?

There was only one way to find out. She tugged the shirt over her head and stumbled from the bed. She found her jeans in a ball on the floor, but had to dig under the covers for her panties.

Her cheeks flushed as she pulled them on, unable to block the memories of the night before. The things she done with him…the things he'd made her feel…

And she had never even gotten to tell him the truth. Last night, in the heat of passion, she was sure she'd have plenty of time to explain first thing in the morning. Telling him the truth wouldn't have made her lies any easier to bear, but surely it would have made this situation a little better.

Before facing Dex, she snuck into the adjoining bathroom and splashed water on her face. She stared for a moment at her reflection. Her skin was pale and splotchy from shock. Her eyes red from lack of sleep. The short chunky haircut stood out in rumpled spikes.

Anxiety sat heavily upon her shoulders. Her emotions felt like they'd been cut out of her heart and trampled by a herd of elephants.

Turning her back on her reflection, she left the sanctuary of Dex's bedroom to face him. She found him in the living room of the guesthouse, with his forearm pressed against the window frame, staring out into the yard.

"Let me explain," she began.

But the look he shot her when he turned around sucked the words from her mouth. Oh, God. How could she explain this? Where could she begin?

"You don't need to explain. It's pretty obvious what happened."

"It is?"

"Obviously you had no idea who the father was. You just thought you could get the most money out of me."

"No. God, no. It was nothing like that. I thought she was yours. I swear I did. I didn't think she could be anyone else's."

"That's not precisely true is it?" He strode toward her, and without thinking she backed away from the threat. "'What if she's not yours?' Those were your exact words when you were trying to get me to give her back to you."

"I may have said that, but I didn't really believe it. I believed she was yours. I was just grasping at straws because I was desperate to get Isabella back. Even when I said it, I believed she was yours."

"But you knew it was a possibility that she wasn't."

"I—" She felt like she was drowning, struggling to re-surface, to get on top of the conversation. But nothing she said would bring her head above water long enough for her to catch her breath. "I suppose I always knew it was a possibility that she wasn't yours. That there could have been someone else."

"Could have been?"

And then her mind, which had been desperately flailing about for something to latch on to, found the life preserver she'd been searching her. "But you said yourself she had to be yours. You said she had your father's eyes."

He let out a bitter, angry chuckle. "She does have my father's eyes. That's because Isabella is my brother's daughter."

Sixteen

"What?" Her question came out as a high-pitched squeak. "Your brother's? Are you serious?"

Dex's mouth was compressed into a thin, humorless line.

Well, apparently this wasn't his idea of a bad joke.

"Your brother? Your brother, Derek?"

In response, he merely handed her the papers he'd been holding.

It took her a long moment to read and make sense of what she was looking at. A detailed and rather extensive test to determine Isabella's paternity with two possible candidates, Dex and Derek. The letter briefly explained that because the two possible fathers were brothers, Isabella shared genetic markers with both of them. However, the test was conclusive. Derek was her father.

No, the joke was on her. And if anyone was laughing it was Jewel.

Jewel who, apparently, had slept with both Dex and Derek the month Isabella was conceived. It wasn't hard to piece together what happened. Jewel had had a crush on Derek. Despite Raina's insistence that he would never sleep with an employee, he obviously had slept with Jewel. When she'd been fired shortly thereafter, Jewel must have slept with Dex as revenge. Her way of proving to herself that Derek meant nothing to her. A few weeks later she'd found herself pregnant with no way of knowing which brother was the father.

Lucy's knees wobbled and gave out, forcing her to sink to the edge of the sofa as the enormity of the situation washed over her.

"I knew she'd slept with you." She was surprised to find herself speaking aloud. But what the hell. In for a penny, in for a pound. "I swear I had no idea she'd slept with anyone else. Let alone your brother."

For an instant, Dex's icy anger flickered with confusion. "What are you talking about?"

She sucked in a deep breath, pressed her hands to her knees and stood. That was the traditional way to face a firing squad, wasn't it?

"I know you're mad." He opened his mouth as if to cut her off, but she held up a hand to stop him. "Maybe even furious. But just let me explain."

"I think you'd better."

"I never slept with Derek."

He pointed to the sheaf of papers. "This rather expensive, scientific test says you did."

"*I* didn't sleep with him. *I'm* not Isabella's mother. I'm her aunt." A frown creased his forehead. Again, she held up her hands, though whether she did it to stave off his questions or as a sign of surrender, she wasn't sure. "My sister, Jewel, is her mother."

He gave a bark of bitter laughter. "I never slept with your sister."

She sighed, running her hand down her face. "She's my twin sister."

"Your twin?"

"Yes. My twin. The night you met my sister, Jewel, fifteen months ago, I was there at the bar. I knew she picked you up. I knew you slept with her. When she turned up pregnant a few months later, I just assumed you were the father."

"And decided to come looking for me?"

"No! It wasn't like that. You have to understand about Jewel. She means well, but she's flighty. Impatient. Impractical. But when she was pregnant with Isabella, she was different. For the first time in her life, she took something seriously. When she said she wanted to raise Isabella, that she was going to turn her life around, I believed her. Obviously, I encouraged her to contact you, to let you know you were going to be a father."

"Of course you did."

She ignored his comment and his sarcasm. It wasn't as if she'd done much to earn his trust. "But she refused. I can now see why. She said she wanted to do this on her own. And the first couple of months of Isabella's life, she did. But lately, she's been increasingly erratic. She and Isabella have lived with me since before Isabella was born. I love Isabella like she's my own daughter."

"Obviously."

"I'd even contacted a lawyer to get full custody of Isabella. And then one morning, I woke up and found them both gone."

"Two weeks ago."

She nodded. "I'm sure you can imagine how I felt. I wanted to believe she'd just gone out for the day, but the more I looked around the condo, the more worried I became. I couldn't tell if she'd taken any of her own clothes, but her makeup was gone. All her toiletries. When I realized Jewel had left Isabella at this house, I just assumed it was because you were the father."

She paused, sat down on the sofa again and rested her head in her hands. How could she explain? How could she possibly make him understand what her thought process had been like in those few panicky hours when she hadn't known whether or not Isabella was okay?

"You have to understand." She looked up at Dex, her expression pleading. "My first concern was for Isabella. I wanted to get her back. And I knew I could pass for Jewel if I changed my hair." She searched his face for any sign of softening. She saw none, so she stumbled ahead in her explanation. "I knew if I could just convince you that I was Jewel, that I was the woman you'd slept with, you'd believe I was Isabella's mother and you'd let me take her."

"And it never occurred to you that I might want to keep her? That I might care that I had a daughter?"

"I didn't know you then. I didn't know anything other than what I'd read in the papers. That you were the playboy rebel. Irresponsible."

His expression tightened, undoubtedly annoyed at the snap judgment she'd made about him.

She forced herself to her feet. If she was going to have to defend her decision, she was going to do it face-to-face. "I had no reason to assume you'd be a better parent than Jewel had. I knew her. She's my sister and I love her. But she abandoned Isabella. For all I knew, you wouldn't do better."

"Surely even I could do better than leaving a baby on the doorstep of a stranger."

His tone, heavy with sarcasm, only proved her arguments weren't swaying him. "Look." Her tone was sharp with anxiety and frustration. He wouldn't give her an inch. "You know how much I love Isabella. You know I'd do anything to protect her."

"Even sleep with me?"

His question hit her like a punch in the stomach. She reeled a step back, desperate for some space. "That's not how it was."

But he didn't let her retreat. He stalked closer, all his anger and frustration visible on his face. "Really? Then how was it? Why don't you explain to me exactly why you thought sleeping with me would help your cause? Did you think if you went to bed with me it would convince me you really were Isabella's mother?"

Her spine stiffened. "Now you're just lashing out. If you're only going to insult me, then there's no point in even discussing this."

She spun on her heel and headed for the door. She was several steps away when he grabbed her by the arm and spun her back to face him.

For just the briefest moment, the closeness of his body called to her. His expression, so tense, so unyielding reminded her of the previous night. Of the way he'd looked, poised above her as her body had writhed with passion.

How could that man—that man with whom she'd felt so close and free—be the same man fighting with her now? How could he accuse her of such awful things?

And why, dear God, hadn't she told him the truth earlier?

In that instant, she might have dropped to her knees and begged for forgiveness, but the moment was melodramatic enough without it.

That part of herself that wanted to supplicate to him evaporated with his next words.

"You're lucky I don't call the police and have you arrested."

For a moment she merely gaped at him, then she tugged her arm away from his. "You're right. I don't know why I did sleep with you."

For the first time that morning, something other than anger flickered across his face. But it was gone before she could even consider the possibility that she'd hurt him.

"Sleep with me? You were ready to marry me."

"I—"

"And how exactly did you think you were going to pull that off?"

"Don't be ridiculous. You know I was never going to marry you. I never said yes."

"Well, you didn't exactly say 'no,' did you?"

"I certainly did. And if you remember correctly, last night I told you we needed to talk. I was going to tell you the truth about Jewel. You're the one who stopped me. You're the one who wouldn't listen."

"And what exactly were you going to do after you'd told me?"

"I was going to leave. I'd realized that I was wrong about you. That you were going to be a good father. That you really did love Isabella."

"Of course I love her, I'm her father."

She knew the second Dex realized what he said was no longer true. A flash of pain so deep crossed his face there was no doubting it.

And that's when she knew she'd well and truly lost.

It didn't matter why she'd lied to him. She'd never convince him that her intentions justified her deception. In the end, he'd been too hurt by what she'd done. It wasn't about trust or deception anymore.

By pretending to be Jewel, she'd convinced him he was Isabella's father. In that short time he'd fallen in love with the girl he believed to be his. Her lie had ripped that dream away from him.

Nothing she could say or do would justify the pain she'd put him through.

All she could do now was step aside and let him mourn his loss. And pray that someday he'd at least understand what she'd done.

"She's not the mother."

Dex planted his hands in the center of Quinn's desk and leaned forward, so he was right in Quinn's face.

Quinn didn't flinch, but quirked an eyebrow. "Who isn't the mother?"

"Lucy. Lucy Alwin isn't Isabella's mother." Dex bit out the words, his rage emanating from every syllable. Overcome by the sudden urge to sweep all the papers off Quinn's desk, Dex forced himself to straighten and shoved his hands into his pockets. "You run a billion-dollar security business. You have legions of people at your disposal. Resources I'm sure I can't even imagine. Besides which, you're one of the smartest men I've ever known. So how the *hell* did one little woman—one actuary—manage to outsmart you?"

By now, Quinn's sardonic expression had faded to one of confusion. "What do you mean she's not Isabella's mother? If she isn't, then who is?"

"Her twin sister."

"Ah." Quinn rocked back in his chair. "That explains it. I would have needed her medical records to have found out. And you said you didn't want me to do anything illegal."

Dex turned away and paced to the far side of Quinn's

office, resisting the desire to yell at Quinn. This wasn't Quinn's fault. No, the only two people to blame here were Dex and Lucy. Which made it all that much harder to bear.

Quinn kept talking, apparently unaware of Dex's inner turmoil. "From a legal standpoint, this is good news. If both sisters were in on the deception, that should make it much easier for you to get custody of the girl."

"No, it won't. Isabella isn't mine."

"Oh."

That single word held a note of understanding that made the anger in Dex's stomach roil. The smug bastard thought he had it all figured out. Dex took little satisfaction in knowing that someday Quinn would meet a woman who would turn his life inside out.

"So that's what this is about," Quinn continued. "You've fallen for this kid and now that you've found out she isn't yours, you're understandably pissed off."

If only it were that simple. The problem was, this wasn't only about losing Isabella. It was also about losing Lucy.

Seventeen

There were times—and this was one of them—when he wondered why he even came in to work. Since this was corporate headquarters, Derek all but insisted at least one of them be there at all times. Yet the reality was, Derek did his job so well from no matter where he was, that Dex often contributed very little to this company in comparison to his brother's endeavors.

Which left Dex way too much time to consider the many years he had ahead of him of having not much to do.

Still, when he heard the door to his office open he didn't appreciate the interruption. Quinn was the only one who would just let himself into his office. And Quinn really should have known better.

"Damn it, Quinn—" But he broke off when he saw not Quinn, but Lucy enter the room.

"Don't blame him. He was going to have me arrested. Or

at least thrown out. But I bullied him mercilessly to convince him to let me up. I pulled out all the stops. Even tears."

As evidence, she held out one of the crisp white handkerchiefs Quinn always kept tucked in his suit pocket.

Dex felt his jaw clench. Despite himself, he couldn't help noticing how good she looked. Which was ridiculous, since she looked horrible. Splotchy complexion, red nose, dark circles under her eyes. And she'd pulled her hair into a stubby ponytail rather than her normal sassy bob.

He should be rejoicing. After all, if things had been different, they'd be engaged right now and soon he'd be trapped in a marriage to a liar. So why did he instead want to cross the room and pull her into his arms?

Somehow, his subconscious must not accept what his conscious mind knew to be true: this woman meant nothing to him.

"Looks like I'll have to review security procedures with Quinn. In the meantime, if he's feeling too sentimental to have you thrown out, I'm sure I can find someone else who isn't." He made to reach for the phone, though he knew he'd never follow through.

Before his hand even touched the handset, Lucy rushed across the room and stopped him by putting her hand on his.

"I only need a few minutes." She held up a duffel bag he hadn't noticed before now. "I just stopped by to drop off this bag of Isabella's clothes. At least…" she hesitated. "At least, that's ostensibly my reason for stopping by."

"What is it you want, Lucy?" Her name came out with a little bit of bite to it. Even speaking her name was a reminder of the lies she'd told.

"To apologize. I'm not very good at owning up to my mistakes. It's just that I…I don't like making them. I've spent all my life trying to be the perfect daughter. The perfect student. The perfect employee. I don't like failing."

She paused to suck in a deep breath, and despite himself, he found his defenses against her weakening.

"Which only makes it harder when you have to admit to making a huge, colossal mistake like the one I made. I know what I did really messed up your life for a few weeks. But you have to know, I really did believe I was doing the right thing for Isabella. I just got so centered on what I thought was right for her, I didn't think about what was right for anybody else."

She flashed him a game little smile, like she'd made a bad joke but wanted him to laugh at it anyway. He didn't. He couldn't laugh at anything, not even bad jokes.

Her eyes narrowed as she looked at him, giving him the impression she was assessing his very soul. And probably finding it lacking.

"You know, Dex, this act may work with other people, but I don't buy it."

"This act?" he asked sardonically.

"You, sitting there behind the desk, so cool. Obviously you want me to believe that all of this means nothing to you. That you haven't been affected by any of this. But I know the truth. I've seen how you are—how you were—with Isabella. You really love her. And it's got to be killing you that she's not your daughter."

Having her here was bad enough. Listening to all this crap about his emotions was more than any man should have to up with. "What exactly is it you want from me, Lucy? If you're expecting some sappy outpouring of emotion, I'm afraid you've come to the wrong man."

"Yes. I suppose I have." Her expression tightened as grim lines settled around her mouth. "Thank goodness I didn't expect that. I guess I just wanted to admit that I was wrong. And to apologize and—"

"And you expect me to forgive you?" A note of bitterness crept into his voice. As much as he hated how weak it made him sound, he kept talking. "You expect me to offer you absolution? Or assuage your guilt?"

"No. Trust me. I'd never expect that. You're not a very forgiving man, Dex. You still haven't forgiven your parents for dragging you around the world when you were kid. Or your brother for not being there when you needed him. I certainly don't expect you to forgive me for this.

"What I want is to make sure Isabella isn't going to pay the price for my mistake." She paused as if waiting for him to say something. When he didn't respond, she sent him a searching look and seemed to find him lacking. She just shook her head. "I bet you haven't even seen Isabella since you found out she's not yours. I bet you can't even look at her."

"Mrs. Hill is with her. If you're implying she isn't getting competent care—"

"Mrs. Hill is more than competent. But Isabella needs people near her who love her. If I can't be there, then she needs her uncle."

He planted his hands on the desk in front of him. "So this is really just another bid to get custody of her?"

If he expected a burst of anger, he was disappointed. She merely shook her head as if disillusioned with him. "You should know me better than that. This isn't about what I want. It's about what's best for Isabella. I don't know your brother. He knows how to run a company, but is he going to be a good father?"

She rounded his desk, got right in his face and stared up at him, her expression pleading.

"I'm not willing to leave it up to chance. I'm going to fight for her." He opened his mouth to protest, but she put her hand on his face, shushing him with her gentle touch. "This can't be a surprise to you. You had to know I'd do this. I'm going to see my lawyer this afternoon. I'm not asking for full custody. I don't think there's a court in the country that would give me that. Just partial custody. But if I don't get it, then it's going to be up to you to make sure your brother has what it takes to be the kind of dad she needs.

"Derek may be a great CEO," she continued. "But he'll probably need help from you to become a great dad. You can't let your past differences get in the way."

"Trust me, Lucy. You're the worst person to be giving me advice about how to live my life."

"No. I'm the best person. I know better than anyone else that you're hardest on the people closest to you. The more you care about them, the less likely you are to forgive them for making mistakes. For being human. But Dex, if you can't forgive other people's mistakes, how are you ever going to forgive your own mistakes? And trust me, this mistake you're about to make—of pushing Isabella out of your life— It's a real doozy. If you don't make the effort to work things out with your brother and then Isabella ends up paying the price, you'll never forgive yourself. I don't want you to have to go through that. I love you too much."

He scoffed. "A bit melodramatic, don't you think?"

She smiled a wry, sad little smile. "You know me, I'm the romantic one." She turned to leave, but stopped just before she reached the door. "Just out of curiosity, *Tom Sawyer?*"

His blank expression was all the answer she needed.

She nodded. "That's what I thought. Just a ruse, huh?"

"You wanted a big romantic gesture."

"Where did you get the copy of the book?"

"I had a couple of boxes in storage. Just stuff from when I was a kid."

"I bet you've never even read it, have you?"

"If I did, I don't remember. How did you guess?"

"Just a hunch." She was hurt but not surprised by his admission. Their whole relationship had been built on lies. Maybe she should be reassured that she wasn't the only one telling them.

Just before closing the door behind her, she looked over her shoulder and said, "You should try reading it sometime. It's a good book. You might find it brings back more of your childhood than you think it will."

He appraised her coolly. "I'm hardly the type to try to reclaim my childhood innocence."

"No. But maybe you should be."

He didn't go looking for *Tom Sawyer*. In fact, if he ever happened upon the damn thing, he'd resolved to toss it in the trash. Burning it held a certain appeal but seemed to give the book more significance than it warranted.

It was pure bad luck then that the same day Lucy had come to his office happened to be the same day Mavis cleaned the guesthouse, top to bottom, during which she must have found the tattered old copy of *Tom Sawyer*, so that when Dex arrived home at just after nine, the first thing he saw was the book, sitting in the middle of the kitchen counter.

The sight of the book stopped him in his tracks, just inside the door. He stared at it as emotions rushed through him. Finally, he swooped across the room, snatched the book from where it sat on the counter and carried it straight to the trash can. He stomped on the trash can's foot pedal and the lid sprang up. He stood there for a long moment, holding the book poised over the fresh white trash bag.

"Damn it," he cursed softly, dropping the book into the otherwise empty trash can. He moved his foot, letting the lid snap closed with a clang of finality.

Then, with forced calm, he grabbed a Shiner out of the fridge, twisted the cap off and didn't even look at the book when he dropped the bottle cap in the trash can. Taking a gulp of beer, he loosened his tie and pulled it off. In the bedroom, he avoided looking at the bed, as he had ever since the night he'd shared it with Lucy.

If Mavis—who came by the guesthouse every day to make the bed and pick up—had noticed that he'd spent the past three nights sleeping on the sofa in front of the TV, she wisely hadn't said anything.

Dex changed into jeans, leaving on his dress shirt but not bothering to tuck it in. Then, with pointed determination, he sat himself down in front of the TV, as he had the past three nights, and grabbed the remote. He scanned through all three-hundred-and-sixty-four channels. Twice.

Before he could make a third round, he happened to glance out the window toward the main house. Lights were on in both the kitchen and the living room. Through the uncurtained window, he caught a glimpse of a form pacing back and forth. Mrs. Hill, he realized, walking with Izzie.

"Isabella, damn it." He sat up, thumped his beer bottle on the table before him and dropped his head into his hands.

She wasn't his. Izzie was the cute nickname a doting father bestowed on his daughter. But he wasn't a father.

Three days he'd known it, and the loss and resentment still burned in his gut. Still kept him up at nights. Which was ridiculous. He'd never wanted to be a father. Hadn't ever wanted a tiny baby girl with copper curls and his father's eyes. Hadn't ever dreamed there'd be a woman he desired so strongly he couldn't even sleep in the bed in which he'd made love to her.

He sure as hell hadn't known that losing them both would be like having his heart ripped out. But they weren't his to keep. They weren't his family.

But—he straightened slowly as the realization hit him—Isabella didn't know that. She didn't know the difference between a mother and an aunt. Between a father and an uncle.

All she knew was that the two people who'd cared for her most were suddenly gone.

No matter how competent Mrs. Hill was, she couldn't make up for the lost love of an aunt or an uncle.

Only a few minutes had passed by the time he made it down the guesthouse stairs and across the yard to the kitchen door.

Mrs. Hill—who had been pacing around the kitchen island, Isabella clutched in her arms—looked up when he entered, a harried expression on her face. Isabella wailed in indignation.

"I'm sorry, Mr. Messina," she blurted out. "I didn't realize you could hear her crying from over in the guesthouse. I can take her back up—"

"No." He interrupted her. "She didn't bother me. How long has she been crying?"

"A couple of hours. It's nothing to worry about," she hastily reassured him. "Babies just need to cry it out sometimes. It's just colic, nothing serious."

Mrs. Hill's words barely registered. His attention was so completely focused on Isabella, he hardly knew Mrs. Hill was there.

It had been days since he'd seen her. Since the morning he'd found out she wasn't his. The morning he'd hired Mrs. Hill to watch her twenty-four hours a day until Derek got back. And then, he'd barely let himself look at her.

Tonight, her tiny face was flushed red from exertion. Tears and snot ran down her cheeks and chin. She'd never looked more beautiful to him.

He crossed to Mrs. Hill and held out his hands. "You could probably use a break."

Mrs. Hill hesitated. "You're not paying me to take breaks. I can handle her."

"I know you can. But it's been pointed out to me lately that I haven't been a very good uncle."

"Nonsense!" Mrs. Hill protested, but she let Dex slip his hands under Isabella's tiny arms and take her into his arms.

Isabella protested by ratcheting her cries up a notch.

"Oh, dear," Mrs. Hill reached for her, but Dex stepped out of her reach.

"We'll be okay. You said yourself there wasn't anything wrong with her. Why don't you go get some rest? I'll come get you if we need anything."

Mrs. Hill twisted her hands together. "Well, if you're sure…" She stood in the doorway a long time before slowly backing away. "She ate about an hour ago so…"

"I'll give her another bottle in an hour or two. Thanks."

As Mrs. Hill disappeared around the corner, he settled Isabella more closely to his chest. He felt her body, warm and fragile in his arms, her tiny hands pushing against him in protest, her cries—quieter now—slowed and softened. The weight of her against his chest seemed to melt something deep inside of him. He felt as though his chest had opened up and she'd slipped right inside of his heart. Like her body had melted into his, become a physical part of him that he'd be unable to function without.

He'd felt that same way the first time he'd fed her and

felt her fall asleep in his arms. That first time he'd ac-knowledged that he was her father.

The sensation—the emotions—were no different for knowing that he wasn't her father. To him, father or uncle felt exactly the same.

He'd still do anything to protect her. Anything to keep her safe and let her know she was loved. To his heart, it didn't matter one bit that she wasn't actually his daughter.

Automatically, he slipped into the slow, rhythmic waltz that had calmed her previously. As her cries slowed and she nuzzled his chest with her tear-dampened face, a realiza-tion rocked through him.

This must be how Lucy felt about her.

It didn't matter that she wasn't her mother. The love and devotion was there, regardless. It hardly mattered who her parents actually where.

Isabella stared up at him from under her tear-spiked lashes. And as he stared back into her blue-gray eyes, he knew just how Lucy felt. He'd do anything to protect this child. Lying? Yep. Even to someone he cared about, if he thought Isabella's health and happiness were at stake.

And then it hit him. The real reason he hadn't yet told Derek he was a father. Dex hadn't decided completely that he *was* going to tell him.

He had to tell Derek, of course, but until he did, the pos-sibility of not doing so still lingered in the back of his mind.

But Lucy was certainly right. Derek wasn't prepared for this. Dex would have to work hard to whip his brother into fatherly shape.

"Don't worry," he murmured to Izzie. "I won't let him screw up too badly."

In response, Izzie merely snuffled and stared up at him. She blinked slowly and he saw a question in her eyes.

"What do you mean, 'What about Lucy?'"

Isabella blinked again, the last of her cries dying out.

"You don't expect me to just forgive her, do you?"

If he didn't know better, he'd have sworn she rolled her eyes at him.

He flicked off the lights in the kitchen and waltzed his way toward the back door as he felt her beginning to relax against him.

Despite his teasing tone with Izzie, Lucy's betrayal still sat heavily on him. But what had she done that he wouldn't have?

She had put Izzie's needs before everything else. Before her own needs. Before his.

All his life he'd resented the fact that his parents hadn't done the same. Could he really blame Lucy for acting exactly in the manner he'd want the mother of his children to act?

As he let himself into the guesthouse, he felt Izzie sigh against his chest, her breath warm and moist at the open collar of his shirt.

"Yeah. I guess you're right."

He crossed to the trash can, popped open the lid and stared at the copy of *Tom Sawyer* lonely in the bottom of the can. He reached in, flicked the bottle cap aside, and pulled the book out.

Eighteen

She'd been summoned to Messina Diamonds. Via her lawyer, no less.

If Dex Messina wants to talk to you without lawyers present, it would be wise to attend, her own lawyer had said. *Down the road, if this case goes to trial, you want it to look like you did everything in your power to settle this amicably.*

As she circled the block for the third time looking for a parking spot, Lucy contemplated what an odd word choice that was. *Amicably.* In the spirit of friendliness.

But things between her and Dex had never been friendly. Tender, passionate, fraught with emotion, yes. Friendly? No.

And at this point, she couldn't imagine anything either of them could say or do that would change things between them.

It all came down to this. She'd lied to him and deceived him. And he'd never be able to forgive her for that. It didn't seem to matter to him that she'd fallen in love with him in the process. Or that he'd lied to her as well, in his own way.

They'd both made mistakes, she rationalized as she rode in the elevator. Too bad she was the only one interested in overcoming their differences. That—she supposed—was what she got for falling in love with such a stubborn man.

At least she could face him having finally talked to Jewel. After all this time, Jewel had returned Lucy's phone calls. It turned out that Isabella's conception had occurred much as Lucy had imagined it. After sleeping with Derek and being fired by him, she'd set out to seduce Dex on a vengeful whim. She'd let Lucy believe he was the father all those months because it was easier than explaining the truth. Just as dumping Isabella on Derek and Dex's doorstep had been easier than facing either man.

On Jewel's part, there had been many tears and a lot of posturing, but she'd never acknowledged that abandoning Isabella was wrong. Lucy had ended the conversation more frustrated with her sister than ever. She could only hope that her impending conversation with Dex would go better.

Within mere minutes of walking into the building, she was being shown into Dex's office. It was empty when the secretary left Lucy alone in it. She stood in the middle of the room for a moment, feeling awkward before propping her hands on her hips and glaring at the empty room.

"Typical," she muttered aloud before crossing to his desk and nosing around unrepentantly.

She stared down at the meticulously organized desk, looking for some clue as to why he'd asked her here today. A laptop sat on one wing of the desk at a ninety-degree angle from an empty in-box. On the corner of the other-wise blank blotter sat a small familiar jewelry box. It looked lonely there on the desk. As if Dex had set it there the evening she'd returned the ring to him.

"Typical," she muttered a second time. Apparently Dex had just left the ring in his office all this time, not even bothering to put it someplace safe.

By the time she heard the door open and close behind her, she was feeling even more disgruntled than she had when she'd first received his summons.

She turned to face him, but her words got momentarily caught in her throat at the sight of him.

"You don't look happy to be here," he observed.

As always, he was dressed impeccably in a navy suit. The crisp white of his dress shirt accented his tan. However, his eyes were lined with exhaustion and his hair looked as if he'd been running his hands through it.

She felt a pang of sympathy for him before repressing the urge to cross the room and rub the tension from his shoulders. Yeah, he'd certainly appreciate that, wouldn't he?

"How should I look? There's not much to be happy about in this situation."

"No. I don't suppose there is."

"And frankly, I can't even imagine why you'd want to see me again. The last time I was here was hardly a successful meeting."

He ignored her comment as if she hadn't even spoken. Which was a bit disappointing, because she was really curious why he'd wanted to see her.

"I received a letter from your lawyer the other day."

"That can't be unexpected. I told you I would try to get partial custody of Isabella."

And she refused to feel the least bit guilty for it, either.

He crossed to his desk and pulled a single sheet of paper from the drawer.

"What surprised me was that it came to me. Instead of Derek."

"Oh." She hadn't even considered to whom her lawyer would send the letter. It hadn't occurred to her to ask.

"Did you think I'd be more sympathetic to your cause?"

"I wouldn't dream of presuming that."

"But—" Again he continued as if she hadn't spoken, though his voice had softened a bit. "I suppose I am."

She blinked in surprise but could think of no response.

"I've given it a great deal of thought. Once Derek finds out Isabella is his and once he learns about your role in all of this, he's unlikely to so much as give you a chance to explain, let alone to be a part of Isabella's life. I may be unforgiving, but Derek is the control junkie in the family. He'll approach raising Isabella like a business venture and he'll see you as a rival. He'll do everything in his considerable power to guarantee you never even see her again."

Listening to Dex's description of Derek, Lucy felt her knees wobble, forcing her to drop to the chair opposite Dex's desk.

"I hope this isn't your idea of a pep talk."

Of course, he hadn't told her anything she didn't already know. Yet somehow hearing him say it made the threat seem all the more real.

"The way I see it, you have only one option." He rounded the desk and came to stand in front of her, hip propped on the edge of his desk, long legs stretched out in front of him.

Once again his sexual charisma slammed into her. Reminding her that more than her relationship with her niece was at stake here. Her heart was in danger, as well.

Though in danger of what, she couldn't really say. He'd already broken her heart, rejected her when she was at her most vulnerable. What more damage could he do?

Bolstered by that thought, she stood, crossed her arms over her chest and faced him head-on. "And what option is that?"

"Marry me."

She laughed outright. A sharp bark of laughter full of incredulity, but not humor. "You're asking me to marry you? Again?"

"Yes."

"What, third time's the charm? You can't be serious."

"I am." He propelled himself away from the desk and took a single step, closing the distance between them. "The third time will be the charm, only if I can do it right this time. Marry me, Lucy. Not because it's the right thing for Isabella but because it's the right thing for me."

The intensity of his expression made her breath catch in her chest. Still, she forced herself to be rational. Not to be manipulated by those romantic tendencies he was all too capable of using against her.

"You mean it's the easy thing for you," she pointed out.

This time, he was the one who laughed. But instead of cynicism, there was genuine warmth in his laughter. "Lucy, when have you ever been easy on me?"

"Good point."

He reached up to cradle her face in his hands. "You drive me crazy. You make me doubt myself and question everything I do. Being married to you definitely won't be easy. But I need you."

Her heart felt tight in her chest. She so desperately wanted to believe him. But she'd been fooled by him before. Been tricked into believing in sincerity when sincerity wasn't there.

"Let me guess. You need someone to pick up your laundry and you think I'll fall for it since you can dangle Isabella in front of me like a carrot."

"No. I need you, Lucy. Not someone else. Just you. You're the only one capable of breaking down these walls I've been building around myself. You're the only one who can teach me how to be an uncle and a husband and a father. You're the only one I want to bear the child I didn't even know I wanted to have. It's got to be you, Lucy. You're the only one up to it."

"Children?" she asked, more than a little in shock.

"You didn't think after teaching me to be a dad I'd be willing to settle for being just an uncle, did you? Besides, Isabella needs cousins."

"Dex, how can you ask me to marry you when you haven't even forgiven me for lying to you about who I was?"

"Who says I haven't forgiven you?"

"Well…" She fumbled for a moment, searching for an answer. "Logic does. I can barely forgive myself for the way I messed up your life, for how my lies hurt you. I thought I was doing the right thing for Isabella, but—"

"Exactly. You were doing what you thought was right for Isabella." He took her hands in his, his thumbs tracing delicate circles around their backs. "All my life I've blamed my parents for not putting our needs before their own. How can I blame you for doing the opposite? Every decision you made, you thought of her first. That's exactly what I'd want from the mother of my children."

"I…I don't know what to say."

"Say 'yes.'" And then his lips quirked into a smile. "A definite yes would be nice this time."

And, oh, dear God, she wanted to. Pure yearning nearly pulled out of her the "yes" he wanted. Only caution held her tongue.

She had to force herself to step away from him. "It's not that I don't want to say 'yes'—"

"Then what is it? Another secret identity you've kept hidden from me? Another child of your sister's you've been pretending was your own?"

Because there was still humor in his voice, she forced herself to smile. But before she could voice her protest, he grabbed the ring box and went down on one knee. Popping the box open with his thumb, he presented it to her.

Nestled within the black velvet of the jeweler's box was a ring, but not the one she'd expected. Set into a simple platinum band was a round, blue-green stone, its surface polished smooth to reveal a pale six-rayed star.

She looked from him to the ring and back. "It's lovely. Is it an opal?"

"No, it's a star sapphire."

"Oh." She wasn't sure what he expected her to say.

"You want to know the real reason I never gave you that damn ring from my father? I don't like diamonds."

"Oh," she repeated, this time with dawning comprehension, as a glimmer of hope pierced her confusion.

"Actually, I hate the things. That particular one more than most. To me, it doesn't represent love, it's just proof of his stubborn tenacity."

"Then why—"

"Why did I give it to Isabella? Because whether or not I like them, isn't the point. That ring is part of her heritage. I may not want it, but someday she probably will. Of course, I could give you some other diamond. But I don't like any of them. I think they're plain and colorless. They're boring. They're not even particularly rare. People only value them because advertising companies have worked hard to make them the symbol of everlasting love."

He stood, took the ring box from her fingers and pulled the ring out. Taking her hand in his, he slid the ring onto her ring figure. "But look at the star sapphire. Look at its brilliant color. Look at the way it moves in the light." He gently twisted her wrist first in one direction, then the other. As he did so, the star seemed to shimmer across the surface of the stone. "It's almost alive. It's enchanting. It's a stone you could look at every day for the rest of your life."

A faint gasp escaped her lips as she twisted her hand, watching the star's progression across the stone.

"Of course, I could just grab a big diamond from the family vault if you'd prefer." He made to remove the ring from her finger.

She jerked her hand away, with a giggle. "No. It's mine now. You're not getting it back that easily."

"But you're still hesitating."

And how could she explain that after he'd gone to such lengths to give her the big gesture, she wanted the little words to go with it. That without them, she couldn't really *believe*.

"I'm just afraid…" She stepped away from him, giving herself a little room. "Look, the woman you think you want doesn't even exist. You were never really attracted to me. You wanted my sister, or rather, what you remembered of her. Some exotic stranger you met in a bar. That was the woman you desired."

He actually had the gall to laugh at her. She felt a stab of pain, deep in her heart. Just when she thought her defenses against him would hold…

"How shallow do you think I am? No, wait. Don't answer that. I already know." He took her chin in his hand and forced her to look up at him. "I'm not some high school boy to be manipulated. I know what I want. And don't flatter yourself. You're not that good of an actress."

Before she could protest, he continued on.

"You never really pulled off pretending to be your sister.

I never mistook you for some good-time party girl I'd picked up in a bar. I never thought you were just some 'exotic stranger'—to use your term. I always knew you weren't the woman I picked up at the bar that night."

"How? What do you—"

"Oh, I believed you were Isabella's mother alright. I believed you were physically the woman I'd slept with. But I knew you were different. I just assumed motherhood had changed you. Transformed you into someone I could imagine loving. You said I'd fallen in love with an illusion."

"I never claimed you'd fallen in love," she protested.

"Ah." Awareness flickered across his face. "No, you didn't, did you? You accused me of feeling attraction. Not love. I bet you still don't even believe I love you."

"I—"

He tilted her chin up to face him more fully, but she refused to meet his gaze.

"The truth is, I barely remember meeting and sleeping with your sister. If you hadn't shown up on my doorstep, I literally never would have given her a second thought. It's you I can't get out of my head. It's you I love."

Once again he cradled her face in his palms. This time, he leaned down to press a kiss to her lips. Unlike every other kiss they'd shared, this one was gentle. A delicate request. Light as air and soft as the morning sun drifting through a window.

When he pulled back, his heart and his love were in his eyes. "Don't make me ask you a fourth time because you know I'm not going to give up this easily."

"Yes." And she kissed him again. "Yes, Dex. I'll marry you."

As he kissed her again—a real Dex kiss this time—she couldn't help but marvel at her luck. All she'd done in the past month was make mistakes. And somehow it had still ended perfectly.

Epilogue

Isabella, now a rambunctious fourteen-month-old, sat in her high chair, swinging her legs back and forth, kicking the base of the table. One hand clutched the handle of a sippy cup, the other a fistful of Cheerios.

Dex shot an exasperated look at Lucy. "I don't think she understands."

Lucy, suppressing a smile, crossed to where he sat in the chair beside Isabella's high chair. She rubbed her hand along his shoulder, soothing the lines of tension in his muscles. He shifted toward her and she automatically stepped between his open legs. "Of course she doesn't understand. Not really."

Dex tugged on her arm, pulling her down onto his knee. She wrapped an arm around his shoulder and leaned into his chest, marveling at his strength. Relishing the feel of his body against hers, so strong and comforting.

Marveling at her luck, as well. This man would do anything for her. Anything for the child she now carried in her belly.

Dex absently ran a hand over her protruding stomach, obviously not even noticing that the muscles were taut with a contraction of early labor. To Isabella, he said, "The new baby will take a lot of our attention at first. But that doesn't mean we love you any less."

Isabella giggled, no doubt amused by her uncle's serious expression and tone. She brought her fist to her mouth and shoveled in the Os. With one still clinging to her lips, she brought the tips of her fingers together in the baby sign for "more."

Lucy put another handful of Cheerios on the tray of Isabella's high chair, her heart so full she thought it might burst. She had more joy in her life than she'd ever imagined. A child on the way. A husband who loved her. A niece she adored and—now that Lucy and Dex had moved into their own house—who lived just around the corner.

She and Dex might not be Isabella's parents, but they were still very much a part of her life. Frankly, Lucy couldn't ask for more.

"You're allowed to be a little jealous of the new baby," Dex was saying to Isabella. "But just remember, he's going to be your cousin. It'll be your job to show him the ropes. And keep him in line. Just don't be too much of a bully."

Not wanting Dex to see how cute she thought his concern was, Lucy turned her face into his neck so he wouldn't see her smile.

A moment later the doorbell rang.

"I wonder who that is."

"It's Mrs. Hill," Lucy told him as she stood. "I—"

"Why is she here?"

"Well, we need someone to watch Isabella," she pointed out gently. "We—"

"I hope you're not planning on going somewhere. Do you have any idea how long it took me to convince Derek to let us have Izzie for the whole evening?"

After a very rocky start, Derek had eventually taken to fatherhood, approaching it with the same steel-jawed determination with which he approached everything. It was more than a little amusing to watch. However, at the moment, she had more pressing matters on her mind.

Lucy exhaled slowly as the contraction faded and the muscles of her belly began to relax. "Remember, we talked about giving birth at home, but the last time I checked you were adamantly opposed." She paused, waiting for comprehension to dawn on Dex's face. When he still looked confused, she continued. "Since I'm pretty sure I'm in labor right now, we probably want to head to the hospital."

"You're in labor?" Dex's face went white.

"Yep."

"Right now?"

She nodded. "It's still early, but you've been so worried about getting to the hospital…"

He stood so quickly he knocked the chair over. Isabella let out a delighted peal of laughter. Lucy held back her own chuckle as she watched a mixture of anxiety, excitement and wonder drift across Dex's face.

They'd already shared so much together and still had so much more to experience. They had a whole lifetime to look forward to. And Lucy planned on enjoying every minute of it.

* * * * *

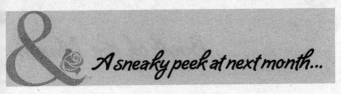

By Request

RELIVE THE ROMANCE WITH THE BEST OF THE BEST

My wish list for next month's titles...

In stores from 21st December 2012:

3 stories in each book - only £5.99!

❑ Swept Away! – Lucy Gordon, Daphne Clair & Joanna Neil

❑ Her Amazing Boss! – Barbara McMahon, Nikki Logan & Anna Cleary

In stores from 4th January 2013:

❑ The Saxon Brides – Tessa Radley

Available at WHSmith, Tesco, Asda, Eason, Amazon and Apple

Just can't wait?

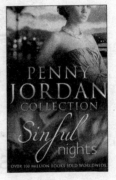

The World of Mills & Boon®

There's a Mills & Boon® series that's perfect for you. We publish ten series and, with new titles every month, you never have to wait long for your favourite to come along.

Blaze®

Scorching hot, sexy reads
4 new stories every month

By Request

Relive the romance with the best of the best
9 new stories every month

Cherish™

Romance to melt the heart every time
12 new stories every month

Desire™

Passionate and dramatic love stories
8 new stories every month

Have Your Say

You've just finished your book.
So what did you think?

We'd love to hear your thoughts on our
'Have your say' online panel
www.millsandboon.co.uk/haveyoursay

- Easy to use
- Short questionnaire
- Chance to win Mills & Boon® goodies

Visit us Online

Tell us what you thought of this book now at
www.millsandboon.co.uk/haveyoursay

YOUR_SAY